# Changed

## Jay Welsby

*Changed*

Copyright © 2017 Jay Welsby

Edited by David M. Good

Cover, Interior Design and Publishing by Tempestuous Erotic Delight
TempestuousDelight.com

Address all inquires to:

Jay Welsby

www.JayWelsbyAuthor.com

ISBN-13: 978-0-9991308-1-0

# Acknowledgments

I would like to first thank God for giving me the gift of storytelling. Without you, none of this could be possible. I thank my mother for always believing in me. Without your encouragement, I wouldn't have gotten this far. I also thank my father for always being a man. R.I.P. Jerry Lamar Wells, Sr. Your example kept me focused.

To my Auntie Jeryl Murphy – thank you for giving me advice about women. I couldn't have written women characteristics without you. And to my Auntie Edythe Murphy – you gave me the opportunity to get myself together during the process of writing this book. Your kindness meant so much to me.

Andria Thomas: thank you for believing in me as a writer. Though we didn't travel the whole road together, you still played a major part in my development as a writer.

Terrell Spencer: you are my "day one" friend who helped with my editing. You were always supportive of whatever I decided to set out to do.

Charlene Glass: thank you for reading over my book. Your keen eyesight caught my many mistakes.

I thank the two arresting officers who lied on my Arrest and Conviction Disclosure form which resulted in my incarceration. The time I spent in jail made me into the writer I am today.

Last, but never least, to all my supporters: thanks for keeping me positive! Once done reading Changed, please leave me a review on Amazon.

# Prologue

Hello, my name is Jacob Richardson, and I'm a degenerate nympho. Oops, I meant to say I'm a corrupted satyriasis. My therapist diagnosed me with the proper term a few years after my marriage. He explained that only a woman could be a nympho. A man, on the other hand, was labeled a satyriasis. By definition, a satyriasis is a man who has uncontrollable sexual urges.

My sexual urges were so bad that I taught myself how to fulfill them at any cost. I've had sex with 3,213 women. I'm not fabricating this either. The reason I know I'm accurate is because I wrote down every woman that I had slept with in my little black book, whether I knew their names or not. I kept my black book secretly hidden away from my wife. I couldn't have her interfere with my sex addiction.

I was a womanizer, to say the least. It had been an ongoing problem since I could remember. Sex and women were on my mind every minute of the day. Any idle time I had was spent on sexual thoughts. I prayed all the time for change, but I knew deep down inside the only way I could change was by force.

My wife, Kimberly Richardson, who everyone called Kim for short, I met while attending Bethune-Cookman University my junior year. I only dated one girl before her. She was a geek who I left behind in high school because she wouldn't put out. Having a high school sweetheart wouldn't be in my near future.

Anyway, Kim was a senior preparing to graduate as a nurse. She was the prettiest girl on the cheerleading team. I was captivated by her long silky straight hair and light brown eyes. She was drop-dead gorgeous without a blemish on her face. She looked like she had never been in a fight before in her life, but rumor had it that she beat up the cheerleader captain for disrespecting her. The word was the cheerleading captain at the time (who was a confused bisexual) continually slapped her on the butt after she told her not to. After speaking to her mother and friends about her awkward situation, she knew something had to be done. Her only two choices were fight or flight. Kim - not being a valley girl - punched her sexual assaulter in the eye during an evening practice. After feeling Kim's right hook, the captain took a leave of absence with a sudden case of pinkeye. From that point on, Kim was the captain of the cheerleading team and all the girls in school knew she wasn't a lesbian.

By the time I started courting Kim, $250,000 was deposited into my bank account. I kept that information from her because I wanted her to believe that I was just a regular college student. We hit it off from the first day we met. It was instant chemistry because we both were from the 305. We had sex after our second date. It took longer than I expected, but it was something about Kim that calmed down the "dawg" in me. It was two weeks to be exact. She was as into me as I was into her. We became an item quickly. With her beauty, intelligence, and decent sex, I made a logical choice. Just like a woman knows who she wants to sleep within a matter of minutes, in the same token, a man knows who his potential wife is at first sight.

We looked good together. Kim being the cheerleading captain and I being a track star made us the envy of the campus. It even got me more pussy because the girls on campus were catty. Most of them wanted to take Kim's place. Or better yet, to do things to spite her. A woman thing, I guess. I played on it.

I almost got caught a couple of times, but I blackmailed every girl who tried to play me. I made it clear that if they so happened to make a mistake and bumped into Kim, I would show their boyfriends all the naked pictures and videos we'd made together. They all held their tongues for the sake of their naïve boyfriends finding out that they were creeping on them.

Kim and I only spent one full year together as lovers at school. We both had apartments off-campus. We would spend nights over each other's places, but of course, she stayed over to my bachelor pad more because it saved her money. Women, I tell you! You can't live with them, but without them, you will have to

# Changed

jack your dick. I never had to worry about that, because If she didn't stay the night, I always had a backup plan.

Honestly, Kim visited my place more because of her financial difficulties. Her mother couldn't always send her money, but what she sent through the mail, helped tremendously. Kim barely got by with her part-time Supervisor job at Wal-Mart. Unlike most college kids who had to eat Ramen Noodles and peanut butter sandwiches to fill their bellies, we shopped at Whole Foods Market. Her mother received $600 in food stamps every month due to the fact she was a genius at picking men who were rolling stones. She would send Kim her EBT card through the mail with $250 left on it. That was good enough.

Out of her four siblings' dads, Kim's father was the only one who stuck around. As a short-order cook in a local diner, he did the best he could to send her money when he could.

From time to time, I would show her the money, but not enough for her to get suspicious of my new-found fortune. I didn't mind helping Kim, because my investment would come back seven-fold. Besides, she was on the verge of graduating with the possibility of starting out with a $70,000 salary.

After graduation, Kim went back home to Miami to start her nursing career. Miami-Jackson Memorial Hospital had plenty of openings for young ambitious nurses who were seeking longevity in the medical field. She had family members to support her in the party city. I, on the other hand, stayed at school fucking all the girls. I hated college, but the girls made me love it. Second, I had to stay in school for at least three years to receive the money my parents left me. They both were murdered in a triple homicide when I was only five years old.

My grandma raised me, and she did a damn good job. I chose to deviate from her guidance once she let me off the porch. It was not her fault how I turned out. She taught me to be humble, but I chose to be arrogant.

I received a scholarship for being able to run fast. "Nigga run, nigga run" was my way out of poverty. The other bullshit I found to be useless in school, other than learning how to market myself. I chose Marketing as my major, unlike the other dumb jocks who mostly majored in degrees that would have them working for someone else for the rest of their lives. I was too independent for that.

The only thing I did responsibly during my college years was not touching the money as much as most financially illiterate 20-year-olds would have. I was an average student, to say the least. I was just happy to pass my classes. I did the bare-minimum to keep my scholarship. C, B, or A, it really didn't matter to me, as long as I passed.

Midway through my senior year, I tore my Achilles tendon while competing in the hundred-meter dash at the biggest track meet of the year. All the prestigious Black colleges were in attendance. In addition to the bleachers being packed, a few Olympic scouts were there. I wanted to impress them, but I did a little too much. I came out of the blocks too fast, and that's when I heard something snap. I knew something was terribly wrong. I fell to the ground immediately. All I could remember was grabbing my ankle to soothe the pain. I must have screamed out "fuck" a hundred times!

I laid on the hot rubber asphalt in agony. The team of doctors and my teammates helped me up off the track. I couldn't put any pressure on my right leg. I didn't need a doctor to tell me that I had torn my Achilles. It was painfully obvious. The MRI the next day showed what I already knew, and from that point on, competing on the collegiate level in track and field was over.

Although I was only a few credits away from graduating, my injury gave me the excuse I finally needed to drop out. No grueling rehabilitation for me. The real reason I went to school was now finally growing interest. Besides while in college, I did a couple of modeling shoots, and all the photographers raved about me. I heard it several times: I "had what it took" to make it big. They said my strong cheekbones and 6'2 lean frame were my meal ticket to success in the modeling world. So, I believed it. Furthermore, I felt like I learned enough about marketing to promote myself. Besides, I could do like the rest of the college dropouts who lied to themselves every year that they would go back. So, I said, "to hell with school" and joined Kim back in Miami.

Once returning home, I got a mortgage for a lovely two-bed condo on Brickell. After a year of testing the water, we were married. Kim was a safe bet. She took the place of my mother who never got a chance to see me grow up. She was a very nurturing woman. We had our problems, but nothing too big. See, I suffered from a slight case of OCD, so everything had to be a certain way in the house. Kim, at times, would leave shit around the house which drove me crazy. I wouldn't necessarily call her lazy, but I hated when she didn't put things back like she found them.

She also couldn't suck dick to save her life! I tried everything in the book to get her to understand. I would leave oral sex porno movies all over the house intentionally for her to see. But, it did nothing but get me cursed out and called disgusting. I even tried to explain to her what I liked, but it went into one ear and out the other. I didn't make too big a deal about it because I had a couple of deep throat specialist on my team just for that.

Lastly, Kim suffered from depression. At times, she would sit in the room by herself gazing out of the window with all the lights off. She wouldn't make a sound. She would just sit in a chair alone looking spaced out. I didn't know this going in, but she didn't know I was a satyriasis either. I did what any real man would do. I got her help.

With counseling and the prescription drug Aripiprazole, Kim could live a regular life. Outside of those few things, Kim was a good wife. She was supportive of me, and my endeavors, and deep down inside that is what made me fall in love with her. She never dressed seductively, but underneath her plain Jane appearance was a woman who had a body like an exotic dancer. She was curvy without a bit of body fat on her stomach.

She could also cook like Trisha Yearwood from the Food Network. There wasn't anything she put into my face that I wouldn't eat. If I weren't into fitness, I would probably look like the Pillsbury Doughboy.

Moreover, she let me be a man. When it came to big decisions, she deferred to me. If she wanted to change her hairdo, she would ask me, "Honey, what do you think about me changing my hair?" If she wanted to use our joint credit card, she would call me if I wasn't around. If there were a problem at work, she would confide in me. If her family had something to say negative about us, she would tell me. I normally would say something that sounded good, and she would go for it.

Furthermore, I loved the fact that she helped the sick. Unfortunately, sometimes her patients died, but somehow, she would figure out a way to keep going on. On top of her compassion, she loved my shitty drawers.

In time, I finally utilized the money my parents left me. I not only used it for us, but I also used it to feed my sex addiction. I bought more things that would get me more pussy, including purchasing a Black Maserati from a police auction. Yes, I drove some poor drug dealer's car who probably got a hundred years for supplying drug addicts with the true American dream: a pipe dream.

Kim and I lived comfortably. She wanted for nothing because I took care of everything. She couldn't tell anyone how much the bills were in the condo because they all came out of my bank account. She was only obligated to pay for her cell phone service, car note, and insurance. Yeah, we were living high off the hog.

My promiscuity grew as I rose to prominence in the modeling industry. My goal was to have sex with 20,000 women, but I never got that far. I will tell you why later.

Anyway, I was an avid reader. But, the sad part about it was, I only read seduction and sex books in my leisure time. I have read books such as *The Art of Seduction, How to Love a Woman, The Kama Sutra*, and *Fifty Shades of Grey,* just to name a few. Oh, I forgot to mention all of Zane's books. Anything that I have read, I have used to my advantage.

I have watched a few porno flicks in my lifetime, but mostly women eating each other out. I wanted to know what made women go crazy about being a lesbian. Or better yet, what made

# Changed

women go from being with a man to falling in love with a woman and never returning to their natural nature. The things I saw women do to each other taught me well. I learned at a young age that most women orgasms came from clitoral stimulation rather than penetration alone. I perfected my skills with everything that I read and experienced. With the knowledge that I had in my hands, it was easy for me to go to a woman's hell, even though I believed in God.

I'm also a third-degree Black belt and a skillful wrestler. Though I was regarded as a "pretty boy," I could kick ass when necessary. I wasn't overly aggressive, but I wasn't a punk either. There wasn't a gun that I couldn't shoot. I visited the gun range frequently. I am a marksman, to say the least. In other words, I could protect a woman, but I couldn't protect her from me. I looked to be sane but deep down inside; I was insane.

I was Eddie Murphy, Bill Bellamy, and Will Smith on steroids. I loved women. I loved the way women felt. I loved the way women smelled. And last, but not least, I loved pussy. I've had sex with all types of women:  Black, White, Hispanic, Haitian, Asian, pretty, ugly, fat, skinny, tall, short, young, old, rich, poor – you name it, I've done it. (When I say young, I mean of the legal age. No R. Kelly over here!) I've had sex with mothers and daughters, sisters and friends. I'm addicted to pussy, worse than a crack head on crack. If I weren't trying so hard to be a supermodel, I would probably try to figure out a way to fuck Michelle Obama. I was a mess!

I have never sold a woman a dream, outside of my wife. The rest, I was somewhat straightforward about sex, or they were straightforward with me. I have learned when a woman likes you, you can't do anything wrong. On the other hand, if she doesn't like you, then everything's wrong. I have heard the saying, "people come into your life for a season," but what they don't say is that same season come back around again. Some women would leave me alone when they were mad at me, but for some odd reason, they would come back around when they needed a fix.

Furthermore, you can have a big house, a sports car, and money, but if a woman doesn't want you, none of that matters. If she decides to deal with you anyway, she is just using you. I could literally cuss a woman out, and still, sleep with her that same night. You try it and see what you get. I was the man!

Anyway, I have been involved in over twenty orgies. I was a part of an elite sex group called AWOP. The acronym had two meanings. One was Ambitious Women of Power. That was the bullshit! The other meaning was why I first joined: Arranged Wild Orgy Parties. AWOPs were put together by a powerful woman from Spain. We met quarterly to have orgies in top-secret locations. Thanks to all the rich so-called elitist women who enjoyed shameful carousals, I could travel and fuck women across the world. With each wild party, the women changed, but my selection didn't. No matter how big the group was, I fucked every woman in the room. I wouldn't deprive any woman the chance for them to feel my dick inside their pussies, no matter what. But the last one. I regretted.

Threesomes came to me as easy as it was for young black males to be locked up in the streets of Miami. I had sex on the regular with desperate housewives. I filled the void where their husbands were neglecting them. While they were busy working long hours, I was busy fucking their wives for long hours. Moreover, boyfriends didn't count. A woman was considered single to me if she didn't have a ring on her finger. Besides, I have never seen an application of any significance that said, "Are you dating?" Nope, it either said Single or Married. Black and white don't lie, but men and women do who play house.

If I found out a man didn't marry his woman after being with her for a long period of time, I would sometimes have sex in their bed out of spite. I got into a couple of fights because of it, but I felt it was necessary. Thank God it was just a tussle instead of my brains staining the carpet floor. Also, if there were kids involved and he still refused to marry her, I would pull off my condom and leave my seeds all over their sheets. I wasn't a Captain Save-a-Hoe, but I would show him why he shouldn't treat his woman like she wasn't worth a ring on her finger. With all of that said, let's get to the story.

# Changed

# Chapter 1
# A Kiss to the Forehead

It was 6:57 a.m. when my phone rang. I was in the better half of my sleep. Normally I would have left my ringer off, but not on this particular morning. I was still tired from a late-night rendezvous. I pretended for one moment not to hear my cell phone ringing, but it continued to no avail. I had three more minutes to rest and needed all three of them.

My first instinct told me who it was on the other line, but I was not quite sure. When I finally decided to look over to my phone which was sitting on top of my nightstand, the caller was just who I thought it would be. The picture ID showed an image of a fat man by the name of Michael Wilson.

I sighed at the picture before answering the phone. I turned to look at my wife, whose back was turned with the covers slightly over her face. I said out loud, just in case she was not asleep, angrily, "Damn it, Michael! It's too early in the morning to be calling me. Hold on, man!" I put the caller on mute.

I peered back once again at my wife to see if she had awakened. She did not budge. Her body was still like a cadaver. We didn't cuddle that night. The late-night shift was taking its toll on Kim's body. It was imperative that I took my conversation to the half bathroom in the living room.

I slowly crept out of the bed. I tip-toed toward the bathroom as I pressed the unmute button.

"Hello," I said with a whisper.

The person on the other end was excited to hear my voice. Once totally in the bathroom, I let the annoying caller have it.

"Goddammit, Michelle! How many times I got to tell you not to call my phone so early in the morning? I promise you, the next time you call my phone this damn early, I will block you."

Michelle giggled.

"What the fuck is so funny Michelle?" I asked.

Once Michelle stopped giggling, she finally answered.

# Changed

"Hey, babe! Don't get bent out of shape. I was just calling to let you know I am ready for my two workouts."

I, still being a little disoriented, rubbed my eyes.

"What two workouts Michelle?" I asked.

The way she breathed through the phone, I could sense her frustration. It was almost like she was shocked. I had so many things going on that sometimes I forgot what day it was.

"You know the TWO workouts I'm talking about. The one at the gym and the workout at my place," she answered.

With my eyes barely opened I responded, "I don't know if I can do both today."

Michelle wasn't having it.

"Listen negro; I pay you good money to train me and fuck me! I don't believe in wasting my money. Jacob, you don't want to lose this contract with me. Only once a month I ask you to fuck me, and the rest of the month I pay you to train me to fuck you. So, get yo ass up, and I will meet you at 8 a.m. sharp because I have shit to do. Oh, tell your wife I said hello," Michelle snapped as she hung up the phone in my ear.

I was furious with her low blow. I slammed my fist down on the white porcelain sink. I threw caution to the wind.

"Hello, hello, HELLO! Biiitttccch!"

If the walls weren't so thick in our condo, Kim would have heard me. Money doesn't buy you happiness, but it does buy good shit. If I were in the hood, Kim would have been stabbing me midway through the conversation.

I took a couple of deep breaths and returned to my bed where Kim was still sound asleep. I was upset that I let Michelle get me out of character. I wondered for a moment if my wife had heard me, but it was obvious the contractors built soundproof walls as advertised. She was exhausted in bed and couldn't hear my outburst. I decided to lie back down for ten more minutes. The same way I got out of the bed, was the same way I got back into it-softly without disturbing Kim's slumber.

The alarm clock went off in my head. The gym was twenty minutes away without traffic. Michelle Cummings was a very demanding woman. She believed in punctuality, and usually, I would not play with her time. However, with her disrespectful words earlier that morning, I did not care.

My beautiful wife was still asleep as I awoke from a few minutes more of rest. Before leaving our condo, I kissed her on her forehead. It was an everyday routine because I still loved my wife despite myself.

I walked out of the door at 7:47. It would take me ten minutes to get to the nearest Dunkin Donuts down the street. Before training anyone, I had to have a caffeine rush. The line at Dunkin Donuts was a bit long, and it would make me a bit late but it did not matter to me. I needed an adrenaline rush. Coffee did the trick every time.

I pulled up to place my order. The cashier spoke through the speaker.

"Wuz yo order?" the young female cashier asked rudely.

She didn't sound like the usual pleasant girl in the drive-thru.

I ordered my usual.

"Can I get a large black coffee?" I yelled through the intercom.

She yelled back, "Yeah, okay!"

Though turned off, I still needed to be hyped before entering LA fitness. I did not want to seem unenergetic entering the gym. Besides, I was late, and I knew the look Michelle would give me.

After speaking to the manager at Dunkin Donuts about their new rude ebonic speaking employee, I made my way to the gym. I walked into the gym at 8:20. I knew Michelle would be furious, but I still walked into the facility with confidence. My head was high, and shoulders square as I walked past the weight machines prepared for the bullshit.

Although Michelle paid me the most money out of all my clients, I still wanted respect from her. She was standing by the free weights on the south side of the gym and did not look too pleased with me as I approached her for our Monday workout session.

"Jacob, how many times do I have to tell you? I can give you my money, but I can't give you my time! You already know that I am a very busy woman. Time is money, and I don't feel like I am getting my money's worth," she said with an attitude.

# Changed

Before exploding, I took a deep breath. I looked Michelle right into her eyes.

"Michelle, number one, don't ever call my phone that time of morning. You know I have a wife, and you will respect her. Number two, you went from almost two hundred pounds of sloppy fat to a hundred and seventy pounds, toned and firm. So, if you're not getting your money's worth, find another trainer. I don't give a shit about what you're paying me. You don't own me. And lastly, I hope yo ass is ready to work because I am going to work it today."

Michelle seemed to be taken aback by how I talked up to her. Her eyes gave me this sensuous look as if it turned her on. Though I was not on her level educational-wise, I was her equal in the alpha department. It probably was refreshing for Michelle to have a man put her in her place. She submitted to me in her own way.

"Okay, goddamn it, let's get started. I don't have any money or time to waste," She said half heartily.

"Alright, bring your butt over here. You are going to work hard today," I demanded.

She now regretted her words to me. I pushed her at every exercise she did. I gave her short breathers in between squats. I made her do exercises that I usually gave to my more athletic clients. She begged for water, but I wasn't having it. I was determined to put her through several vigorous exercises that would exhaust her body.

The session was over after an hour and a half. Michelle was exhausted and fatigued. Out of the two years, I had been training her, I never worked her that hard. She tried to catch her breath but had a tough time breathing. I finally gave her permission to drink some water from the fountain that was a couple of feet away. Michelle could barely walk, but she found the strength to make it to the water fountain. She sweated from head to toe. I did not care. I wanted to burn her out to the point she would not want to go back to her place later. I had other plans for the earlier part of the afternoon. Michelle would be pushing my time if I went over to her place. I stood back with a grin on my face as she staggered.

When she returned and saw the smirk on my face, she snapped at me. "I hate you! Let's go, Jacob. I have some work for you to do around my house."

I was surprised that she still wanted to go back to her place for another session. The 47-year-old still had a lot of stamina left. Some younger women I trained did not possess the same activity level she had. I knew at that moment; I would be late for my meeting with my agent. I texted him, explaining that I would be late. I then turned back to Michelle, regretting ever telling her that intense sex was another form of exercising.

After showering at the gym, we headed back to her place for the second workout.

"Give me that dick, Jacob! Give me that dick, Jacob!" Michelle screamed.

I pulled her hair and slapped her on the derriere without any emotions. I didn't care if I bruised her backside out. It was obvious that she liked it because she kept throwing it back. I wanted to ravage her body.

"I told yo ass bout calling my got damn house so got damn early in the morning! See what you get? Yeah, you gettin' this mean dick ain't cha? You hear me, woman, when I'm, talking to you? Keep throwing that pussy back!" I said to inflict pain on her.

"This is yo pussy babe! This is yo pussy!" She screamed back.

I realized in the short time dealing with Michelle that I had her dick-whipped. At Michelle's age, it would've been hard to find someone that could match my skills in her age bracket. No matter how much she fussed and cursed me out, I knew she would always want to have sex with me. I was sure that I set the gold standard for sex in her mind. I knew exactly what to do to her every time we had sex. When she wanted me to make love, she would act appreciative. But, when she wanted me to fuck her, she would act like a bitch.

She knew she couldn't have me. I also knew she did not want me either. I was too young for her. I was just her sex toy without batteries. It was perfect. fucking with no strings attached and we both knew we could not be exclusive. Being the President of

# Changed

Ebony Healthy Organic Skin Care put a hold on Michelle's social life. It seemed like she looked forward to our workout sessions. Though she would never tell me, I believed she cherished every moment with me. My ego was big enough for the both of us, and to feed mine was to starve hers.

I did not enjoy every session with Michelle, but on this day, it felt good pounding her saditty ass. Michelle seemed to enjoy every minute of it. Whatever alcohol or bad foods she ate over the weekend were being sweated out with every stroke I gave her.

Michelle had already had two orgasms and was looking for one more. I hadn't nutted yet, mainly because I taught myself to think about difficult math equations in my head to stop myself from having an untimely orgasm, so I was still nice and hard in my magnum condom.

I knew I had at least thirty more minutes to be on Michelle's clock. She did not believe in being cheated out of her time. I decided the best way to make her cum again was by eating her pussy. I told her to flip her body to the opposite side of the headboard. With her head facing the bottom of the bed and her legs opened facing the other; I prepared her body for her final climax. I began positioning my body in a handstand as she was caught up in the rapture of lust.

I was now able to do shoulder pushups, but my purpose was not to exercise. Michelle pushed her lower body forward towards the headboard so my tongue could reach closer to her labia. With her legs fully extended backward over her head, I dipped my head down with my hard tongue stretching towards her clit. My taste buds were ready for an acquired meal. Michelle closed her eyes to embrace the pleasure she was about to receive. With the strength in my body, I was able to balance myself while licking Michelle's clit, which drove her crazy.

I noticed her studying my well-defined back. Michelle was addicted to muscles, and my lean muscular physique was worth every dime she paid me. When I needed a breather, I would push myself back up. And when I was ready to go back down, I would push myself back down. Michelle writhed in pure ecstasy. I licked her sensitive spot repeatedly. She moaned loud, and her body squirmed throughout the bed. Before she came, she screamed out to our Savior's name in vain,

"Oh Jesus! Oh Jesus! Oh, Jesus!!!"

She finally reached her final climax. I had completed my mission. It was time to "get mines" before I left. She knew exactly what to do. Michelle bent over to show the roundness of her ass, thanks to me. It was still firm at her age. It was easy for me to slide in because she was very much still wet after she busted her nut. It took less than two minutes for me to pull out and take my condom off and fertilize her backside with sperm.

Once the session was done, I made it clear that I didn't have time to stay. I quickly gathered my clothes. Cuddling was definitely out of the question. Michelle stared at the ceiling while I got dressed. She was used to me by now. Some Mondays I spent a little time with her, and some Mondays I couldn't. Michelle had gotten what she needed and did not care if I stayed or if I left.

"Michelle, I'm in a rush, I will see you at eight tomorrow," I said.

Michelle, with a smile on her face, said, "Okay, babe. I will see you tomorrow. I am sorry for disrespecting your wife. She is a lucky woman."

I looked back at her with disdain on my face as I walked out of her bedroom. I took off from Michelle's building parking garage like a madman. I quickly picked up the phone and called my agent and best friend, Benny Mackenzie, better known as Mr. Greatness. He answered the phone.

"Benny, I am sorry, I am running a little late. I got caught up," I explained.

Benny laughed as he spoke, "Man, I know what day it is. On the second Monday of every month, you have to have sex with that rich lonely bitch Michelle. All that success and she still got to pay for dick. That's a crying shame. Hey, that's what that independent thinking shit will get you. You thought I forgot what you do on the side? Nigga, I remember everything. Get your gigolo ass over to the spot so we can discuss your next shoot. You are moving up in the world homie. Me and Todd are waiting for you."

# Changed

I maneuvered through traffic, as I was excited to know where my next gig would be. Things had finally started back picking up. Modeling had been an uphill battle, but I never showed it on my face. Besides, with all my side hustles, financially I did not struggle. Benny was finally getting me a few gigs, and I was now being exposed throughout the modeling world. It looked like I was finally going to make my breakthrough.

I entered Sonny's Bar and Grill to find the odd couple, Benny and Todd, sitting at a booth out from everyone else. They were my childhood friends. We all grew up in a neighborhood in Miami called Little Haiti together. Benny was 6'4" and blacker than a Tarbaby. He weighed around 330 pounds with a full beard and bald head. No matter where Benny went, he made his presence felt.

Todd Clermont, on the other hand, was the dwarf in the crew. He only stood 5'6" and was a small-built man with a receding hairline. He was the geek in the crew. Todd was book smart but street dumb. He graduated in the top 5 percent of our class. However, he was dead last in common sense.

Benny protected me through my adolescence and I always stole Todd's girls. To this day, I still wronged him. I was sleeping with Todd's wife Simone from time to time. For the last couple of years, his Scandalous-ass wife Simone snuck around with me. I personally thought I was helping their marriage out. Along with a small dick, Todd suffered from erectile dysfunction which made Simone take to me. She had a high sex drive, and Todd couldn't satisfy her. Yeah, with the help from Viagra, Todd could get himself up, but for some odd reason, he would forget to fill his prescription. That was when I usually received a call for my services. Poor guy. Me and Simone agreed to keep it a secret, and so far, so good.

Simone was a Jezebel to her heart. Everything she did was for personal gain. She was manipulative and deceitful. The only reason she married Todd was for security. Other than that, she wouldn't have looked his way. As for Todd, he wanted Simone bad. Back in high school, he would carry her books to class to only find out that she ran after boys who didn't want her. Once they got what they wanted, she was a thing of the past. Her behavior persisted in her adulthood. Good guys weren't good enough, and bad guys made her day. After being drug to a river a couple of times, Simone finally wanted a good man. So, she thought. After all the abusive relationships and being cheated on numerous times, she was a woman scorned. By the time Todd and Simone ran into each other again, she was damaged goods.

Todd had made it big with a hedge fund investment group. He was the top dog at Mary and Murphy's investment firm. He clocked-in close to seven figures a year. He also let me get a piece of the action. I had a significant amount of money tied in with him.

Simone saw him coming a mile away. By Todd being shorter than her, unattractive, and having a thumb-size penis, she finally found a man who wouldn't cheat on her. Todd took her and her daughter Sasha in. He treated Sasha like she was his own. Nevertheless, Simone made sure to get pregnant as fast as possible. She didn't want to wait to see if Todd would marry her to secure her legacy. They named their son Albert. From my point of view, she should have named him Pawn because that was all he was on her chessboard.

After Benny and I pleaded with him not to marry her, the fool did it anyway. For most of their marriage, I have been fucking Simone in motels, hotels, cars, parks, bathrooms, and the list goes on. She was spontaneous with me but boring with him.

Her texts to him were like this:

"You left the lights on."

"You forgot to take the garbage out."

"I need you to stop by the grocery store."

"Don't forget to pick up the kids."

Her texts to me went something like this:

"Do you want me to send you a picture of me naked with the lights on?"

"Todd was garbage, can we meet later for a fix?"

"I got a cucumber from the grocery store. It got me thinking about you."

"Todd and the kids are gone, I can't wait to see you this weekend."

# Changed

Every chance she got, she accused Todd of cheating. She would go through his phone at will to find nothing. Simone even got to the point that she accused him of sleeping with the secretary at work who was 68 years old with a humpback. Simone was sinister. She projected the things that she was doing onto Todd. He was just a good guy who fell in love with a cunning bitch.

Benny, on the other hand, had a swinger for a wife. Patricia was a plumped, shapely White woman. They would go out together hunting for other couples to have sex with. Benny was the only person I knew who had more threesomes than me. I don't know how he could watch another man have sex with his wife, but different strokes for different folks, I guess.

Benny once told me that Patricia's skin color didn't matter. His old saying was, "love those who love you." During his college years playing offensive guard at Texas University which was diverse, the sistahs didn't look his way. Weighing over 300 pounds and being broke didn't help him either. While being looked over by his own kind, a white country girl from Illinois fell in love with him. Once he and Patricia started being on the scene together, black girls would roll their eyes at him. He was annoyed and amused at the same time because none of them were checking for him when he was single.

Patricia's father, who ran several businesses, helped Benny start his own. He opened many doors for Benny, and he prospered. He thanked him by marrying his daughter after graduating from college.

Anyway, Benny was my agent and a damn good one. He opened doors that I couldn't get through without his help. He was the Black version of "Rich Dad, Poor Dad". If Todd was the man with books, Benny was the entrepreneurial guru. Outside of managing me, he had his hands in real-estate, lucrative investments, and a reliance management company. He was The Man in my eyes.

Anyway, it was Happy Hour, and for Benny and Todd, drinking could happen at any hour. Todd was drinking his usual Scotch on the rocks, and Benny sipped on Remy Martin without any chaser. Todd scooted over to make room for me. I sat across from Benny because I wanted to look directly into his eyes when he broke the news. Benny smiled at me, which gave me every indication that he found me a nice gig.

"Jacob, are you ready for this?" He started.
I stared at Benny with my eyes focused, nodding my head up and down.

"Curly Shantel's agent wants you in her next video shoot. The video will be directed by Jonny Ross. You will be her love interest. I think the song is called, *You Ain't Bout Nothing But You Feel So Good.*  Of course, you will have your shirt off to show them muscles of yours. It will be this upcoming Saturday morning, and they're willing to pay you $2,000 for a one-day shoot."

I held back my joy because I did not want to seem like this was not supposed to happen. I had been working hard my entire adult life to reach the spotlight. Day in and day out of sending my portfolio out was finally paying off. Working to death in the gym didn't hurt either.

I nodded as I replied, "That's great Benny! I appreciate you getting me this gig. So, where in Atlanta is the shoot going to take place?"

"No sunny boy! You don't have to go anywhere. She isn't doing her video in her hometown; she's bringing her talents to South Beach. You don't have to pack or do anything. Maybe one bag because you have a free one-night stay at a hotel near where they are filming just in case the video isn't done in one day. All you have to do is look slim and fit, and the rest is on the videographer!" Benny explained.

Though Benny was only two years older than me, he always talked to me like I was a little brother. And no matter how big I've gotten in the modeling business, I still gave Benny my respect, despite our small age difference. He was that good.

I was elated with the news. Though I would've liked to have traveled to Atlanta for the video, doing work at home saved me money and time. Besides, I would not have to cancel my clients who depended on me to train them.

"Jacob, you can't show up late like you always do for our meetings. I know you are a playboy and all, but you can't miss out on this opportunity behind some ass. Your wife is gonna kill yo ass one day. I don't know how she hasn't figured you out yet," Benny finished.

I was quiet until Benny was completely done blasting me. I normally did not expose my marriage to anyone, but I decided since the day was a big day for me, I felt the need to loosen up with my two longtime friends whom I trusted with my life.

"Listen man, the only reason Kim hasn't caught me in my shit is that I'm the same way every day. I think Steve Harvey said it best, 'act like a man and think like a woman,'" I said but was quickly interrupted by Todd.

"Jacob, it's 'Act Like A Lady, Think Like A Man'. I swear you were dropped on your head when you were younger," Todd said trying to be funny.

I stuck my middle finger up at him and continued, "Like I was saying, if a woman cheats, you will never know until she falls in love with the other man. I took on their persona. I don't change, no matter what happens during my day. I wake up every morning and kiss Kim on her forehead. No matter how tired I am, when I get home, if she wants to have sex, we have sex. It is what it is. My phone is so rigged that sometimes it's hard for me to get into it. She knows I'm a model, so she doesn't trip about me having female friends. Sometimes she shows a little jealousy, but overall she stays out of my way"

"You have to be kidding," interrupted Todd, while Benny just listened.

"I have no emotional attachment with any of the women I've slept with. Half of them don't care that I have a wife. The other half don't know that I have a wife. Most of them don't even know my real name. I don't deal with any type of social media. Therefore that keeps me out of the drama loop." I explained.

"So, you are saying that she does not question you on anything? I can't believe that!" Todd exclaimed.

"Kim can't tell me how much any of the bills are in the condo because I pay them all directly out of my bank account. So, with that being said, she is well taken care of. And in my book, that is all that matters. She just doesn't know I ain't shit!" I said as they burst out laughing.

Todd replied, "Okay, I get it, Jacob. You are a good dawg. You will protect the house, but at the same time shit on the front lawn. Be careful Jacob, Kim is a good woman and you would not want to lose her to some smooth-talking cat with all the good lines in the world."

With the utmost confidence, I said, "Kim ain't going anywhere. My wife is beautiful and I know men try to talk to her all the time, but they ain't me."

Benny then joined in the attack. "Jacob, you ain't been shit since high school. Not only did you fuck half the girls in school, but you was also fucking your teacher."

Todd laughed because he remembered the story.

Benny continued, "Yeah, you was fucking Mrs. Smith. That poor lady almost left her husband for you. She damn near lost her job if you didn't transfer to another school. You went from fucking all the girls at Northwestern to fucking all the girls at Norland High School. Again, Jacob, you ain't shit."

I could not help but put a smirk on my face. Both were telling the truth about me. In my arrogance, all I could say was, "Well, I didn't force anyone to do anything that they didn't want to do."

Benny looked to be no longer amused by my infidelity. "Okay, Jacob enough talk about your genius as a good cheat. Your career is on the line. The video is this weekend. Just be on time. If you ever watched Curly Shantel's reality show, you will know that she doesn't play." He said as I nodded okay.

It was getting late, so I decided to part ways with my, by then, drunken buddies. I left with excitement all over. I was about to get the exposure that I needed. It had been a long time coming. It was going to be a win-win situation. It was now time for me to start making the money I wanted to make. Hustling as a personal fitness trainer was paying the bills, but now I was ready to make it big in the modeling world. I wanted to be the next Tyson Bedford. With hard work, I would be a bigger supermodel than he was.

When I got home, Kim was in the kitchen cooking a healthy meal. I could smell the aroma from fresh vegetables and oven-baked

# Changed

salmon filling the air as I walked in. It always felt normal when Kim had the day off to cook. Both of us agreed to eat healthy for the rest of our lives. Every now and then we would cheat, but for the most part, we stayed on course.

I could not hold back the big news as I wrapped my arms around Kim's waist and kissed her on the cheek. As I pulled her close to me, I broke the news, "Babe, you won't believe this, Curly Shantel chose me personally to be in her next video." She turned around and hugged my neck and reached up on her tip-toes to kiss me on the lips. No matter how many women I slept with, none of them made me feel like Kim did.

Jacob, I am so proud of you!" she said with excitement in her voice. She continued with an approving look, "I know you have been waiting for a big break, and God has seen it fit to keep blessing you with opportunities to move forward with your career. Jacob, you said you could do this, and you are doing it. Not many men can speak on something and do it at the same time. I love you, babe! Now, go take a shower because I cooked your favorite. The food will be ready for you when you get out. Would you like a glass of wine with your meal to celebrate?" she asked.

I normally would not have a drink during the week because I disciplined myself that way but today was different, "Okay babe, I will have one glass of wine with you," I said as I was entering the bathroom.

Once I finished taking a shower, I walked out to the dining room to see a scrumptious meal sitting on the dinner table. Kim sat at the table with a tank top on without a bra. I could see her nipples erected through the ribs of her white tank top. She also had on Pink boy shorts from Victoria Secret. With the relief of not dealing with patients at the hospital, Kim looked like she just wanted to relax with me. Our schedules were so conflicting that we barely had time to spend with each other. We cherished every moment together.

After saying a short prayer, we both began to chow down. I was half-way through my meal before uttering my first words to Kim.

"Babe, so how have things been going at the hospital?"

Before answering, she finished chewing her food completely.

"Well, being a nurse is being a nurse. I'm on my feet all day and dealing with patients isn't always easy. However, I love what I do." She explained

"Well babe, I'm happy that you are passionate about being a nurse. Don't worry about your feet tonight. I will massage them. And to add to it, I will rub your booty until you go to sleep" I replied.

She chuckled, "Jacob you're so sweet. I wish my hours were different, so we could spend more time together. I hate working on the weekends, but I'm just happy to be getting paid to help people," she explained.

I concurred with her. I knew I had a special woman on my hands, and I hated the fact that I cheated on her all the time. I believed any man who was in their right mind would cherish a woman of Kimberly's caliber, but I wasn't in my right mind. I had a demon whore inside me that controlled me at all times.

"Kim in due time things will get better. I promise one day you won't have to work as hard. Until then, will you settle for a foot and butt massage?" I asked sincerely. "Okay Jacob," she said sipping her last little bit of wine. I rubbed and massaged her butt and feet until Kim went to sleep.

# Chapter 2
# Golden Opportunities

It was a sunny Saturday morning on South Beach. The sun was shining brightly without a cloud in sight, but as usual, I was running late. Damn Crystal and Redbulls! I knew I shouldn't have said anything to her at the mall. I needed some shoes and slipped into some new pussy. *Bad dick*, I thought to myself.

I pulled up to see everyone was ready. I saw Curly Shantel talking to the director, and she looked furious. As I walked closer, I overheard Curly Shantel suggesting to Jonny Ross to have me thrown off the set, but I came with my game face and was ready to work.

Jonny Ross asked her, "Do you want me to send him back? He can be replaced."

Once she took a good look at me, Curly Shantel replied, "No. I will keep him but go and talk to him." Either she felt sorry for me or thought I was perfect for the part. You never know with divas. Anyway, He walked over to me with an unpleasant look on his face. "Hey man! You were about to be replaced! Go to the dressing room. We don't have a lot of time for this shoot. Lisa, your makeup artist, is waiting on you," he said with a frown on his face. I gave him a cold stare back but didn't say anything because I didn't want to ruin my opportunity.

I walked to a small dressing room where Lisa was waiting for me. The door was opened, so I didn't have to knock. She had a powder brush in one hand and in the other, a makeup palette. I sat down quickly. Time was of the essence. I did not take notice of Lisa until she turned my neck towards her to apply the makeup to my face.

She was beautiful. Her brown skin was clear and smooth, which proved to me that she was a master of her craft. She had a cute narrow face. Her long dark-brown hair was wavy like

Pocahontas. Her black dress fitted perfectly. It was covered partially by an apron that couldn't hide her hips.

I sat tranquil as she applied the makeup to my face. The bright lights from the mirror shined on my face. I vainly looked into the mirror to notice that the makeup enhanced the structure in my cheekbones. I was pleased so far.

I noticed Lisa looking at me as she applied more makeup. It wasn't just a professional look either. I could tell the difference between a woman who was interested in me or not. Her smile and the twinkle in her eyes gave it away. It made me spark up a conversation with her.

"So how long have you been doing this beautiful?"

She giggled then answered.

"Well sir, I have been doing makeup for over ten years. As a little girl, I always wanted to do makeup," she said while applying the makeup to my face. "Do you have any more questions?" She said with gazing eyes.

I smiled before asking the next question. "Are you taken?" I asked with curiosity.

"You are bold, sir. I see you're straightforward. Well, I don't have time to talk about that now, but after the shoot, we might be able to talk." She said. I knew at that point I could get her. I thanked her for her nice work and proceeded to the video shoot.

Curly Shantel and Jonny Ross were going over a couple of scenes as I walked up. "Hello, how are you doing Ms. Shantel," I said with a smile on my face. Curly Shantel smiled back, but not for long. It was time to shoot the first scene of the video. It took place on the rooftop of a hotel. There were white beach chairs scattered all across the pool deck. Jonny Ross started setting the scene. The first scene took place by the poolside. Curly Shantel was instructed by the director to lie back on one of the beach chairs with her feet straight out.

Jonny Ross explained to me that I would be rubbing her feet in this scene. With the very thought going through my head, I forced my hormones to calm down. As she sat back on the beach chair, Shantel's beautiful legs took center stage. They were well-toned and did not possess any scars or cuts. I was ready to rub those babies with the suntan lotion that was next to her beach chair. I was mesmerized by them but stayed focused on the task at hand.

Once both of us were in our proper positions, the director proceeded to tell his film crew to begin playing the music. Once everyone was in place, Jonny Ross shouted action! Curly Shantel acted like she was relaxing on the beach chair without a care in the world. I started walking towards her as her shirtless waiter. My chest stuck out as I got closer to her with grapes on a small tray in my hand. Curly Shantel began lip-syncing once I stood in front of her. I leaned towards her with the grapes then pulled one off with a long stem and placed it in her mouth. She chewed on it seductively. I was so turned on. *Dammit,* I thought, *if she only knew what I wanted to do to her at that moment.*

Once she finished eating a few of the grapes, she began lip-syncing again. Everything was going according to plan. I was acting the part which made the first scene go smoothly. There were a few cuts on the first half of the video shoot, but not that many. It was a tribute to my acting coach. Like the saying goes, practice makes perfect.

At break, I wanted to seize the opportunity to get closer to Lisa, who was standing on set spectating. I did not want everyone to know what I was up to. I looked up to see that Lisa was staring at me, so I gestured with my eyes for her to meet back at the dressing room. She obliged me with her eye contact. There was a little Sushi spot on the corner of 14 Street and Collins. I figured we could grab something to eat and head back to my hotel. It would be perfect. All I needed to know was did she drink.

Once in the dressing room, I came on to Lisa. "So, Lisa would you like to go out and grab a bite to eat after the shoot?"

Lisa gave me an untrusting eye, and said, "Boy, I have to go home. I have things to do."

I learned a long time ago if a woman plays hard to get, don't waiver. Some women like to be challenged. Acting like I didn't hear anything she said, I proceeded to say, "Lisa, I tell you what, let's just get one drink, some food and leave. I know a great Sushi spot on Collins. They have a two for one special during Happy Hour. My treat." I wanted to make things simple. The word treat will just about work with any woman. As long as she doesn't have to pay for anything, even a loser has the chance to be successful.

"Okay, Jacob. Just one drink, but I have things to do," Lisa responded.

Three drinks later, Lisa was telling me her whole life story. She was a single parent with two boys. Her youngest son was eleven and was great at sports. Her oldest son was 15 and suffered from a learning disability. With the money she made on the side from doing makeup at random events, she used for a tutor for him. Lisa worked at least 70 hours a week to cover her expenses. If she was not working, she was sleeping. If she was not asleep, she was busy with her sons. And if she was not busy with her sons, she was busy helping her elderly mother. Listening to her, I could tell she was an overworked mom who needed some dick. And mine was getting harder and harder every time I stared at her pretty face.

Lisa explained that her first son was from a wannabe rapper who never could get his life together. He claimed to be the next big thing, but he couldn't hold his own without her help. Finally fed up, she sent him back home to his momma's house. She went on to say that he still makes music out of his mother's garage at the age of 35 without making any real income. Lisa didn't have the heart to put him on child support, besides she knew it would be better for him to give her money from his bootleg CD hustle. She said he was a good man, but he had nothing to offer but dreams. And at her age, she didn't have time to wait.

Lisa was married when she had her second son. He was an older successful man who gave her a sense of security. She thought she finally got it right, but she had it all wrong. Her husband had the right status, but he thought his money was the way to love her. He spent long hours at his job. She explained that their sex life was terrible because he barely made time for it. His idea of having sex was falling asleep while doing it.

Lisa went on to say that she grew tired of it and would talk to him often about it, but she still found herself on top of him while he was asleep. She would have to get off of him and lie in bed next to him masturbating. She said she couldn't take it anymore. The divorce papers were on the table. He tried to rectify things after he found out she was leaving, but it was too late. Once she was finished telling me about her ordeals, I knew it was time to act.

"So, Lisa with all that being said, have you dated since your divorce?" I questioned.

The look on her face spoke volumes. I knew I hit a nerve. She paused before she answered. "Yes, I have been on a couple of wasted dates. I wished I would have stayed home. But, what can you do when you are a single parent looking for a man to help you raise two boys? I don't know much about being a man, but, I try to understand. I have been raising my two without any help from their fathers. You know the story about my first son's father. And the other is still mad about me leaving him. It isn't my fault that he decided to work all the time instead of making time to fulfill my needs.

Anyway, I show up to all of my younger son's games. He is good at football and baseball. I be tired out of my mind, but I make time. It's a damn shame his father lives only 30 minutes away from the park our son plays at, and he won't show up to one game. I used to cry about it, but I have gotten stronger over time. If he thinks the little bit of money, he gives me for our son accounts for spending time, he is sadly mistaken. I'm not worried because when my son gets older, we shall see who wants to spend time. Kids do not understand a father not being there for them. To be honest, I am looking for a good man for me and a father figure for my sons. I just can't be with any kinda man," Lisa broke it down.

After listening to Lisa intensely, I found the angle to get between her legs. I quickly became empathic towards her. I thought of something that she would like to hear. "I understand Lisa. My father wasn't there for me either. Every holiday I would sit by the window waiting on him. But he never showed up. He only showed up for one of my birthdays. He didn't even bring a gift. He was a poor excuse for a father and I grew up hating him. I couldn't understand why he didn't want to be around me. I made good

# Changed

grades and for the most part, I didn't get into trouble. My mom did everything for me. She was mom and dad. I felt sad for her. But, being the strong woman that she was, she never showed signs of being overwhelmed. I promised when I got older that I wouldn't be like my dad. I haven't had kids yet, but I know damn well I won't be like him. It will be an honor for me to be a dad one day," I said halfway telling the truth.

Lisa hung on to my every word. I knew I had her. Some of the shit I said was true, but the rest was bullshit. It didn't bother me, because both of us were bringing our representatives to the table. She could have been lying too. Who the hell knew? Anyway, she grew closer to me. She took her last sip of Apple Martini and put her hand on top of my hand to console me. I relaxed because it was now time to persuade her to come to my hotel room.

"Look, Lisa, as a model, I travel a lot. I don't know where I'm gonna be from one day to the next. Sitting here right now in front of you, I'm attracted to you physically. I believe in being up front. My room is upstairs. I would hate to spend another night alone. When I travel, I find myself being tormented by staring at the ceiling as a way to cope with my loneliness at night. So, Lisa, I was wondering if you would come up and keep me company? I promise I won't pressure you to do anything you don't want to do," I said trying to sound sincere.

Lisa looked shocked and blown away by my words.

"Jacob, are you serious? What type of woman do you think I am? I am just meeting you, and this is how you are coming at me?! Do you think I'm a hoe?"

I had a feeling this was coming, but once again, I was not afraid to challenge her. Besides I was happy that she didn't make it so easy. I probably would have been more afraid of her if she didn't put up any kind of resistance.

"No Lisa, I don't see you like any of those things. You are a beautiful woman. I don't know you, but you seem like a woman who respects herself. I'm not asking you to compromise your self-respect, but what I will say is you probably are a woman who needs to let her hair down from time to time. All I'm saying is that this may be a moment to loosen up. I promise I won't do anything that you won't let me do," I explained

At this point, it was either she was gonna come upstairs or not. If she resisted, I would stop my pursuit. This would go from persuasion to begging. There isn't anything worse or more humiliating than a man begging. I had to keep my dignity because I didn't know when the next time we would work together. I would not feel right in front of her knowing that I begged her for something that I was getting freely at home.

"Okay Jacob, I will go upstairs with you under one condition. Don't try me. I'm not a floozy. No touching or sexual passes." She persisted.

I looked her right in her eyes, and said, "No problem Lisa."

As usual, I used one of the oldest tricks in the book. I told her that I "need to take a shower real quick." She seemed to be a little uneasy about me taking a shower while she was in the room, but she was relaxed once I took my clothes into the bathroom with me. That was all a part of the plan. I did that to disarm her with the belief that I would get dressed in the bathroom. My trick was to walk out with my towel on to awaken her sexual senses. Once I walked out with my towel on and abs showing, it would be a done deal. Lisa would be no different than the other women I did it too before.

"Lisa put your hands over your eyes. I forgot something in the room!" I shouted out of the shower.

Lisa echoed back, "I'm grown. I don't need to put my hands over my eyes. You ain't got nothing I want."

I knew at that point we were gonna have sex. Well, I kinda knew when she came upstairs, but anything can happen. I refused to get a date rape charge. Anyway, I stepped out of the shower and proceeded to the bedroom. Lisa was sitting on the edge of the bed sipping on the last of her drink. I walked out trying to look as sexy as possible. Little drops of water were still running down my chest. This was done intentionally as well. From the look on her face, it was working.

"Well, well, well Jacob! What is all of that?" she said curiously. I paused for a moment, so she could get a full view.

# Changed

"This is nothing," I said humbly.

There is always a time to turn arrogance on and off. And at that moment I thought I'd let my body do the talking instead of my mouth. It was obvious that she was turned on. I continued to pretend like I was looking for something in the room. From my peripheral vision, I saw her lustful eyes staring me down. As I walked back to the bathroom, Lisa grabbed at my towel and pulled me close to her. I was surprised, but not really. She began slipping her hands down my towel. I pulled back a bit to throw her off. I pretended not to like it.

"Lisa, what are you doing?" I said sounding annoyed.

Lisa looked at me like the lustful demon took over her soul. Lisa looked me deep into my eyes and said, "Shut up!"

The Lisa that I spoke to earlier wasn't the same Lisa I was talking to now. She began pulling my towel apart. Her eyes were big when she stared at my semi-erected penis and her mouth watered. Maybe she thought my dick was steak and wanted to swallow it whole.

She looked me in my eyes and said, "Do you mind?"

I smiled, and said, "Do whatever you feel."

Lisa put my dick into her mouth and began sucking it slowly. The sensation felt so good. She took her time with every motion of her tongue and lips. As time went on, she started building up spit in her mouth which made my dick sloppy wet. At first, I tried not to look down, but the noises she made, I couldn't help it. I found myself staring down into her eyes as she stared back at me. It looked like her arousal grew more and more as she showed off her oral skills. The veins on my dick began popping out. It became stronger and longer with Lisa engulfing it. I enjoyed her mouthpiece. Once Lisa knew she had me fully erected, she swallowed my dick deeper down her throat. It was like her soul had been possessed by Superhead. She had me moaning like a lil bitch. With Lisa's unwavering attempt to put my entire dick down her esophagus, I lost control of the gentleman in me. I grabbed her by the back of her head and shoved my dick down her throat deeper. I could not believe she didn't pull back from me. The freak was slowly coming out of her. From the look of things, she didn't mind. She was a beast!

I was to the point where I was about to ejaculate in her mouth, but I managed to hold myself back. I again thought about a few difficult math equations. I gave her a look as to say enough is enough. She pulled away and began to pull herself up. It was time for the real part. From the look of things, she didn't want anything reciprocated. I wanted her badly. To say I was aroused was an understatement. When she got up off her knees, I helped her undress and stared at her body. It was perfect for a woman in her 30's. Whatever she was doing at her age was paying off. I approached her with care. I didn't want to seem too anxious though my hard on said otherwise. I pulled her close to me and kissed her in the mouth passionately. It didn't bother me that she had just sucked my dick before. It was my dick anyway! My tongue went down her throat. I massaged and grabbed her ass as I tongue kissed her. I felt the front of her vagina rubbing against my dick. It felt good. My manhood was ready to go up into her, but first, she asked the million-dollar question.

"Do you have a condom?"

I looked down at my pants.

"Yeah," I said simply.

She pinched her lips as to say let's get it on. I rolled it on where I stood, while Lisa laid back onto the bed with her legs wide open. The lips of her vagina spoke to me. I didn't hesitate. Her eyes then summoned me. I rushed into the bed like a convict that just got out. I crawled on top of her. I gently placed my tongue on the left side of her neck. Her body quivered as I passionately sucked her neck. I didn't suck hard because; I didn't know her lifestyle outside of what we were doing at that moment. She grabbed my back tightly. It was hot and heavy. I then moved my tongue down to her shoulder blade then to her breast. I licked each one slowly. I then took turns sucking them. I could feel her nipples getting harder in my mouth. She moaned for me and began to stroke my dick. She placed the tip of my dick directly on her clit. Her vagina began to soak. It was time to stick it in. It felt good entering her vagina. She was wet, yet tight. There isn't anything better than a tight pussy.

I started stroking slowly. I didn't want her to feel any pain at first. I wanted her to know what pleasure was. My goal was to reward her for being a hard-working woman with multiple orgasms. I took my time. I moved my pelvis like I was a Jamaican. I wasn't much of a dancer, but I could wine in the bed. Our bodies intertwined together like a game of Twister. The chemistry was there and I let her know who was in charge with my deep penetration.

Within 10 minutes, I felt the sperm in my penis building up. I had to think fast, so I pulled out. Lisa was feeling so good to me. I had to get myself together fast and come up with a quick excuse. She stared at me as if something was wrong.

"Lisa, it's your turn to do whatever you want to do to me," I said needing a short break before exploding inside of her.

Lisa wasn't bashful at all. With the strength in her body, she turned me over on my back. I saw that she was ready to be the aggressor.

"Jacob, I hope your motorcycle is insured because I am about to do some damage," she said with a nasty tone.

I didn't know what was in store with her comment, but I went along with it. "Sure, I am insured. I hope you have full coverage as well, because this ride may get rough." I said to match her wit.

She stood up over me, so I could get a good look at her goods. Her hairless camel toe smiled at me. It looked like her pussy lips were ready to shove my whole cucumber down its throat. She slowly descended her body down towards my hard dick. She was ready to show her riding skills. Everything up to that point was pleasurable, and I didn't see why this would be any different. She was so wet that she slid down my pole easily. I was harder than a trigonometry problem without having a calculator. Lisa had good balance and posture as she rode my manhood reverse cowgirl style. I placed my hands underneath her ass to hold her up in a proper riding position. The way she rode me, I knew that not only did she look like she was in great shape, but her actions exceeded the look. Lisa could ride a dick. She took no mercy on me as I drove every inch of myself into her. After a while, I could see that either she was getting tired or wanted to cum when she laid the back of her head on my chest. After a short breather, she turned her body in the normal riding style. Lisa started grinding her thigh on top of mine. The sensation made her grind harder and harder until she started moaning loudly. I could feel her convulsions trembling through her body. She finally had an orgasm.

After another short break, we went at it again, and we both came twice. The sex was so good that it knocked both of us out. I woke up around 5:30. My arms were wrapped around Lisa's body. I removed them and quickly jumped up. Like always, I was ready to go. So, I did what I always did after an one nightstand. "Lisa, I have to go," I said as I got up.

Lisa looked to be confused. "So, Jacob, you gonna just have sex with me without asking if I want to be contacted by you or not?" She questioned.

I was prepared to answer because I've been down this road plenty times before. "Lisa, I don't mind exchanging numbers," I said. I was a softy at times when it came to women's feelings.

She reached down to her purse and pulled out her cell phone. "So, your number is…? And don't lie," she persisted.

I gave her my real number. Just as I thought, she called my number on the spot. I felt my phone vibrate in my pants pocket. I pulled it out just to show her that I gave her my real number. "Jacob that is my number. Don't be a stranger and don't be afraid to use it," she stated.

I smiled and said, "How could I forget."

I hugged Lisa and told her she could stay at the hotel if she didn't feel like driving back home. I promised that I would come back knowing damn well I was lying. As I made my way down the hallway, I did what I've done many times before, I erased her number immediately then blocked it. What was done was done. I never hesitate to move on to the next one. Yeah, it seemed like I was a heartless asshole, but my wife came first. I couldn't deal with any real attachments. I wasn't going to play with Lisa's

# Changed

feelings nor the idea of playing stepdaddy. She would get over it like the rest of them did.

# Chapter 3
# The More Things Change

Some Wednesdays were all the same. I received a phone call from my little sister that was always in need of something. It took Mary Jo at least three days to recover from the weekend of doing drugs and feeling sorry for herself to contact me. She was a party girl with four kids. She didn't have to be in a club to party either. If it wasn't the mollies and weed that got the best of her, it was the alcohol: liquor, cheap wine, or beer, it didn't really matter. If her loser boyfriend Frank were home during the weekend of her intoxication, they would argue and fight. Frank was a small-time pusher for one of the biggest drug dealers in Dade County. Like a fool, she fell in love with him. He had nothing to offer other than excuses. Even through the black eyes and verbal abuse, she stayed with him.

During the week, Mary Jo could be a half-decent mother, but once the weekend hit her children were more neglected than a dog tied to a doghouse without water. Mary Jo wasn't really my sister, but I claimed her as such because she grew up next door to me. Ironically, we never had sex. Though I had an extraordinary sex addiction; I could never bring myself to have sex with her. I did have some morals.

Growing up, her brother was my best friend. Unfortunately, he was hit by a stray bullet and killed when he was only 12. I vowed to stay in Mary Jo's life since he was gone. I kind of regretted it, because it was something always going on with her. Mary Jo, who was a single parent, always needed something because she couldn't keep a job. She had her first two kids before graduating from high school. Unbelievably she graduated with a diploma. However, she had two more kids shortly after finishing school. Her first baby daddy is waiting to be executed. The second one was murdered. Mary Jo sure knew how to pick 'em. And Frank, who should 've had a bullet in his head years ago, wasn't any better.

# Changed

"Jacob, wuz up?" Mary Jo said. That was the usual start to a long counseling session.

"Nothing sis. Talk to me?"

Mary Jo, as usual, took a long breath before speaking. "How are you and your wife doing?" She said, not sounding like she really cared. Nevertheless, she did have a little manners before asking for what she really wanted.

"We are doing fine," I replied.

What came next was what I expected from the beginning. "Jacob, I'm a lil behind on my light bill. These kids love to leave the lights on. I tell their bad asses all the damn time to leave the lights off, but they don't listen. They're so damn hard-headed," she said with distress.

I had to take a deep breath. I knew at that point the burden fell solely upon my shoulders. I had to ask, "What about Frank? Isn't he working now?"

Mary Jo, as usual, defended the piece of shit. "Well Frank was working, but he said 'em pussy ass crackaz was gettin to him. So, he quit," she explained.

I wasn't surprised at all. Mary Jo was addicted to thugs who couldn't do anything for her besides give her hard dick and a collect call from jail.

"Mary Jo, when will you get it? Every man that you have falling in love with means you no good. You mean to tell me that this nigga you lay up with every night can't pay a light bill? I told you growing up, your self-esteem is more precious than gold, never relinquish it to anyone. Which part of that message you don't get? I need to make you a shirt with that message, so it will remind you of how you should feel about yourself. But, anyway, how much do you need?" I painfully asked.

She paused for a second. I knew at that point, it was going to be big. "Well Jacob, I am behind two months. The light bill is $400. I only have $30. I will pay you back. I promise," she said.

I felt insulted by her insincere gesture. The last time Mary Jo paid me back for anything was when her brother was still alive. It was a piece of chewing gum I gave her. She, in turn, gave me half of hers' later.

"Mary Jo, I am not worried about you paying me back. My concern is this sorry ass nigga you got living with you. Mary Jo, when will you learn that you are the woman and he is the man? A man's job is to take care of you and not you taking care of him!" I finished.

As usual, it went into one ear and out of the other. She suffered from captain save-a-nigga complex. As bad as I wanted to say that it was Frank's responsibility to pay the light bill, I had to do something. And that was to go into my pockets. "Okay, sis. I will come by this evening. You need to check that nigga before I do. I'm getting tired of him going from job to job. You know he thinks he's a gangsta?" I said with anger.

I hung up feeling disturbed. I couldn't ever understand my sister. Crazy couldn't explain her actions. I then thought about all the women I was dealing with that had the same problem and I kind of understood. Sorry ass niggaz who could pull their dicks out at a drop of a dime but couldn't offer their gurls a dime. How many women who were victimized by this, I would never know. I just knew this was an epidemic that researchers needed to research. My only job was to fuck them good and send them home to a life they didn't want to live.

I had to make a short stop to the ATM before going to Mary Jo's duplex. There was a Bank of America right around the corner. It was the only bank in the majority Black neighborhood. I pulled up feeling lucky because no one was in sight. I took my Glock 45 off the safety before getting out of my car. I didn't want to take any chances, even though I have never been robbed before. I made a quick withdrawal without any incident. I sped off to Mary Jo's place. She stayed in one of the roughest places in Little Haiti. I wasn't worried because she only moved two blocks away from where I grew up at. Most of the people I knew were still there. I felt comfortable in my old stomping grounds. I never felt any jealousy from the fellaz in the neighborhood. The chicken heads who did not want to give me any when I was a bumpy faced kid all wanted to give me some now. Out of spite, I wouldn't even acknowledge their passes towards me.

# Changed

Anyway, I parked in Mary Jo's front yard. It was the only place I could park because she kept her broke down Chevy Impala in the parkway. The transmission blew a couple of months ago. She was waiting for her tax return to fix it. That was at least four months away. She either used public transportation or bummed a ride. My sister was something else.

As I got out of the car, I heard my name being called from across the street.

"Hey, Jacob!" I looked around to see who it could be. The strange, seductive voice screamed out again, "Jacob, this is me Kiki."

I stared across the street into the dark to see Kiki standing by her car talking on the phone. "Wuz up Kiki?" I said waving back at her. I didn't want to start a conversation with her because Kiki would've talked my head off with her new-found love for the Lord. It was God this, and God that. But I remembered a time before God came into the picture…

\*\*\*

When we were teenagers, my boys and I ran the train on Kiki. It was four of us. I think that was how me, Benny, and, Todd, got so close. Benny's cousin who was visiting from Georgia rounded off the bunch. Kiki's mother was a teacher. One day during the usual school week, Kiki's mother had to work on teacher's workday. School was out for us, and there wasn't anything but mischief running through our minds. Kiki was a bored only child who liked to watch porno flicks alone at home while her mother wasn't home. She was a nympho from what I heard. As we walked by her house, she came out of the door with some short gym shorts on and a cut off t-shirt. She was developed for a sixteen-year-old and we all looked at each other with amazement.

"Hey, Jacob, do you see what I see," Todd said.

I looked back at him and said, "Yes, I see hard nipples and a camel toe. It is phat!" I looked over dead into her eyes and didn't shy away from her. She looked directly back at mine. I knew at that moment something was going to happen. I didn't know what, but I just knew something was gonna happen.

"Hey, where are y'all going?" She yelled out.

To be honest, we really didn't know, but I had to think of something. I yelled back, "We going to the corner store!" She smirked and told me to come here. I could see a little jealousy in the fellaz' eyes, but nevertheless, I went over to her by myself. They stared at her like some little perverts as I walked up to her.

"Jacob, I need to tell you something in your ear." Kiki stood every bit of 5'4, so I had to lean down to hear the discreet message. "Jacob, go to the store and get four condoms. I have a surprise foe y'all when y'all get back. Don't tell them anything. If you say something, I won't do it," she said with freakiness in her voice. My dick immediately got hard. My eyes got bigger than Omar Epps's.

I quickly rushed back over to the fellaz. "Don't ask me anything. Let's hurry up and go to the store," I persisted. They all gave me a weird look, so I started trotting towards the corner store to get the condoms. I knew they would fellow behind me. They kept trying to ask me what Kiki said. I just ignored them.

We made it to Best Value Market in record-breaking time. I prayed Ms. Gloria wasn't working the register. She was a real bitch! She worked with her feelings on her shoulders. If her old man had her upset, everyone who walked through the door would know it. If they were on good terms, she would be happy go lucky. This morning it looked like she was happy because she smiled when we passed the counter. Good dick can change a woman's attitude. We walked to the back to grab two-for-a-dollar chips and four hot sausages. As usual, Benny had the money. He sponsored the food, but before walking away from the counter, I blurted out to Ms. Gloria, "We need four rubbers." The fellaz looked shocked.

She looked baffled. "Boy, what do you need four condoms for? Y'all lil penises can't even fit in one. Y'all must be blowing them up with water," she said as she laughed at the idea of us having sex.

I was pissed and ready to get back to Kiki. "Yeah, Ms. Gloria, we are gonna blow them up and throw em at police cars. Can we just get the condoms?" I said sarcastically.

# Changed

She didn't take too kindly to my words. "Get these damn condoms! Make sure to put them on so y'all little dicks don't fall off," she said with an attitude.

Benny paid for them, and we quickly rushed out of the door. I heard her mumble out as the door was closing, "These young gurls nowadays are some real tramps. If I were there mammies, I would beat their asses!"

We speed-walked in the middle of the street as if it was a treadmill. Our hormones raced with the possibility of knowing we all were gonna get some. "Jacob, we got four rubbers because we all are gonna get some right?" Todd said with naïve excitement.

I didn't want to say anything, but the cat was out of the bag once they all saw Benny buy the condoms. "Listen, y'all need to keep it cool. Kiki said she will do us all if I kept it quiet. Let me do the talking and we all might get some. Even your lame ass Todd," I said with the intention of embarrassing him. Todd sighed but continued running with the pack of horny wolves.

All the fellaz had their special talents, but at that time, I was the only one who knew how to talk to girls. Benny and I had the most experience with girls but they trusted me to get them all some. It was an honor for me at my young age.

As we approached Kiki's house, she wasn't anywhere in sight. We stopped a couple of feet away from her house; right on the corner to be exact. We huddled up, and I presented the plan. "Okay fellaz, this is the moment of truth. Let me go up to the house by myself to talk to her. Once I put my game down, she will let me in. I will give y'all the signal to come in behind me. Just stay right here," I finished.

They all stood together in the hot sun waiting for my go-ahead. I looked around before approaching Kiki's house. I wanted to make sure none of the neighbors were watching. It was around ten in the morning and most of the adults in the neighborhood were at work or probably still sleep. Either way, it went, I didn't want to get Kiki killed for letting our nasty young asses in her place. Before ringing her doorbell, I looked back again. No cars drove by and the fellaz were still standing together waiting on me. I rang the doorbell. I heard the echo from the doorbell go through the house through the front door. I waited a second before ringing it again. I rubbed my cheek wondering if she left or was playing with us. I was a little irritated, but I rang the doorbell one more time. It would be the last time. But this time I heard a sound of feet walking over tile. I prayed no one else was home besides Kiki. I got a little nervous as I heard the person approaching the door. I took a deep breath.

I saw an eye looking through the peephole. It looked like the person didn't take long to figure out who I was. "Who is it?" the person asked in a deep voice.

I said with a little hesitation, "It's Jacob."

Kiki opened the door laughing with only a towel on. "Silly I knew it was you. I was just seeing if you would have answered. Boy, if that were my momma, she would have cussed your butt out for being in front of her door," she said with laughter in her voice.

Her poor sense of humor went over my head. There was something else my mind was focused on. My eyes lusted at Kiki standing in front of me in a towel. Her hair was curly, and body dripped of water from the shower. I stared at her before saying one word. She looked back at me with lustful eyes. "So, Jacob where are the rest of your friends?" she said sounding disappointed.

*This actually was gonna happen,* I thought to myself. "They're right there," I told her.

She peeped out to see all of their horny asses waiting on the corner of her house. "Jacob, come in and tell them to go around to the back door. I don't need my noisy neighbors to see them outside of my mom's house," she insisted.

I looked over and gave them the signal to go around back. They proceeded quickly through her front yard to the back fence. They pulled up the unlocked lock and went to the backyard. By then, Kiki and I walked through her house to the den. She opened the back door where they all were waiting and quickly ushered them in. It wasn't any time for us to look around because she told us to go to her backroom. There were two rooms on the same

# Changed

side adjacent to a door that seemed to be the bathroom. She opened the first door which I figured to be her room.

We all walked in together to find pink walls with black actors, rappers, and R&B singers pined up throughout her room. And a noise that sounded like sex on her TV. We all looked back at the TV with disbelief. She was playing a porno film on her DVD player. It was one woman with a group of men. All of them had big dicks. It wasn't any confusion at that point. The Porno movie confirmed what she brought us in her room for. It was about to GO DOWN!

"So, what are y'all waiting on? Pull out y'all dicks," Kiki commanded.

We all stood in shock once again. We were prepared to get down but weren't prepared for Kiki's aggressiveness. "What? Y'all scared to pull out y'all dicks?" She said demanding.

I wasn't afraid, so I pulled down my pants first. After breaking the Ice, the rest of the fellaz started pulling down theirs. By us being young teens, it took us a matter of seconds to get hard. I spoke up, "So, now that you see us, it's time for us to see you," I said pretending to be the leader.

Kiki didn't give it a second thought. She dropped her towel in a flash. We all were astonished by her body. Her breast stood up nicely. She had no stomach with a small bush to go along with nice hips and ass. Kiki dropping her towel in front of us made me know that she knew exactly what she wanted. We pulled closer to her as she dropped to her knees without us saying anything to her. With our dicks in our hands, we stood over her. One by one, she put our penises in her mouth. She sucked one after another. I was kind of uncomfortable being in a room with my friends with their dicks out, but the moment called for it.

Kiki began rubbing herself as she gave each one of us the business. She was an amateur at best, but for four horny little boys, it was good enough. I kept feeling her teeth, but I really didn't give a damn. No one else looked like they minded either. She was trying to portray what she saw on the porno flick. As she did her thing, she would have one of our penises in her mouth and stroked two others with her hands. Whoever wasn't getting their dick sucked or stroked would rub her pussy. Her nipples stood up like two rockets ready to be launched. Benny being more experienced because of his age began eating her pussy while Benny's cousin put his dick in her mouth. Kiki's legs were shaking and the room began getting hotter. It felt like a hundred degrees. I was ready to stick my dick in her. I started rolling on my condom. I told Benny to move. When he pulled his head up, it looked like his mouth had a mouthful of clear slime. Once he stepped to the side, I put my dick inside of Kiki's tight pussy. Her body jerked. She moaned as to say it was in. I began stroking. She moaned but not for long because Benny put his dick in her mouth. It was getting more and more intense. Kiki looked like she was enjoying it more than us. I just kept stroking as Benny stuffed his dick back and forth down her throat. She could barely breathe but kept swallowing his dick. Wow, I couldn't believe Kiki was like that. Once everyone saw me inside of her, they started putting their condoms on. Todd took his turn next. He dived in and started humping fast. I knew at that point; he would probably be bad at sex forever.

We all took our turns with Kiki, leaving her with a wide open pussy. When the moment arose for all of us, she let us all ejaculate on her face. She looked like a glazed donut when it was all said and done. We quickly got dressed and left Kiki on the floor soaking in cum.

As we ran down the street, they called Kiki everything in the book. They said things like nasty bitch, raggedy hoe, and slut bucket to name a few. I thought otherwise, but I kept my thoughts to myself. I didn't really want the fellaz to know how I felt. They wouldn't understand.

See, I knew me, and Kiki had something in common. She just understood herself at an early age. She was a free spirit. I thought what she did took courage and a strong sense of self. Unlike some nymphos, she acted out on her fantasy. She didn't hide behind what society said was right or wrong. There are only two types of sexual beings in the world: the ones who act out their sexual fantasies, and those who masturbate to them. Kiki and I were the ones who acted ours out.

# Changed

Unfortunately, Benny's cousin found out the hard way about messing with a nymphomaniac. He doubled back. He started dating Kiki on the regular. His captain save-hoe-ass fell in love with Kiki, even though we gangbanged her. Benny pleaded with him to leave her alone. His cousin wasn't hearing it. Three years later they tied the knot. One year after their marriage, a bullet was put into his head. He came home early from his security job to find her being gangbanged by nine men on their new furniture he had just brought. He pulled his gun and killed one while injuring another. But, one of them managed to get to his gun and put a bullet in Benny's cousin's head before he could fire again. Blood stains were all over their brand-new Rooms-to-Go sofa. It made *The Miami Herald* local page. Benny cried for days. He talked for weeks about how stupid his cousin was for trying to change a hoe into a housewife.

The power of the pussy could make a smart man dumb. He wasn't pissed because he got murdered, but because he got murdered behind a nymphomaniac. it was his cousin's first piece of pussy. Not every man knows how to handle good pussy. Benny's cousin's funeral was so sad... but I helped one of his female cousins get over it upstairs in their grandma's bathroom during the repast. I didn't think there was anything wrong with giving her some dick to help her get past her grief. I thought it was an honorable thing to do.

Kiki's next husband didn't get a chance to read about his new wife. He was a lame from Green Bay, Wisconsin. He went to the University of Miami for grad school. They met while they were both ordering coffee from Starbucks. He wanted her, and she saw potential. His backpack and well-spoken voice didn't make her jump. His studies in college were what caught her interest. He raved about how he was going to be a great lawyer, and she lied about how she wanted more out of life. It was a match from hell. Not knowing any better, he walked down the aisle with Kiki. She had rehabilitated a bit, but the demon whore was in her. She went from having sex with dozens of men to only two at a time.

After finding God, she hooked up with the preacher and deacon at Purity Christian Church. She went to church every chance she got. The poor guy from Green Bay thought he had a God-fearing woman, but he had a nympho.

***

I was jarred back to the present when I heard, "Jacob come in!" It was Mary Jo shouting from her front door. I took one more look at Kiki and walked back to the house where Mary Jo was standing. The kids were running around as usual. The house was a mess. Toys and food were everywhere. Mary Jo was one of the sorriest women in America. I couldn't understand how a woman, who only worked part-time, was not able to clean her house. The kids didn't make it any better. Their idea of cleaning was throwing stuff everywhere.

"Chad, bring yo' ass here and clean dis shit up! I'm tied of yo' ass leavin' shit round the house. Chadrick, sit yo' muthafuckin' ass down somewhere! I told you to stop running through my got damn house!" She screamed from the top of her lungs.

Kevonna, the only girl, made a mess of her pork 'n beans and rice. It was scattered all over the table. Her mouth was covered in pork 'n bean sauce. Little Kevin crawled on the stained carpet with a pissy pamper on. Mary Jo's kids ran her. She knew how to have them, but she didn't know how to control them.

She named all her kids after their fathers. Chadrick Sr. was a hitman for the ruthless John Doe gang. He carried out a hit on a key witness during the John Doe trial. He was later arrested and almost beaten to death by Federal Marshalls. He was found guilty of racketeering and capital murder. He is still on death row awaiting his promise of a lobster and steak dinner before being injected with potassium chloride. Kevin Sr, on the other hand, was killed during a drug deal that went wrong. He decided that he would rob his plug with his friend. What he didn't know was his friend was as greedy as he was. He put a bullet in the back of his head while Kevin was counting the stolen money.

Frank, her new sorry ass boyfriend, wasn't any better. Besides being a small-time drug dealer, he had a serious gambling problem. As fast as he made the money was how fast it went to the gambling house. With the losers that Mary Jo chose to

# Changed

date, I was forced to be her kids' father figure. I tried my best to be in their lives, but I had my own life to live.

"Jacob, thank you for coming by," Mary Jo said. I didn't want to sit down. I didn't have time to chit-chat. I just wanted to do what I came for.

"Mary Jo, I don't have time to stay. I need to make a move."

I handed her an envelope with money inside. I didn't want Mary Jo and her kids to suffer riding the train. I gave her not only the money for the lights but enough to fix her raggedy-ass car. I had the money to do it, so I did it. She didn't know how much I gave her. I found out later that Frank beat her up because he couldn't believe I gave her money without having sex with her. I wanted to beat him up again but stayed out of it. (I'd whipped his ass before for putting his hands on her, but she went back.) From that point on, I stayed out of their quarrels.

# Chapter 4
# Get Away

Modeling and being a personal trainer were finally coming together. I was happy, and so was Kim. Kim had a birthday coming up. We began planning a Bae-cation spot as the summer approached. The Bahamas seemed like a wonderful place to go. Kim was in the best shape of her life. My gut feeling told me she wanted to put on a bikini to walk the beautiful beaches of Nassau. The Bahamas islands would be perfect for her big day. I was delighted to make some real strides in my marriage finally. Kim deserved it. I knew the hospital was burning her out. On some occasions, if she wasn't working, she was sleeping most of the day. It was time for both of us to take a break from our careers. I Kim was more than happy to do so. She had vacation time coming up, and The Bahamas would be the perfect opportunity to use it.

I made a call to Benny, who was my travel agent as well. He booked the cruise and hotel. We were set. I made a promise to myself I wouldn't cheat while on vacation. I prayed to God it would work.

A three-day trip was set. We would be staying at the luxurious Atlantis Hotel. From the looks of it on the internet and the awesome things I heard about it, it would be a great weekend. The sunny beaches of Nassau and seafood would put my mind on Heaven's door. No irritating phone calls from my clients or worrying about what model shoot I would have to do next. My grind life would be on pause, and my relax life would take center stage.

Kim also was ready to get away from the hustle and bustle of hospital life. We both were drained. Our cruise was set for 8 AM sharp. We only stayed a couple of miles away from the port of Miami. I gave Kim my credit card to go shopping for both of us. We needed travel bags and beach clothing. The weekend would be dedicated to her.

I wanted her to have complete control over the trip. I let my Alpha male guard down. I would be the submissive one that weekend. I didn't want any control. It was Kim's turn to have her way. I thought it was a nice gesture on my part. The funny thing about women is that they want control, but don't want control. I don't know if that makes sense, but what does?

Anyway, we were ready Thursday morning for a trip that I believe would draw us closer together. I didn't trust my Maserati in anyone else's hands, so we took the shuttle bus down to the port. It was early, so there wasn't much traffic to fight with. We arrived on the dock of Carnival Cruise line at 6:45 AM. It gave us plenty of time to check our bags. The calmness of the moment gave us peace, and we were glad to get away from Miami. Miami was a nice place to live, but like any place, we needed to get away.

We sat side by side on the bench with our morning beverages. I had my cup of Joe and Kim had her sugarless green tea. As we sipped, I closed my eyes thinking about the beautiful sandy beaches of The Bahamas. I thought about all the romantic things I wanted to do with Kim. It would be just my babe and me. I even took it upon myself to leave my phone home. Do not disturb was an understatement. Kim would be the only thing I would focus on. She needed it, and I needed it. Though I have been with Kim for at least seven years, at times, we loved each other but didn't *love* each other. We spent a lot of time apart. And when we were together, it was like we were on a ticking time clock. *Tick tock, tick tock* was all I' heard in my mind when we had time alone. It was a price to pay for being an ambitious couple. And that was time. Thank God, we didn't have kids, but that was on the horizon.

There was an announcement over the intercom. "All o' board! All o' board!"

We picked up the small belongings we had and headed for the ship. As we were boarding, I noticed a lot of people traveling from different ethnic backgrounds.

The Carnival Vista was huge. The extravagant ship had so much to offer. It had bars, shopping stores, a beautiful lobby, an eloquent restaurant area, and water slides – the works! I was definitely getting my money's worth.

# Changed

We made our way up to our cabin room. It was a lovely spa suite. Room 12202 was on the twelfth deck. The hallways were private to keep unwanted traffic from coming in and out. Inside the room was a king-size bed. The sheets were white with turquoise green trimming that almost matched the color of the ocean, which was visible from the sliding glass doors. There were two wooden nightstands with lamps on each side of the bed. In front of the bed was a 42-inch flat-screen TV mounted to the wall staring down at us. Underneath the TV was a huge mirror just in case, we wanted to have sex with the lights on. There was a sofa with a coffee table in front of it next to the bed. It matched the colors in the room. The bathroom wasn't anything to write home about, but the whirlpool tub made up for it. The cabin had a huge balcony that had beach chairs to feel the breeze that combated the summer heat. I was proud of myself: I'd did it big for Kim's birthday weekend.

After putting our bags away, we decided to go down for a few drinks. Kim wasn't much of a drinker, but to bring her birthday in, getting drunk wasn't a difficult choice to make. I liked when Kim drank because it brought out her spontaneous and wild side. Throughout our relationship, I never mentioned what she did the next day. I respected her enough not to embarrass her. She wasn't the freakiest woman I had ever been with, but the freak did come out when she got tipsy.

On our way to the bar, we walked through a casino. I didn't think once to gamble. I always thought it was a waste of money. I had better things to do with mine. As we continued to walk, we noticed the restaurants, nice gift shops, and upscale shopping stores. Carnival was definitely well put together. We finally found a bar that wasn't too packed. The bartender greeted us with a nice smile.

"What are you two beautiful people having today?" He asked.

I let Kim order hers first.

"I want something sweet. Is there anything that you would recommend?" she asked.

"The pineapple cooler is a perfect choice. We mix a little

real pineapple fruit and rum to give it an authentic taste. Trust me; you're gonna love it," the bartender replied.

She agreed to it. My drink wasn't that complex. "Let me get a Long Island Ice Tea," I requested.

"One Pineapple Cooler and Long Island Ice Tea coming up." He said with enthusiasm.

Our drinks were done in a matter of minutes. They looked good. The bartender put an umbrella, a slice of lemon, and pineapple on our drink rim. I quickly threw my decorations in the garbage as we walked away.

We then made our way up to the top deck where all the festivities were going on. The sun was beaming. It had to be in the mid-'90s, but it didn't keep the crowd of people from enjoying themselves. Women were walking around in bikinis and men in the swim trunks. The kids slid down the slides screaming their lungs out. The splashes were so big that anyone who was standing next to the pool got the business. As I gazed over the deck, I saw a group of Carnival cruise line dancers entertaining the spectators. Some of the people joined in. If they weren't dancing, they clapped.

Kim and I walked over to where the guard rails were to see dolphins following the ship. It sounded like they were laughing and cheering us on. We both smiled and waved at the dolphins. As the dolphins raced against the ship, I grabbed Kim's hand. My wife looked so good in her yellow sundress. It accentuated her curves. The thong she wore made her cute butt clap with every step. She had on some cute sunglasses and a sporty straw hat. The trimming in the hat matched the color in her dress perfectly. My navy-blue polo linen shirt and khaki shorts didn't match her warm color dress, but the way I held her hand with my wedding band and her huge diamond shining, anyone could see that we were a married couple.

After staring down at the ocean for a while, Kim did something unusual. She started walking towards the group of people who were dancing. I followed her in curiosity. Once she got close to the partiers, she stopped in her tracks. Then Kim did the unthinkable: she started dancing with the crowd! I couldn't believe

# Changed

that my wife was dancing with total strangers. That wasn't like Kim. She was a very coy woman when it came to being in the public's eyes. I guess a drink and the eve of her birthday was slowly bringing out the other side of Kim. I didn't want to be a spoilsport, so Me and my two left feet joined in, and we danced the evening away.

***

After one too many drinks and burning feet, we decided to go back to the room. We both jumped on the bed together. We were exhausted but refused to take a nap. Our bellies growled. I looked over the room service menu. Lobster tails, mash potatoes, and asparagus sounded really good.

"Kim, how does lobster tails sound?" I asked.

"That will be okay, honey," she said back.

"Pinot Grigio or Riesling?" I asked.

"Pinot Grigio will be fine." She answered.

I placed the order. I figured it would take a while before our food came up. Before becoming too lazy, Kim and I jumped into the shower. I scrubbed Kim down from head to toe. I didn't miss a spot. I washed her face, scrubbed up under her arms, cleaned up under her breast, rubbed her stomach, cleansed her vagina, and placed the soapy rag between each toe. I waxed on and waxed off her backside. When I got down past her lower back, I soaked her butt. I took my time passionately massaging it. I squeezed the soap out of the rag that made the suds run down her legs. Once done completely bathing Kim down, I withdrew from her.

I washed myself down as she rinsed herself off. I didn't want to put any burden on her. I wanted to cater to Kim on her soon-to-be birthday. I didn't have time to bask into any romanticism for myself because the food would be coming up sooner or later.

Once we were out of the tub, I carefully dried her off. I made sure to get every wet spot on her body. Every drip that descended from her body, I caught with the towel. The bathroom was full of steam. The mirror was fogged up, and steam from the hot shower escaped into the bedroom. I wanted my wife right then and there but held myself back. I gracefully walked out of the bathroom to let Kim handle her womanly business. Almost a half an hour later, she came out of the bathroom in a black sexy lingerie that was barely covered by a dark silky robe. My manhood quickly arose while watching her walk towards me. She laid on top of my chest. I held her tightly while rubbing her arm. We both closed our eyes waiting on our dinner to come. Our stomachs continued to growl. Ten minutes later came a knock on the door.

"Room service!" the person yelled from outside the door. We slowly got up. I threw on a robe and walked to the door to open it. There was a young Black man at the door with nappy hair standing in front of me. He was still well-groomed with a fade on the side. I thought about how far African-American men had come. At one point, a Black man had to have a clean-cut to enter through the corporate door, but times had changed. Afrocentric hairstyles were accepted. The subservient ways of the old Negros were out the door.

I greeted the young man with a tip that I placed in his hand. He smiled at the twenty dollars that I gave him. I told him he could leave the cart with me. He looked concern so I grabbed ten more dollars from my wallet to give him to relieve his troubled face. He took the money and ran. I scrolled the cart carefully to the middle of the room because of the burning two candles that sat on top of it. I opened the lid of our entrees. The aroma from the steam left a pleasant smell in the air. On the bottom of the cart was a bottle of Kracher's Pinot Grigio in a bucket of ice.

I wanted to serve Kim. I told her to go out on the balcony. Along with the beach chairs were a small table with four patio chairs. I pulled one out for her. I carefully placed the burning candles on the table. I then put her entrée in front of her with the wine glass. I poured the Pinot Grigio into her empty glass. After pouring her glass a little over half-full, I then poured mine. I sat the bottle of wine in the middle of the table. I grabbed my tray and sat down with my beautiful wife.

After saying a short grace, I said what I felt.

# Changed

"I love you, Kim. I really wanted to make your birthday special. I hope I'm doing a good job."

Kim giggled like she was in puppy-love. "Jacob, I love you, too. You're doing a great job. I'm so happy you are my husband. You treat me like a queen. Sometimes I don't know what to do," she expressed.

If I were white, my cheeks would've been red. "Babe, I just want the best for you," I said leaning over to kiss her.

After I pecked Kim on her lips, the true romance began. Using my fork and knife, I pulled the muscle from the lobster's shell and began cutting it up into pieces. Still using my fork, I feed her piece by piece. She grinned with each bite. I patiently waited for her to get done chewing before I placed any more food into her mouth. I followed the lobster up with the mashed potatoes. I only put a mouthful in at a time. I was only able to feed her a few asparagus tips before she stopped me.

"Honey, thank you, but eat your food. It will get cold."

"Okay, babe, but I wanted to cater to you," I replied.

"Honey, it's okay. I'm a big girl. I can feed myself. I want you to enjoy your food, too," she persisted.

I took heed. I sat down and started eating my food. The waves hit against the ship creating a loud splash sound. The stars were out, and it was a full moon. The moon looked like the sun of the night because of how bright it shined. There were still a few clouds lingering around in the darkness of the night. The burning candles fought diligently with the wind. They managed not to go out.

The lobsters melted in my mouth. The perfect blend of butter and garlic made the mashed potatoes delicious. The asparaguses were bland, but it went well with the meal.

We sipped on the wine as we ate our food. I looked to see a shooting star. I told Kim to look up to see it. She smiled and began clapping. It was her night.

"Kim make a wish," I said.

Kim looked like she was caught off guard.

"Kim, you know they say you should make a wish when there's a shooting star."

"I don't know what to wish for Jacob," she said.

"Babe, just wish for something," I replied.

"Okay, Jacob. I wish that we stay together forever."

I wanted forever with Kim, too. But I had a problem to solve first.

"You make a wish now Jacob." She said.

"Kim not only do I want forever with you, but I also want to be able to afford you a lifestyle that any woman will envy," I said.

"Jacob, money isn't important to me. I got me. I just want you in my life forever," she explained.

"Then forever it is," I replied.

Kim hugged me with excitement. I hugged her back tightly. Her soft body felt good in my arms. I started kissing her all over. It was getting heated. I caressed her butt. I then kissed her passionately. Our tongues intertwined. We fondled each other. I knew at that point; I couldn't hold back. Kim began stepping backward towards the beach chairs. She sat down and opened her legs. I slowly pulled her see-through thong off. I put my head between her legs like stuffing in a turkey hole. I didn't hesitate to pull the skin back on her vagina to get to the clitoris. I licked her clit slowly. I grabbed her right breast while doing so. She squirmed as I made her kitty cat the top priority. I didn't bother to come up for air. I promised myself I wouldn't stop until she had an orgasm. I rotated my tongue as I slid two fingers into her promised land. I rubbed them rapidly against her G-spot.

I asked, "Babe how does it feel?"

"It feels really good," she replied.

I then asked, "Do you want me to suck it?"

"Yes, babe suck my clit!" She replied.

Then I asked, "Babe do you love it when I eat you out?"

"Yes, babe I love when you eat my pussy! Keep licking it, babe!" She moaned out.

After keeping a study rhythm, she finally climaxed as I continued to lick through her orgasm.

"Happy birthday bae!" I said with her juicy wetness dripping from my lips.

"Thank you, Jacob. I love you," she replied.

"You're welcome honey," I said.

Kim took a moment to get herself together. She shook in the beach chair. Once she was able to stop shaking, Kim wiped the tears from her eyes. She then reached for my wood. I pulled back. I didn't want her to do anything to me. I wanted to spoil her body. I

# Changed

got on top of her and thrust my tongue down her throat again. I held my chocolate thunder in my hand before sticking it in. When it went in, it felt like the first time we made love. Kim grabbed my back tightly.

"Jacob, that's what I'm talking about," she said as she pushed her body towards me.

"That's what you like babe?" I asked.

"Yeeesss!" She replied.

I made love to my wife until the candles finally blew out. We lay sweaty on the beach chair. I held her as we blacked out. We woke up to her phone ringing. The sun beamed on our naked bodies. Kim quickly ran back into the room to answer the phone. I guess everyone wanted to wish her a happy birthday.

I got up soon after. I walked into the room to hear her talking to her mother. Kim seemed to be happy. I told her to tell her mother hello as I went to the bathroom. I jumped into the shower. I didn't take long. I walked out of the bathroom with water still dripping from my body. I walked back out on the balcony to see that we were close to Atlantis. The Islands were beautiful. I couldn't help but be amazed at the scenery. It was getting closer to time to get off the ship. I interrupted Kim's conversation.

"Babe, we're approaching the Island. We got to get breakfast."

"Okay honey. Let me finish up talking to my mother," she said covering up the phone.

Once she got done talking to her mother, Kim jumped into the shower. An hour later, she was ready to go down for breakfast. There was a long line, but it quickly moved. Once we got our breakfast, we sat at a booth. We ran through the oatmeal, cereal, boil eggs, and turkey patties swiftly. Passengers were leaving the boat. We didn't want to be left behind. We went back to the room to gather our stuff.

We stepped down the steep staircase with the other travelers. I put my sunglasses on. I didn't want to get into trouble for staring. Getting slapped while on an Island would be uncivilized. I couldn't take any chances.

The natives waved from down below. Everyone looked like they had adventure and curiosity in their eyes. The moment we reached land, we were greeted by two beautiful chocolate latte skinned Island women. My dark shades kept me from having Kim's handprint on my face. After being greeted by two goddesses, we walked over to get our luggage. We left the ship to get on a shuttle bus. We rode through the beautiful Island of

Nassau. It was weird seeing the steering wheel on the opposite side of a standard made American car. Even driving on the opposite side of the road was strange.

Anyway, we saw Atlantis in front of us as we made our way across the bridge. There were palm trees everywhere and clear blue water surrounding the gigantic peach color hotel that resembled a palace. As we got closer to Atlantis, a sense of peace came over me like no other. I wasn't worried about my sexual urges. Kim was truly my security blanket. She protected me from myself. Though my eyes would flirt with the Ray-Ban hiding them, I wouldn't dare entertain any idea of sleeping with another woman while being with my wife on her birthday weekend. I was going to be on my best behavior.

The shuttle bus pulled up to the hotel a little past 10:30 AM. We all filed out of the bus. The driver took everyone's bags off the shuttle. I tipped him once we received our luggage. We then walked into the lobby area. The interior structure of the massive hotel was amazing. We walked through four pillars that were carved into an abstract sculpture. The ceiling had shells molded on it. The well-patterned marble floors looked as if they were polished that morning. I truly was impressed.

After checking in at the front desk, we made our way to the room. The bellman followed behind us with our luggage. He rode up with us to the eleventh floor. Once we got to our room, he took our luggage off. I gave him a tip for his service. Then Kim and I unpacked some of our belongings. The room at Atlantis was similar to the one on the Carnival Vista, but not as exclusive. The view from the window was over the beach. From the look of things, everyone on the beach was just relaxing watching the waves hit the shore. There were a few people in the water, but the majority looked to be cooling out. It was early, but I saw a few vacationers walking around with drinks in their hands.

Kim and I went down to tour the Island. It was hot, but a beautiful afternoon. We did our best to avoid getting a sunburn by walking closely by the shade. The palm trees protected us from the sun's rays, leaves flapping from the small breeze that swooped through the sky. My sunglasses were now being used for exactly what they were made for. Kim had on suntan lotion and another straw hat that was different from the one on the boat. Though a little tan wouldn't have hurt either one of us, coming back home like a burnt cookie wasn't a part of the plan.

# Changed

We decided that we would try to do everything we could on the Island in three days. Our efforts didn't go in vain. We went snorkeling, jet skiing, hang gliding, and horseback riding in the shallow part of the beach. Also, we took advantage of the water parks. We dropped 60 feet straight down from the Mayan Temple. It was really a leap of faith. We then raced each other on the Challenger Slide. Of course, Kim was mad that I beat her. The Surge gave us a break from using our bodies to slide with. Water inner-tubes were used to slide down this slide. We went from another vertical drop to twisting and turning as we passed through a flash flood. The Serpent Slide went from a high-speed ride on a double tube to a calm and slow ride through a tunnel full of sharks. Kim was scared shitless! I was a little petrified but maintained my composure. I couldn't let Kim see me being scared. A man thing, I guess. After riding a few more slides, we ate.

We stuffed our faces with Bahamian cuisine. We ate fresh conch straight out of the ocean. I could tell the difference from the conch that was shipped out compared to the ones that came right from the sea. We also ate a ton of other seafood: shellfish, shrimp, lobster, crab, scallops, and calamari. We also had tropical fruits, cocoa rice and beans, and cabbage. We ate like two fishers who threw their nets out and caught everything good from the sea.

To curve my sex addiction, we had sex three times a day all three days. We made love in the morning on the bed. We fucked on the couch in the afternoon. And we had passionate sex in the ocean at night. Kim was so good that I didn't even think to cheat one time. She even got oral sex right. Tequila really brought the best out of her. On one day out of the three, she made me tap out. Unlike me, she made sure to let me know. It kind of bothered me because I was used to making women go to sleep after a night with me. I had to admit that Kim got the best of me.

*** 

The weekend in the Bahamas was everything that we needed. The trip ended too fast, but what a weekend! It was time to go back to work, but first I needed to rest. My body was in overdrive and I wanted to relax for the rest of the day.

"Jacob, I'm about to take a shower. Are you gonna get in with me?" Kim asked. My body was shutting down. I couldn't move it. I felt like I had just taken a Flexeril. Right before my eyes closed completely, I yelled back, "Honey, I'll be there in a minute." The next thing I knew, I woke up with slob on the side of my lip. And like that, the trip was over.

# Chapter 5
# Back to Being Me

We had a blast, but it was time to get back to reality. When I came home, I checked my phone and had over 40 messages. I was exhausted from listening to all of them. It was mostly clients and Mary Jo complaining as usual. The best message was from Benny. He explained that the Curley Shantel video would be premiering tonight on *BET* at 8 pm. It also was going to be playing on *MTV's Jam of the Week*. After a nice weekend with my wife, I thought it couldn't get any better. My cup was running over with joy. Once I broke the news to Kim, she called in to take another day off. It would be just us two watching the video together. But first, we needed to rest. Both our bodies were tired from the trip and still feeling the motion of the sea.

\*\*\*

The alarm went off at 7:15 that night, and I woke up grudgingly. I was hungry like a weed head. I looked over to see Kim still fighting her sleep. Long days and the trip must have done something awful to Kim's body. She sighed as she forced herself up yawning.

"Honey turn on the TV. I'm going to the kitchen to get something to snack on. Do you want something?" I asked as I got out of the bed.

"Yes, bring me back some potato chips, fruit, and juice," she replied.

I quickly rushed to the kitchen to prepare a quick snack as I heard the TV being cut on. I could hear the Channel 7 news coming on. There wasn't ever good news on Channel 7. Some Black person did this, and some Black person did that was the usual headline. I walked back into the room with the chips, fruit, and juice for both of us. Neither one of us was in the mood to cook, bake, or microwave anything. Something easy would do.

It was 30 minutes before the premiere, so it gave us enough time to catch up with the news. Bloodshed was in the streets of Miami. Another murder in the Pork and Beans Projects; a man killed in front of his son in Overtown; a drive-by shooting in Miami Gardens; and another Cuban official embezzled money. "Different day, same shit!"

There wasn't anything new up under the Sun in Sunny South Florida. I wished the real Miami could be like South Beach with hot chics walking around in bikinis with drinks in their hands, but the gutter part of Miami wasn't like that. It was a real revolving door of senseless violence. Anyone who made it out of the hoods of Miami, God blessed their souls.

I was tired of the depressing news so I told Kim to change the channel. BET was 15 minutes away from showing the world premiere. We sat up and ate until the video came on. Eight o'clock finally hit and it was time for the premiere to come on. My eyes got big as I heard the announcer say, "Curley Shantel has the jam of the week." We both laid back and waited. I laid humbly next to Kim. I didn't want her to see my excitement or nervousness on my face. I wanted Kim to be proud of me. One minute into the video, I got the exact opposite. Kim's enthusiasm quickly turned to a frown as we watched the video.

"Jacob, do you honestly think I want to see some woman on top of you? There must be something I'm missing. I understand you have a career that will make you deal with different women, but I don't want to see this. My man with another woman draped all over him. Who do you think I am? I respect what you do, but don't ask me to sit down with you and watch it!" Kim said pouring out her heart to me.

I was completely lost, so I had to douse the fire. "Kim, you're trippin'! You are the only woman I love. This is just a video. This is how I make my money. That woman is just an entertainer. She wanted me to do the video so why are you trippin'?" I persisted.

Kim was still hot up under the collar and didn't want to hear anything I was saying. There wasn't anything that I could do to ease her mind, so I let her vent. "Jacob, I am your woman, and it ain't always easy dealing with you. I know modeling brings you attention from women. I knew what I was getting into before we got married, but please don't throw it in my face," she finished.

Though I didn't understand, I did what any man would do when he wants to shut his wife up. "Okay babe, I'm sorry. I didn't know how this would affect you, but I understand your point of view," I finished hoping to alleviate the situation. If you ever want to make a woman feel empowered, just tell her she is right even when she is wrong.

Right after the brief argument, my phone rang. It was Benny. As I was answering, Kim stared at me in disappointment. If looks could kill, Kim would've shot me and stood over me to finish me off.

"Benny, wuz up?" I said.

I heard the enthusiasm in his voice, "Baby boy get ready for this one. Polo finally wants you to pose in their underwear. I got you a deal for $3,500 a shoot. It's possible you can negotiate when you get there. I told you one step at a time. You are going to be a big-time model like I said you would. You don't have to thank me. Just be on time Monday. Your plane leaves for New York at 7:30 am. It is time for you to be on top," he finished.

I was overwhelmed with joy even though Kim was still fuming. "Benny, no I must thank you. You have been not only a good friend but a good agent. You have opened doors for me that wasn't there for me a couple of years ago. I do appreciate your work," I said a little choked up.

With a brief moment of silence, I knew Benny took in everything I said. I felt appreciated. "Man, Jacob I don't need all that mushy stuff. Just go to New York and shine son," he stated. I laid back with relief on my face. It was time to take my career to the next level.

I was excited about my new opportunity to wear Polo underwear. Growing up in such an impoverished neighborhood like Lil Haiti, I would have never thought I would be modeling in underwear that my grandmother once bought me as a Christmas gift.

Kim was trippin', and it made me start thinking about something else. Latoya started crossing my mind. I had been seeing Latoya for most of my marriage. Latoya wasn't anything like my wife. She represented my dark side. Though Kim was everything I wanted, Latoya was everything I needed. Our sexual appetites were just about the same. You would think a good wife is everything a man wants, but sometimes a little unruliness is just what the doctor ordered. Unlike most women who got good dick and went crazy, Latoya had pussy control. No matter how great our sex was, she never got into her feelings. Sex was sex to Latoya. She really was the female version of me. She was the nightmare that most wives dreamed about, a bitch that would do everything that they wouldn't do in the bed without a problem. Latoya and I've had several threesomes together. We would get gurls together. Furthermore, if a newcomer came into King of Diamonds Gentlemen's club, she would let me break her in.

She was the top earner at the strip club, so she had the top pickings of the baddest bitches. Latoya looked like she came from buildabitch.com. She was the definition of fine. She was dark and sexy with swag. She kept her hair in finger waves to represent her stage name, Black Betty Boop. Her fine was different from women who didn't work out. A lot of women at King of Diamonds paraded around with butt injections, but none of them could touch Latoya. Her body was a work of art.

I put Latoya's body on another level by training her. Her ass wasn't injected with all the bullshit women were taking. It was as natural as Serena William's butt was. After working out with Latoya for about a year, she went from the typical hood fast food fine to snatching an NBA player fine. Her stomach went from having no definition to flat as an ironing board. She emphasized over and over that she didn't want to look like a man. I assured her that with clean dieting and hard work she wouldn't remotely look like a man. So, she dumped Churches Chicken, Popeyes, and KFC for baked chicken without barbeque sauce. Smoothies became her snack between meals. She hated me at first for it but thanked me later.

# Changed

Her biggest problem was late night cravings for Oreo cookie ice cream. It was a bad habit she picked up during her pregnancy. She would cry herself to sleep without it. But, over time with my motivational texts, she kicked that habit, too. In the words of Latoya, she became "a salad eating bitch," once I got her on a proper dieting program. I told her if she wanted to make top dollar at King of Diamonds, she would have to sacrifice something. So, she gave up her unhealthy lifestyle for a healthy one. I explained to her that it would be a younger dancer showing up to the club hungry to take food out of her mouth.

Fast forward to the next day, Kim told me some good news. She was called into work to do a double shift. A few nurses called out. All I could think about was a late-night rendezvous with Latoya. Kim was preparing herself in the other room for work. As usual, she would put her nurse uniforms on the iron board for me to iron as she got herself together to take a shower. Even after having great sex the whole weekend, the demon whore in me still was thirsty for more.

But, before I could go on another rampage, I had to iron Kim's scrubs. No matter what was going on with us, my heart always made me want to spoil her. And no matter how long we had been together, Kim never had to iron her clothes. It was my way of saying thanks for cooking for me: even when she was dirt tired, she would still find the strength to cook for us. I thought the least I could do was keep her clothes wrinkle-free. If I wasn't a dawg, I could be a good man. Maybe when I reached my goal of 20,000 women, I would stop.

"Jacob, pass me a towel!" Kim shouted from the shower. I stopped ironing and grabbed a towel from the hamper.

"Here you go honey," I said.

She grabbed it and started wiping herself down. As I watched her, I started reminiscing about us taking a shower together on the cruise. And now I was thinking about being with another woman. There was something seriously wrong with me.

Kim threw her clothes on in a matter of minutes. I gave her a pop kiss, and she was out of the door. Duty called her and Latoya's booty called me. The minute the door closed, Latoya was on my mind. I gave it a few minutes before calling my favorite side chic. Everything that Kim wasn't she was. And I liked it.

"Latoya!" I said with one word.

"Yes, Jacob," she said as seductively as the first time we fucked. Latoya knew just what I wanted.

"Do you know what's on my mind?" I said as if she didn't know.

"Jacob, I know that voice from anywhere. You want some booty, don't you? I might have to take a rain check tonight. I'm a lil tied. I've been doing a double shift all week. You know I ain't trying to strip forever like the rest of 'em dumb ass hoes. I'm trynna get somewhere. A bitch need a break. Probably in a month, I'll get my own boutique shop. Plus, I got my eyes on a couple halfway houses. A bitch gotta change. I'm tied of niggaz feeling on me and bitches hating on me. I'm just tied," she said sounding tired.

I believe she was tired, but when I got around her, someway, somehow, I always lifted her spirits as well as lifted her up literally. I knew if she didn't want to fuck or have company, she wouldn't have answered the phone.

The one weakness I knew Latoya had was crabs. Her whole life would stop for a bucket of crabs. It didn't matter if it was those cheap little blue crabs or the large red snow crabs. Crabs were her kryptonite. I quickly played the crab card.

"Naw, Latoya, I wasn't calling you for a booty call. I'm headed to Captain Crabs and was wondering did you want me to drop off a bucket for you and Jimmy." Jimmy was her 10-year old son. His father didn't want to be bothered with him after Latoya stop opening her legs after she caught him cheating a bunch of times.

"Jimmy isn't here. Since I knew I would be working overtime this week, I let him stay with his grandma. I knew I would be too tied to take him to school. So, I'm home just relaxing with my pillow on the couch and a glass of Moscato," she said leaving me an opening.

I had to think fast. "Well, Latoya, I know you didn't cook anything because your son is gone," Latoya wouldn't have cooked even if lil Jimmy was home. They ate out all the time.

# Changed

"Jacob, why are you doing this shit? You know how I'm about crabs. Well, I guess so. But nigga, I'm tied, so don't come over here thinkin' you are gonna get some," she said non-convincingly.

Latoya knew how to please me. She had only two jobs in her life. One was being a stripper, and the other was playing men out of their money. Most would think that she sold her body for money being a stripper, but that wasn't Latoya's style. The secret to Latoya's success came from always making a man feel like one day he was gonna get some. In other words, she made them chase the cat, while she ran up their credit cards and lowered their bank accounts. She did it all with a smile on her face.

Latoya was the only woman I knew who could throw her pussy up to the Sun and it would become a solar eclipse. I've walked out of her place many nights with cramps in my toes after her fellatio. I hated to say it, but she was better in bed than my wife. What Kim felt to be an obligation, Latoya did with pride. What it took for my wife to do drunk, Latoya did easily sober. She was plain nasty. The two things I knew that would keep a man's attention was a woman who could cook and a freak in the bed. What Latoya couldn't do in the kitchen, she made up for in the bed. I was ready for Latoya's nastiness.

****

I finally got to Latoya's apartment in Hallandale Beach. She had a lovely place in a secluded area. Latoya came a long way from the mean streets of Opa-Locka. Gunfire and crack heads were replaced by peaceful evenings and friendly Jewish neighbors. I pulled into the back of her condo building to the guest parking. I always kept my car out of sight, just in case someone spotted my Maserati. Plus, I didn't want any of her stalkers to know she had company. I wasn't a hundred percent sure if she had any, but my gut told me she had a few. I refused to be the nigga that got killed at the side chic's place while the wife is sitting at home wondering what the hell went on. How would that look to Kim? I hated to even think about it. Anyway, I quickly made a move to her place. I hit the buzzer twice before she opened the door. She stood before me in a Betty Boop shirt and some booty shorts that was partially covered by a robe. I tried to pay more attention to her nicely done finger waves, but my eyes quickly went down to her camel toe. It was too phat to miss. The smell of Dove and body spray enticed me even more. She caught me looking but it was a common practice when I got close to Latoya.

"Jacob, you always stare at my body when you're around me. All you wanna do is have sex with me," she said with a stone look on her face.

Once again, I had to play it off. "What do you mean? I was looking to see if you had been keeping up with your workout regimen."

"Jacob, I ain't stupid by a long shot. Bring yo crazy ass in." Latoya said with a smirk on her face.

I walked in and placed the bucket of garlic crabs on her dining room table. I could tell she was hungry by the way she rushed into the kitchen to grab some plastic plates. She came back in a flash. We sat down at the table and began crunching down on the well-seasoned crabs.

It felt good being in my ratchet friend company again. It was something about being around a hood chic that made me feel comfortable. I couldn't explain it. Maybe, growing up in the hood was part of the reason. I was more laid back when I was with Latoya. I didn't have to act like a husband. It was always fun and spontaneous when we were together. Unlike Kim, Latoya had a foul mouth. She kept me up with the pulse of the streets. I was so far removed from the streets that at times I felt out of touch. No matter how long I stayed away from her, she would quickly catch me up with what was going on in the underworld. Tonight, wasn't one of her nights that she wanted to talk about the streets. Latoya had something more pressing on her mind.

"So, Jacob, how're things going at home?" she asked being nosy.

I've known for a long time that Latoya liked me in her own way, but deep down inside I wasn't her type. Latoya was accustomed to ex-cons and streets dudes. I could never live up to her expectations of being either. I was a man all day, but I could

# Changed

never be a thug. I honestly think she liked me because of our sexual compatibility and maybe thought I could be a good role model for her son. But other than that, I couldn't be her man. I couldn't get into things like her previous boyfriends did. The ones in her past were straight criminals. Latoya was the type who wasn't afraid to speak her mind to anyone; in that case, she needed a man who wasn't scared to have her back. I couldn't fault her for the way she acted. Her mother, raising five children on her own, taught her how to live in the fast lane. A man to her was nothing more than a cash cow. She explained to Latoya at an early age that if a man laid up with her, he better be paying her. So, with that mentality being instilled in her, Latoya never learned how to love. It was all about money, money, money! I was the only exception.

Interestingly, Latoya never asked me for anything other than to speak to her son about being a man. What she and I did was based on mutual attraction. I didn't have to give her money or take her out for us to enjoy an evening in bed. On some occasions, we didn't have to do anything sexually. She was my getaway. I trusted her with the one thing that I didn't trust my wife with - and that was my life. If some unforeseen incident happened, I trusted her more than my wife to have my back. Crazy, right?

"Me and Kim are doing well. Why'd you ask?" I replied with a small amount of curiosity.

"Jacob, you already know how I am. I was just wondering. Besides, I don't need yo ass asking me for a place to stay just in case you and Kim get into it behind yo dawgish ass ways. Me and my husband don't have any room for you," she concluded sarcastically.

Sadly, she was talking about her son. Latoya just wasn't wifey material, nor did she care to be. Part of what she said was true. I remember some shit in my psychology class that Sigmund Freud said about the Oedipus Complex. It was something to the effect about a baby boy would want to one day kill his father to have sex with his mother. That old white man must have snorted a ton of coke when he came up with that one. Nevertheless, he was on to something. It was just different for Black folks.

In many of our homes, there wasn't a father around for a young Black male to murder for the love of his mother. Actually, young Black boys who grew up in the hood didn't have a hard time fighting for their mother's affection because their father was removed from the home whether by the government or the streets. In general, Black boys filled the void that their fathers left. The boy became his mother's everything. He is a child when she needs someone to scold, but her man when she is incapable of doing a man's job. One of the biggest burdens a young Black boy face is being told he is the man of the house. Once a Black boy hears that he grows up thinking he is in charge of his mother's wellbeing. When mama doesn't have a date, he becomes her date. When mama doesn't have anyone to talk to about her problems, he has to listen. When mama doesn't have a man in the house when she hears creepy noises at the front door in the middle of the night, he has to go check it. When mama talks about having her own house one day, in the mind of her son, it is his responsibility to get it for her.

Moreover, if the boy doesn't leave the house once he becomes an adult, mama cripples him by saying it's okay for him to stay with her until he gets himself together. And depending on his will to leave the nest, he might be there until his mother's dying day or go out searching for another woman to be his mother all over again. He'll ask her for the keys to her house, keys to her car, some money out of her paycheck, and ask her to cook and wash his clothes. Just like mama did.

Anyway, I digress. We finished the crabs just about the same time. I wasn't really full because crabs weren't filling, but they were good. Latoya, on the other hand, looked to be nice and full. It was now time for the second-best part of the night. Latoya picked up both of our plates filled with crab shells and threw them in the garbage. She then proceeded to her bedroom. She came back with a joint in her hand. It was time to get high. I wasn't a weed head but getting high never hurt anybody. I didn't smoke unless I was about to fuck. Weed was only used as an aphrodisiac. Latoya was the first woman I smoked with. She was always freakier and more open-minded when she smoked. I was curious about what made her so sexually in tune with herself when she smoked compared to when she didn't. I finally gave in one day, and the rest was history.

We hit the joint a few times before Latoya said sarcastically, "Jacob, so you just came over here to be kind to me, huh?"

I knew this was coming. It was late, and it wasn't like we were gonna be watching the eleven o'clock news. "Well, to be honest, you know I miss going down the tunnel of love. Plus, I haven't gone back door in a while," I said with as much sincerity I could muster out of my mouth.

Latoya busted out laughing. "So, your wife ain't handling her business in the bed? Did you get the anal lubricant I told you 'bout?" she asked with an inquisitive look on her face.

The look I gave her said plain as day, *even if I did, Kim still wouldn't do it.*

Latoya let it pass and continued, "So, you come to me because you want out of me what she won't do for you. I bet even if she did, you would still cheat. I don't think I will ever get married after seeing the shit men do."

Latoya loved to play innocent before we had sex.

"Well, we are married from the hip down," I said in the hopes of lightning up the mood.

I could see she was upset by me referring to her body as my personal gain. She looked me directly in my eyes, "Jacob, you are stupid," she said busting out laughing.

Thank God my words worked. She looked back into my eyes again with a serious face.

"So, Jacob, you wanna fuck me?"

I chuckled. "Of course, I do. It's been a while."

The anticipation was overbearing. I jumped up and rushed at Latoya. She pushed me back.

"Jacob don't rush it," she insisted.

I was hot and bothered and really wanted Latoya bad. My patience was growing thin. However, Latoya had something in store.

"Jacob, go into my room and take off your clothes and rub yourself down with the oil on my nightstand. I'll be in there in a minute," she said.

I didn't hesitate. I went into her room and took off my clothes. I laid on top of her bed and put on the sweet almond oil she had on the nightstand. I began rubbing myself down quickly. It was something different. As a man, it was always a turn on when a woman suggested something sexual to do.

Latoya came into the bedroom. "Jacob, you look like a shiny chocolate candy bar. I hope you can satisfy me. Now rub yourself down some mo' in front of me!" She commanded.

I paused at first but took heed to her request. I began rubbing myself down as Latoya stood in front of me with her robe still on unclosed. I took my time rubbing myself down. I rubbed every inch of my body as seductively as possible. My muscles glossed as if I was running for Mr. Universe. I looked deep into her eyes as I stroked my dick with the oil. The weed had her looking like a sexy Black China doll. She licked her tongue with each stroke I took. I wanted her, and by the way, she was looking at me, she wanted me, too.

With her slanted eyes, she looked directly in my eyes as she began removing her robe slowly. Latoya's braless nipples pointed through her shirt like a beehive. She then pulled her Betty Boop shirt off. Her breasts were stunning, and her areolas were three times the size of a quarter. Her nipples were erect. I was ready to suck on 'em. That would come later. I just stared at her pretty dark skin while I continued to stroke my dick. She then removed her shorts. Her hips were banging, and the pussy print from her panties looked delicious. Once she finally removed her boy shorts, there was one last obstacle left. I was ready to see what Victoria's Secret hid. Though Latoya looked great in her red lace panties, I wasn't laying in the bed naked just for a peep show. Latoya looked into my eyes to see that I was done with the theatrics. Seeing my impatience look, she finally took off her panties. She smiled at me as I still stroked my dick watching her heavily tattooed body. I felt the urge to get up and take her right where she stood. I was overly turned on. I took one moment to stare at her voluptuous body.

Her tattoos enhanced her sexiness. Her body was a canvas of graffiti. Latoya in the nude looked like an exhibit from Art Basel. Each tattoo had its own meaning. From the neck down, there was an expression of her past and present ideas. Not one patron at the strip club would've ever taken the time to notice or cared what Latoya was trying to convey in her tattoos or how intelligent she was. However, being long-time fuck buddies, I knew very well what each one meant. Every tattoo was a contradiction of her life. They said who she once was, and who she was becoming.

Anyway, Latoya was completely naked. I laid in the bed covered in oil with a hard-on. The weed had kicked into overdrive: my dick felt harder than when I didn't have weed in my system. I didn't want Latoya to make a move towards me until my third eye got a complete view of her naked body. I told her to come here, and she slowly crept onto the front of her King size bed like a lioness who had spotted her prey. Her lips watered as if she spotted a zebra. Our eyes met as she came closer. The lust in my body grew fonder as she finally reached her destination. Simultaneously, she grabbed my dick with her right hand and kissed me. We both opened our mouths to let our tongues go wild. With my tongue down her throat, she stroked my oily dick with passion. We tongue wrestled for a while before I began biting down on her bottom lip. I bit down on it hard, but not hard enough to cause a puncture into her pretty little lips. In pure ecstasy, she pulled away with her head and eyes rolling to the back. Latoya looked like she was caught up in the rapture of lust. I reached my hands down by her pussy as she pulled her body closer to me. I rubbed her clit with gentle aggression. In no time, I felt her wetness. Latoya vaginal lubrication showered my drowning fingers which would make it easier for my dick to penetrate when the time presented itself. She continued grinding her pussy on my fingers to stimulate her vagina. From the expression on her face, she was enjoying herself.

She then grabbed my hand and brought it up towards her mouth. The same two fingers that I used to rub her clit were the same two fingers that she used to put into her mouth. She sucked them as if she imagined that they were another dick in her mouth. She sucked while I aggressively grabbed her breast with my other hand. I didn't know if my dick was harder or her pussy was wetter, but the foreplay was off the hook.

Latoya stopped sucking my fingers. There was something more interesting on her mind. The dick was calling her. She gave me one last kiss and began licking on my chest. Latoya's sexuality grew stronger. She slowly licked around my chest nipple. It felt weird at first, but I was high, so I went with it. She then bit down on them one at a time. I must admit, it felt so good that I clenched my teeth. With saliva on the tip of her tongue, Latoya then combed my abdomen. Without care of the oils in her mouth, she licked and kissed all over my six-pack. She then went down to my belly button and began making a circular motion with her tongue. My back rose up to assure her that she was doing a great job. Her gentle tongue made my eyes close as I knew what was next. Her head moved down even further as her tongue now engaged my groin. She had no problem getting to my dick because there weren't any pubic hairs to be found. As a model, I had to get a wax every week. Boy, did it hurt, but it was worth it: it felt so good when a woman's tongue grazed across the bare area.

My dick was fully erect and ready for Latoya's baptism. She then looked me directly in my eyes before turning into her alter ego, Nasty Bitch. Her stage name was Black Betty Boop, but in bed, Nasty Bitch represented everything nasty about Latoya. She was a freak. I was just lucky to be getting some.

The lust in her eyes showed that she was ready to suck my dick. I closed my eyes to prepare myself for the massacre she was about to do to my dick. She started at the tip of my head with a little tongue action. She swirled her tongue around the top of my penis before engulfing it. I felt my temperature go up an extra notch. The oil was sweating from my body like I was sitting in the sauna for hours. Latoya wasn't shy when it came to giving head. After putting my dick down her throat, she quickly came back up gasping for air. She looked me directly in my eyes to let me know that was only the appetizer before the entree. Latoya wasn't the type to give you everything at once. Her cheerful play and patient attitude were what drove me crazy.

I thought I was the master of seduction until I met Latoya. She was good at capturing the mood. She proceeded to suck the top of my head again and did so with the perfect pace. She was only warming up. I made myself more comfortable by relaxing my legs. I caught a cramp the last time Latoya gave me head. Once fully relaxed, Latoya's mouth went further down. She had to be at halfway down my dick when I felt the saliva building up in her mouth. With the build-up, my manhood drowned in warm wetness. The noises Latoya made with her mouth was unparalleled. She slob on my popsicle as if her life depended on it. I tossed my head from side to side on the pillow. Between the head and weed, it felt like the veins in my dick was gonna burst. After slobbering all over my dick, she abruptly pulled away. I opened my eyes momentarily to see what happened. She had something to say. And what she told me, no other woman had ever said to me before.

"Look in my eyes when I suck yo dick!" Latoya said as she went back down. Only this time, she did the full Monty.

"Mmmmmm!" Was all I could say.

She deep throated me as I watched her intensely. She was down so far that I felt her lips on my groin. The drool showered down, and my toes curled again. I couldn't look at her anymore. My head went back into the pillow. I tossed and turned again. She had no mercy on me as she sucked my dick up and down. Her deep throat was crazy good. For a moment, I wish my wife was there to see how it was supposed to be done. She then caressed my balls as she gagged on my dick. The sounds of gagging noises turned me on even more. I felt myself cumming, so I quickly grabbed her by the head and pushed her away from my manhood. Cumming too fast would have ruined the moment. I needed a break.

"So, Jacob, you can't handle it? You lil punk," she said poking at me.

After a short breather, the volcano of cum calmed down. I was now ready for Latoya's freaky ass. I slipped my magnum on. Driven by lust, I laid Latoya down on her back. She pulled back her pussy lips for me to stick my dick in. It went in with ease because it felt like the levee broke on her vaginal walls. After a couple of strokes, my dick felt like it was drowning, but the strength of my boat kept me afloat during the storm of her wetness. I could tell from the start; lubrication wouldn't be needed at all that night. The THC from the weed made me feel like we were as one. The chemistry was there, and every stroke I gave her had a meaning. I put my hands underneath her ass, so I could bring our bodies closer as she let me have my way. It felt like my dick was doing the cha-cha with her pussy. No matter how she moved, I automatically caught on to her rhythm.

Sex was always best when words didn't have to be spoken. The mind and body already know what the other person's body wants. Intuitively, Latoya and I had that in common. I pulled my dick out of her pussy to prepare myself for the next position. I laid on my back with my dick standing straight up waiting for her to get on top. I imagined her being a jockey saddling up to ride her Stallion. Once Latoya was fully on top of me with a soaking pussy, I launched my dick inside of her. I took one look at her and said, "Are you ready to win the Kentucky Derby?"

Not having a clue of what I was talking about, she simply said, "Yes!"

We were then off to the races. With the strength in her legs, she was able to lift herself up and down my dick. Her squats at the gym were paying off. I was able to match her intensity by pushing my dick up in her when she came down and pulled my dick down when she came up. Her ass made a juicy noise. It sounded like the echoes of tomatoes being smashed at the La Tomatina Festival in Bunol. What made it more sensual was her small breasts bouncing as she went up and down my dick.

With her right hand pressed down on my chest, Latoya looked like she wanted to take complete control of the situation. I knew Latoya well. From the look on her face, she wanted to fuck me without my participation. I made my body motionless with a standstill dick. She wanted to work, so I let her. It was like her pussy opened even more. She slid up and down with the grace of a gymnast. I found myself in awe of her athleticism. I gave nothing of myself outside of a hard dick. That moment in her dominance over me was all she needed. If I even attempted to put my hand on her, she would slap it away. I believed in her mind; my dick really became her stallion that she was riding to victory. The only physical thing I was allowed to do was make a fuck face. Over time, I became bored with playing dead. I wanted to feel alive and contribute to our sexual encounter. I wasn't into necrophilia sex. I was tired of being treated like a corpse. It was time to move on.

Latoya only had two ways to cum; either orally or anally. There was no in-between. Latoya was a freak for anal sex. No matter how many times I've penetrated her vagina, she never got off like she did when we had anal sex. In the wee hours of the night, it was time for me to take back control.

With my hands grabbing her arms we said our dialog, "Latoya, are you ready to open the back door?"

Latoya looked down at me with a smile, "Who's at the back door?"

"Jacob."

"Jacob who?" She asked.

I giggled, "Jacob Dick."

With seduction in her face, she said, "Jacob Dick what do you want?"

"Jacob Dick was wondering would you let me in your back door?"

And as usual, the dialog ended the same way.

"Yes, Jacob Dick. I will let you into my backdoor."

It was getting late, we both wanted to cum, so Latoya got off my dick and bent over for doggy style. On average, I believe most men and women liked doggy style. It's something about that position that intensifies sex. I have done many different sexual positions, but doggy style was always gonna be a classic in my book.

Latoya turned her body to face the headboard. She took the face down, ass up position. Her pussy looked like a swollen peach protruding from the back. Though Latoya liked anal sex, I still had to take it easy on her. I always had to fuck Latoya's pussy first before penetrating her asshole. Though she liked anal, it was still a delicate area. There would not be any ramming on my part, at least not at the beginning. I would have to take my time at first.

I gave her one look, and she said, "The anal ease is in the top dresser drawer."

I quickly grabbed it. Since I haven't had anal sex in a while to the default of my wife, I was a bit anxious. I took one hard stare at Latoya's apple bottom before I put my dick inside her pussy. It slid in nice and easy. It was still wet with a little tightness. I went in hard. It was like the weed said, "Go hard, or go home." I'd come too far to go home, so I went hard.

Latoya threw it back as I pushed my dick in. We were in sequence again. Her snapper was biting like a Sunday morning fishing trip on a boat in the Florida Keys. Her ass clapped for an encore. I oblige by sticking my dick in her deeper and deeper. I felt sweat pouring from my forehead. I was all the way in. It was time to put the icing on the cake, or shall I say, the anal ease in her anus. I grabbed it off the bed and poured a little in her butt hole. I let it marinate for a moment before pushing my index finger in it. Once I pierced her asshole, Latoya jumped a little. I fingered her tight booty hole as gently as possible. After a few strokes of my fingering, she became comfortable. So, with my dick in her pussy, index finger in her asshole and two fingers in her mouth, Latoya's sexual senses went in full throttle. She pushed her butt back and forth. It was like she wanted to feel the pressure of my dick in her pussy and finger in her ass. The real freak was now coming out. Nasty Bitch finally took over Latoya's body.

"Ja-Ja-cob-fuuuck me! Fuuucckk me harder!" She said seducing me even further.

"Okay, Latoya! I will stop playing with you. I see you want this dick." I said thrusting my dick further in.

"Yes, Jacob that is it. That is it!" She screamed back.

"Are you ready?" I asked

"Yes Jacob, I'm ready!" She shouted

# Changed

Her asshole had to be well bathed with anal ease by now, so it was time to take her to the Promised Land. I pulled my dick out of her pussy. It made a farting sound, so I guess I had handled my business. I took a moment to glaze her booty hole a little more with the anal ease before I stroked it. The head of my dick began penetrating her anus slowly. She pushed forward slightly, but that was the usual process before she let me go in fully. I put it in inch by inch before the pain subsided. With each pump, it seemed like her anus became numb to the pain. Latoya was now enjoying the pleasure of anal sex. With the tightness, my dick felt the satisfaction of her asshole. Before long, my aggression took over. I pulled her hair as I went deeper and deeper into her forbidden hole.

Latoya was getting into it. She placed her hands on her butt cheeks and opened them up as wide as possible. The sweat from my body descended onto her lower back which flowed down her backside unto her anal hole like a river headed downstream. The more I pulled her short hair, the more she wanted. I added slapping her ass to intensify our erotic pleasure. As I penetrated her anus, she reached between her legs and started finger fucking herself. I couldn't control myself anymore. It felt too good. I hope she was ready to cum or be left out.

I screamed out, "I'm bout to cum!"

I hoped that my warning helped her to prepare for her own orgasm.

With her head pressed deeply into her pillow, I heard Latoya mumble, "Don't pull it out!"

Just the sound of that made me explode inside of her asshole.

"I'm cummin'; I'm cummin'," I said as I felt a shiver come through my body. The nut was so intense that I felt like I was between life and death. If I were an elderly man, I probably would have died from a heart attack. It was that intense.

Latoya rubbed her clitoris harder as I couldn't move anymore. I was stuck. She continued to go for hers. After playing with her pussy for a moment, she started to shake as she reached her climax We both fell to the bed. The euphoria from us both cummin' ended the night on a high note. By then, I needed a short nap. I looked over to see on Latoya's alarm clock that it was 4:15 AM. I couldn't believe that we had sex for four hours. I only had two hours to take a quick nap. I hit the alarm clock on my phone for 6:00 AM and went to sleep.

I jumped up at 6:00 AM but didn't get out of the bed until 6:10. I didn't have time to wash my dick. Latoya was knocked out. I left 200 dollars on her dresser drawer hoping it was enough to get her hair done over. In a matter of minutes, I was in my car pulling off. I was praying that I-95 wasn't jammed packed. I only had roughly 2 hours to get home before Kim would walk in the door with her scrubs on. I had to think quickly. I would have to either take the freeway, which could 've had an early morning accident or deal with the lights on Biscayne Boulevard. I turned on the radio to hear the traffic report. Steve Harvey had just finished picking fun at Nephew Tommy. I laughed but stayed focus on the traffic update.

"Expect a 30-minute delay on I-95 South Bound lanes due to a three-car accident. Two lanes are closed till further notice," the traffic reporter reported.

I took a deep breath because I knew I would have to catch every light going down Biscayne. The traffic wasn't that bad. I caught a few green lights. On occasion, I would run into a couple of yellow lights, but I drove through them as if they were still green. I was willing to risk getting a traffic ticket to make it home before Kim. I didn't want to explain myself or give her any idea that I might be out doing something that I wasn't supposed to be doing. It was a task being able to have sex with so many women and never getting caught by my wife.

*** 

Kim's career choice gave me every possibility to get away with cheating. Kim's schedule fit just the way I needed it to be. She worked four days a week with three days off. Her schedule would fluctuate sometimes, but she mostly worked through the weekend. No matter what, it was always four days on and three days off. She made it even easier by posting her work week on the refrigerator as a reminder. I believe I paid more attention to it than she did. On the first three days, she did twelve hours, and on the last day, she did a half a day. She normally worked from 7 PM until 7 AM Friday, Saturday, and Sunday; and on Monday, she worked half a day.

With Kim's schedule, the opportunities were always there. From Friday until Sunday, I felt like a single man with a wedding ring. I had a lot of space to do whatever I wanted. During my alone time, I found out that two ambitious people in a marriage resulted in less sex. Kim and I only had sex twice a week, and that's if she wasn't too tired. If I was lucky, I might get some three times a week. I would complain only as a smokescreen to cover up what I was really doing. If it were up to me, I would have sex with Kim at least seven times a week and at least five times a day. But, how could I tell her that?

Anyway, I did what any sensible man would do in my position: I found other women who would fulfill my needs. I've jacked off only one time in my whole life. Once I caught my nut, I felt like it was a waste of time. In my opinion, it took away the ability of going out and getting it. I definitely was a hunter. Or better yet, women culled me - I was tall, dark, and handsome.

Furthermore, I knew the best way to get caught cheating was by having an affair and changing my behavior. There is no way in the hell a man can continuously have sex with the same woman and not have feelings for her. Matter of fact, a man could grow to love his side chic more than his main lady. In my opinion, there were far greater advantages to having a side chic than meets the eye. Typically, side chics do whatever it takes to keep her dude happy, and the woman at home does everything to piss him off. A side chic is a relief from some of the bullshit a complacent woman at home will put a man through. A woman who is too comfortable will always put herself in a position to be cheated on. A side chic doesn't really come with any real responsibility outside of helping her with a few bills or paying for miscellaneous things, such as nails, hairdos, outfits, or just a meal. Finding the right woman who isn't looking for commitment could be so much fun. But most times, women will eventually want more, and that could be a real problem at home, so I avoided women who I thought were bold enough to show up to my doorstep.

To keep myself looking like I was a faithful man, I kept my behavior the same around Kim. I used the art of deception to keep her in the dark, away from what I was really up to. I kept my routine the same when we were home together. I gave her all the attention she needed when we spent time alone, but when she went to work, my mind shifted to new pussy. Furthermore, I made sure to block certain women's phone calls and text messages. No matter how hard they tried to contact me, I showed them no love. They would hear from my voicemail:

> *You have reached Jacob Richardson. I'm sorry that I can't come to the phone right now. Please leave a detailed message and I will get back to you as soon as possible.*

The text messages were filtered through an app I downloaded. Nothing got through to me other than what I wanted to get through. Moreover, usually, the few women that I dealt with, I put their names up under a male name. Christine was Chris, Keisha was Keith and Shantae was Shawn for example. I also never put a lock on my phone; Kim was able to access it at any time. I never got nervous when she picked up my cell phone. It was so rigged that it would take a computer geek to hack into it.

I was a disciplined cheater. I knew if I made one false move, Kim would be on my ass like flies on shit. The worst thing I could do was get caught cheating. If Kim ever found out, that would be it. I needed her blind trust to get away with what I was doing. If I ever lost her trust, I would lose control. She would become untrusting of everything that I did. I knew the less a woman trusted, the harder it was to cheat. Just as hard as I worked to be with other women was just as hard as I had to work to hide it from my wife. I couldn't afford that with my sexual urges.

On certain nights that I felt obligated to be with Kim and miss out on some new pussy, I would start an argument. Though my wife didn't give me a reason to argue, I would make up one. I

# Changed

remembor one time, I got a text on my app from a chic that I wanted to hit but couldn't respond because my wife was sitting right next to me. I had to come up with an argument. I decided to excuse myself to the kitchen to grab a snack. While I walked into the kitchen, I tried to figure out an argument. I combed the kitchen to see what I could complain about. I couldn't find a damn thing! The cabinets were clean. The stove was spotless. The refrigerator was in order. I kept searching. I looked on top of the refrigerator to find my excuse. Kim left the wire string off the bread again. It was perfect.

Kim yelled into the kitchen, "Jacob, did you find what you're looking for?"

*I sure did*, I thought to myself. I walked into the living room angrily. "Kim, how many times do I have to tell you don't leave the bread opened?"

I knew the way I said it to her, Kim would get upset. It would start an argument, and I would storm out.

"Jacob, number one, don't talk to me like that. I'm not one of your floozies you train at the gym. You will not speak to me like that," she screamed back to me.

Kim wasn't a punk by a long shot. I quickly backed down, but I wasn't done badgering her.

"Ok Kim, I'm sorry for my tone, but you know how I feel about the bread being opened. The pressure from modeling is getting to me, I need to take a breather. Besides you know how I am about eating out of bread that has been opened. Anything can get into it. You know I'm a germaphobe. You and I both know I hate being sick. That will stop me from getting this money," I said with the sincerest face as possible.

Kim looked at me with an attitude, but once what I said sunk in, her facial expression changed.

"Jacob, I understand you are dealing with a lot of pressure, but don't take it out on me. I'm sorry for leaving that stupid wire thingy off the bread. I will do better, but please don't talk to me like that," she said taking a deep breath.

I stood quietly. "Jacob, you may be right. Go hit the gym or something to get the pressure off your mind. I'll cook tonight. Don't stay out too late so your food doesn't get cold."

It kept everything in my body from laughing. "Okay, honey. Thank you for your understanding," as I went into the bedroom to grab my gym bag. I waited until I walked down the end of the hallway to text my new pussy.

***

That was just one of my episodes on how I used an argument to get out of the house. Anyway, I needed to make it home before Kim did. I was able to maneuver through traffic and now had about an hour to get home. For some odd reason, I was feeling a little guilty. I usually didn't feel this way after creeping out with another woman. I couldn't understand what was going on with me, but I decided to stop by a grocery store before making it home. I quickly made a turn in a shopping plaza that had a newly built Publix. I ran inside to buy roses. The guilt I felt inside made me find the prettiest bouquet as possible. I paid for them and rushed back out to my car.

I made it home shortly after my short pit stop. I drove through the parking garage, peeping to see if Kim's silver-blue Porsche Cayenne was parked. Her space was still empty. Thank God because I didn't want to explain myself.

I spoke to the security guard as I hustled towards the elevator. I pressed the button to the 18th floor praying that there wouldn't be too many stops. The elevator swiftly moved until it reached the tenth floor. It stopped. A beautiful Latino woman entered with her Yorkshire Terrier hanging its head out of her Louis Vuitton purse.

"Good morning!" she spoke.

I said, "Good morning! What floor are you going too?"

She kissed her dog in the mouth before answering, "The Penthouse Suite. Thank you!"

I pressed the button, and we were off. I stepped back and looked at her from the back. She was a beautiful senorita who looked like she was well taken care of. Her body was fit. From the looks of things, she looked like she had got her early morning workout on in the Condo's gym. There was sweat still on her back. The tenth floor always had people in and out of it. It was the hot spot for meeting people who worked out. They had common ground. The morning was the usual crowd of retirees and business people with time to stay in shape. The evening was for the working class who wanted to get it in before going to bed. I never used it because I made my living in LA Fitness. Besides, I didn't want to get too familiar with anyone in the building. I didn't believe in eating where I shitted. But I could see that the gym was doing her body some good. She probably had a rich man taking care of her. I'd seen her once or twice in passing with a tall Spaniard dude who looked to be well off. Anyway, the elevator finally made it to the 18th floor.

"Ok, enjoy your morning," I said as I walked out of the elevator.

I walked through the door still feeling a sense of guilt. The bouquet of flowers didn't feel like enough. I looked down at my watch to see that I had about 45 minutes – Kim would be walking through the door at eight. I decided to cook breakfast for her. But first, I had to get the sex off my body.

I jumped into the shower and scrubbed myself down. I scrubbed so hard that it felt like I was peeling my skin off. Once I purged myself of sex, I hopped out of the shower feeling refreshed. I decided not to put any clothes on. I thought it would be better to cook her an omelet with oatmeal in a towel.

I took out four eggs from the refrigerator, along with green pepper, red pepper, onion, sliced cheese, and some leftover steak. I was gonna make Kim the best Omelet ever out of guilt. Anyway, I sliced and diced the onions and peppers. I poured the 4 eggs into the skillet. I let them cook for a few minutes before putting the meat and vegetables on top of the frying eggs. I placed the cheese on the left side and steak and vegetables on the right side of nearly cooked eggs. The omelet cooked perfectly. I covered the omelet for at least one minute before turning it which allowed me to put the apple cinnamon oatmeal into the microwave. I pulled two small glass cups from the cabinet. There couldn't be breakfast without Tropicana Orange juice. I poured the two cups quickly so that I could get back to the omelet which looked to be a yellowish brown color. I rushed over to do the most difficult part. One false move, the omelet would be ruined. It took years of practice to learn how to flip a perfect omelet, and this morning, my skills would be put to the test. I was pushed for time. "come on babe!" I said as I managed to get the spatula underneath the flat egg. I eased it up carefully. I made sure to go slowly so it didn't break. It made it over without breaking. I was well pleased and now wondering when Kim would walk through the door. I cut the omelet in half. It was more than enough for both of us. I place them on each of our plates. Then I felt something again. It was guilt. I couldn't shake it. *What the hell was wrong with me?*

Anyway, after placing the two cups of Tropicana Orange Juice and omelet on the table, I kept wondering when Kim would walk through the door; it was a bit after eight. I took my oatmeal out of the microwave and put hers in. I just prayed she would be walking through the door. It would have spoiled the surprise if I had picked up the phone and called her. I just proceeded with the task at hand. I placed the rest of the breakfast on the dining room table. The aroma filled the kitchen. I could smell greatness in the air. Cooking wasn't my forte, but I was great at cooking breakfast.

I felt like something was missing. It hit me; strawberries with brown sugar as a dipping sauce would complete the beautiful display.

As I opened the refrigerator to reach for the strawberries, I heard the lock turn. Kim walked through the door looking exhausted. When she looked at me, I smiled. She then looked down at me with a towel on and strawberries in my hand, a sign of relief went over her face. She began to giggle.

"Jacob, what are you doing half-naked in the kitchen with strawberries in your hand?"

"I read in Reader's Digest that women like hot butt naked men in the kitchen cooking breakfast."

She chuckled again, "Jacob, you're crazy!!"

I looked her directly into her eyes and said, "Yeah, I'm crazy about you! Come here, babe."

# Changed

I kissed and hugged her with strawberries in my hand. I took one and put it in her mouth. It really would have been a special moment if I didn't do what I did the night before. As she rested her head on my chest, I felt guilt pulsating through my body. Was I getting soft or what?

*by* _____

# Chapter 6
# The Big Apple

Monday morning, I was sitting my ass in Fort Lauderdale Airport with mostly White people waiting on an Airplane going to New York. I guess it was too early for Black folks to be up for a flight. I sat by myself thinking about how far I've come. I was living a dream just like the only man that I ever admired: Tyson Bedford. He had the most influence on my life. Tyson's impeccable impact on the modeling world for young Black men kept me with the hope that I would be great just like him one day. And the brand that I first saw him in was about to give me the same opportunity to shine. I then wondered if I would meet Ralph Lauren. I guess I would find out when I landed in the Big Apple.

"Please get your tickets ready with your boarding pass in your hands. Flight 38 is ready to board," the pretty announcer said over the microphone.

I was so excited. It would be my first time going to New York. I quickly grabbed my carry-on bags and stood in line. The flight attendant standing at the podium checked my boarding pass with a sparkling smile.

"Ok, Mr. Richardson, enjoy your trip to New York."

I smiled back and said, "I hope New York is ready for me!"

I proceeded down the tunnel with my destiny on my mind. I felt like I had the whole Miami and Haitian community on my back. I wasn't afraid to represent where I was from. Miami would no longer be just represented by South Beach and the "First 48 hours". It would have a new star other than Dwyane Wade? I wondered if "Jacob" County would ever catch on?

Once I entered the door of the plane, I was greeted by another pretty stewardess whose smile was as engaging as the first flight attendant in the waiting area. I looked down at my ticket to see exactly where I sat. I requested a window seat online, so I had a nigga moment in my head. *No one betta be sitting in my seat*, was my first thought. Once I got closer to where I was sitting, my first thought was actually a mindless one because seat E06 was empty. I took my seat realizing I left my earphones at home. I then wondered who would be sitting next to me. With my luck, it would probably be some fat ugly woman with stank breath who would want to talk to me the whole flight. I turned my head to look out the window and took a deep breath to prepare my mind for a three-hour flight. I had a big breakfast earlier that morning, and the dreadful nigga-itis was slowly making me drowsy. Before I could close my eyes fully, I heard a kid's voice.

"Wuz up sir?" He asked which forced my eyes to open.

It was a little Jewish teenager with a kippah on the top of his head. He was frail with freckles on his face, but his clothing had a hip-hop appeal to them, and he had a pair of Jordan's on to match his urban outfit.

"Hi, my name is Brad Lewinsky. What's your name?" the kid asked me as he leaned towards me to shake my hand. I was taken aback by his boldness to start a conversation.

"My name is Jacob Richardson. So, you're traveling alone?" I asked shaking little Brad's hand.

"Yeah, once a month I travel from New York to Miami because that's where my mother lives. My father and mother got a divorce 2 years ago. I guess they agreed that I would live with my father to learn the Jewish tradition and go to Miami with my mother to forget all of it. My dad is strict, and my mother lets me have my freedom," Brad finished. I thought, *His parents were crazy as hell to let him fly by himself.*

I was about to say something back before the flight attendant interrupted with instructions on how to survive just in case the plane crashed or landed in the water. She went over a couple of procedures before I turned my attention back to Brad. I would've been the first to drown because I didn't listen to anything the flight attendant said.

"So, Brad, you live in New York with your dad, and you go visit your mom in Miami? I guess you have the best of both worlds," I stated.

# Changed

Brad put a smile on his face and said, "I guess so. I can do this for the rest of my life. New York is fast pace, and Miami is the vacation of vacations. The beaches are beautiful, and the girls are pretty," young Brad finished.

Brad seemed like a cool little teenager. I was about to judge him because of his Kippah, but I was wrong. I thanked God for a mouthpiece. If people couldn't talk, everyone would be judged from how they looked. Brad was a true example of, "you can't judge a book by its cover." Although Brad sounded like a smart kid to talk to, my body needed rest.

I explained to him, "Well, Brad. I'm glad that you enjoyed my city. And you're right, the women are pretty, and the beaches are great. But, check this out Brad, I'm about to get some shut eye."

Brad looked like a lonely child that needed some attention. "Okay, but I have one question before you go to sleep."

He waited for me to say okay. "Go ahead," I said.

"So why are you going to my city?" He said being sarcastic.

I smirked, "I'm going to your city to do a photo shoot."

He began taking his Beats by Dre out of his book bag as he simply replied, "Okay."

I didn't want to be rude to the kid, but I needed some sleep. I fell asleep quickly, thinking about how I would pose in Polo's underwear.

It didn't take long for my dream to be interrupted. "I'm leaning on any nigga intervening with the sound of my money machine-in, my cup running over with hundreds, I'm one of the best niggas that done it, six digits and running. Y'all niggas don't want it," Brad rapped to the beat drumming in his earphones.

I woke up livid. I pulled one of his earphones off of his ears.

"Brad, you are too loud, and can't you see that I'm Black?" I said scolding him.

Brad seemed to be a little startled, but not unnerved. "I'm sorry Mr. Richardson, but I am a big Jay-Z fan. He's a lyrical genius and entrepreneur," Brad said giving Jay-Z his props.

Trying to be understanding for Brad's love of rap music, I simply said, "Brad, yeah Jay-Z is cool, but I'm trying to get some sleep. Besides I don't like you using the word 'nigga' around me."

It was like a light bulb went off in Brad's head when I said that.

"Though the 'N' word carries a negative connotation, Tupac said it means, 'Never Ignorant Getting Goals Accomplished,'" Brad said being a smart aleck.

I responded fast, "Where did you hear that at?"

Brad didn't hesitate, "The internet! You can find anything you want to know on the internet." For crying out loud, this kid was too smart.

"Brad, that's cool that you learned that on the internet, but please don't say the 'N' word around me. It is offensive," I said with an angry pro-black face.

Brad repeated sorry again and promised he would find a different song to listen to. I gave him a nudge to let him know if he didn't bother me, I wouldn't bother him. Back to sleep, I went.

"Jigga, what's my muthafucking name? Jigga, who I'm rolling with? My niccaz?" He rapped out loud again. I woke up and snatched off his earphone.

"Brad, didn't I just tell you not to say the word 'nigga'?" I said in my most meanness voice. He put his hands up in fear, but once again he didn't back down.

"My bad Mr. Richardson, but I didn't say the N word. I said nicca. I took the two Gs out, so I wouldn't offend you again. I can't help that I'm a big Jay-Z fan! Jewish people love listening to rap music too. Unfortunately, a lot of the best rap songs uses the "N" word. I'm not trying to be disrespectful; I'm only repeating what the words say," he expressed. I thought for the first time in my life how much rap music gave little snobbish suburban white kids their First Amendment right to say nigga either in front or behind African-Americans backs. Some only repeated what they heard.

"Well do you have anything else to play?" trying my best to work with him.

He looked down at his playlist. "Mr. Richardson, I sure do. I have Tupac, Nas, and Biggie downloaded to my phone."

# Changed

I was at a loss for words. "So, kid, how do you know all those legends and you're only a teenager? You weren't even born in that era," I finished.

Brad looked at me with confidence. "Mr. Richardson, my mother loves their music. When my dad wasn't around, she would play rap music. My dad is what you call a traditional Jewish man, but my mother, on the other hand, was totally opposite. My mother has a lot of hood in her. She grew up in a house where some of the men in the family weren't so nice. Matter of fact, I think some of the old timers were associated with the Italian mob. Jewish men couldn't be Made Men in the La Cosa Nostra, but they could still be mobsters. I believe the reason my dad fell in love with my mother was because of her toughness. My dad was laid back, and my mother was the Hellraiser," Brad explained.

I was surprised to know that it was Brad's mother who put him on to Hip-Hop and not his dad.

"So, you mean to tell me that it was your mom, and not your dad who introduced you to the kings of rap? Wow! Yo mama is gangsta" I said.

Brad ruminated over the question for a few seconds before responding.

"Mr. Richardson, you're right. I never thought about it like that. I guess my mother is the cool one out of the two," he said analyzing his parents.

I probed more into his hip-hop knowledge. "So, Brad, who're your top five rappers?" I questioned.

The look on his face said he had been waiting for someone to ask him that forever. "You might disagree, but these are my top five rappers of all time: Jay-Z, Tupac, Nas, Biggie, and Eminem."

I was perplexed by Brad's answer. Anyone who loved rap music would know that Tupac was the greatest rapper of all time. Not only was he a rapper, but a great poet as well. Also, who could forget him as Bishop in the movie *Juice*? Furthermore, he was a revolutionist who wanted drastic changes done by the government through his Thuglife message.

This kid went from being cool to being lame. Being curious to why he chose Jay-Z over Tupac, I asked, "So why did you put

Jay-Z first and Tupac second? Everyone knows if Tupac were alive, there wouldn't be a Jay-Z." It was like a light went off in Brad's head when I said that.

"I beg to differ. Some people are destined to be great no matter what obstacles may come their way. Jay-Z is one of those exceptions. Tupac had his uprise, but Jay-Z had the right idea. Guns will never take over America, but capital and politics will. The oldest rule in the book is, 'He who controls the gold, makes the rules.' You can open people's minds with poetry, but it doesn't solve the problems that your people have been dealing with for years. It's called financial literacy. Research shows that though Jewish people make up only 4% of America's population, most control the majority of the wealth in this country.

On the other hand, Blacks make up 13% of America's population, and African-Americans are almost dead last when it comes to obtaining assets that will grow for future generations. Matter of fact, African-Americans are the highest consumers in this country, and when it comes to investing, business development, and real-estate holdings, African-Americans are at the bottom of the totem pole. I'm not trying to be harsh Mr. Richardson. I'm only stating facts. Don't get me wrong, I do love Tupac's music, but I think Jay-Z had the better perspective on capitalism. America is based on capitalism. I can't explain it any other way.

Furthermore, I find it to be interesting that every successful Black entertainer who makes something out of themselves are always associated with the Illuminati? Why isn't any of the wealthy White billionaires like Bill Gates, Warren Buffett, and Mark Zuckerberg being exposed for being a part of the same evils? If you tell someone being successful is evil, what do you think they will inspire to be? Moreover, if your people use slavery as an excuse to fail, then what else are they going to do besides fail?

Jewish people and Black people have been put through some of the worst torment in history, but we handled it differently. Some African-Americans ran to the government for help, but Jewish People ran to each other for support. When they told Jewish people, they were not allowed on South Beach, instead of protesting and boycotting the beach, they just bought it. Your people can have the same power. It's more of you than us in this country. If African-Americans pulled their resources together, your people would be so powerful in this country – more than uppity Whites. And those same Whites would have to respect the new paradigm shift. Whites don't fear an educated Black man because he has less of a chance of hitting them across their heads at an ATM. However, Whites will fear a group of Black men who have a financial understanding because those men can own and run banks. AND the ATM where he gets his money.

Mr. Richardson imagine a bunch of financially educated Black men in suits walking down the Yellow Brick Road to Wall Street to tell White folks to their faces, 'There's a new sheriff in town.' The looks on their faces would be priceless. Black people would then be known for residing in the highest places instead of the lowest places. People of color make up 45% of the prison system, but only make up less than 5% of the Senate.

Truth be told, no one knows who is in the Illuminati unless they are affiliated with it. But, if your people believe that being successful is associated with evil, your race is in trouble," Brad finished.

I was shocked by the knowledge the young kid had. I felt ashamed that I never thought about the Black struggle that way. I found myself pondering over everything that Brad had said. My brain was in overdrive. I started thinking about what I could do as a Haitian-American to help my people. Up to that point, my only thoughts were selfish. Pussy and being a big-time supermodel were the only things that mattered to me. For the first time in my life, I had thoughts of making a difference. I wasn't quite sure what it would be, but I knew after speaking to Brad, I had to find my purpose.

Damn it, why did God send this kid my way? Well, until I found out what I was supposed to be doing, I was gonna still be a slave to pussy and my career.

"Brad, you have an interesting way of looking at things."

I would have never thought in a million years that a Jewish kid would have such a unique perspective on the Black movement, more so than some Pro-Blacks did. For years, I believed the Black movement was about complaining about slavery and how it affected us as a people, but now listening to Brad, I gathered it was time to come up with a new ideology in the struggle of being respected as an African-American. Every opportunity that was given by a country that so-called hated us, was for us to take full advantage of. I thought that was the best way to fight back. Focusing so much on pass transgression, was like concentrating on an ex, when the new girl needed more attention. I wanted to one day become a progressive Black man instead of one who lived in the past.

Having such an intellectual conversation, I began getting sleepy again. My brain was stimulated. But Brad seemed like the type who didn't know when or how to stop talking.

"Brad, I really like your perspective. It's different and motivational. I promise you, if I can be the vessel of change for my Haitian and Black people, I will. But, with that being said, I need to rest. I have an important meeting tomorrow morning, and I can't go into it unenergetic," I explained.

Brad took it well even though the look on his face said he'd like to continue. "Okay, Mr. Richardson," he said looking like a sick puppy. It took no time at all for me to go back to sleep.

I woke up to, "Please put your seat belts on. We are about to land at Kennedy Airport. I hope everyone enjoyed their flight," the pilot said over the intercom.

I looked out of the window to see buildings, skyscrapers, and the apartment's right next to each other. It looked like they didn't have any space between them. I couldn't see any grass or trees. From the plane, it seemed like New York was busy and congested. Although I was a little disoriented from my nap, I still enjoyed my amazing view of New York City from thousands of feet above. I was ready to get off the plane and venture out. I would make the best of the next 2 1/2 days in the Big Apple.

We finally landed. I grabbed my bag and was off to the races to the baggage area. Some of the people who I got a slight glance of while on the plane were recognizable at the baggage claim. It took a while, but the luggage started to come out slowly.

# Changed

Waiting on luggage was like waiting on Lotto numbers to come out. It never came out quite right.

Brad's travel bag came out in the first group of luggage. He grabbed his bag and headed out. I hoped my bag would come out before he left. After at least 15 minutes of waiting patiently, my luggage finally came out on the conveyer belt. I grabbed my bags quickly as I walked with a little pep in my step towards the window glass doors to find a taxi. I wondered where Brad was at. I walked out of Kennedy Airport to the sun shining and blue skies. It was a beautiful Monday morning in New York, and the rush was on. The traffic at the airport was bumper to bumper so I knew it wouldn't be a problem catching a taxi to my hotel. But, before being in a rush to catch a cab, I wanted to see if I could find Brad. I turned every which way to see if I could find him. I couldn't spot him. I gave up on the idea. Before I started my way towards a taxis area, I felt a tap on my shoulder.

"Mr. Richardson, were you looking for me?" Brad said with a smile on his face.

"Yes, Brad I was looking for you. I wanted to thank you for the conversation on the plane. You have a real head on your shoulders. But I do have one question before I go. Why are you so concerned with Black people?" I said being curious again.

Brad went through the same emotion as he did before. "Well, Mr. Richardson, my great-grandfather was a freedom rider. He hated racism and wanted African-Americans to have the same rights as everyone else. Though he stood out like a sore thumb when he marched among Black protesters during the Civil Rights Movement, he still stood up for what he believed in, no matter how many times he was called an 'N'-lover by redneck bystanders. He always quoted Martin Luther King Jr., 'Stand for something or fall for anything.' That quote became his motto. His way of thinking was passed down to my grandfather then my dad and now me," Brad finished.

I was happy that there were kids like Brad in the world. At that point, I knew the next generation would be okay.

"Mr. Richardson, I want to tell you something before you go."

"Okay Brad," I said.

"Mr. Richardson, you will be a famous model one day. Just remember, a life without purpose will not amount to anything you accomplish if you don't change things around you. If you do one day find your purpose, you will be hated for challenging the status quo, and loved if you don't. Nothing will ever change if a man doesn't stand up for what he believes in. The kids in school sometimes tried to bully me because I represent a threat to their belief system. But I don't have to worry about that because I know judo. My dad paid for my classes, so I wouldn't be a wimp in my cause for change. From the day I started talking, he knew that I couldn't be weak. So, Mr. Richardson, I wish you well in all your future endeavors. And can I please have your email? Maybe one day we can speak via email," Brad stated, sounding so encouraging.

I gave Brad my email and wished him well. A man pulled up in a Ford Escort.

"Mr. Richardson that is my dad."

"Okay, Brad. I have a safe trip home." I said.

I watched him walk to his dad's car like a big brother. Once I saw him get into the small Ford Escort, I found a taxi. The driver asked me where I was going while putting my bags into the taxi's trunk. I told him, and we were off to Manhattan. I wanted to enjoy the view, so I kept my eyes glued to the window. As we drove out of Queens, I noticed homes were built differently from homes in Florida. They were beautiful but too close to each other for my liking. I thought Miami cheated people out of land, but New York took the cake.

The traffic was heavy which I knew the driver appreciated. We approached a toll plaza before going over the Manhattan Bridge. I thought for a moment that he would ask me to pay the fair. However, we went through with his taxi pass. As we traveled over the bridge, I stared at the East River with unlimited possibilities. The bridge was surrounded by water. I was a little uncomfortable, but my trust in the Lord got me through it.

As we approached Manhattan, the buildings got taller and taller. Downtown Miami had buildings, but they didn't compare to

# Changed

the gigantic skyscrapers that filled the skies of New York. I was overwhelmed, and little anxiety crept in as we got closer to Manhattan. But I wasn't gonna let fear get into my way. All the hard work I put in wouldn't be overshadowed by doubt.

It took 45 minutes for the cab to reach the Belmont hotel in Manhattan. Of course, the taxi driver drove away with a healthy $50 in his pocket. The only tip I could give him was to drive safe to his next destination. The hotel wasn't anything like I expected. There wasn't any bellman waiting in front of the Belmont to handle my bags nor valet parking attendances. I felt cheated from the start. But I wasn't paying for it. There was a young White girl who poorly wore her uniform at the front desk. With her tag leaning, Rebecca asked, "Hello sir, welcome to the Belmont. Will you be staying for more than one night?"

I started reaching for my wallet before answering. "Yes, I will be staying for more than one night," I said trying to be pleasant.

She smiled and asked for my ID and itinerary. I gave it to her. Once she saw that everything was cleared, she gave me my card key.

"Sir, you are in room 303. You can take the elevator to the third floor." I looked over to the carts sitting by the entrance door and decided to take my bags up.

Even the elevator looked to be antiquated. Nevertheless, I got on the elevator praying that claustrophobia wouldn't kick in. The inside of the elevator needed to be remodeled. I pressed the 3rd-floor button, and that's when the adventure began. The elevator made a loud noise as it seemed to be cranking up. It shook as I ascended to the third floor. My heart dropped. When it finally stopped on my floor, my heartbeat went back to its normal pace.

My room was a couple of doors down from the elevator. I put my card into the slot for the little green light to buzz me in. When I walked into the room, my mouth dropped to the floor. Room 303 looked more like a prison cell than a stay-in for a soon to be supermodel. The room was a little bigger than a six by eight cell. The bed looked similar to the one I had growing up in at my

Grandmother's house. The closet was tiny. It was built more for a child than an adult. The bathroom didn't make things any better. I've seen bathrooms in the projects that were more desirable.

"How could Ralph Lauren do this to me?"

I would give him a piece of my mind tomorrow. But today, I would make the best of it. I had enough money to leave but didn't want to seem ungrateful. There was no way I would let a crappy hole in the wall get the best of me. I decided not to take any of my clothes out of the suitcase. To calm me down, I called Kim.

"Hello," Kim said on the other end.

I sighed with relief when she answered the phone. It was early afternoon, and normally Kim would be asleep this time of day.

"Kim, you wouldn't believe this. Ralph Lauren put me up in a raggedy hotel. Bae, I feel like an inmate. How can he think so little of me?" I said in disgust.

I was hoping Kim knew what to say to get my thoughts back right. I was in a terrible state of mind. She didn't disappoint.

"Jacob, calm down. It isn't the end of the world. You are not up there for the hotel. You are up there to meet with the modeling agency. I'm pretty sure Ralph Lauren has nothing to do with this. This is an opportunity of a lifetime. Don't blow it, Jacob," Kim said sounding comforting.

As bad as I wanted to be upset, Kim's words sunk in.

"Well Kim, I'm still going to give them a piece of my mind."

Kim huffed. "Jacob, you can't be serious. Be happy that you were invited to New York for free. Just relax. If you don't like the room, go be a tourist instead of a complainer," Kim finished.

Lord, I hated when she was always right.

"You know something Kim, you're right. I guess this jail cell will make me appreciate my freedom in New York. I love you, babe. I'll call you later. I plan on doing a little shopping while I am out here – size eight right?" I confirmed her size like I didn't know which sizes and cuts accentuated her curves just the way I like them.

Kim laughed. "Jacob, you know I like to try my clothes on before I buy them. I'm a curvy gurl! But you know I love whatever you bring, and I'm going to wear it just for you!" as we said our goodbyes.

I decided the best thing for me to do was to take a nap. I was still sleepy and exhausted from the flight. My body had yet to get its proper rest. I looked around the tiny room once again in disgust, but I knew I had to make the best of it. Along with my eyes getting heavy, my jaw muscles began popping from yawning. The nigga-itis part two was beginning.

I woke up around 3:05 PM to my phone ringing. I grudgingly got up. I stared down at my cell phone to see a 212-area code. I knew it had to be someone from the modeling agency. I picked up the call.

"Hello, may I speak to Jacob Richardson," the caller said.

I wiped the cold from my eyes as I answered, "Yes, this is me. Whom am I speaking to?"

The caller replied, "This is Marty Grey from the modeling agency that requested you. I hope everything is fine. We need to meet with you tomorrow morning at 8:30 AM sharp. We'll go over the contract, and if you approve of it, you'll be doing a photo shoot for Polo's new underwear line. Are you familiar with the subway stations?"

I responded, "Well, I've never been to New York before so I'm a little lost."

Without hesitation, Marty Grey said, "Mr. Richardson, all you have to do is follow the itinerary. All the instructions are there. New York City has the best transit system in the world. You won't have a problem getting here." I felt confident after hanging the phone up with Mr. Grey about my ability to get around Manhattan.

My body felt well rested. It was now time to take a bite out of the Big Apple. I walked into the bathroom, and my slight case of OCD kicked in. There wasn't any way I would take a shower in that bathtub. I called down to the front desk to see if I could get housekeeping to come and clean the bathroom up. The young girl at the front desk said that the housekeeping staff was off. I was pissed but quickly moved on. I decided I would do it myself. I remembered when I was riding up to the hotel; I saw a CVS on the corner. It looked close enough to walk to. I jumped out of bed and made my way down the stairs to the lobby. I walked past the front desk without speaking to the clerk who went from looking sloppy to just plain old tired. I made my way out the door trying to remember exactly which direction I saw the CVS. I knew once I got to the corner of the sidewalk, it would either be on my right or left side. Once I got to the corner, I saw the CVS on the right corner of the Belmont. It looked to be close enough that I would get there in a couple of minutes. I proceeded to walk and paid attention to the buildings and streets names and numbers. My grandmother always taught me growing up to know my surroundings.

I made it to the CVS in no time. I didn't waste any time looking for cleaning products. I asked one of the older employees in a red vest to point me in the right direction for them. I grabbed the Clorox bleach and mold stain remover. Down the same aisle, I found a scrub brush for the tub and the bathroom tile walls. I grabbed an extra-large pack of yellow gloves and found a cheap toothbrush to clean the sink. I was now fully prepared to clean the bathroom to my liking. There were three people ahead of me in the checkout line. I looked over to see if the other cashier was opened, but she was rushing to go on break. I guessed I would have to be patient. The first lady in line had a small carrying bag in her hand filled with hygiene products. The next person didn't have anything in his hands. I figured he was there to buy a pack of cigarettes. The last person was an elderly Black man who had a loaf of bread in his right hand, Orange Juice underneath the same arm, and eggs in his left hand. The first two customers purchased their products fast. The cashier seemed as if she was trying to move up or get a bonus from CVS with her swiftness. The elderly Black man walked up slowly looking a little uncertain. He took his time putting his items on the counter. The cashier put them through as soon as she got them. The total came up to $7.08. The old man seemed to be a little confused. I gazed into his hand to see that he was a bit short.

"Young lady the last time I paid $6.48 for the same things, and that was just last week," the elderly man said with frustration.

# Changed

He must not have paid attention to the price change. It was obvious that he had been paying the same price for a long time. I didn't have any patience at that point. I wanted to get back to the hotel in time to clean the bathroom and get the hell out of there.

"Excuse me, sir, if you don't mind, I will give you the rest of the change," I said.

The cashier looked at me with a smile, and the senior man permitted me. I took care of his minor problem. He said thanks as he gathered his stuff and walked out. The cashier had me in and out as she did the other patrons.

I made it back to the hotel in no time. My only focus was the task at hand. I didn't waste any time. I took the cleaning products out of the bag. I ripped open the plastic bag containing the yellow gloves, and they fit perfectly. I grabbed the brushes as if I was a part of Belmont's housekeeping staff. I took a deep breath before I started cleaning. I put my back and elbow into cleaning. I scrubbed as if my life depended on it. I wasn't about to take a shower in a tub that I considered to be subpar. It was like I could see the glaze shining on the white porcelain tub as I scrubbed. Once I was done, I went over it again. When I was well pleased, I turned my attention to the bathroom tile walls and put the same effort in. When I was finally done with the bathroom, I stared at my work and congratulated myself on a job well done. I had to make sure my bathing area was cleaned thoroughly.

Once I was done with my unexpected workout, I prepared myself to take a shower. Thank God, I brought all my own bathing items. I had my black soap, shower gel, towels, toothpaste and toothbrush on deck. There wasn't any way I would be using any of the hotel's amenities. I had trust issues. I put my clothes on the bed before taking a shower. I didn't want to wear anything special for the first night in New York, but I still wanted to be fashionable. I just wanted to take a quick view of the city. Time was of the essence because I had to be up early in the morning to go to the modeling agency without a real clue of where it was.

I took a quick shower, grabbed my wrinkle-free Armani Exchange shirt and shorts off of the bed, along with my burnt orange Rick Owens sneakers that matched to a T. I looked like a

Texas Longhorn fan. It was an expensive casual look. I sprayed a little Tom Ford Tobacco Vanille as I walked out of my room.

Only a couple feet down was my nemesis. I dreaded getting back onto the elevator. I pressed the down button. It was about to be another adventure. I stood in front of the elevator praying that the ride down would be better than the one going up. The elevator shortly arrived after I pressed the button. The door opened. My heart began beating rapidly. My feelings of being stuck in it overtook my mind. I investigated the elevator as if it was the black hole of doom. I've ridden in some shaky elevators before, but not like this. I was at a crossroads of being a man or a coward. It was either me or the elevator. The elevator door suddenly started closing as I wondered if I should get back into it. I put my arm in between the closing doors to stop them. They opened back up. It bought me more time to decide what I should do. I took a deep breath before stepping in. My right foot stepped in, but my left was too scared to move. I pulled my right foot back and stared at the black hole of doom again to see if I could muster up the courage to walk back in. I felt like some little wimp ready to confront a bully. The fear grew enormously, as I knew that the elevator would be closing in any second. I repeated the famous words of Franklin D. Roosevelt, *the only thing we have to fear is fear itself*. It sounded good to say as I let the elevator doors close without me on it. I couldn't bring myself to get back on after the first experience. I got punk'ed by an elevator. The only thing that I could be proud of was that there wasn't anyone around to see an elevator take my manhood. I chalked up my losses and took the stairs. It was only three flights. For an athletic person like myself, it wouldn't be so bad.

I was downstairs in no time. I went out on the side of the hotel. The subway was only two blocks down from the Belmont. It was gonna be my first time on a subway. I was a little nervous but enthusiastic at the same time. Even though it was late in the evening, the subway was packed with people. I paid my fare and entered where the train tracks were located. I wanted to ask someone for help, but my pride made me look at the directory first. It was somewhat confusing, but I managed to see what train went

# Changed

to Times Square. It was a straight shot. I was pleased that I didn't have to change trains; that would have made things more difficult than they already were. There was a train passing every five minutes.

My train arrived less than 15 minutes later. I boarded with the rest of the people in a rush to get where ever they were going. The subway was stuffy and crowded. To avoid the pushing and shoving, I simply wrapped my hands around the first pole I could see. From the seats to the poles, there wasn't any space to wiggle. Though it wasn't much space to move, people still managed to mind their own business. No one spoke to each other no matter how close they were. It was almost complete silence outside of the train making noise. Being on a New York subway was different from what I was accustomed to in Miami. Yeah, Miami wasn't the friendliest place in the world, but the people on this train acted like they had something stuck up their asses. The haves had on suits with satchel bags hanging from their shoulders, and the have-nots looked like they had been beaten up by life. The rough-around-the-edges young hoodlums didn't associate with the dorky school boys. The ghetto fabulous chics rolled their eyes at the hard-working 9 to 5 women. I gathered from the looks of things New York was about minding your own damn business! I decided to do as the Romans did. I didn't want to get cursed out just from smiling at someone. I just kept observing without staring. I then noticed a few women were standing up while some men sat. I thought what kind of sleazeballs would let women stand up while they sat down? I guess some men just didn't have any gentlemen in them. I had to ignore it before it made me upset. My temper calmed down once I heard, "Times Square, next stop." I sighed in relief. The train stopped, and most of the passengers on the train got off.

We were off to the races. I didn't know where I was going so I followed the crowd. Times Square was easy to see. The lights were bright. It was the best light show I had ever seen in my life. The light bulbs were huge. I had seen Times Square many times on TV but seeing it in person didn't do it any justice. It was like the 8th Wonder of the World. Excitement flowed through my body. I was ready to see the lights up close. They obscured the strength of the stars as they weakly glared in the midst of the night.

From the moment I entered Times Square, I made it so obvious that I was a tourist. My eyes were wide opened, and I couldn't stop staring up at the skyscrapers' lights that illuminated the streets of Manhattan. Being impressed was an understatement. It was breathtaking. Taxis and cars were moving up and down the streets. There also were people walking at a fast pace as if it was still daytime. The pace was so different from Miami. The pedestrians who walked the sidewalks of Times Square looked like every step had importance to them. There were homeless people who put on a show at whatever capacity to earn their daily keep. Real New Yorkers would tolerate no handouts. The people in suits looked as if they were rushing to get to their nightly business meetings. There were stores everywhere for anyone who was interested in shopping. I made sure to stop by Express to grab Kim a few dresses and jeans. It always was easy to shop for her because she liked simple things.

Anyway, Times Square offered a man everything he could ever want. The only difference was it offered it flamboyantly. The more I walked with enthusiasm, the more my stomach growled. I hadn't eaten anything since breakfast that morning. I had to breakfast before my stomach would think that religion was the reason that it was not digesting any food.

I always wanted to eat a pizza from New York. Though not healthy for my 6-pack, I couldn't resist the fact that I always wanted to taste a New York deep dish pizza. Now where to find one was going to be the difficult part. I could have googled it, but I didn't want to go to a pizzeria that wasn't the best in Times Square. If finding it was gonna be hard, asking someone who knew would be even harder. New Yorkers just didn't look that friendly to me. I thought the best thing to do was to find someone who looked Italian. Call it stereotyping, but it only made sense. Hell, if I was White, I would ask someone Black where to find a good soul food restaurant. I wondered for a moment if I should look for someone with tan skin, a big nose, and a silk suit. Once again, I wasn't trying to be a stereotypical asshole; I just wanted the best deep-dish pizza New York City had to offer.

On my search for a pizzeria, I kept trying to draw images of an Italian in my head. I thought of Michael Corleone from "The Godfather." Then Joe Pesci's character from "Good Fellas." Then Robert De Nero's character in "Casino," popped into my head. With those descriptions in my mind, I was on the hunt for an Italian who looked like a wise guy. I walked with a decent pace with shopping bags in my hands to keep up with the crowd. I got a chance to window shop as I passed stores and boutiques on my pursuit for pizza happiness. I gazed through the crowd hoping to find someone who looked Italian. The more I walked, the less likely it became that I would find someone who could help me. I was ready to throw in the towel until I saw two men standing up next to what appeared to be a nice size pizzeria. One was smoking a cigarette, and the other was talking on the phone. The opened shirts and gold chains made me believe that I had found what I was looking for. If they were Italians, I would kill two birds with one stone. As I approached them, I wondered if they were gonna be like the gangsters from the Godfather. "If yo Black ass don't want to sleep with the fishes, don't ask us where a pizzeria is." Or like the short Italian dude from Eddie Murphy's Raw, "Yeah, moolie I know where a pizzeria is. If I show your Nigger-ass where it is at, you're gonna pay for my pizza. Then you'll watch me eat it right in yo nigger face. What do you think about that moolie?" If so, that definitely wouldn't have been a good experience.

"Good evening fellas. Is this a good pizza spot?" I asked while pointing up at Sal's Pizza Parlor.

They both looked at each other. "Brotha, this is the pizzeria of pizzerias. You must be new to Times Square?" The one smoking the cigarette asked.

"Yeah."

He said with excitement, "Man, you don't know what you're missing. This pizzeria is the best in town. My Uncle Louie used to own this joint years ago. He turned it over to his son, who's my cousin - Little Louie, who's done an even better job than the old man. I come here three times a week out of respect for my uncle and to eat a helluva pizza. I promise you; you won't be disappointed."

With the confirmation that I needed, I was ready to patronize Sal's Pizza Parlor. It was beautiful on the inside. It had a welcoming feel to it. People smiled at me as I waited in line to reserve a table to eat. The hostess had a few people in front of me, but it didn't look like the wait would be too long. I was just ready to eat. My stomach was still doing backflips. It made noises, but not enough for the people surrounding me to hear. The hostess finally asked me how many people would be seated. I said, "only me." Being alone got me a seat at the bar. It was fine by me. I just needed to eat something to calm my stomach.

The bartender acted fast. He quickly placed a coaster out in front of me.

"Good evening, my name is Marco, and I will be taking your order. Would you like to start with a drink?" He questioned.

Well, it definitely wasn't a night that I would be drinking, so I ordered the next best thing.

"Could I get a bottle of Boss water and two slices of Pepperoni pizza? And Marco while you're at it, could I also get the best salad that Sal's Pizza has to offer?"

Marco smiled and said, "I have just the salad for you, and your pizzas will be hot and fresh when they come out."

Thus far, the customer service was off the charts. The atmosphere was friendly, and I didn't feel uncomfortable at all being around such an auspicious crowd.

No one seemed to care that I was one of the few Blacks patronizing Sal's that night. The people sitting at the bar were too busy watching the New York Yankees to notice that I'd sat down. One guy drinking a Becks beer nodded his head, gesturing welcome once he spotted me. He quickly turned back to his friends cheering the hometown team on. The Yankees were up by one on their hated rivals, the Boston Red Sox. The top of the order was coming up to bat in the bottom of the fifth inning. I wasn't much of a baseball fan, but I glanced up at the TV hanging over the bar with curiosity because their enthusiastic energy rubbed off on me. I instantly became a New York Yankees fan.

# Changed

Well, at least for that night. You would have thought it was a playoff game with the amount of noise that was being made at the bar. Just as I got into the game, the bar back brought out the salad. It looked pretty good. I was hungry. It could have been green grass with horse manure sprinkled on top of it, and I probably would have still eaten it. I jumped right into it. The spinach, kale, cucumber, red tomatoes, balsamic vinegar, olive oil, lemon juice, sea salt, ground pepper, and garlic powder was devoured in seconds.

After eating one of the best salads ever, my stomach acted as if it was disappointed by its continuous grumbling. What made matters worse, I was drinking water that had zero calories. It was going to be a rough few minutes before the pizzas came out. I just prayed that it wouldn't take too long. The bartender brought more beers for Yankee fanatics who were now calm because the top of the order struck out in order. I could see the disgust all over their faces with the game heading into the top of the sixth inning. The loud talking became mumbles.

Just as my stomach was turning again, the bar back came out with my two pepperoni pizzas steaming. The smoke ascended from both of them. He placed the slices in front of me with the pepperoni sizzling and cheese melting. The deep-dish pizza crust was golden brown. Perfection was the only word I could think of. The first bite I took was to die for. I was in pizza euphoria if it was such a thing. I just knew I wouldn't ever look at another pizza the same. I was hungry but wouldn't be foolish enough to eat these two precious babies too fast. I wanted to cherish every moment. Besides, they were too hot just to rush it. I let them sit for a while before I took another bite. I didn't want to burn my lips off.

The Red Sox went up by one run without any outs. The Yankees looked like they were going to blow the game. The team chemistry was in disarray. The pitching wasn't as crisp as it was when I first tuned in. Anyway, the pepperoni pizzas finally cool down. I bit back into the same one that I put down earlier. The warmth of the pizza went through my body. It tasted so good in my stomach, I could feel the cheese and pepperoni being digested. My hunger became obsolete after every bite. My stomach was finally being satisfied. But the sad part about it, the pleasure didn't last that long. No matter how slow I tried to eat two slices of pepperoni pizzas, the fact remained that I was a grown man who was starving eating them. They were done quicker than I expected. I kind of wanted another slice, but I thought better of it. had to keep my six-pack intact for the photoshoot the next day. If I had a choice to eat or have a six-pack, I would probably choose to starve.

I paid my bill and left a healthy tip for Marco. I looked up at the TV for the last time to see that the Red Sox had scored again. The friends looked dejected. It didn't stop the beers from coming though.

I politely walked out of Sal's Pizza Parlor feeling better. It was amazing to see what a bite to eat could do. I walked with a sense of urgency. I was no longer interested in looking around Times Square. Time just wouldn't permit it. I needed to get back to the hotel and get some more rest. This time I would take advantage of Google Maps. I put 'subway' into my search engine, and it popped up. It was only a couple of minutes away. I moved expeditiously through the crowd. I made it to the Subway station in no time. I paid my fare and went through the entrance. The train pulled up shortly after I entered. I made my way on the train to find a seat as soon as I walked on. The train wasn't crowded like earlier. Ironically, there was more noise being made with fewer people on the train than before. Maybe the night owls were more comfortable around each other. I just sat quietly. I didn't want to be disturbed, and I didn't want to disturb anyone.

In a matter of minutes, the train stopped at my destination, and I rushed off the train. If Guinness World record was present, I would have established a new world record for how fast I got back to the Belmont from the subway station. I trotted up the staircase to my room. From my room to the shower. And from the shower to the bed.

# Chapter 7
# The Big Day

I woke up the next day with a burst of energy. I fell out of the bed doing pushups. It was one of my routines when I couldn't go to the gym. I did four sets of 50 pushups, then immediately started in on my sit-ups. I did ten sets of 60 in one-minute blocks with a minute break between. So, it took me all of 20 minutes to complete 600 sit-ups. Man, I felt awesome after my short morning workout.

I jumped in and out of the shower. Time was of the essence. My dress clothes were already on the bed. I thought since I would be meeting with Ralph Lauren's model agents, it would be a good look to wear the brand. With a twist on the words of the late and great Biggie Smalls, I was "Polo down to the socks."

I wore a plaid long sleeve shirt with an array of cool colors which blended in perfectly with my Diplomat blue slacks. The blue Polo symbol in the dress shirt was the same color as my slacks which accentuated my attire. Also, my brown belt matched with my brown and white golf polo shoes. My color coordination didn't stop there. To swag it out, even more, I wore a pair of Argyles diamond socks that matched the key colors in my outfit. Then the icing on the cake was my leather satchel bag that matched the brown in my belt and shoes. I was swagalicious.

I walked out of the Belmont looking like a million bucks. My self-esteem was on blast. There wasn't anyone who could tell me that I wasn't the man. Before heading to the subway, I had to find some breakfast. I remembered seeing a Mom and Pop store located in the same area as the CVS. I made a quick stop to grab something to eat. Though the little spot had a dine-in area, I decided take-out would be best. I ordered a breakfast sandwich to go. It was toasted wheat bread with two scrambled eggs, turkey sausage, and cheese in the middle. I paid $4.76 with a dollar tip and was on my way. I managed to eat it cleanly as I made my way back towards the subway station. Of course, the breakfast sandwich was done before I got there, and it was good.

The morning crowd was bigger than the one I had dealt with the day before. Plus, it was louder because the students were vociferous while waiting for the train to take them to school. They all seemed to be hyper. Most of them looked like they were either in high school or college. The longer the train took, the louder it got. I could barely hear myself think with all the noise. Although the commotion was loud, I still had to pay close attention to the trains that were coming and going. I couldn't afford to be late for my interview. In the nick of time, a train pulled up. I was lucky to get on the train that left most of the loudmouth kids behind.

The morning train ride was no different than the evening one. I had to hold on to a pole once again. Ironically, I landed next to a beautiful Asian woman who was talking on her phone with earplugs on. I tried my best not to stare. Knowing me, I would have tried to fuck her at the next stop. I was in New York on business that couldn't be disturbed by my perversion. When she finally looked my way, there was a short connection. She even smiled at me. I turned my head quickly to give her the indication that I wasn't interested. My mentality at that point was fuck then or leave it alone. My career was on the line and for the first time in a long time, I wouldn't let pussy get the best of me. Though the thought of rolling her little Asian ass up like an egg roll did cross my mind, I didn't have time for it.

With my head slightly turned, I could see her staring at me from my peripheral, but I acted like I didn't see her. I couldn't resist the flirting game though. I turned my head back towards her to see if she had the courage to look me directly in my eyes. As I thought, she turned her head before I could catch her. Unfortunately, our little flirting game had to end because my stop was next. I didn't even bother to look her way again. I had to remind myself that this trip to New York was about business and would stay that way.

# Changed

I stepped off the train with a mission in mind. I repeated to myself, "I will be the next Polo model. I will be the next Polo model. I will be the next Polo model."

I had to convince myself of my worthiness because anxiety was running through my body at full steam. The agency was only a half-block away from the subway station. It wouldn't be long before I would be sitting in front of Mr. Grey, who controlled my fate. I wanted to wow him, but at the same time, I wanted to be myself. The closer I got to the building, the more nervous I became. I said a short prayer before I entered NYC Model Network, Inc. I thought of my grandma's favorite verse from the 23 Psalm, "The Lord is my Shepard, I shall not want," to calm me down. And with that simple prayer, I gained my strength and confidence back.

A security guard was waiting at his post for people entering the building. Everyone who walked into NYC Model Network had to sign in before they could make their way towards the elevators. From the looks of things, the guard looked like he took his job seriously. I told him that I was there for an interview with Marty Grey. From his security phone, he made a call-up to Mr. Grey to verify who I was. In no time, the security guard was asking me for my ID and to sign in. I gave him my information and signed my name. He then pointed me towards the elevators. He told me that it was on the 44th floor. As I walked towards the elevators, I thought to myself, *44 floors*? I prayed that the elevator wasn't like the one at the Belmont. I took a deep breath as I pressed the arrow going up. I stood in front of the elevator with caution in my heart. It arrived without a soul on it. On the inside was nothing like the elevator at the Belmont. It looked new. The glass mirrors were crystal clear. The handrails were sparkling silver. The floor was made of six-by-six turquoise porcelain tile. The light fixtures embedded into the ceiling were bright. I felt a little at ease as I stood in it. As the elevator went up, it didn't rock one time. It was one of the smoothest rides I'd ever taken on an elevator. Whatever paranoia I had was gone. I walked out of the elevator with even more confidence.

The modeling agency was directly to the right of the elevator. I walked through the door with my head up. I was greeted by a secretary who looked bright-eyed and bushy-tailed. She stood up and shook my hand.

"Your name sir?" She asked as if she didn't know it already.

Without hesitating, I said, "Jacob Richardson."

She smiled at me then said, "Good morning Mr. Richardson! Mr. Grey is waiting for you. I will notify him that you are here."

She advised me to take a seat. I sat on a brown leather sofa thinking about what I would say. I thought about something else my grandma used to tell me, "If God is for you who can be against you?"

I then heard a voice say, "Mr. Richardson!" The well-dressed gentlemen said.

"Yes sir, I am Jacob Richardson."

The man gave me a welcoming smile. "Hello, Mr. Richardson! I'm Marty Grey. You can follow me back to my office."

We walked down the hall to his office. As I walked into his office, I noticed another man was sitting behind an office desk.

"Mr. Richardson, this is my colleague, Scott Fitzgerald. I know this is none of your business, but he was named after the famous Novelist F. Scott Fitzgerald," he laughed while introducing us.

I did a fake laugh because I had no idea who he was talking about. High school and college were a blur.

Down to business, we went. "So, Jacob, to be honest, the photoshoot is yours. I have seen some of your work, and Scott and I were impressed. Ralph Lauren is looking for new models for his upcoming underwear line. Now, are you interested?"

Without a second thought, "Yes, Mr. Grey. It will be an honor."

He smiled again and said, "Mr. Richardson, you are our man. Did you bring your portfolio?"

I reached down to my satchel to grab them. "Yes, Mr. Grey, I have my portfolio."

# Changed

I turned it over to them. They studied over the photos assiduously. With the expression on their faces, I knew then it was a numbers game. Mr. Grey looked up first.

"Mr. Richardson, we are ready to make you an offer. Do you have a number in your head that you would be satisfied with?" Mr. Grey asked with a serious look on his face.

I was taken aback and really didn't know what to say. However, I did do a little research on what top models made. The numbers were staggering for a top model. A male supermodel could earn up to a million dollars in a year. I knew to make myself equal to a supermodel was ridiculous, but I was on the spot.

I blurted out, "Seven thousand a shoot!"

They both chuckled. Mr. Grey scratched his head with a smirk on his face. "Mr. Richardson, I like your style, but seven thousand is too much for your first major photoshoot with our company. I'm pretty sure with experience, you will be able to ask for more than $7,000, but as for now, how does $4,000 sound for a day's shoot?"

At that time, $4,000 was the most I had ever been offered for a single photo shoot.

"Mr. Grey, how about $4,500?" I said with a counter offer.

They both looked at each other again and chuckled.

"Mr. Richardson, I admire your confidence and boldness. I tell you what; we can do $4,300 at the most. Do we have ourselves a deal?" Mr. Grey said looking me directly in my eyes.

I didn't hesitate, "Yes, Mr. Grey we have a deal."

After confirming the deal, I took photos in Ralph Lauren's Polo underwear the same day. It was a dream come true. The two photographers were very professional. They made sure to get the most out of every pose they instructed me to do. If they saw that I was uncomfortable, one of the photographers would take the time to explain to me what they were looking for. It was a little aggravating just because I wanted to get every pose right. The more we got into the photo shoot, the more relaxed I became. Things started coming to me naturally. My muscles weren't as tense as they were at the beginning. No matter which way they asked me to position my body or face, they made sure I held every pose properly. I had done quite a few photoshoots beforehand, but nothing on this level. The lighting was perfect. After letting go of my nerves, I stood in the bright lights with confidence and nothing but a pair of underwear on. The jockey cup I wore was to cover up my real penis print from showing. It enhanced what I was already working with. The makeup I wore matched close enough with my skin tone. My short morning workout had me looking like David's body chiseled from the hands of Michelangelo in stone. I was done with the photoshoot in two hours. There was a check waiting for me the minute I got dressed. I picked it up with a letter of thanks from the receptionist. I couldn't believe I got paid $4,300 for just 2 hours of work!

Back at the hotel room, I wanted to get some rest before heading back to Miami. I took it all in before picking up the phone to call anyone. I needed a moment to thank God for His many blessings. I couldn't say that I believed in any religion, but I knew there was an entity out there that was greater than me who pulled the strings.

After my short prayer, I wanted to call Kim. But first I had to call Benny.

After two rings, "Jacob, my man, how did it go?" Benny said with enthusiasm.

I couldn't hold back my joy. "Benny, we did it! The photoshoot went very well. I think I impressed the photographers as well as the agency. I believe they will call me for more work. I'm not sure but I am pleased with today's photoshoot."

Benny started laughing on the other line.

"Jacob, man, you found a fine time to be humble. You know you are arrogant as hell! Don't change who you are after one major photo shoot. And, yes, my boy, you did impress them. I received a phone call from Mr. Grey, a little bit before you called. He wants you to do more work for NYCM. Jacob, get ready to do some real work. I guarantee you will be working a lot after this. Oh, by the way, you are about to start traveling. So, get your bags ready. I'll holla at you when you get home," Benny finished.

The confirmation that I received from Benny gave me a sense of relief. I fell back onto the bed with security. My years of hard work, sweat, and pain was finally manifesting itself. I had to tell Kim. But, the phone rang, and Michael's face popped up. *Dammit*, I thought to myself. I forgot I told her that I was coming to New York.

"Hello, Jacob! I hope your trip to New York was worth it," Michelle said sounding sarcastic.

I wouldn't let her get up under my skin. "Yep, it is Michelle. NYCM is prepared to sign me," I finished.

Michelle was quiet for a moment. Then she went on to say, "Well, Jacob, I'm not getting another trainer. You are it. I don't want another man or woman to train me. So, if I must travel just to get trained and fucked, I guess I will have a ton of frequent flyer miles to use. I need to travel anyway."

Michelle never seemed to amaze me. She always wanted her way.

"Michelle, look, I can't promise you anything. You know modeling is my first priority. Personal training is just to keep me afloat so when the day comes that I am overbooked for modeling gigs, that will be the day we can't train or fuck," I said in a serious tone.

I could hear her alpha female complex deflating in her sigh. "Jacob, you betta stop playing with me. You will continue training and fucking me until I say stop. So, with that being said, congratulations and I will see you when you get home," Michelle said as she hung up the phone in my ear, again.

I wanted to call her back and cuss her out, but I was in too much of a good mood to do so. I wasn't gonna let her craziness affect my day. I would take care of her when I got back home.

I wasted no time dwelling on Michelle's comments; it was time to call Kim. I just hoped she wasn't asleep. The phone rang four times before going to her voicemail. I left a brief message before hanging up. My emotions quickly became uneasy because I wanted the woman who lived through the struggle with me to answer the phone. No one knew better than Kim what I've been through until this point in my modeling career. As I was getting down on myself, the phone rang. I rushed to answer it.

"Hey, honey, I'm sorry that I missed your call. I was resting. So how did the shoot go?" Kim asked sounding half asleep.

Without hesitating, I exaggerated it, "Well, babe, I blew them away. They were in awe of me. It was easy money and they have invited me back to do more photoshoots. It is finally time for us to go to the next level."

I always wanted to make Kim feel secure with my career choices. No matter what I dealt with as a model, I kept the bad parts out. All she knew was that I was striving in a business that discriminated against people based on how they looked.

"Jacob, that's good. I'm happy for you. I can't wait until you get home. I miss you," Kim said.

Chills went through my body. "Babe, I miss you too. I brought you a few things. I hope you like them," I said smiling.

She simply replied, "I'm pretty sure I will."

"Well, babe, I am going to let you get some sleep. I will see you when I get home," I said as we said our goodbyes.

I laid my head onto the pillow staring at the ceiling thinking that I needed some pussy to celebrate my breakthrough. I thought about the white girl at the front desk but thought better of it. She just didn't turn me on. She looked unkempt, but the thought crossed my mind. I decided to pass on the idea. I would just get some shut-eye.

I woke up the next morning with my dick in the front desk clerk's mouth. She fell asleep with it in her mouth. I couldn't resist it. I didn't have sex with her, but I did get some Becky before heading to the airport. I woke her up by pulling my dick out of her mouth. We didn't say anything to each other as she grabbed her stuff and snuck out the door.

What else was I supposed to do? I'm Jacob Richardson.

I slept through the whole flight home. I was ready to get back to Miami. I felt a sense of success as I exited the plane. But before I could take a victory lap, my phone rang. I forgot it was Wednesday. Old faithful was on the other line.

"Good morning Mary Joe. What's on your mind?" I asked not really wanting to know the answer.

# Changed

She went right into it. "Frank slapped me last night in front of my kids! I called the police on his muthafuckin' ass. The police caught his stupid ass driving with a suspended license, dope, and all the money he was supposed to give me for my sons' football uniforms. And no I'm stuck without any money. They need to do something other than get into trouble. What their dads did, they ain't gonna do. Over my dead body will I let dem fall victim to the streets. The only thing I have going for myself right now is the majority of my bills are paid. But I don't have any money saved for their uniforms. I just don't know what to do!" Mary Jo cried.

Yeah, she knew what to do. She knew to call me. Jacob "Captain Save Mary Jo's Ass" Richardson.

"Okay, Mary Jo, how much do you need?" I grudgingly asked.

I could hear over the phone that Mary Jo was breathing easier. "I need at least $600 for their football pads, helmets and cleats, and game uniforms," she finished.

I paused. I thought to myself, *game uniform*?

"Mary Jo, you need money for game uniforms?" I questioned.

"Yeah, Jacob, they're charging for game uniforms, too. I thought it was crazy, but that's what they told me."

Mary Jo was lucky I had it.

"Okay, Mary Jo, when I come home, I'll come see you. Oh yeah, by the way, I'm gonna have a word with Frank whenever he gets his ass out of jail," I said feeling the burden of being a good friend.

Mary Jo was silent. It seemed like she was conflicted by my wiliness to confront Frank, but I didn't give a damn. He was a loser and Mary Jo just couldn't see it. Without making a comment about Frank, she simply said, "Thank you so much, Jacob," as we ended the call.

Once I had my bags in hand, I called for an Uber. It arrived in less than five minutes. The traffic wasn't bad so I made it home in good time.

I came home to see that almost everything was in order. Kim had left a bowl with milk and Honey Bunches of Oats residue in the sink. I figured that she had a bowl of cereal and was too tired to put it in the dishwasher. I was kind of upset about it, but I figured this time I wouldn't make a big fuss about it. I looked down at the trash can to see that she had eaten carry outs the whole time I was gone. Mostly Chinese boxes filled the garbage. I walked over to see a letter on the stove stating, "Jacob, there are leftovers in the refrigerator if you are hungry. I love you."

I checked the refrigerator to see that there was a box of Chinese food. I was too tired to eat. I needed more rest. I walked to the bedroom to find Kim still sleeping soundly. The long hours at the hospital kept Kim comatose. I didn't want to disturb her sleep so I kissed her on the forehead and went to sleep next to her.

# Chapter 8
# Trainer

We woke up together around 3:30 PM. We kissed each other before getting out of the bed. It felt really good being back home with Kim. I honestly missed her. It was just something about Kim. I just wished it was something about me that could stop me from having sex with other women.

Kim said, "Babe, I missed you. I hated being here by myself. I missed your company."

I smiled back and replied, "Kim, I missed you more. I felt alone in that hotel room. I couldn't wait to get back home to you."

Kim put a silly look on her face.

"Whatever Jacob, you probably was surrounded by beautiful women that looked way better than me," Kim inquired.

No matter how secure a woman appears to be, there was always some type of doubt somewhere.

"Kim, I don't care how many beautiful women I'm around, they'll never be you. Besides, half of their asses ain't married. I choose you to be with for the rest of my life," I finished in the hope of bringing comfort to her heart.

I saw her face relax. It was the best time to take a shower together.

"Babe, let's get into the shower," I said.

She looked me in the eyes and said, "Okay, Jacob. But we are not having sex. I have to get ready for work," she persisted.

As we took a shower, I noticed Kim had put on a little weight. I wondered after a 3-day trip how she could put so much weight on. Kim could eat anything and never gain weight.

"Kim, it looks like you put on weight?" I said being inquisitive.

Kim looked down at herself and said, "I guess so. I work so much that I don't have time to pay attention. Plus, I sleep for the most part of the day. But it also could be happy pounds. They say when a woman's happy, she gains weight. Or maybe, it's a combination of all three," she finished vaguely.

I thought for a moment if she was pregnant. But after putting six and a half gallons of sperm in her over the years, I thought it couldn't be that. We were so busy with our careers that we never talked about planning for a family. Then I thought about how we went ham in the Bahamas. I wondered again but didn't believe it.

"I guess I have to get back into the gym," Kim suggested.

I wanted to agree with Kim without telling her that she was getting fat.

"Kim, I love you just the way you are, but the gym never hurt anyone," I said as passively as possible.

The shower ended right there. As Kim walked out of the shower, I said, "Your weight does make your ass look bigger."

She grinned and looked back to check it out. She noticed it, too. "Yeah, it is a little bigger," she replied.

She then began clapping it. I smacked it! Her butt jiggled. I was turned on. I begged her for a few minutes for some, but she resisted. With Kim, her job came first. I knew she would leave me home with the blue balls. I and blue balls were worse enemies. She left me home with a hard-on.

****

After handling my blue balls problem with some random chic at a bar, I came home around 1:30 AM. I had to be up for an early morning workout session. I needed to rest, badly. It was gonna be a hectic week. I had a full schedule ahead of me. By the time Kim would be getting home, I would be leaving out.

I got a few hours of sleep before hearing the doorknob turn. It was Kim coming home from work. I had overslept. The late nights were starting to catch up with me. I was in and out of the shower. I kissed Kim as I walked out of the door. I didn't have time for any conversation of any sort. I wanted to have a good breakfast before I made it to the gym.

I decided to go to Jackson Soul food in Overtown. It was one of my old stomping grounds when I was growing up. I never took Kim to it. She would have blown up my spot. Jackson Soul

# Changed

Food gave me the opportunity to stay relevant in the hood. The neighborhood restaurant brought all walks of life together. Hoodrats, gamblers, dope boys, robbers, city workers, longshoremen, police, and professionals all mingled under one roof. I would ear-hustle to hear what was going on in the streets. It was mostly the same gossip. Who said this and who said that; who was beefing with who; who was sleeping with who; and who killed who were the morning topics.

The waitresses treated me well because I had slept with a few of them. Word got around fast among the waitresses who were only looking to get a good fuck and a few dollars. It didn't matter how many Longshoremen or ballers who were ahead of me, I always got taken care of quickly. Today wouldn't be any different as one of the servicers who I regretted sleeping with approached me. I sat alone, so the flirting was inevitable.

"So, Jacob what are you ordering this morning?" Tina asked with a flirtatious tone.

I ordered my usual salmon croquettes and grits as we exchanged fuck faces. After she took my order, I noticed as she walked off that Tina had put a little extra in her walk to entice me. I wasn't going for it. She always asked me to come back and fuck her again, but I couldn't bring myself to do it. We fucked only once because her house was dirty. She had shit everywhere. I couldn't tolerate a woman who kept a nasty house. Her house was so filthy that we handled business on her back porch. She had some good pussy, but her place turned me off.

As I tried to forget about how despicable Tina's house was, she walked out of the back kitchen with my food in her hands. I kept staring at her hands holding my food. Something suddenly came over me, and I was no longer hungry. Just the thought of how dirty her house was made me sick to my stomach. There was no way in the hell I could eat after visualizing her nasty ass house. I needed a way out, and I knew just what to do. She placed the food on the table. I had to put my acting skills to use.

"Say, Tina, I can't stay and eat," I said with as much panic on my face as possible.

Tina looked concerned. "Jacob, what's wrong?"

"Something came up. I got to leave immediately," I said with a straight face.

Sometimes it's better to tell a lie than the truth. I honestly couldn't tell her the reason I couldn't eat my breakfast was that the thought of her nasty ass house made me lose my appetite. No. Saying the less hurtful thing was always the best thing to do when dealing with a person's feelings. So, I just made up some random shit and rolled.

I paid her just because and I walked out of Jackson Soul Food with my stomach still growling. Nevertheless, I found a homeless man to give my doggy plate. I decided that I would get a meal replacement shake at LA fitness. It would just have to get me through the morning until snack time.

***

After six hours of training, I was done. All my clients worked out hard. I got less complaining and more working out. I guess everyone was happy with the results they were seeing. Their bodies were changing for the better. My client Diana was one of my oldest clients. At 55, she went from 230 pounds to 195 pounds in a year-and-a-half. Another client, Rick, who couldn't do 2 pull-ups when we first started, was now able to do ten a set. Another client, Steven, who couldn't bench press 150 pounds was now able to lift 230 pounds 10 times. Caroline, who had a flat butt on her first day starting with me at the gym, now was bootilicious after doing intense squats and spin. I was proud of not only my clients but myself. I took pride in being a personal trainer. It wasn't anything better than seeing someone's progress in fitness.

I gave all of them meal plans that I came up with for their specific body types. Some wanted to gain muscle, and some wanted to tone up. It didn't matter what they were trying to accomplish body wise; I had the perfect workout and meal plan for them.

If they wanted to see muscle gain, I would put them on a high protein diet. They would have to eat six times a day. I instructed them to eat boiled eggs, oatmeal, and any meat of their choice in the morning. Eleven was snack time. A Snack could be either a protein shake or bar or two peanut butter sandwiches.

# Changed

Lunch was either salmon or baked chicken. The sides could only be brown rice or pasta. Around three in the afternoon, they would have to eat another snack. If they were tired of eating peanut butter and protein bars, I would advise them to eat plain peanuts. Their last meal would be at seven sharp. They could eat a little red meat for muscle gain but not a lot. Fish, lamb, or chicken was usually their last supper of the night.

Their weight training consisted of lifting heavy. Reps were low, and weights were to the max. No matter what muscles they were working, it was always done to its maximum potential. Every workout was done to failure. It was no such thing as a count. Each rep was done until it couldn't be done anymore. I still incorporated cardio into their workouts just to keep them in shape. All weights and no cardio equal a person who can't wipe his or her ass. I wasn't building stiff robots; I was building agile athletes.

Moreover, if I had clients who wanted to tone up, they would still have to eat six times a day, but not heavy foods. The breakfast would stay the same. However, snacks and meals were totally something else. They literately had to become vegetarians overnight. The only snacks they could have were fruits or salads. They couldn't eat any greens that didn't have any nutritional values. Romaine, house lettuce, and those stupid looking maroon leaves were not allowed in any salads. Only kale and spinach were acceptable. Grill chicken breast and tuna were the only meats that could be added. Also, I told them that red meats were the devil to toning up. I explained to them that red meats took too long to digest. I had them replace red meats that contained proteins with soy products that had the same nutritional value. Their workouts consisted of mostly cardio and light weights. Their reps were high, and weightlifting was light. On some days, they didn't have to use weights at all. All of them had to jog for miles on end. I instructed them to jog or walk at least six miles, five times out of the week. On occasion, I would jog with them if my schedule for the week wasn't overbearing. If I jogged with them, there wasn't any such thing as a treadmill. I hated treadmills because of the potential for sheen splits. I preferred jogging against the elements. I loved jogging with them in the early morning as the sun arose. I wanted to see the sweat rolling from their faces. They hated me for it but loved seeing the results. That was my only job. I believed if they didn't hate me then I wasn't doing a good job as a trainer.

Every two weeks I would weigh my clients, so they could see their progress. I could tell which ones followed my meal plans closely and those who deviated from it – the ones whose progress was slow as hell were the cheaters. For some, it wasn't the training; it was the eating part that held them back. I didn't put them down for it. I just tried to keep encouraging them. Over time, all of my clients showed results which in turn brought me more clients. I was booked up for the year. I couldn't take any more clients. If I didn't have to maintain my lifestyle, I would probably have trained people for free. But the way my lifestyle was set up, I couldn't afford to.

***

Before going home, I stopped by Mary Jo's place. I dropped the money off and checked her face out. She still had a bruise on her cheek. My temperature boiled.

"Mary Jo, why do you deal with this loser? It's not like he really does shit for you!" I questioned with anger.

She held her head down with shame. I touched her shoulder to comfort her. I could see tears coming down her right cheek. It was the same one Frank had slapped.

Mary Jo replied, "Jacob, I promise I'm gonna leave dat fuck boy alone. I can take just about anything, but when he hit me in front of my kids, dat was it!"

She sounded serious. I wanted to believe Mary Jo, but her history with men didn't give me any comfort. Every man that she had been with before Frank all put their hands on her. She was caught up in a vicious cycle of physical and emotional abuse.

"When Frank gets out, he's gonna have to see me," I said with anger in my eyes.

She shook her head. "No Jacob, I got this. You have a whole career ahead of you. You're gonna make it big. I will not let what me and Frank have going on get you in trouble," she finished.

# Changed

I rubbed the tears from her cheek. I put my fingers under her chin to lift her head. I looked her in the eyes.

"I made a promise to your brother that I would watch over you. And that won't change. Just let Frank know that I want to see him," I finished.

Her eyes got big. "No Jacob, I won't tell him nothing. Frank is scary. He keeps a gun on him at all times. I don't want anything to happen to you," she cried.

I wanted to go back and forth with her, but I did what was best. I simply replied, "Okay."

I handed her the envelope with sadness in my heart. I knew deep down inside that when Frank got out; Mary Jo would be right back with him.

# Chapter 9
# Tree Nan Lanmo

I dreaded my parents' birthdays. Both were the hardest days of my life. One hit me more than the other, but I respectfully went to the cemetery on both birthdays. June 15 tore me down more emotionally than October 5. The drive to the gravesite was the longest drive I made twice a year. I always drove alone. Being their only child, I didn't have any siblings to lean on. I was far removed from my family after my grandma passed. I didn't even ask Kim to go with me. I never wanted her to see me in that state of mind. It had been over twenty-two years ago since their deaths, and I still haven't gotten over it.

As usual, at the beginning of the summer, it was raining. The roads were slippery, and my windshield wipers fought the downpour of raindrops. I could barely see, but I managed to arrive at Graceland Memorial Park safely.

I drove slowly through the graveyard to make sure I didn't miss the exact spot they were buried. My landmark was always the tallest pine tree in Graceland Memorial. I called it "Tree nan Lanmo," which meant the tree of death in Creole. I saw it as I drove about 50 yards down. The tree still looked as strong as it did when my parents were first lowered into the ground. I stopped at the stop sign before turning the corner headed in the direction of the tree. I pulled up to the side of the road next to the grassy fields that contained what was and what used to be. I grabbed my umbrella and two bouquets of roses from the back seat. I released the large size black umbrella as I stepped out of the car and into a puddle of water.

An eerie feeling came over me as the raindrops fell from the deep indigo skies; it was as if it knew it would make me even more depressed. Nevertheless, I had to make my journey to see the people who conceived me.

I walked through the muggy meadows with torment in my heart. I had to lift my legs high to avoid my Prada shoes drowning in a pool of water. My socks had already been penetrated by water. As I drew nearer to the first gravestone, I thought how much I hated the month of June.

I stood in front of the tombstone for a while in the pouring down rain before making one move. I always had to get myself mentally prepared before looking down to read the caption on the stone of dead. I looked over it slowly. It simply read "Esther Jean-Baptiste, October 5, 1967, till December 21, 1991." There wasn't anything else said after that. My mother's family was very poor so they did the best they could to give her a proper burial. As I always did, I stood at her gravestone for a few minutes before placing the bouquet of roses on top of her grave. I would always give her headstone a firm stare before making my departure.

"Rest in peace mom," I said as I walked off.

I headed towards my father's tombstone. I splashed water all over my pants as I struggled through the soggy grass. He was only a couple of feet away from my mother's grave. In the background, I could hear thunder echoing and saw lightning tearing through the sky as I approached my father's grave. The loud banging noise didn't scare me, nor did the lightning bolts that cracked the skies. The rain had already drenched me. I had nothing else to do but pay my respects.

I just wanted to get the moment over. My father's tombstone was no different than my mother's. It read in plain English, "Pierre Jean-Baptiste, June 15, 1957, till December 21, 1991." His family was poor as well.

It was a big mess as to why my mother and father weren't buried next to each other. My mother's family fought with my father's family over their burial. It was too much for my mother's family to handle my father murdering her and the man she was seeing in cold blood, then killing himself. Although I was there when it happened, I only knew a little about the story behind it. I honestly didn't care to know.

I was only five years old when it happened. It was a blur. Everything happened so fast. The only time I thought about it was

# Changed

when I had to visit my parents at the grave site. No matter how hard I tried not to think about it, I saw blood every time I stared down at their tombstones. I saw my mother's body lying lifeless on top of a pool of blood. The guy she was seeing at the time, lay half-naked on the floor with bullet wounds everywhere. My father was near the guy with his head split open from a self-inflicted wound.

I was in the other room when it happened. I always felt like it was my mother's fault that my parents weren't here. Just the mere thought of that tragic night had my heart filled with a mix of rage, pain, and despair.

I couldn't bear to think about it anymore. I just wanted to say my piece to my father and leave.

"Dad, I love you. I wish you were here to see me. I'm finally moving up in the modeling world. I know if you were here, you would be so proud of me. But since you're not, I know you're smiling down on me from heaven. I will continue to push myself no matter what as you once did."

The thunder crackled, interrupting me for a moment. Once it subsided, I continued," Well dad, it's raining cats and dogs! I'll be back in October to see you again. Thank you for giving me life," I said with sorrow in my voice.

The drive home wasn't easy. I always felt down leaving my parents grave. To make matters worse, the rain didn't let up. It had been over two decades since their deaths, yet the same feelings were still there. The sense of emptiness that couldn't ever be replaced by anyone. The thoughts of "what if" plagued my mind as I made my way home. I was too overwhelmed to stop and get anything to eat. I wanted to lay down with my despair.

I came home to see that Kim was laid back on the bed watching some Lifetime show. She looked up at me with understanding eyes. I put my head down like a sick puppy. She reached her arms out for me. As a broken man, I walked towards her for comfort. I laid in her arms like a weeping child who needed his mother's touch. She embraced me, soggy clothes and all. I hated Kim seeing me like this, but I had nowhere else to turn. Kim was my only outlet. As my wife, Kim always stepped up when it mattered most. God, I love this woman!

Before I fell asleep in her lap, I prayed silently. *Lord Jesus, please help me to stop cheating on my wife.*

# Changed

# Chapter 10
# The Fellaz

It had been months since the last time I hung out with the fellaz. I needed to get out with my true-blue friends. I gave Benny a call first.

"Man, wuz up Jacob?" Benny said on the other line.

"Hey, Benny what do you have to do on Saturday?" I asked.

Benny took a moment before answering as if he had to think about it. "Jacob, as of now, I have nothing to do. Wuz up?"

"Well man, I've been going through some stuff and need to get out. I think Club LIV is gonna be popping this weekend. Do you wanna get out?" I asked.

"You know something Jacob, I think that'd be a good idea. I haven't been out in a while, so let's do it," Benny said with enthusiasm in his voice. "Okay man, it sounds like a plan," he said as we hung up.

I then called Todd. "Wuz up Jacob?" He asked.

"Todd, would you ask your wife for permission to go out Saturday?" I said.

Todd took immediate offense. "Jacob, fuck you! You're just lucky Kim doesn't see yo ass for who you are," he said with anger.

I knew I could get a rise out of him.

"I was just joking with yo sensitive ass, Todd. Man, anyway, I want you to go out Saturday with Benny and me. We're going to LIV," I finished.

I was really hoping Todd's wife would give him permission to go out. She was a real controlling bitch! Well, not with me. Anyway, she controlled Todd's every movement. She had his passwords to his phone, Facebook, Twitter, and Instagram accounts. He had to call her every time he took a break at work. She had access to all his bank accounts.

To make matters worse, he had a curfew when he went out. Todd was pussy whipped to the third power. His backbone

# Changed

was as fragile as someone who has osteoporosis. Simone kept tabs on Todd so he could be blinded to what she was doing behind his back. And what she was doing was doing me every chance she got.

"Jacob, I will let you know. You know the weekends are family time. I'm pretty sure it will be cool, but let me see first," he said.

His wife would definitely be getting a text from me. "Todd, I'm not worried, you will be with us Saturday night," I finished before we hung up.

***

Saturday morning came with the biggest surprise ever! Kim had taken the weekend off because she wasn't feeling well. Her stomach had been hurting all week long. She kept Pepto Bismol by the nightstand. I thought it would be best to stay home with her until I went out later that night.

I went into the kitchen to hookup some breakfast. I made her favorite: French toast, chicken sausage, and eggs sunny side up. I put a little powdered sugar on top of the golden-brown French toast. It was perfect. I walked into the room to see Kim was finally waking up. I brought her food on a tray. She sat up to eat. I placed a towel over her lap before putting the tray down. I laid next to her with a smile on my face. I wanted to see the aroma hit her nose. But I got the opposite effect of what I wanted.

"Honey, I'm starting to feel nauseous."

What happened next threw me for a loop. Before I could tell what was going on, she began regurgitating uncontrollably. The vomit almost got into my face, but I moved out of the way in the nick of time. The bed sheets and uneaten breakfast weren't so lucky. I quickly grabbed the small trash can next to the bed. She grabbed her chest and began vomiting inside of the trash can. I put my hands on her back to comfort her as much as I could.

"Babe, what's wrong, what's wrong?" I screamed at the top of my lungs.

The vomit was coming out so fast that she couldn't speak. I was freaking out.

"Kim, please tell me what I need to do?" I questioned in hopes of getting an answer.

Kim just wouldn't stop throwing up no matter what I said. She managed to gesture to me that she was okay by waving her finger. I decided to stay by her side until she stopped gagging.

So, after a couple of minutes of letting out everything that she ate the night before and then some, Kim finally stopped. She wiped her mouth with her hands. I went into the restroom to grab a towel. I handed it to her. She wiped the rest of the vomit off her mouth and lips. It was gross. We stared at each other with vomit splattered all over her nightgown. We both were slow to speak. Then she said it.

"Jacob, I think I'm pregnant. All of the signs are there. I have been gaining weight lately. I can't stop eating. I'm sleepy for no reason. My stomach won't stop hurting me. I should have known better," Kim said as if she failed herself as a nurse.

I was shocked! As I heard the words of pregnancy coming out of Kim's mouth, all I could think was, *Wow!* I was gonna be a daddy.

"Jacob, go to the store and buy a pregnancy test. Make sure not to buy a cheap one. Sometimes they're not accurate," she persisted.

I rushed out of the door in the same clothes that I wore to bed. I walked through CVS in a tank top, pajama pants, and slippers. One of the women clerks showed me where the pregnancy tests were. I looked through all of the cheap shit to find the First Response brand. I grabbed the most expensive one I could find. It had a curve on the tip of it. I guessed for more comfort. I didn't have time to ask the woman clerk who showed me where it was for any information. I trusted the price. I paid for it and quickly made my way back home.

I walked back into the house to see that Kim never left the room. She was turned to the side with the covers over her head. She must have found the strength somehow to remove the disgusting bed sheets for cleaner ones. It looked like she'd thrown up again. I felt so bad for my babe.

"Jacob, is that you?" she asked from up under sheets.

I pulled closer to her. "Yes sweetheart, it's me."

She pulled the sheets off her head.

"Did you find a good pregnancy test?" She asked.

"Yes, sweetheart."

We made our way to the bathroom. Once there, Kim made a request.

"Jacob, if you don't mind, I'd like to do this alone."

I was taken aback, but I guessed a woman had to do what a woman had to do.

"Are you sure?" I questioned.

She nodded her head to the affirmative, so I walked out of the bathroom feeling as helpless as I did when she was vomiting. She closed the door.

She shouted from behind the bathroom door, "I'll call you in once I get done so we can watch the pregnancy test together."

I tried sitting on the edge of the bed with patience but couldn't. I paced up and down the bedroom. I couldn't stand still to save my life. I was consumed with a million and one thoughts. There wasn't anything that I could do to calm myself down. Every stupid thought I could imagine went through my head.

*Is Kim really pregnant?*

*Would I be a good father?*

*Is it a boy or girl?*

*Is the baby gonna be healthy?*

Finally, Kim emerged from the bathroom.

"Jacob let's watch it together," Kim said.

I was as nervous as a two-dollar prostitute at an STD clinic waiting for her results. The pregnancy test sat on top of the bathroom granite counter top. It was the main attraction of the morning. I hugged Kim as we waited patiently. I then kissed her on the forehead to reassure her that I was there for her. She laid her head on my chest as I rubbed her back. Then the moment of truth came. We looked down at the pregnancy test to see two red lines appear. I held her in my arms harder.

"Kim, we're having a baby!" I screamed with joy.

It couldn't have happened at a better time. I was 28 years old with a modeling career on the rise. My credit score was at eight hundred and my bank account was solid. It wasn't like I was some young punk who couldn't take care of his child. I wasn't afraid of the responsibility. Furthermore, I didn't have a child out of wedlock. No one could ever call my child a bastard.

"Jacob, are you ready to be a father?" Kim asked.

I didn't have to think. "Kim, I am so happy right now! I've been ready. I just didn't know the day, but I am happy it's here," I said with enthusiasm in my voice.

Kim started crying tears of joy. I just wanted to relax with her for the rest of the day. We laid back down on the bed together. As we laid together, Kim looked pressed.

"Babe, what's bothering you," I questioned.

Kim spoke, "Jacob, I won't say anything yet to my family. When I go back to work, I'll make sure. I'll get all of the tests done there to make it official."

I concurred. I then began rubbing her belly. The love I felt was unreal. I honestly couldn't describe it other than thinking of a child who was eating his favorite ice cream.

I rubbed Kim stomach until she fell asleep. I stayed up a little while longer but went to sleep shortly after.

Around 7:00 PM my phone rang. I jumped up out of my sleep. It was Benny calling me. I'd forgotten all about going out. Kim looked like she was still in a deep sleep.

"Benny, wuz up?" I asked.

"Jacob, my man are we still going out tonight?" He asked.

I thought about it. Would it be wrong if I went out or would it be better if I stayed home was the question?

"Benny give me one second. I'll call you back and let you know," I said with uncertainty.

"Okay man, but I got my clothes ready and pressed," Benny finished.

With indecision in my heart, I turned to Kim. After thinking about it, I decided that it would be best if I left it up to her. She was still sleeping. I didn't want to wake her up, but I needed an answer. So, I kissed her hard on the forehead in the hopes of waking her up. As I thought, Kim woke up out of her sleep.

"Jacob, why did you kiss me so hard?" Kim questioned.

I couldn't make it obvious. "I kissed you like that because I love you so much. Please don't be upset with me," I said in hopes of making her smile.

"Jacob, I don't feel good, and you're playing with me," she said giggling.

I was relieved. It was time to drop the bomb on her.

"Kim, before I found out the news that we're having a baby, I planned on going out with the fellaz tonight. Is it okay with you?" I asked in hopes that she would say yes.

Kim gave me a blank stare. "Jacob, I could say, no but I won't. You're a grown man who should understand that I'm pregnant. However, I won't stop you from going out with your boys. Just know I will need you around the house for this process. This is my first time being pregnant, and I will need all the help I can get," Kim finished.

I thanked God for giving me such a loving and understanding woman. "Kim, I promise I will give you all the help you need around the house. Plus, anything you need me to do, just let me know," I said, knowing damn well I was going out to turn up.

I asked her the same question again just to make sure. She said yes again.

I called Benny back.

"Yo, Benny it's on! I have something to tell you when we meet later," I said.

Benny was his usual calm self. "Okay man. I know it will be something else," he finished.

Shortly after hanging up the phone with Benny, I called Todd. "Wuz up Todd? Did you get permission?" I asked being funny.

Todd sighed. "Jacob, what day do you pick during the week to not be an asshole?" Todd replied.

I always got under Todd's skin. "Todd, I'm only an asshole to you because you are my good buddy. Anyway, my brotha, are you going out tonight?" I asked without the sarcasm.

"Yeah man. I'll get out tonight. Simone didn't even put up a fight. What time do you want to meet up?" he asked.

I replied, "Around ten is cool. By the way, I have some news."

Todd came back, "Kim finally came to her senses. She's divorcing yo raggedy ass. Good for her."

I laughed. "No, Napoleon. It's better news than that. I'll tell you when we meet up," I said before hanging up. It was time to get ready.

I looked through the closet to see what I hadn't worn in a while or what I haven't worn at all. I had so many clothes. I promised myself that I would one day go down to a homeless shelter and give most of my old clothes away. Until then, Yeezy would do for the night. All black would be the theme. I never thought in a million years that I would buy a shirt for almost a thousand dollars with holes in it. Kanye West took fashion to another level with a God-awful looking clothing line. But fashion was my thang, and if the 'it crowd' said that Yeezy brand was it, then it was my look. Besides, I didn't mind supporting a brotha in fashion. There weren't that many of us out there. So, if I could support high-end clothing lines such as Gucci, Louis Vuitton, and Tom Ford, why couldn't I support Kanye West's crazy ass!

I stared at myself in the mirror. I looked like a million bucks in a holey black shirt. I was ready to hit the streets. I turned around to ask Kim how I looked.

"Honey, you look like an extra in Roots. If I weren't sick, I would probably come hangout with the fellaz. You wouldn't mind right Jacob?" Kim asked testing me.

I had to smirk. "Kim, you don't want to hang out with the fellaz. All we do is kick the bobo."

I said trying not to sound appealing. Kim gave me a cold stare. "What is kicking the 'bobo' mean?" Kim asked.

# Changed

Lord, this woman wanted to know slang. I wondered how do I explain "kicking the bobo"? Okay, I had it. "Kicking the bobo, simply means men talking shit," I explained.

I couldn't think of any other way of explaining it.

Kim replied, "Talking crap? That's what kicking the bobo means? So, you mean to tell me that men hang out to talk crap? That doesn't sound right Jacob." Kim insisted.

Kim was trippin'. I needed to get out of the house. I didn't want to be late meeting the fellaz.

"Kim, I can't explain it any other way. Besides, you said it would be okay if I go out. Don't trip now," I said with my chest out.

Kim sighed. "I guess Jacob. Remember no phone numbers and come home at a reasonable time," Kim finished.

I had nothing else to say but, "Okay honey. If you need me, call me. I will leave my phone on vibrate."

After the interrogation, I made my way to South Beach. There was traffic crossing the bridge. It looked like everyone and their momma was trying to get to the beach. It was bumper to bumper. The whole ride over the bridge was aggravating because it was one stop after another. But I made it and headed towards the club scene.

The traffic wasn't as bad, once I made a turn on Washington Ave. There were people walking up and down the street. The lines were long at every club I passed. The clothing stores were closed, but the pizza eateries were busy. It was funny what alcohol and overpriced South Beach weed could do to one's stomach on a late night.

The nightlife was about to begin. I was ready! I wouldn't stay out late because Kim was back home with my baby in her stomach. I even thought to behave myself. I wondered how that would turn out as I pulled up to Club LIV.

Benny and Todd had already arrived. I saw Todd's Benz parked next to Benny's Corvette in the VIP area. Ironically, there was an open parking space next to their vehicles. If I knew Benny well, he paid the valet parker to hold that parking space for me. He was such a playa. I placed my wedding band in the glove compartment. I didn't need to have on a deal breaker just in case I met a cutie. I jumped out of my car ready.

As the valet took my keys to park my car, I thought about how three Haitian-Americans rose from poverty. While most from the old neighborhood took to the streets to earn their way, we decided to take the road less traveled. Though we came from a drug infested community, Little Haiti never got the best of us. We stayed clear of the streets. Yes, we all were clowned for our mixed-matched clothes by African-Americans in school who put so much worth into their stylish fashion, but it never made us once think about being criminals. Our parents instilled hard work into us from day one. My grandma would literally beat education into me. Benny and Todd's parents were no different. And through hard work and education, three Haitian-Americans were afforded the opportunity to park their Luxury cars VIP in front of Club LIV. God bless America!

"Jacob, come on man. The security guard is waiting for us in the VIP line," Benny shouted impatiently.

I walked over to them smoothly. There were bitches everywhere and I didn't want them to see me rushing as if I was a flunky.

As I approached Benny and Todd, Benny said, "Jacob, you walk slower than molasses pouring out."

I brushed him off and began walking towards the club. The regular line to get in was a mile long. Bitches looked uncomfortable in their heels. A couple of them were prancing back and forth as they complained on the phone about how long the line was. The men looked more uncomfortable. Some looked as if they were ready to rush the gorillas in suits guarding the front entrance. But the security guards weren't having it. Besides, there were cops all around. If one of them would have gotten too unruly, it probably would have been another unarmed Black man dead, and another police officer getting off. I could see the disdain on their faces as we walked towards the VIP line. A security guard was waiting in a black suit for us. He greeted Benny with a handshake.

# Changed

"Mr. Greatness, I'm glad to see you back," the well-groomed security guard said.

Benny greeted him back, "Well, you know I wouldn't stay away too long. These are my two friends. They are with me," Benny explained.

He shook our hands and we all entered. Benny wasn't the type who liked to wait on anything. He made friends in high places to ensure that he didn't. A bouncer frisked us as we walked in. I always felt violated when a man searched my balls, but better that than walking around the club like cowboys in the Wild Wild West!

Once done with the security guard checkpoint, we stepped upstairs to the VIP area. There were bouncers surrounding it. They were even bigger than the ones downstairs. They all looked like Colossus in black suits with the training of kick-a-nigga-ass-quick-if-he-gets-outta-line. They checked our wristbands and once confirmed we were okay, one of the bouncers opened the red rope for us to walk into the VIP area. The ambiance was on point. There was a table with bottles of liquor in the ice waiting on us. We sat down to see there were hotties everywhere. Their hair was long and skirts short. They were dancing as if they were strippers. I guessed the privileged life could bring the freak out of any bitch! Some of them danced with each other. Ass rubbed on pussy in front of my eyes as they held their drinks in the air to celebrate the good life. My dick was provoked, but I didn't want to get out of control so early. I thought of Kim's pregnancy, my child in her stomach, which eventually calmed down.

I turned my head to see that ballers filled the VIP. No one looked like a leech. They were well-dressed gentlemen from every ethnic background. They were pouring expensive liquor and champagne in their glasses. Some had bitches at their tables helping them indulge. It looked like it would be a wild night.

Benny lit his cigar. I hated the smell of cigars and cigarettes but adjusted by sitting closer to the edge of the table.

"So, what are y'all fellaz drinking tonight? I got brown or white," he asked.

The old saying popped into my head, "Brown will have you down, and white will have you right." I looked over at the Remy

Martin and D'usse. Then I looked over at the Ciroc and Patron. It was a hard decision, but I stuck with my first thought.

"Ciroc sounds good to me," I said.

Todd chose the opposite. Not sure if it was out of spite, but Remy was his choice. It was far from his usual Scotch taste, but I believe he could manage it. Benny, on the other hand, went with the D'usse. We said cheers, and the real night started. We bobbed our heads to the music. Future had the whole club rocking. The night was young, but the pussy circulating in the club was of age. I contemplated if I should go after some ass or keep my dick in my pants. It was a tough decision. I wanted to walk around but kept my cool. I just sipped on my drink with wondering eyes.

The bitches in VIP appeared to be thirsty. It looked like they were trying to get free drinks and lie about life. Then I saw *her* on the dance floor. But before I could make a move, Todd started screaming some lame shit in my ear. "Jacob, this is a really nice club. I'm glad you invited me out," Todd screamed in my ear.

I was like *what the fuck* in my mind, but I held back, remembering in an instant that I was responsible for getting his lame ass out of the house. "Todd, you're right. This is a really nice club. Do you see the bitches in here?" I replied.

Todd glanced through the VIP before he answered. "Yeah, man there are some ho's in the house!" He said trying to be funny.

We both laughed because Todd usually had a terrible sense of humor. It must have been the alcohol or not being up under Simone's foot. Whatever the case was, it felt good to be out with my childhood friends.

Benny was in his own world. Benny always wanted to look like the man when we were out. I didn't mind because, without him, there would be no me.

The entire time this was going on, I kept my eyes on *her*. I watched *her* walk across the dance floor with a small group of chics. Though all of her friends were decent, *she* stood out. I didn't want to lose her. Todd kept yapping in my ears.

# Changed

"Me and Simone are thinking about getting a business together. We plan on leasing out a building to do tax service in. It'll be lucrative for the both of us. We know a lot of people and it will be a great side business," Todd finished yelling in my ear.

I was starting to get annoyed. I wanted to say, "*the business would probably be a good idea without his wife's name on it. Your wife is as scandalous as they come. Your marriage is a total farce. She doesn't have any real love for you. She only has sex with you because yall live together. Simone once told me when you get on top of her; she had to imagine it was me to get through it. But now you are stuck with a gold-digging bitch who has no good intention for you. Security is all she needs from you. However, when she needs some dick, she calls me. If you ever get divorced, Simone will get half your shit plus child support for Albert. Your foolish ass should've made her sign a prenup.*"

"So, what do you think Jacob?" Todd questioned.

I really didn't know what to say because I was too busy eyeballing the finest chic in the club. I had to have *her*. "Todd that sounds like a great idea," I said lying through my teeth.

I poured another cup of Ciroc before excusing myself from the table. I walked out of the VIP and headed towards the dance floor. As I stepped down the stairs, I noticed *she* and her friends were headed to the bar. It was perfect. I squeezed through the crowd. People were grooving all over the place. The walk over to the bar wasn't easy. I had to start and stop as if I was in morning traffic. I hoped by the time I got there; *she* wouldn't have ordered her drink yet.

I finally made it to the bar. Her friends were in front of her ordering drinks. I wanted to get closer to see if what I saw from upstairs was real. I stood behind her. I looked her up and down. I could see that she had an expensive taste from her dress to her heels. I tapped her on the shoulder.

"Excuse me, Miss, what are you drinking?" I said with the utmost confidence.

I looked her directly in her eyes. The way she looked back at me, I knew I had a chance.

She smiled before saying, "I'm drinking Patron with a twist of lime juice."

She was talking my language. Benny had a bottle upstairs, but I didn't want to be so quick to invite her up. She could've been crazy. I wanted to see what my game could find out.

"Okay, babe! Would you like a double shot?" I asked smoothly in her ear.

She grinned, and said, "Okay."

I introduced myself to the fine woman. She looked as if she was mixed of Asian, Brazilian, and Black. It wasn't any words to describe the foxy momma. All I could think of was exotic.

"My name is Terrence," I said using one of my many aliases.

She gave me a pleasant smile as she finally introduced herself back. "My name is Amber. Me and my friends are visiting from California."

Her friends finally got their drinks, and there was room for me to move into the bar. Her friends first wanted to be nosy.

"Amber, who is this fine man standing in front of you, gurl?" One of the less attractive ones asked. Amber grabbed my arm, acting territorial.

"This is Terrence, and he is buying me a drink. There are still some gentlemen in the world," she said like a dense hopeless romantic. If she kept it up, having sex with her would be easier than I thought.

One of her friends said out loud, "He would be more of a gentleman if he bought all of us drinks."

Amber looked at her like *bitch, please*. I bought only her a drink. Her girlfriends remained close to the bar sipping on tropical rainbow drinks embellished by umbrellas sticking out of them. Amber stayed close to her friends but even closer to me. She began sipping on her drink while gyrating to the music.

The club was getting crunk! People were dancing everywhere. The excitement got to me. Not wanting to seem like a wallflower, I began two-stepping. Amber backed her butt up on me. I then pushed up on her. She started grinding on me. The friction of her ass rubbing on my dick made me aroused. I could tell that she didn't have on any panties because of how her ass moved in her dress. I quickly got back to my senses. I didn't want to mess up the grove because of a little booty rubbing on me. I backed up but continued to dance.

I stayed in rhythm with her seductive dancing. I whispered into her ear, "I know this sounds corny, but what's your sign?"

Amber leaned back and said simply, "What an original line. I thought you would have come a little better than that Mr. Gentleman. Woo me, Terrence. I'm a sapiosexual," she said sarcastically.

I laughed and thought of a better way to present myself. I didn't know what sapiosexual meant, but I went for it.

"Amber, do you know anything about astrology? I think chemistry is everything. And if two signs don't match, it won't work," I said in hopes that I met her challenge.

It looked like Amber had exhaled. She smiled and turned to me and spoke softly into my ear, "Terrence, I will give you a pass on that one. I'm impressed," she said in a giddy voice.

It was now time for me to work my magic. "So, what do you know about compatibility with Zodiac signs?"

I said probing for answers. Amber turned back around and rubbed her ass harder against me.

"Well, I'm a Taurus," she finished without any other explanation.

I was taken aback by her answer.

"Amber, is that all you're gonna say?" I questioned.

Amber turned around to me.

"Terrence, I'm not a dumb chic. If you're gonna ask me about astrology that would mean that you know something about it. So, tell me about myself Mr. Astrologist," she said being difficult.

It didn't take much for me to spit it out. "Before I start, you have on Giuseppe Zanotti heels. The clementine dress you're wearing is designed by Jackie O Belted Sheath, and it's a Gabardine. Two nice choices. The dress accentuates your curves and your heels bring attention to your beautiful legs. Now for your sign. Well, you are stubborn as a bull. You hate depending on others. Financially you will never let that happen because most Taurus's are good with money. You are lazy when others tell you what to do but have so much energy when it comes to doing your own thing. Last but not least, you hate change. Change makes you feel uncomfortable because you are used to whatever the status quo," I finished confidently.

She bit her lips and gazed into my eyes. I looked back deeply into hers. That was the moment that I knew I could fuck her.

"Terrence, you just read my whole life out. Besides not being able to change. That is one trait I don't possess. I am forever changing, growing, and evolving. Are you a Taurus?" she asked back.

"No, actually I'm a Scorpio," I said leaving it just like that.

Amber looked at me strangely.

"So Terrence, that's all you're gonna say?" She asked with a puzzled look on her face.

Yeah, I was being petty.

"Amber, I'm not a dumb dude. I'm going to take an educated guess that you know something about astrology. I bet you can tell me about myself without thinking." I finished waiting for the magic to start. She giggled.

"Okay, Terrence. Here goes nothing. You don't believe in giving up. You are a fierce competitor, and that's why losing isn't an option. You are a control freak, but at the same time, very loyal. And being loyal will make you go after anyone who betrays you. You are also manipulative. The only way a Scorpio gets its way is by manipulating everything in his favor. Oh, by the way, a Taurus and Scorpio are sexually compatible. When we fuck, we fuck!" She ended with so much passion in her voice.

My mouth almost dropped, but I held my composure. I couldn't let her see my excitement. My dick, on the other hand, didn't get the Keep-It-Cool memo. I felt it growing in my pants.

"Well, everything that you said Amber is true, but one thing," I said. She looked at me with anticipation. "The part about being manipulative. People have one or two choices when a Scorpio tries to impose their will on them. Either use common sense to see through the bullshit or become a victim of the bullshit. Furthermore, I've never been with a Taurus to know what you're talking about. I haven't been that lucky," I said lying through my teeth.

The truth was I had had my share of Taurus. I could have been considered a cowboy because of all the bulls I had lassoed over the years. Amber would be no different than the rest.

Amber had finished her drink. It was time to keep the train moving. I looked over at her friends' really good. They were all decent besides one. It was three of them, and that was suitable for Benny and Todd who were still in the VIP section.

"Amber, I must apologize to you. Me and my friends are actually in the VIP area upstairs. If you would like, you and your friends can come up. We have bottles so don't worry about spending any more money," I said.

From the look on her face, it sounded better than the music being played through the sound system. She huddled up her gurls to tell them the good news. With no objection from her friends, we headed towards the VIP area. The crowd was even larger than before. I held Amber's hand as we slid through the mob of people dancing like it was no tomorrow. A couple of ignorant dudes tried grabbing at her friends, but they quickly stopped the ambush by pulling away and cussing them out. It was no need for me to interfere. We made it to the VIP without any real incident.

Benny and Todd were still sitting down sipping on their drinks. Their eyes got big when they saw me walking towards them with four women. Todd looked like he wanted to jump out of his seat. Before they could open their mouths, I crossed my fingers to form the letter T. If I lied to a chic about my name, I would use hand gestures so they would not blow my cover. Over the years, Benny and Todd caught on to my sign language. For example, if I chose the name Clarance, I would curve my fingers into a C shape. Or if I used Vince, I would put two fingers up in a V shape. Benny was always on point, but sometimes Todd would fuck up at times. I couldn't afford his mess up tonight. I made sure to look him right in his face as I did it.

"Terrence, who are these lovely looking ladies?" Benny said as we approached the table. With my cover not being blown, I let the introduction begin.

"This is Mr. Greatness and Todd. Sorry I didn't get y'all's names. Amber never introduced y'all," I said poking fun at Amber. She gave me a look that could kill. Nevertheless, they began introducing themselves.

"Hello, my name is Latasha. How are you?" "My name is Shelia." "Hey, my name is Tina." "And I'm Amber." "Yo boy Terrence invited us up," they said with hugs and handshakes.

We then sat down to enjoy some drinks. Everyone took their proper space at the table. Since Benny looked like the man in charge, two of the gurls sat on each side of him. The ugly one sat next to Todd. Amber took the cake by sitting on my lap. I was a little uncomfortable because I prayed the few friends Kim had were not in the club. But I immediately remembered that my wife was a hermit. Though she did have a small circle of friends, they were either homebodies or settled down. I was safe.

Benny and Todd barely drank any of the alcohol. There was plenty of poison to go around. Benny, without any hesitation, offered the ladies drinks. He didn't have to tell them twice because they went right in. They poured nice glasses without much chaser. It looked like we all had a chance to get lucky. Even Todd's lame-ass had a possibility. Medusa was all over him. Benny continued to smoke his cigar as if he was Rick Ross being videoed with vixens surrounding him in the VIP. It was turned up. I felt Amber massaging her butt on my dick. I was so tempted to pull her dress up and slide my manhood between her legs, but that time would come later.

I decided to get to know Amber better.

"So, Amber what do you do for a living?" I asked. She answered, "Well I have over twenty investment properties, which can be a headache. If you pick the wrong tenants, it can be a mess. Repairs are costly, but I wouldn't change it for the world. I also own three salons. They all do well. Everything that I own enables me to travel. I love traveling! Terrence, do you travel?" She asked.

# Changed

I wondered if I should reveal myself or not. It was gonna be a one nightstand anyway.

"Yes, I do travel from time to time. I do a little modeling so sometimes I have to take flights across the country. I would like to travel more. In time I will," I finished.

Amber poured another drink of Patron with even less chaser than before. It was her third cup. I didn't know how many she'd had prior to us meeting, but I could tell she was feeling the effects. She started grinding harder on me than before. I felt her dress coming up. I placed my hand on her ass just to see what she would say. She didn't say anything. My dick became more excited. Her eyes looked as if she wanted me to take her right there. I still kept my cool.

"Terrence, now that I think about it, you do look like a model. You are a gorgeous man. So how is it being a model?" She asked.

This was my moment to brag but thought better of it. "Well Amber, it has been a humbling experience. There are so many models in the industry. I just get in where I fit in," I said modestly.

Amber put her arm around my neck. She looked me straight into my eyes.

"Terrence, I like a humble man. That's a real turn on in my book. I hate when men brag. They try to make themselves seem like they're more than what they really are. For some women that's a turn on. But for me, it's a red flag to run. Terrence, I'm so tired of little dick arrogant men who can't fuck! I think when a man brag, it's because he is trying to overcompensate for having a little dick."

I almost spit my drink out. The conversation was getting closer and closer to what I wanted. I thought about pouring another drink but thought better of it. I didn't want to be sloppy or catch a driving back over the bridge. Miami Beach cops were dick heads. Not only would I get a DUI, but I would also probably get a nigger-stay-away-from-Miami-Beach beat-down along with it. I didn't have time for that bullshit.

"Amber, are you driving tonight?" I asked.

With tipsy eyes, she said, "No! Why do you ask?"

"Well, I noticed you've had quite a few drinks, so I just wanted to know if you'd be alright getting back to your hotel."

Amber gave me a peculiar look.

"You are such the gentleman now, aren't you? You want to make sure I get back to my hotel safely. How cute is that. Mr. Gentleman? I am perfectly fine. Besides, we're not driving. Uber, babe Uber!" She said slurring a little.

I turned to see that Benny and Todd were turnt up! Amber's friends were all over them. It was good seeing my childhood friends enjoying themselves. Todd was on Cloud 9. Though the chic he was dancing with would probably look better with a brown paper bag over her face, her body was banging. Benny on the other hand, looked like he would be bringing home some fresh meat to his wife. They loved having new sexual partners in the bed. Swingers never cheated alone, they always cheated together.

I stayed focused on the task at hand. Amber drunk her glass of Patron quickly. She poured another drink. I was astonished that she could drink so much liquor. I could see that she was going to be inebriated sooner or later. The alcohol could only do one of two things to her. She would either be sleepy or horny as hell. The way Amber was grinding on me, sleep had to be the last thing on her mind.

The music in the club got faster and louder, and the VIP was off the chain. Even the players at their tables were bumping to the music. I checked my watch to see that it was 12:24am. If I was going to make a move, it would have to be now.

I whispered into Amber's ear, "So Amber, how do you feel about getting out of here?"

She gave me a crazy look while still arousing my dick with friction from grinding on me.

"Terrence, I thought you were a gentleman? Why are you talking to me like I'm a hoe?"

I thought of something clever to come back with. "Amber, I would never come at you like a hoe. Let's be honest, we have few things in common. Besides, you're here on vacation. Best thing about a vacation is going back home with a story to tell. And if you let me have you for one night, that story may be the greatest story ever told. Plus, you never know what will come out of this," I finished hoping to spark her interest.

Amber laughed hard as hell as she tossed her drink up. I could see in her eyes she was feeling me. But like any woman who didn't want to be perceived as a hoe, she made it more difficult than it needed to be.

"Terrence that greatest story told was corny as hell. I do understand what you are saying, but wouldn't that make me seem easy?" She asked.

That was the opening that I needed. No man in his right mind would ever tell a woman that she is being a hoe for having sex on the first night – at least, not to her face. It could have been a nun asking me the same question. I would've told her that she was doing god's work.

"Amber, that wouldn't make you a hoe, it only means you know what you want. Being grown sometimes means making grown-up choices. If you're feeling hot, why let it fizzle? So, let's get out of here. I think your fire needs some wood to keep the flames burning," I said in an effort to get her to see things my way.

She rolled her eyes. "Terrence, it has been so long since I did something spontaneous. My pursuit of happiness has made me so unhappy. Everything I do now is safe. I'm bored with safe. I don't take any risks anymore. I do miss that side of me. I'm really thinking about it Terrence," she said with an indecisive look on her face.

She grinded one more time on me before saying the magic words: "So, what about my friends?"

Checkmate.

"I'm pretty sure they know how to get back to the hotel. Besides, they're occupied with my friends. My friends are gentlemen just like me, so they'll give them a ride back to the hotel if necessary," I finished.

To build up her courage, Amber gulped down the rest of her drink. It was obvious that she was with it.

"Okay, Terrence. You better not be a murderer. I know mixed martial arts," she said as a fair warning.

I took heed. "No babe, I'm not crazy, though I like doing crazy things."

She staggered over to her friends to give them an excuse as to why she was leaving. They were damn near drunk as well. Her friends gave her their blessings and continued to be naughty with my boys. As she was finishing up with her friends, I spoke to Benny and Todd. They knew what time it was. There wasn't anything to be said. They told me to text them once I got home.

Once it was confirmed that we were leaving together, Amber and I made our way out of the club. It was more packed than before. Thankfully, we could exit out the back door of VIP. I gave the Security dap as I walked out.

Amber was able to walk on her power even though the alcohol had her staggering. I pulled her close to me. She placed one arm around my waist. I held her up. I kept my eyes on her as we made our way to the car. The further we walked, the harder it became for her to walk in her expensive heels. She took them off. She tried walking in her bare feet, but it wasn't plausible after we had to step off the sidewalk onto the rough, rocky road. I decided to be a gentleman once again. I picked her up. She wrapped her arms around my neck.

"Terrence, you truly are a gentleman," she said as I carried her to the car which was only a couple feet away.

The valet attendants were waiting. A few women who walked passed us yelled out loud, "How romantic. Chivalry isn't dead!"

I wasn't trying to get any cool points. The attendant brought my keys. I tipped him ten dollars, and we were on our way. To where I didn't have any idea.

I drove thinking about where to go. Amber looked like she was coming in and out of her drunkenness. Once she fully got herself together, she reached to turn on the radio, and 99 Jamz had the Quiet Storm on. An old Keith Sweat song was playing. Amber seemed to be a bit too young to know about *Right and a Wrong Way,* but she knew the lyrics. She slumped her body down into my black leather seat and put her hands in the air damn near reaching my car roof. She sang to the top of her lungs when it got to what seemed to be her favorite part.

*You may be young, but you're ready (Ready to learn) you're not a little girl, you're a woman (Take my hands), Let me tell you, baby, I'm yours for the taken.* She sang as if she was at a Keith Sweat concert.

She looked over at me and said, "Terrence, are you ready to teach me something new?"

I was surprised by her readiness.

"Well Amber, if you're ready to learn, I'm the best teacher on the planet," I replied.

She giggled.

"So, nigga, you telling me that you're the Lebron James of sex?"

I never looked at it that way. I simply said, "Yes. I would be that."

She gave me a crazy look. "So it's like dat?" She questioned curiously.

I gave her a stone look. From that point, she knew I wasn't playing.

Without any more delay, Amber put her hands down my pants. She stroked my dick as I drove down Washington Avenue, headed towards Ocean drive.

She leaned over to me and whispered into my ear, "Terrence, this is nice. Can I suck it?" She said as the alcohol spoke for her.

I needed somewhere to park. And I needed somewhere to park fast.

"Sure, you can, as long as you don't bite it," I said sarcastically.

Her response was even better, "I promise I won't bite it, but I will nibble on it."

It was hard concentrating on the road with Amber jacking my dick and her legs open in the passenger seat. I turned off Washington Ave with one light to go to Ocean Drive.

I found the perfect spot. The location was discrete. There was someone pulling out as we drove up. I thought for a moment this was to perfect to be true. Once we parked, I finally got a chance to look at Amber. She was as beautiful as she looked in the club. She continued to stroke my dick. We both were turned on. I placed my hand right on her pussy. It was phat and bald. I could feel the lips on her pussy getting wet as I gently rubbed them. She then pulled my dick out of my pants. Nine inches of my manhood was about to go down her throat. It was heating up. Ironically, one of my favorite oldies came on. The host Freddie Cruz was out doing himself. Stevie Wonder's *Overjoyed* set the tone. I kept wondering why things were so perfect. It really didn't matter as I put my tongue down Amber's throat.

The French kiss went perfectly with Stevie Wonder's soulful voice. I was in awe with how well Amber kissed. I wondered what other skills she had. Before I let her give me head, I asked the question of questions.

"Are you sure?" I asked staring into her eyes.

She looked at me then down at my dick.

"Terrence, I'm sure," she replied.

Once it was confirmed that it was consensual, I turned off the recorder on my phone. I had trust issues. I would never put myself in a situation where a woman could call rape.

I prepared myself for some head. But before I laid back, I had one more thing on my mind. Amber sat in the other seat looking like Pavlov's salivating dog. Her lips looked so juicy. Right before she got ready to go down, I asked one more question.

"So Amber, what does the word sapiosexual mean?"

She giggled. "You're being silly Terrence. I'm about to suck your dick and you're asking me what sapiosexual mean? You're such the word."

My face was serious. "I never heard the word before. I just wanted to know the meaning of it," I said.

Amber began stroking my dick even harder. She looked like my brief interruption of untimely questions was interfering with her taste buds.

As she began to go down to suck my dick, Amber said it means, "Someone who finds intelligence attractive."

# Changed

But before she made it down, she puked in my face. I couldn't believe it! Throw up got all over my face, clothes, and the interior of my car. Pissed was an understatement. The alcohol finally overpowered her stomach. I wanted to call her every stankin' ass bitch in the book but couldn't. It was simply unintelligent to be in a car with a woman I hardly knew. My wife was in bed at home with our baby in her belly, and I was out with some breezy trying to get my rocks off.

"Amber it's okay. Are you okay?" I asked as I wiped the puke out of my face.

Amber looked awful and ashamed.

"Terrence, I'm so very sorry. I wasn't aware of how much I drank. I completely understand how you feel. You can just drop me off at the hotel." She said in embarrassment. I started the car, and we were off to her hotel.

I dropped her off at Eden Roc down Collins Ave. Before walking into the hotel, she looked back with tears in her eyes.

"Terrence, I'm really, really sorry."

I told her it was okay once again as I drove off. I was distraught leaving South Beach. This had to be one of the worst nights I ever had in my life. I needed to clean myself up before I got home. Luckily it was only 1:15 in the morning. The time I thought I would be fucking, I would instead be scrubbing my car and washing my clothes. Now the problem was trying to find somewhere to wash at. It was late, and I needed to find a 24-hour wash house. I used Google maps to locate one. There was one in Liberty City. I pressed on the gas.

As I drove, I wondered how a perfect night could go so wrong. Everything was going better than I thought then bang! Bitch throws up on me! I couldn't figure out what went wrong. Why didn't it happen? Then I thought about *why did my wife's throw up miss me earlier that morning, but some random chic I barely knew puked right in my face later that night? Was it karma? Was it God trying to tell me something?* I was confused. I couldn't place my finger on it. But for the first time in a long time, I was starting to have a conscience. My mind was slowly changing. I wasn't sure if

I was ready to change, but the thought was now starting to cross my mind.

With so many thoughts racing through my mind, it was difficult to focus. I didn't have time to be retrospective. I needed to make it home in a timely matter without puke stains all over me. Plus, the odor in the car was unbearable. Having the windows down didn't help. The smell was so horrible that it made *me* feel like throwing up. I thought chitt'lin' smelled bad until I had to drive miles with the unpleasant smell of regurgitation reeking through my car.

The only good thing was I had entered the city. The wash house was only a few miles away. I needed to get out of my smelly clothes and some way, or another clean the interior of my car. Now how could I kill two birds with one stone in the wee hours of the morning was gonna be the trick.

As I pulled up to Greg's 24-Hour Laundromat, there was a homeless man casually sitting on a milk crate underneath a No Loitering sign. I figured I could wash and dry my clothes while the homeless man cleaned out the inside of my car. I wasn't quite sure if he would do it, but it was worth taking a shot.

"Excuse me my man; would you like to make some money?" I asked.

The way his face lit up, my words seemed liked music to his ears. He wasn't that big but very toned. He looked to be in his fifties with a beard white as snow. He looked like he could have been a pimp back in his day. The tracks in his arms were visible. Heroin must have gotten the best of him, like most of the Macks from those days. The price of prostituting lost girls was severe.

"I sure would good brotha. What do you want me to do?" He asked with excitement.

"I just need you to clean the inside of my car," I replied.

I opened the door, so he could see the task at hand. He carefully surveyed the mess in the car. Without hesitation, he made his decision.

"Say, man, just give me $10.00, and I'll make the interior of your car spotless. Now, do you have anything in your car that I can use to clean it?"

# Changed

"I have some cleaning stuff in my trunk," I replied.

I always kept cleaning products in my trunk, just in case. Tonight, was a prime example of "just in case".

"Hey man, I'll give you $20.00 instead of $10.00 if you do a good job," I said.

He gave me the biggest smile with his no teeth ass. "I will have yo car looking like new." He claimed.

I gave him the cleaning products from my back trunk. He was off and running. I proceeded to make my way to the Laundromat. There was an older Black woman sitting at the front counter. I thought how brave it was for an older woman to be working this time of night in the heart of the city.

"Young man, can I help you?" She asked as she stared at the puke on my clothes.

I was in a rush. I didn't look to see if the machines took change or cards.

"Ma'am, do these machines take quarters?" I asked.

"No, young man. You'll have to buy a card for $5.00, then put money on it," she explained.

*Lord Jesus, why me?* I thought to myself. Why things weren't simple like they were when I was growing up.

"Okay, Ma'am. Where do I pay for my card at?" I asked being a little irritated.

"Young man, you pay right here with me. I'll give you the card. Now, how much would you like to pay on it?" She asked.

I only had to wash my outfit. One load shouldn't cost too much. "Will $5 cover the cost of one load?" I questioned.

In a sweet old voice, she said, "Yes honey. You will have some change left on your card when you're done."

I asked her where the bathroom was. She told me it was in the back of Laundromat. I had to get out of my stinking ass clothes. I smelled terrible. Once in the bathroom, I pulled my clothes off. All I had on was a tank top and boxers. I hid away from the elderly lady. There were washing machines in the back that could hide my half naked rump. I couldn't let her see me like that. I still respected my elders, even though I had a few cougars in my time. Besides, I didn't want her to call the police on me for indecent exposure.

The washer seemed like it was taking forever to wash my clothes. There wasn't anything I could do about it. I just kept my eyes on her. She looked like she was busy looking over some paperwork. Twenty-five minutes later, my clothes were done. I quickly took them out and snuck over to the dryers which were in the back as well. I threw my Yeezy's in with hopes they wouldn't shrink. I don't know which one I stared at more, my watch or the dryer rotating my clothes. It was pushing 2:30. All I could think about was getting home. I wondered if Kim was up or not.

Finally, the clothes stopped. It was 2:45. I saw the old lady moving from behind the counter. She was headed my way. "Honey, is everything okay back there?" She asked loudly. I quickly grabbed my clothes out of the dryer. I threw my clothes on faster than a man hearing a husband coming home too early from work after having sex with his wife. Everything fit as if they were new. "Yes ma'am, I'm okay," I yelled back. There was an opening in the back of the Laundromat. I made a dash for it. I screamed out, "Thank you, mamma, for everything," as I exited the wash house.

The homeless man was waiting by my car. He opened the door for me to see his work. It was unbelievable the job he did. It looked like nothing ever happened. Instead of giving him twenty dollars, I gave him fifty dollars. He acted like he had hit the lotto.

I was out. I couldn't smell anything but the pleasant fragrance of cherries. I was in a rush again getting home. This was becoming a common theme in my life. Do something wrong to disrespect my wife and then rush home to cover it up. With a child on the way, I needed to do better by Kim. She didn't deserve my crap. It wasn't like I didn't know what I was doing to her. Instead of being an upfront husband, I hid behind my habitual adultery ways. What was I to do? There had to be something, but I didn't know what. It was ridiculous to think that I could keep going on this way.

I pulled up to my Condo complex at 3:27 am. It wasn't a bad time. I didn't have to come up with an off the wall story. I had

# Changed

a lie for every question. But, just not this time. Over the years I mastered the art of remembering every lie I ever told. However, this time it wouldn't take much to get through the third degree.

Before I went inside the building, I sprayed some cologne on me. I then got out of the car and started jogging down the sidewalk to a nearby gas station. I needed to mix the sweat with the cologne, so it seemed like I didn't wash my clothes. Once I got to the gas station, I spoke to a man who was smoking a Black and Mild. I wanted the scent from the smoke to get onto my clothes. Once I got done talking to him about nothing, I walked inside the gas station to get some gum. After getting a pack of Doublemint, I was ready to go home. I smelled like a club with chewing gum diluting the impact of alcohol breath.

I walked into our dark condo without making much noise. I didn't know if Kim was up or not. I crept into the bedroom hoping not to disturb her. As I thought, she was asleep. I took off my clothes and put them into the dirty clothes hamper. I went into the bathroom to brush my teeth. I then jumped into the bed next to Kim. With the events of the night, I was compelled to put my arms around her. I felt so ashamed.

It was starting to be unbearable being Jacob Richardson. I had an excellent wife in Kim, but something in me had to change for our marriage to work long term. I seriously wanted to keep my family together. Man can't live on bread alone. Nor could he live without love. I wondered if Kim ever caught me, would she leave me on the spot. If so, I couldn't blame her. I would leave me, too. I didn't want Kim to divorce me; paying alimony and child support wasn't the way to go. I needed to come up with something.

Kim started moving as I held her. She began waking up.

"So, Jacob, how was the club?" She asked hardly awake.

I took a deep breath. "Babe, it wasn't all dat. That's why I'm home early," I said.

Kim began wiping her eyes. "What time is it?" She asked.

I had only been laying with her 30 minutes.

"It's a little after 4:00 babe. I've been laying in the bed with you for a while. You were sleeping pretty hard," I replied.

Kim yawned. "Jacob, I don't want you hanging out late while I'm pregnant. I'll really need your help during this process. I don't want to slip into any type of depression during the next couple of months. You understand my situation better than anyone else. I'll have to check with my doctor to see if it's okay to take my anti-depression pills while pregnant. Hopefully, I can, but if not, I need to come up with an alternative. This process won't be easy without your understanding Jacob." Kim reiterated.

I reassured her that I would slow down. I didn't want my wife to have a bad pregnancy nor a miscarriage because of my behavior.

"Babe, I will do everything in my power to be here for you and the baby. Anything that you need me to do, I will do. I will make every doctor's appointment. I will even go to your breathing classes. I won't let you down," I said trying my best to be sincere.

I needed to talk to someone. I needed some good advice. Surprisingly, Benny nor Todd were my first choices. I thought a female's advice would be best. Since my mother and grandmother had passed, I could only turn to one other woman who understood me. I would make that phone call in the morning. Or whatever was left of the morning when I woke up. Before I fell to sleep, it crossed my mind that I didn't tell Benny and Todd that Kim was pregnant. Worrying about sex always got my mind off of what was really important.

# Changed

# Chapter 11
# Talking It Out

"Good morning Latoya! Can you talk?" I asked hoping she wasn't busy.

"Jacob, give me five minutes and I will call you back," she said.

I sighed, but I had to understand. I was headed to 36th street and 7th Avenue to Moore Park to do a morning cardio workout with a few of my clients. I wanted to speak to Latoya before I started my training session. I pulled up to the park to see that my clients were waiting on the track. They were warming up. As I parked, my phone rang. I answered it quickly.

"Hello!"

"Jacob, wuz up?" Latoya asked.

"Latoya, what are your plans for next weekend?" I asked in hopes that she would be free.

"Well, at night you know I have to go to the club and shake my money maker – bills gotta get paid. But before that, I don't really have any plans," She replied.

"Cool. Latoya, I really need to talk to you. Let's do brunch at Houston's. It will be on me." I said.

She giggled. "Jacob, you know I don't pay for food. I'll see you Saturday. Around two will be good for me," she said.

The time was set. I hoped that Latoya could point me in the right direction.

\*\*\*

The waiter directed me to my seat. It was 2:00 PM on the dot. I had a feeling that Latoya would be late. How late she would be was the question.

The waiter poured me a glass of water and sat a basket of bread on the table. He then placed two menus down before attending other tables. I looked over the menu while staring out the window. I hoped that Latoya would make it to the restaurant in a reasonable time. I sipped on the water and nibbled on the hard bread. Butter couldn't make it taste better. But I ate it anyway. I wanted to start with an appetizer. Looking through the appetizers, the clam chowder caught my eyes. After a hard training session in the morning, I needed the full entrée. As the waiter came back to my table, I saw Latoya walking in.

She had on some short cut off jean shorts with a white tank top without a bra. Her nipples poked out. Her brown suede heels went well with her Louis Vuitton purse. Even when she didn't try, Latoya had so much sex appeal. I could see the men at their tables trying to take a sneak glimpse of her from the corner of their eyes as she walked towards me even though their women sat across from them. It was ridiculous how much attention she brought to herself. It was amazing what a lil ass and a cute face could do for a woman. But the last thing on my mind was her sexiness. I needed to talk.

"Jacob, I'm sorry for being late. Traffic was terrible on my way here," she explained.

I brushed it off. "Latoya don't worry about it. I would like to thank you for coming. Would you like an appetizer," I asked?

"Yes, the clam chowder is really good here," she said.

"I was just about to order it," I replied.

I gave the waiter our orders. In addition to the two clam chowders, I ordered Houston's specialty exquisite cuisine: two filet mignon - medium rare, two lobster tails, garlic mashed potatoes, and a side of key lime pie for dessert. Latoya concurred with me. The waiter took our orders to the back. It was time to talk.

"So, Jacob, what do you want to talk to me about? Latoya questioned.

I almost got cold feet, but quickly gathered myself. I had to get this off my chest.

"Latoya, I feel like I'm going through a change," I said.

Latoya looked confused. "Jacob, what are you talkin' bout?" She questioned again.

# Changed

"Latoya, I guess what I am trying to say is I wanna do better by my wife. My heart is changing. I'm starting to think sleeping around with all these women isn't cool," I responded.

Latoya had a strange look on her face. "Jacob, you don't say? So, you finally figured out that you wanna be a real husband?" She asked sarcastically.

"I'm not joking Latoya. Something has come over me. I'm beginning to feel guilty about sleeping around. Kim is pregnant, and I need to do better as a husband and soon to be father. Plus, I don't wanna be a baby daddy paying child support to get weekend visits. That shit ain't for me," I said.

Latoya was about to say something, but the waiter appeared with our appetizers. The brief interruption gave both of us time to think. We said a quiet prayer to ourselves before continuing our conversation.

"Well Jacob, you have to start with you. Nothing changes without you renewing your mind. Congratulation by the way."

I went on to say, "Thank you but Latoya, what do you mean about renewing my mind?"

"Renewing your mind simply means lose your old ways of thinking and replace them with new ones. Most people can't move forward in life because they can't escape their past or bad behaviors," Latoya finished.

I sat quietly before responding.

"Latoya, I'm not sure if I can change. I'm so used to being me. Ever since I can remember, pussy has controlled my mind. I don't go a minute, hour, or day without thinking about how I can get some more," I explained. Latoya's mouth dropped. She then shook her head.

"Jacob that is the most pathetic shit I have ever heard in my life. You can't be serious. I know you like having sex, but I didn't know it was that serious. You need help. Have you ever thought about going to church?"

*Church,* I thought to myself? I didn't even think of that. I wondered if it would work.

"Latoya, you might be on to something. I haven't been to church in a while. Kim always asks me to go, but I never have the time. Or better yet, I never made time for it. I guess it wouldn't hurt to try."

Latoya gave me consoling eyes. She honestly understood me. Our relationship had always been sex and friendship. A true fuck buddy indeed. Today, in particular, her friendship meant more than her opening her legs. Before Latoya dropped the bomb on me, the waiter brought out the entrees.

"Jacob, we can't have sex anymore. You need to do better by your wife. I refuse to be a part of the problem anymore," Latoya said.

"Latoya, what do you mean we can't have sex anymore? You don't remember taking the oath of being fuck buddies forever?" I said in distress.

Latoya replied, "Dat the shit I'm talkin' 'bout. Jacob, how you gonna change if you still wanna have sex with me? Let it go, Jacob. Besides, I met someone I like. I need more than just a fuck thang. Me and my son need more," Latoya expressed.

In the end, that was the wisest choice Latoya could've ever made in her life. I couldn't help but respect her mind. She was right; it was time to move on from just having sex with her. It was only right that she found someone who was truly interested in her. My intention was nothing more than sex and friendship. Nothing else would come of it.

"Latoya, that's cool. I do understand. Though I would miss that banging ass body and good pussy, it's time for you to be with someone who wants more. Besides, your son needs a man full time in his life," I said with sadness in my voice.

It was a somber moment, but we both knew it would be best.

"Jacob, you know that you're my dude. We'll always be friends no matter what. I'll be there for you when no else will be. That's a promise," she said as she kissed my cheeks.

We finished off the remainder of our entrees. We talked a few minutes more. From the sounds of things, it looked like both of us were headed in the right direction. We slowly ate our desserts. It felt like we wouldn't see each other again. Once we were done

# Changed

with the Key Lime pies, we said our goodbyes. I knew at the point; I wouldn't see Latoya again until I needed her.

# Chapter 12
# Back to Church

In the middle of the week, I suggested to Kim that we should go to church. She couldn't believe that I brought it up. She was more than willing to go. It had been a while since we went together. Though I didn't make time for church, Kim went at least three times a month no matter her workweek. She tried to get me to go on numerous occasions, but I always rejected her request. Someway or somehow, I came up with an excuse. The man I had become was nothing like the boy my grandma raised.

"Jacob, what made you want to go to church," Kim asked, interrupting my train of thought.

I couldn't tell her the whole truth. So, I settled for a little white lie. "Well, I'm going through changes, thinking about how to be a good father. My father never had the opportunity to raise me because of his untimely death. I honestly don't know how to be a father. I'm not saying that church will make me a better father, but it will be a good start to a long journey."

I finished sort of telling the truth. Kim had a big smile on her face. She so wanted us to be a family that attended church together. She never forced church on me, but I did understand the good in it, even though I found every which way not to go.

"Jacob don't worry. You will make a good father!" Kim exclaimed.

She left the bedroom calling every female friend and family member she could think of about us going to church together. I could see the joy on her face. I was kind of proud of myself. I wish I could have told her the real reason, but what woman in their right mind would understand?

Sunday morning came with all of Kim's favorite gospel songs. I didn't mind because the music was peaceful and inspiring. I looked through the closet to find my Sunday best. I had a cream color Armani Exchange suit that I hadn't worn in a while. I picked out a purple tie to go with it. I coordinated the rest of the accessories to match the subtle colors in my suit. Kim matched me with a pretty purple dress. She looked stunning! The color purple made my wife glow. My heart skipped a beat. I couldn't help but stare at her.

"Jacob, what are you staring at?" Kim asked.

I replied with a smirk on my face, "Kimberly Richardson, you look great in purple! If I haven't complimented you lately, let me be the first to say that I'm sorry. In that dress, you take my breath away."

Kim blushed. "Boy, you are crazy. But, thank you. You don't look bad yourself. Jacob let's get out of here. It's late. We are not doing Black people time today. Let's make it to church on time."

I grabbed my keys, and we were out the door. On our way to church, Hot 105 had on gospel music. It kept the mood spiritual. Yolanda Adam's "The *Battle is Not Yours,*" was followed by Hezekiah Walker's "God Favored Me," then Marvin Sapp's "My Testimony," fed our souls as I drove quickly to get to church in a reasonable time. Kim sat in the passenger seat singing her little head off. I didn't know much about gospel music, but my wife, on the other hand, knew every song that came on. One thing about a black woman is no matter how much hell she raised; she will still pray and sing. Kim was no different. Though we didn't fight much, we had our moments. But no matter what, she read her Bible and prayed. Those values were instilled in her by her mother. The apple doesn't fall too far from the tree. There were many things to love about Kim but staying positive in her spirituality was one of the things that I loved the most about her.

We arrived at New Hope Baptist Church at 11:15. We were 15 minutes late, but in Black folk's time, we were early. The parking lot wasn't packed yet. Thank God, we found a spot close enough to walk from. New Hope was one of the biggest churches in Miami. First Sundays were the worst days to be late because the parking was horrendous. An uninformed church goer would find themselves walking two football fields just to get to the entrance.

# Changed

We walked in holding hands. Some polite ushers met Kim and me at the double glass doors. They greeted us with smiles and handshakes. It felt so pleasant. They passed us pamphlets before pointing us towards two other elderly female ushers standing in front of the entrance of the seating area. They greeted us with smiles as well. They pointed us to the opened seats which were closer to the podium in front of the church. The way people stared at us as we walked down the aisle, it almost felt like we were royalty. Royal Blue was just a name of a color, but purple really represented royalty. Kim and I looked like a king and queen scrolling down the aisle.

The people that were seated in the fourth row made room for us to join them. We sat down just in time for the opening chorus. A young lady vocalist stepped to the microphone and hit the first note perfectly. The choir came in right after she woke up the whole church with her soprano vocal cords that pierced the airway. I felt a sensation like no other going through my body as the young lady poured her heart into the rendition of Tasha Cobbs "Break Every Chain." Kim sang the song word for word. I, on the other hand, didn't know one single word, but I still clapped with enthusiasm! My feet tapped uncontrollably. It felt like the old days when my grandma used to take me to church. Women jumped up throughout the church singing along with the gifted female performer. Men soon followed. Young and old all sang together in unison. The vocalist finished the song using a range of vocal styles. She went to the highest pitch of soprano to medium alto, then to the lowest bass as she possibly could. It was an uproar of applause when the choir rested behind her.

Church was starting on a high note. There were a few announcements that went right on schedule. The main topic was about helping the community and improvements that needed to be done to the church - the usual church rhetoric. I knew before the offering plate would be passed out, it would be special benevolence just for that. After the announcer was done with her pleading for help, the choir resumed their position again. This time it was only the musicians and the chorus. They played a jazzy yet uplifting version of "Hold On, I'm Comin'." The church lit up like a firecracker. The electricity in the building was contagious! I even stood up alongside Kim as we clapped and sung with everyone else. I felt my wife's aura taking over my body. It was moments like this that made me proud to fellowship with Kim.

After dancing and hollering at the top of our lungs, it all ceased in preparation to pay tithes and offerings. We were all told to rise in prayer. Pastor Victor D. Collier led the prayer from the podium. He emphasized the importance of tithing. Kim went into her purse to grab her checkbook. She wrote out a check and placed it in an envelope. I, on the other hand, had cash on me. It wasn't ten percent of what I earned for the week, but it was close enough. Besides, I recalled giving a few homeless people money throughout the week. I thought that should count towards my tithe.

After Pastor Victor D. Collier finished his short speech, we were told to bring our tithes and offerings to the stage. I guessed they didn't pass trays around anymore. Good, because I didn't want to pay anything else. The nerve of some churches.

The ushers lined us up in an orderly fashion. The band started playing traveling music. I stood up next to Kim praying that I didn't see any fine women walking by our row. Sure enough, some of the women who walked by had their cleavage hanging out. Lord, Jesus, the racks I saw had my manhood jumping in my pants. My mouth watered as the sweet taste of melons crossed my mind.

On top of that, some of them had on dresses so tight that I could see every curve on their body. Booties were bouncing more than a little kid jumping in a bounce house. I began praying to myself as Kim stood in front of me. My hormones raced.

It was divine intervention when the usher directed our row to go forward to the front of the church. I walked behind Kim towards the two huge woven brown baskets. Kim and I placed our envelopes into the baskets and proceeded back to our seats. I was relieved. I didn't want the pressure of seeing all those fine women; it would get in the way of the Word.

Once everyone gave what they could, Pastor Victor D. Collier stood for his message. The church sat quietly waiting for his sermon.

# Changed

"Church, please turn to Romans 12:2," he instructed.

He waited for everyone to find the verse. Though the scripture was clearly displayed on the huge projector, he still stood patiently waiting for everyone to find it in their Bibles. Once he saw that everyone found their place, he began.

"Do not be conformed to this world, but be transformed by the renewal of your mind, that by testing you may discern what is the will of God, what is good and acceptable and perfect."

Once he was done with the reading of the scripture, I thought, *there goes that word again, renewal of the mind.* I guess Pastor Victor D. Collier was gonna finally explain what I didn't understand.

He went on to say, "No one can go on living without changing. How you start isn't the same way you're supposed to finish. In life, we all are going to make mistakes, but we can't let those mistakes consume us. Though we are born into sin, it doesn't mean we can't live righteous in this world of corruption. The world will say do this and that, but in God's eyes, you are living in sin if you are not living by the Word. The ungodly will pay a dear price at the end. Heaven is hard to get into, but hell is so easy to go to. My true believers, please change your ways before it is too late."

Pastor continued, "Don't believe you are not a sinner if you are sinning. The world will make you think that you're doing right when you're doing wrong. You can't hide behind sin because God sees everything. You can fool people, but you can't fool God. You will be judged according to your deeds. Romans 6:23 says, 'For the wages of sin is death, but the gift of God is eternal life.' You must decide what side you are on."

The church was quiet as he picked up steam, "And for the people that steal, all of y'all will lose everything sevenfold. If you don't know what seven-fold means, it simply means you will lose more than what you took. You must earn what you want! Committing crimes is for the lazy mind. Oh yeah, I haven't forgotten about the people who live a life of adultery. Why did you get married? It's unfair to the person you married. Who are you to disrespect the vows you took? You have men sleeping with this woman and that woman. An outside baby isn't the only thing that you can get! Can I get an Amen from somebody?"

Someone shouted out, "Amen Pastor!", and another screamed, "Weellll!"

Duly encouraged, Pastor went on, "I will leave you folks with this. Bad behavior plus a stubborn mind equals ignorance. Everything starts in the mind. God can only help those who are ready to change. Change starts within. You must renew your mind by doing things that you're not accustomed to. A true believer will take the road less traveled, but wrongdoers will be among the popular. You can start off wrong, but that doesn't mean you can't finish right. Give yourselves to God before the devil gets a hold of you. I'm done, hallelujah!"

The whole church went into an uproar. The church screamed for God's mercy. Pastor Victor D. Collier captivated the men and mesmerized the women. I could hear cries of "Hallelujah!" echoing throughout the church. People jumped and danced. Some caught the Holy Ghost as if the spirit of God entered New Hope Baptist church. It was a scene for the ages.

My spirit was stimulated. I didn't know much about screaming and shouting in church, but my insides hollered for spiritual growth. I grabbed Kim's hand to comfort her. Kim looked like the Holy Spirit paralyzed her as she prayed silently. I also found it to be difficult to move. Pastor Victor D. Collier's words penetrated my soul. I held Kim's hand more firmly as we both felt the spirit in the building. It was epic. Tissues had to be distributed throughout the church to wipe the tears of guilt. The church stood for at least 15 minutes before everyone took their seats.

Pastor Victor D. Collier drank a glass of water before closing the church service with the benediction. I didn't want to get caught up with bumper to bumper church traffic. I signaled to Kim that it was time to leave. We kindly excused ourselves in shame. It was nothing worse than walking out of church while the preacher hadn't finished his sermon, but my patience was low for traffic jams.

We made our way to the car feeling spiritually enlighten. I kissed Kim on the forehead before opening the door for her. I walked over to the other side, peeking into the back window to see Kim reaching over to make sure the car door was unlocked. I pulled out of New Hope Baptist church feeling like I had work to do. I couldn't continue living life promiscuously. I also knew I couldn't do it on my own. I needed God to help me.

"So, Jacob, what did you think about the church service?" Kim asked.

I still was in some sort of trance. But I snapped out of it after Kim asked me the same question again.

"I'm sorry babe, but I was just thinking about how much I missed going to church. It was great! I think we need to go more often," I finished.

Kim smiled from ear to ear. A woman who has some spirituality love going to church with her man. It is a part of bonding.

"Yes, church was great. But Jacob, what did you take from Pastor Collier's sermon?" She asked going further into the first question.

Once again telling the truth was on the line. And once again, I told a little white lie.

"Well, Kim I need to change for the better. I'm not perfect though I strive to be the best that I can be," I said, then quickly changed the subject.

"So, what do you want to eat?" I said in hopes to get her mind off me.

"Let's go to a buffet. Ever since I found out that I'm pregnant, I've been over hungry," she said giggling.

It was the perfect subject changer. Food and pregnancy went together better than sugar and Kool-Aid. I suggested a nice soul food spot a few miles from the church.

On our way, I decided to play Maxwell's greatest hits. My gurl loved Maxwell! It was something about his music that made Kim tranquil. We both sang his hits as we made our way through the city. Miami Gardens seemed to be calm. It was around 2:00. I guess everyone was in the house watching the Miami Dolphins game, praying that they made the playoffs this year. It would be tough for a franchise which played in the AFC East where Tom

Brady and the New England Patriots ruled. The only NFL team to ever go undefeated was cursed.

As we turned on the corner of 95 street and 22 Avenue, I saw Frank and his crew hanging out in front of a convenience store. He must have made bond. All the nostalgia I felt earlier went out of the window. I made an abrupt turn into the store, which was nothing more than a front for a gambling operation. I whipped into a parking space in front of the store. I grabbed my 45mm Glock from my glove compartment. I placed it underneath my dress shirt. Unconsciously, I said "datz the nigga who slapped my sister." Kim started panicking. She screamed, but I ignored her. I rushed out of the car, slamming the door behind me.

I left Kim in the car confused. I was too heated to care. I stepped to Frank who was holding a point spread line sheet with aggression. Where I was from, being diplomatic could have gotten me slapped in the face. I didn't want to give Frank the impression that I was soft.

"Hey, Frank I got a bet for you," I said as I approached him.

Frank looked confused. The two smoked out young teenagers standing behind him looked to be more interested in street rep than finishing high school. They started holding their position like henchmen.

"Jacob lay it on me," he said actually thinking that I was talking about sports betting.

I replied, "The next time you put your hands on Mary Jo, I bet I beat yo' ass from where you're standing to American Airline Arena!"

Frank was taken aback but didn't back down.

"Jacob, who the fuck do you think you're talking too? Nigga, you know my M.O.," he said trying to scare me.

I wasn't impressed nor afraid. "Yeah, Frank I know yo' M.O. You a po' hustla. You're a disgrace to crime. You can't stay out of jail 'cuz you a poor excuse for a drug dealer. Every dime you get, you gamble it. By the way, ain't dat your boss man's money you're using to gamble with? You a peon in the scheme of things," I said in an effort to embarrass him in front of his flunkies.

# Changed

Frank wasn't the type to be put to shame in front of anybody, so he stepped closer to me as I expected. He was so close to me that I could smell cigarettes on his breath. I didn't make a move for my gun. My gut told me not to.

"Listen hear fuckboy! Don't worry 'bout what I do with Bloc's money. The next time you come 'round here 'bout a bitch, I will kill you where you stand. I don't know what the fuck these metrosexual niggaz think they are nowadays. Don't you have somewhere to go to put your makeup on at?"

He said as his young flunkies laughed. I smirked at him. Rage took over me!

"Frank, if you think that I'm a pretty boy, this should be an easy win. Last I checked, the only men I know to be punks are those who hit women. And that is something that I have never done. But I do know someone who did." I said as I balled up my fist.

The young teenage losers started reaching in their pants. I was too heated even to care. As World War III was about to happen, Kim jumped out of the car.

"Y'all, please don't do this!" she yelled desperately.

I yelled back, "Get back in the car!"

During the confusion, one of the Arab's clerks stormed out of the store with a gun visible.

"Frank, get yo' ass out of here. I don't want any trouble in front of my store. You know what's going on in here," The Arab screamed.

Frank turned in disgust. "Shut the fuck up pussy ass A-rab! I got this."

He turned back to me. I still stood firm and unafraid.

"Jacob, I will see you again. It won't be pretty when I do," he warned me.

I simply replied, "A real nigga fight with his fists, punks pull out guns. Which one are you?" I said as I walked cautiously back to the car.

When I pulled off, that was when the real fighting started.

"Jacob, what the hell were you thinking about? I'm pregnant, and you left me in the car behind some female that isn't your real blood relative. You could have gotten yourself killed. And for what? The way you were acting, you make me think it's something more than a guardian angel relationship!"

With my adrenaline on overdrive, I lost it.

"Look, Kim; I don't know what you're talking about! How many times do I have to go over that I made a promise to Mary Jo's brother a long time ago! I don't give a damn what you think my relationship is with Mary Jo! Just know I won't let anything happen to her," I finished screaming from the top of my lungs.

Kim wasn't having it. "Jacob, you can't be serious! You will not take another bitch over me any day of the week! I'm your wife! And you will not disrespect me, Jacob!" She screamed back.

I knew I had to put my foot down at that point. Once a woman starts believing that she can raise her voice when she feels like it, a man's manhood will always be challenged. And there was no way in hell I was about to let Kim take mine.

"Kim lower your voice! I will not tolerate you screaming at me! Okay, I'm wrong for raising mine, but we will talk to each other in a lower tone," I said calming down.

Kim started crying. Tears were always a weak point for me. Kim didn't cry often, but when she did, I turned softer than cotton candy. I went from the Incredible Hulk to Dr. Phil almost simultaneously.

"Kim, I will never disrespect you for another woman. But you know the deal. That poor excuse of a man is hitting Mary Jo in front of her kids. I can't sit back as her guardian angel and let that happen. Kim, please respect me as a man. I wouldn't do anything to hurt you," I said.

Kim seemed to be a little abrasive towards everything that I said, but her tears didn't pour as much.

"Jacob, just take me home. I don't feel like eating anymore," she persisted.

I didn't utter a word. I knew at that time it would be best to drive quietly. Our nerves were shot. Trying to discuss the situation would only lead to another argument. I cut the music back up to change the mood in the car. It really didn't change anything

# Changed

because Kim sat sobbing. I kept my eyes on the road. It was complete silence the whole ride home.

We walked into the house as if we had never gone to church earlier that morning. The Holy Spirit had come and gone. It felt like it was all for nothing. The darkness in the house made the melancholy more prevalent. Kim said nothing as she walked into the bedroom. I didn't bother to walk behind her. I simply laid on the couch uncovered. I didn't need a blanket to comfort me because the temperature in my body was hot enough to heat the whole condo. I didn't know if it was life or death with Frank and me, but what I did know was if he hit Mary Jo again, I would beat his ass where he stood. The anger in my heart made me grow tired. Before I fell asleep in disgust, I said a short prayer.

**d**

# Chapter 13
# Renewing the Mind

Two months had passed since the incident with Frank, which helped the process of healing between Kim and me. The best part about it, I kept my dick in my pants. Kim was the only one who got the business. Also, I managed to dodge Michelle's sexual requests with two sick notes. She called me a liar, but oh well, what could she do? Latoya was behind me, though I did miss her sexy ass. It was for the best. All the other women who harassed me for sex, I ignored. If it weren't about modeling or personal training, I would simply send those calls straight to voicemail. I honestly was proud of myself. Change was a-coming. I finally felt like a real husband. I haven't lied to Kim in two months. I even spent more time with her. Becoming a father surely had a lot to do with it.

She was not showing as of yet, but we prepared ourselves as if the delivery was right around the corner. Without knowing if it was a boy or girl, we bounced names around to each other. Nothing serious, but it became a part of our talks. Kim gave me the right to name the baby if it was a boy and I gave her the same right if it was a girl. In addition to baby's names being tossed around, I took it upon myself to start a college fund for my unborn seed. *Better now than later*, I thought. I was enthusiastic about the whole process of pregnancy. I wanted to be the best father that I could be.

Kim continued to work at the hospital as she always had done. Those long weekends where I used to sneak out, I was now home on the couch feeling lonely. Being faithful for the first time in my life felt a little odd. Normally when I got bored, my dick found interesting things for us to do. But not at this point and time. On late nights, I would find myself channel surfing. Nothing could keep my attention long other than *Sports Center*. When I wasn't watching highlights for the umpteenth time, I would clean the

# Changed

whole house. After cleaning the entire house, I would clean it again. My OCD was kicking into turbo due to my free time. I couldn't see how people could sit home all day and do nothing.

After mastering the art of boredom, I started working out at home. I bought a pull-up bar to hang on the bedroom door frame. I would do pull-ups until my muscles failed. I would also incorporate leg-ups to keep my abs firm. My nightly workouts while Kim was gone kept my mind occupied. Moreover, if the weather permitted, I would jog at night. I chose different parks and trails to jog at to keep myself from becoming complacent. My conditioning and stamina got better over time. Not that I needed it, but my fat percentage went down as well.

I used my time wisely because I knew I wouldn't be sitting home for long. Modeling was still my top priority, but it was good to be home with Kim. The less she did, the better I felt. She reminded me all the time that pregnancy wasn't a handicap, but a blessing from God. It went in one ear and out the other. I found myself cooking more. I would look up recipes just to keep Kim out of the kitchen. After a couple of failed attempts to take Kim's place in the kitchen, we decided going out to eat would be better.

\*\*\*

We came up with an idea to start back dating again. On her off days, Kim and I went out to paint the town red. I took her to expensive restaurants which obviously I never took any other woman to before. I chauffeured her as far away from Miami as I possibly could. We mingled mostly in the Broward and West Palm Beach city limits. On occasions, we would take a 3-hour drive to Orlando just to get away. If we so happened to stay in Miami, we would drive down to the beautiful Florida Keys.

I almost got caught on one of my dates with Kim when I made the mistake of not venturing out of Miami-Dade County. I assumed it was a discreet location. It was a ducked-off spot in the corner of nowhere in Miami Springs. It was in a majority Hispanic community that I thought could keep me out of sight of any woman who made my list. It was wishful thinking. As I was sitting down eating with Kim, a Cuban chic I had laid the wood on came in with some muscle-bound dude with a shirt tight enough to cut off his blood circulation. As I recalled she was trying to be my girl. Not only did she try to get with me, but the bitch was loco! The night we had sex, she begged for a golden shower while barking like a dog in the tub. So, after watering the lawn, she got upset when I couldn't piss anymore. She started barking louder for more. She kept trying to get me to drink water to erupt my bladder. I couldn't take it. I loved freaks, but her freakiness was unbecoming. I couldn't wait to block her number once we were done.

I tried hiding my face, but she saw me. As her dude was checking on their reservation, she turned and stared at me with disdain. I believe if her dude wasn't present, she would have walked right over to me in front of Kim and poured a glass of water on top of my head. To ease the tension, I excused myself to the restroom.

I prayed as I went to the restroom that she would politely sit down with her dude and relax. I took the longest pee in history. I wasn't in any rush to leave the urinal. It got the best of me. I must have shook my penis for at least a minute before zipping up my pants. I then washed my hands staring in the mirror thinking about what I would say if she tried to blow my spot up. From a logical stand point, I should've been fine, but dealing with a crazy chic, anything could happen. I sure wasn't about to let that happen. I figured the worst that could have happened was knocking her dude out and calling her delusional in front of my wife just in case things got out of hand. For the sake of my marriage, I was willing to do anything.

I walked out of the restroom with confidence that I could get past this insane situation. But as I walked out, the loco Latina was waiting on me in the hallway of the restroom area.

"So, Clarence, did you think that you were gonna just pee on me and leave?" She said in a low tone not wanting either of our dates to hear.

"Gurl, what are you talkin' 'bout?" I said trying to sound confused.

# Changed

"Clarence, you know what the fuck I'm talkin' 'bout. How dare you make me believe that you wanted something more with me? If you just wanted to fuck, you could have just said that" she expressed angrily.

"Check this out Chica, I'm here with my wife. I don't have time for this shit. We fucked and it was whack! Besides you're with that Ricky Martin look-alike outside. Please go entertain him before I find a bone," I said in hopes to get her ass out of my face.

She was pissed! Before going off, she glimpsed at my wedding ring, "Okay, asshole! I'll make a deal with you. You get your ass outta here or I'll go to your table and tell your wife about how much of a piece of shit you really are. And for an added bonus, I'll scream rape just because. Who do you think the court will believe, a cheating nigger like your ass or a sweet innocent Latina like me?" She said intentionally insulting me.

"Fuck you! You barking bitch!" I said in retaliation.

"Get out of here Clarence before I tell your wife that you're nothing more than a cheat!" She said cutting no corners.

I walked back to Kim with my head down and the Chihuahua pranced back to her date, who would probably be painting her face yellow later on that night.

"Kim, let's get out of here. I think I have food poisoning!" I said.

Kim stared at me crazy.

"Jacob, you hardly ate anything. I think that food poisoning takes a little longer than that." Kim replied.

"I don't know what it is, but I don't feel good," I said as I waved for the waiter.

He came over with the tab and a doggy bag. I didn't go on with Kim. I paid then simply grabbed our stuff and walked out the restaurant feeling humiliated.

As we drove home, I thought again about being called a cheat. This woman didn't even know my real name other than Clarence the cheat. I didn't want to be labeled that, but at the rate that I was going, it was inevitable to be called just that. I looked over to Kim to see that she was sleeping in the passenger seat. She had no idea who she was riding with. I identified myself to her years ago that I would be her future husband, but deep down inside I was nothing more than a con artist in a tuxedo. I was the Bernie Madoff of cheating. Prison wouldn't be a harsh enough sentence if Kim ever caught me.

It was a close call in the restaurant, but I managed to make it out. Karma felt like it was catching up to me.

# Chapter 14
# Time Speeds By

The months went by fast. I had since slowed down with the dating idea. I wasn't gonna get caught that way. Kim was starting to deal with fatigue and back pain from the pregnancy. I became her errand boy. In between training in the afternoon, I did anything Kim needed me to do. She took good advantage. The women and men at the post office knew me by my first name. Kim's mother saw me once a week for something. In addition to some of the ridiculous places I had to go, I also got a detailed grocery list every two weeks.

Furthermore, Kim's cravings were out of control. It didn't matter what time of day or night it was, she had to have either butter pecan ice cream or apple pie. Kim's cravings were so bad that she woke me up one morning at 3:00 AM for an apple pie. I couldn't believe it! *Three o' clock in the morning and this woman wanted some damn apple pie?!* But with redemption on my mind, I went out and got it.

I was still on my good boy status. It had been almost four months since I slept with another woman. I was starting to get the shakes at night. It wasn't easy going cold turkey. I still refused to watch porno movies to get off. Kim saved my life because she stayed horny. I never knew that pregnancy could make a woman so ready for sex. Kim was my unsung hero. But even with that, I still found myself thinking about other women. It was hard controlling my urges. I did everything possible to stay in the house or to make sure I was with Kim to sustain my urges.

While suppressing my sexual urges, I got the best news ever. The ultrasound showed that we were having a little boy. I couldn't believe it. I was having a little boy! The greatest thing a woman could bring to a man was a boy. I stood proudly as I watched the screen with Kim. I saw his little dick. I would one day have to teach him how not to be like me. I would teach him to be the total opposite. I would teach him to be a one-woman-man. The

# Changed

amount of energy that I had spent hiding the truth, I would teach him to use it to master the crossover dribble, or how to play shortstop while learning to swing at a curveball. Running track could also be a possibility, but I preferred a sport that paid out of the gates. I just wondered what name the sportscasters would call him...

Since I was in charge of naming him, I went through many names before coming up with one. At first, I thought of African names like Amadi, Ebo, Jahi, and Talib, but couldn't bring myself to do it. Then I thought about Muslim names such as Abdul-Azim, Ashraf, Aydin, and Akram but didn't want my son to be negatively labeled. Then I thought about Haitians names that could fit like Jean, Pierre, Sidney, and Zhedd, but I remembered my name being changed after my parent's death.

Then I thought of a simple, but profound name: Michael. A lot of outstanding people had the first name, Michael. Michael Jordan was the greatest basketball player ever to play the game. (Sorry, Kobe.) Mike Tyson before biting off Evander Holyfield's ear off was considered to be one of the greatest heavyweight boxers ever. I couldn't forget about the best entertainer in the world: Michael Jackson! Two-hundred-fifty million albums sold nationwide. Pure greatest! (Now, did he touch those kids was another story.) And last, but not least: Michelangelo! He was one of the greatest artists of all time. I wondered how he painted the Sistine Chapel on his back. Anyway, my son's name would be Michael Pierre Richardson. Kim didn't have a problem with the name. Now, I had four more months to wait to see my little man.

\*\*\*

Every chance I got, I rubbed Kim's stomach while repeating Michael's name. Kim would smile when I did it. We were getting closer. Every now and then, Kim would have her moments. She would cry for no reason. She was no longer allowed to take her depression pills because they could've affected the baby. I monitored her as well as the doctors. I needed her to stay stable in the mind while carrying our child. It was imperative that I kept Kim cool and calm. Her happiness was so important to the survival of our little one. There wasn't a woman worth enough to destroy my child's birth. So I thought.

One night while looking through my email, the devil showed up. I had been doing well for most of Kim's pregnancy until I came across two messages. As I was scrolling through my messages, I saw one from my old college flame, Melissa Turner. It said she was now changing her last name to Evans. My old track mate Carl Evans was marrying my old dorm room jump off. On the weekends, she would sneak into my dorm room through the back door while my dormies looked out. She loved seeing me in my track warm-up suit. She would pack her majorette outfit in her hoe bag. She loved wearing it before we had sex. It was her way of role-playing. I was always down.

I couldn't believe she was marrying this asshole. The truth was, Carl was marrying my leftovers. After a track meet, I told him how freaky Melissa was in bed. This idiot went behind my back and had sex with her. Instead of passing her along to the boys, this ass wipe fell in love with her. He made Melissa his gurl. I never confronted him because he could've been a pussy and told Kim. It wasn't worth the risk.

Moreover, another reason I didn't like Carl was that he always bragged about being faster than me. He was the fastest male athlete in the entire school. I always came up second to him. And he made sure to let me know every chance he got. I thought I was arrogant until I met him.

Before opening the message, I thought, *Why would Melissa reach out to me after so many years?* I pressed on it.

> *Dear Jacob Richardson,*
> *I hope everything is fine. Carl and I have decided to get married. I'm sorry if this is last minute, but we want to send you an invitation. We are getting married next month on August 9$^{th}$. If you would like to attend, please email me your address. It has been such a long time since we last saw one another. I cherished those moments back in the dorm room. Lol! I know I shouldn't be speaking this way, but how could I forget you in your warm-up suit? Anyway, I*

# Changed

*convinced Carl to invite all of his old track team buddies just to see you. He didn't mention anything when I said your name. I guess it doesn't matter anymore to him that we used to date. If you are interested in attending, please call me this week at 305-786-7788. I really need to talk to you.*

*Sincerely,*
*Melissa Turner*

After reading Melissa's message, I wondered if she wanted to have sex again. The message she sent had all of the indications, but I wasn't quite sure. Furthermore, if she did, why would she want to have sex with me if she was getting married? I thought for a moment; *this had to be the devil in disguise.* Lucifer, the son of the morning, came to me via email at night. I had been behaving myself for months, so why now? So, my dick could veto every thought I had of staying monogamous? It gave an executive order to be released back into the wild. I fought the temptation by quickly scrolling down to my other messages.

As I scrolled down further, it didn't get any better. I saw a message from AWOP. AWOP was founded in 2005 by a woman from Spain named Olivia Gomez. She was the quintessential woman who made her fortune selling red heels. Her expensive woman's shoe brand, Rojo, only carried a variety of red heels which propelled her to the *Forbes* Top 20 Richest Women in the World list. Her net worth was estimated at $4.2 billion. She had powerful influence throughout all Hispanic regions. If Columbia couldn't get a shipment of cocaine past the water patrol, Olivia handled it. If the Mexican cartel found it hard to get past the borders with guns, Olivia handled it. If Cuban drug lords' keys were intersected before making it to the Florida shores, Olivia handled it. If a corrupted Hispanic official were looking to take a political office, Olivia handled it.

Olivia could be business savvy and ruthless at the same time. She also had a passion for investing. She grew up dirt poor in the small city called Extremadura in Spain. It was on the border of Portugal. For centuries, the Extremadura unemployment rate was around 30%. Her parents couldn't afford to keep her, so she was left at the front door of an orphanage to fend for herself. She got into a lot of fights while being harbored at Mother Teresa's Home for Little Stars. Even though Olivia did well with defending herself, she was even better with math and creative arts. The staff members at the orphanage took notice. When anyone new came into the orphanage seeking to adopt, Olivia's name was always mentioned first. Gabriel and Sofia Gomez finally adopted her. They were an older couple who wanted to have kids, but unfortunately, Mrs. Gomez couldn't have any. The only alternative they had at ever being parents was through adoption. Therefore, Olivia was given a home.

Olivia fit right in. She did well in school and did her chores around the house without being asked twice. The Gomez's took to her as if she was their daughter. They even changed her last name to theirs to make Olivia feel like she was a part of the family. They didn't keep any secrets from her. They used to always tell her even though she came from a poor background; she could be anything she wanted to be. Olivia discovered what her true talent was one day when she watched the Wizard of Oz for the first time. Dorothy in her red ruby slippers caught the attention of Olivia's imagination. She vowed to herself that she would design only red heels for women.

The Gomez's sent her to the best fashion design school in Spain. Olivia excelled in all her classes. She graduated in the top ten percent of her class. But shortly after finishing school, Mr. Gomez became sick. The insidious disease cancer ripped through his body. He died within months, and Mrs. Gomez died shortly after of a broken heart. With the small fortune they left behind, Olivia was able to use it to launch her brand *Rojo*. She never looked back. *Rojo* went from a bunch of red shoes being stored in a small room to having over 100 stores worldwide. *Rojo* was synonymous with Red Bottoms and available at only the high-end women's shoe stores.

With all the success Olivia had, she still gave back in her own fashion. Understanding without help she wouldn't be where she was, Olivia decided to start an organization to invest in

# Changed

women's small businesses. She would find women from all across the world to invest in their projects if they could come up with a decent business plan. She would have to see some growth or revenue before giving out one single penny. Moreover, the women who she chose would have to work out as a part of the prerequisite. Her philosophy was, "The better a woman looked, the better chance of her making money." Lastly, age was a requirement. The women who were seeking monetary help for their businesses couldn't be younger than 35 years old, but no older than 55 years of age. In Olivia's mind, that was the proper age range for a smart business-minded woman and the right old age of a cougar.

Though Olivia had everything a woman could want, she never settled down. At the age of 50 and being one of the richest women in the world, she had never been married. Nor did she ever want to. She loved young dick too much to get involved seriously but was old enough to know better than to marry one. To pay palimony or alimony to a man who she only wanted something physical from was preposterous in her mind. Therefore, she would fuck her young hotties and brush them off.

Her organization AWOP was based on business and pleasure. Every four months, Olivia would hold a workshop with the women she chose. Once the business meetings were done, the fun would begin. Since her cup of tea was young men, her tastes trickled down to the other women. All of them knew what they were getting into before they signed on. Some were married and some were not. It didn't matter because all of the women knew that they were gonna get dicked down for the weekend after a tedious set of meetings.

Olivia would arrange an orgy with the hottest young men she could find. The men's ages ranged from 20 to 30 years old. The pay was $5000 for each man. I was on the borderline at my age. Olivia always made sure I made the cut. She liked her coffee caramel brown. I fit the description perfectly.

I wondered for a moment if I should attend or not. I left it up in the air before closing my computer down. *Why me?* I asked again. *Poor Kim,* I thought to myself. I was doing so well for us,

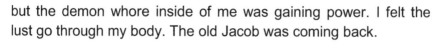

but the demon whore inside of me was gaining power. I felt the lust go through my body. The old Jacob was coming back.

_ d

# Chapter 15
# Old Flame

I decided to call Melissa on hump day. It was a beautiful Wednesday afternoon in Miami. It was around noon. I figured she wouldn't be busy.

She picked up immediately, "Hello!"

I didn't hesitate, "Wuz up Melissa?" I said hoping she recognized my voice.

"Jacob is this you?" she asked.

It felt good that she still kind of knew my voice.

"Yep, this is me, Jacob."

"It's so good to hear from you after all these years. I miss you, friend! How have you been?" She asked.

"I've been good. I'm still pursuing my modeling career and doing a little personal training on the side," I said.

I knew her next question was coming.

"So, how are you and Kim doing?" She asked being nosey.

"Well, we're still holding on strong. We've been married for six years," I said, not wanting to go into any more details.

I could hear her breathing changing through the phone. "Well, as you know, I and Carl are getting married. I would like for you to attend. Is that cool?" She questioned.

It was time to find out why she wanted to see me so badly.

"I will attend, but my question is why do you want to see me?" I inquired.

She paused before answering. "Well, Jacob, it's like this. I love Carl to pieces, but he's killing me in the bed. He is totally inadequate sexually. He can't last over two minutes. No matter what we do, he always cums too fast. His head is okay, but his dick is terrible! I'm more a penetration girl than a lick it up one. I thought over time he would get better, but it hasn't happened yet. Don't get me wrong, he's a good man, but his untimely ejaculations are ruining my sex life. Outside of the bad sex, he's a great provider. But enough is enough."

# Changed

I'd heard enough, but she kept on going. It was like she was at her last confession, and I was the priest. "Despite it all, I'm still gonna marry him. I hope one-day things change, but until then I need some good dick before I get married. I would hate to anticipate something wonderful for our honeymoon only to be disappointed by a two-minute brotha. I can't take it, Jacob! So, I was wondering could you give me some good-good before I get married?" She asked without an apology.

I tried to gather all the information that she laid out for me. It was coming too fast, but I got her point.

"So, you mean to tell me that you want to fuck me for the last time? Why me Melissa?" I asked wanting to know the answer.

"Jacob, I never cheated on Carl in my life. I stayed faithful through it all, even though I wasn't being satisfied in bed. I replaced what he couldn't do in bed with sex toys. Those toys became my best friends. I loved when he had to travel with his company so I could masturbate in peace. The toys felt so good that I started hating when Carl wanted to have sex with me. I damn near cried one night when my batteries went dead. I drove damn near 20 minutes to find some AA batteries. Shit was that real."

Man, I'd heard enough, but Melissa had only gotten started. "Now, I must admit that I have cheated with other men, but nothing physically. While placing my best friend on my clitoris, I would watch Brian Pumper, Lex Steel, Justin Slayers, Rico Long, and how could I forget Wesley Pipes crazy talking ass on porn. A gurl got to do what a gurl got to do."

Finally, Melissa ended with, "Anyway, so Jacob, will you give me some good-good or not?"

I laughed. "Okay, so how are we supposed to pull this off?" I asked in disbelief.

She mapped out the perfect plan. Before hanging up, she told me to bring my old warm-up suit.

My head was spinning. So, the night of the bachelor and bachelorette party, we were gonna sneak out to a hotel she reserved under an alias. It was probably a girlfriend who knew her sexual frustration. Anyway, she would go to her bachelorette party, and I would attend the bachelor party. Melissa instructed me to stay at the party until she texted me. That would be my cue to leave.

***

Carl's Best Man did a great job finding some of the finest strippers in Miami. I wasn't interested. I was more interested in having sex with my rival's wife. The strippers performed for the dollars that were being thrown at them. Carl was all in as if he forgot he was getting married the next day. I watched the activities from afar. I saw him walk to the back of the rented-out house with two strippers. All his homies in the living room cheered him on. A couple of my old track buddies tried to talk to me, but the music was too loud for me to hear them. It gave me the opportunity to shy off. I felt my phone vibrating in my pocket. I looked at my cell phone to see Melissa left a text.

"Jacob, I'm about to leave this spot. I'm tired of watching these muscle-bound men in bikini underwear dancing around slinging their dicks. Not my cup of tea. Is Carl occupied?"

I texted her back, "Yep, he is occupied."

Melissa responded, "Good. Okay, you can meet me at the Diplomat. You don't have to say anything to the people at the front desk. Just come up to room 2401. I will be waiting."

I replied, "Okay."

I sat around for a minute before making my exit. I didn't say anything to anyone as I made my way to my car. I hit I-95 North headed to Hollywood. It wasn't too far from where the bachelor party was being held. All I could think about was waxing Melissa's ass. It had been years since I put it on her. I was ready to see what old pussy felt like. It would probably be like taking an old couch to be reupholstered. And the way Melissa sounded over the phone, she needed more than just an upgrade. Bad sex in a marriage was a tough pill to swallow. Anyone can lie to themselves that it's possible to do, but the fact of the matter is no one wants to suffer like that. I wouldn't wish bad sex on my worst enemy.

As I pulled up to the Diplomat Beach Resort, my phone vibrated. It was a text from Melissa.

# Changed

"Jacob, we don't have much time. My gurl is covering for me at the party. I'm ready. There's no need to play. I will leave the door opened."

I texted back, "Okay."

I pulled up to the elaborate hotel. It was above shoulders the finest hotel on the whole Hollywood Beach Boulevard strip. The windows on the outside matched the color of the beach that was behind it. There was a connector in the middle of the two gigantic buildings. It was something to stop and admire, but I didn't have time to become one of its many spectators. I was in a rush. I grabbed my track warm-up suit out of the back of my car. I didn't have time to put it on when I got up to Melissa's hotel room. I squeezed into it in the front seat of my car. It still fits like a glove. I was on my way.

I walked through the Diplomat without looking at the front desk clerks in their faces. I moved quickly through the beautiful array of palm trees that were planted inside the lobby. I was astonished by the elegance of the hotel's interior design. The modern wood finished furniture went well with the beige shiny marble floors. It was upscale and presented class for those who could afford to stay there. I made my way to the elevator. I pressed the number 24 and was there in no time. I walked calmly down the hallway to Melissa's room not knowing what to expect. Her room door was cracked. I eased the door opened. I walked into the room with the acoustic sounds of India Arie's "Ready for Love" playing at a medium volume. The lights were dimmed. I looked straight ahead to see Melissa's silhouette in front of a curtain covering a huge window in a majorette pose holding something that resembled a baton. As "Ready for Love" went to its first verse, Melissa broke her pose. She started walking towards me dancing seductively. She shifted her hips from side to side while twirling an object that I couldn't recognize.

I turned my eyes slightly to see the king size bed covered with white sheets. I thought to myself; *This could get messy.* There was a sofa a couple of feet away from the bed. I thought that could be a perfect place to bend Melissa over. The candlelight flames gave the hotel room a sensual atmosphere. The fumes coming from the burning candles smelled like peppermint, caramel, and tropical berry combined. The aroma gave the room a tropical island scent. I felt like I was in a massage parlor/jazz lounge. Melissa went out of her way to set the mood.

Melissa did her dirty dance until she got close to me. She stood in front of me looking almost the same as she did when we used to mess around in college. She looked me directly in my face as if she saw a ghost. Her eyes were so tempting. Then she raised her right arm holding the object that I was so curious about. She put it to her mouth and licked the tip of it.

"Hey Jacob, this is my best friend. I hope you don't mind if he tags along?" She asked in a nasty filthy voice.

Once visible, I was able to distinguish that she had the Hitachi Magic Wand vibrator in her hand. That bad boy could keep an independent woman who hated sweat dripping on top of her single forever. It originally came from Japan. It actually was made for massaging sore areas of the body. However, one night a widow who was a part of the HMW researched department decided to take her workload home. She discovered one night while masturbating and looking at her deceased husband's picture that the Magic Wand vibrator could be used for more than soothing an aching muscle. She placed the vibrator on her clit, and the rest was history. Her horny night improved HMW's bottom line exponentially. It was patented and trademarked in April of 1968. Though FDA approved the Hibachi Magic Wand as a therapeutic electric massager, most women found a better use for it on their clits.

*** 

Anyway, I replied, "I don't mind."

She then put the top of the vibrator to her lips. I was intrigued.

"Jacob, you still look good in your warm-ups. Some things won't ever change about you, I see," she stated.

I continued the clever conversation by saying, "Well, I got to stay in the gym. I found the fountain of youth in there. You look like you drink from the same fountain."

# Changed

"Yes, I do get to the gym from time to time, if Carl isn't too tired to watch the kids," she replied stepping back.

Melissa started removing her majorette leotard outfit slowly. It was amazing that she could still fit into it 10 years later. She looked so sexy lifting her shoulders up to pull down the slinky sleeves of the leotard. Her breasts drooped down a bit, but they still had some youth to them. She next pulled her leotard even further down for me to see her stomach. It had a few stretch marks, but I couldn't expect anything more from a woman who had children. Once she pulled down her entire role play outfit, I stared at her, biting my lips.

"So, what do you think, Jacob?" She asked.

"Melissa, you still got it going on. Nothing has really changed. You actually got finer over time, like fine wine," I said to make her feel comfortable.

"Thank you Jacob, but now it's your turn," she said in anticipation.

I didn't hesitate. I seized the moment by slowly removing my warm-up suit. Without a rush, I started unzipping my uniform. I only exposed my chest for her to see. She made a sexy "umm" sound. I kept going. I pulled the top of the warm-up jacket off. She gazed at my upper torso. Then her eyes roamed down to my abs. She then put her hands on them.

"This is nice Jacob. They've gotten more defined since school," She said.

I laughed but stayed modest. "Thanks," I replied.

"So, Jacob, what are you waiting on? Take off the rest," She insisted.

I obeyed her wishes by continuing to take off my warm-up pants. My dick pointed at her like she was the chosen one. She then grabbed my manhood in her hand. She began stroking it as Prince's, "Insatiable" played through her phone. I looked into her eyes, feeling the pleasure of her stroking my meat. I felt the intensity of her hands. I pushed her back to let her know it wasn't about me. I then pulled her close by grabbing her ass tightly.

"Well, since you brought your best friend, I guess you'll have your first threesome," I said jokingly.

She bit her lips in excitement. I then pushed her back onto the bed while she still held on to the vibrator like a receiver holding on to a football after a hard hit.

"Jacob, why are you being so rough?" She said.

"I know it's been some years, but last I checked, Melissa, you like it rough," I replied.

Melissa said nothing. Her eyes rolled back. She placed the Magic Wand on her clitoris and began going to work. I tried to approach her, but she stopped me midway.

"Jacob don't touch me. Just stand there and jack your dick," she insisted.

What else could I do besides follow her orders? I started stroking my dick in front of her without shame. She watched me as she got off. The vibrator looked as if it was taking over her body. She moaned from the top of her lungs. Her eyes rolled back even more. There wasn't anything I or anyone else could do about the sensation that she was feeling. Erotica was the only word I could describe what Melissa was feeling. I saw the tears falling from her eyes while her body impulsively quivered. I couldn't help but smile as she enjoyed herself. I became just as aroused with her arousal. She had one convulsion after another. Tears continued to roll down uncontrollably. Her orgasms seemed like they didn't want to be disturbed. So, I waited patiently masturbating by myself.

She finally called me over to get into the midst of the fun.

"Jacob, come stick your dick in my mouth," she requested.

It was the moment I was waiting for. I climbed up on top of the bed. She opened her mouth wide while continuing to vibrate her clit. Without hands, she put the top of my glans in her mouth. She didn't waste any time by playing with it. Melissa began gobbling my dick down like she was at a Thanksgiving dinner. I could see the passion in her eyes. From my observation, it looked like she was excited to be in my mix again. Melissa gave me the impression that this was something that she needed to do with every slurp. I wasn't sure if Carl was handling his business in bed, but boy Melissa was sure giving me the business with her deep throat. I gazed down at her while she continued to massage her clit with the vibrator. Her pussy looked wetter and wetter. It seemed like it had been glazed with KY Jelly lube, but it was only her body producing the creamy discharge.

I pulled my dick out of her mouth.

"Melissa, are you ready for some good-good?" I asked, playing on what she said earlier.

She seemed to be disoriented after her multiple orgasms.

After she pushed the hair out of her face, she gathered herself.

"Jacob, I'm over ready for some of your good-good," Melissa said as she cocked her legs open on the edge of the bed.

She wanted it really bad! I threw on my condom. I then slipped my dick inside her vagina without any problems. She was too wet even to try to pull the tight pussy trick. There wasn't anything from stopping her vaginal canal from flooding.

I took full pumps inside of her. I pulled my manhood completely out and stuck it all the way back in. I held her down by her shoulders. I didn't want her to make any movements. I wanted full control of her body. I held her down with delicate force. She tried wiggling, but my strength overpowered any attempt to escape. I started dicking her down harder. I gave her all I had. Every inch I had penetrated every inch of her sugar walls. I felt her insides drenching my dick. I wanted more but from a different position.

I then turned her body over while my dick was still inside of her. The thick white creamy secretion started building up around her vulva. It almost reminded me of a little sloppy child with ice cream stuck around his lips. I kept stroking passionately.

She hollered, "Jacob, fuck this pussy! Fuck this pussy!"

My dick felt like it was in paradise. The sex was off the chain. Melissa's cookie felt so good that I started feeling my sperm racing towards the finish line. I pulled out to stop the flow. Once I was able to prevent myself from climaxing, I put my dick back inside of her. I became more aggressive as I saw that it was making Melissa hotter and hotter.

"I hope you're ready for this ride?" I said with no regard for her physical well-being. I put my hands underneath her ass and began lifting her up. I was able to balance myself with her 160-

pound body frame in my hands. I slowly walked her over to the window while she held me tightly. I opened the curtain with one hand while holding her. I then purposely pushed her butt cheeks against the window. Her booty left a nice impression for anyone who could see from the parking lot. I began stroking her right there. Just the mere fact of the possibility that people could have been watching from afar, I believed turned her on even more.

"Jacob, please fuck me good! Fuck this pussy! Go deeper and deeper!"

"So, you really want this dick?"

"Yes, Jacob, I really want this dick!"

"What a slut wants is what a slut gets," I said.

My disrespectful choice of words pushed her over the edge.

"Slut? Who you calling a slut?" She said.

"Yeah, I'm calling you a nasty ass slut," I replied.

With lust in her eyes, she said, "I'll show you who is a slut."

She demanded that I put her down. Once her feet were able to touch the floor, she put her finger to my lips. Melissa then put her other finger to her own lips as if to say I got this.

"Jacob, I hope you can handle this pussy from the back? Imma shows you how a slut fucks."

Without hesitation, I slapped her on the ass and said, "Get your nasty ass over to the couch then!"

She walked over to the couch and bent over. She put her hands on her butt cheeks and opened them. It was a beautiful sight to see. Her pussy looked ready for more. It pulsated before my eyes. It cried to me *come get me, daddy.* I walked over to her holding my time-ticking dick in my hand. I slapped her backside before thrusting my rock-hard dick inside of her wet pussy. I went ham from the jump. I didn't give her any mercy. I gave her all my dick as she threw back her pussy. Her ass cheeks jiggled like Jell-O pudding.

I began pulling her hair. Melissa's head jerked back, but she didn't pull away. There was a mirror on the wall that let me see her face, and her expression looked in between pleasure and plain. The pussy felt juicier than before. The fume of sex reeked throughout the hotel room. Sweat poured down my body onto Melissa's booty. I honestly couldn't hold my composure anymore.

"Melissa, I fuck you better than your fiancé Carl?" I asked throwing her for a loop.

I knew she wasn't ready for that one. She resisted from saying anything, so I said it again.

"I fuck you better than your fiancé Carl, right?"

I questioned with more pressure for the truth. She squirmed even more, but I kept a tight grip on her hair.

"Jacob, why are you making me do this?" She questioned back, almost teary-eyed.

"It doesn't matter why I'm doing this. Tell the truth. I fuck you better than your fiancé Carl?" I asked again.

A tear came down Melissa's left cheek.

"Yes Jacob, you fuck me better than Carl!" She screamed.

"I said do I fuck you better than your fiancé Carl!

"Yes, Jacob!"

"Yes, Jacob what?"

"You fuck me better than my fiancé Carl!"

Hearing her say that I fucked her better than her fiancé Carl wasn't good enough for me. I drove my dick into her even harder.

"Say I fuck you better than your fiancé Carl! And you love it!" I said as I gave it to her.

With contempt on her face, she said the magic words, "Yes Jacob, you fuck me better than my fiancé Carl! And I love it!" I jerked her head toward me; then tongue kissed her. I could no longer hold my nut.

I screamed, "I'm cumming, I'm cumming!"

She yelled back, "I'm cumming, too!" I pulled off my condom as she leaped to the floor like a cheetah. She opened her mouth anticipating cum. I sautéed her lips with my fresh thick milky semen. Melissa then sucked the life out of me with sperm dripping from the side of her mouth. With cum on her face and down her throat, I found myself blinking in and out. She sucked me up so good that I had to push her head away from me. Once I gather myself, I went to the bathroom to grab a hand towel to clean her face.

Melissa had to get back to her bachelorette party. We both jumped into the shower together. We didn't have time to rub each other down with soap. We scrubbed ourselves down individually. Once done washing our asses, we hopped out of the shower. Melissa brushed and gargled her mouth. We got dressed in no time. Before walking out of the hotel room, I asked Melissa how she was able to get away from the party.

She simply said, "My longtime friend who knows my sexual frustration all too well, purposely poured wine on my blouse. We made it look like an accident. I bitched at her in front of everybody. She looked humiliated, and I looked like an angry bitch. It was easy for me to leave the party undetected. Just in case anyone became suspicious, my alibi would be everyone knows that it takes me a year and a day to get dressed," she finished.

I put a smirk on my face. "I guess you have it all planned out Melissa, just like your marriage," I said being facetious. She ignored my poor sense of humor.

"I guess so, Jacob. Thank you for taking care of my needs. I hope your wife didn't mind me borrowing you for a night," she said being as sarcastic as I was.

*Touché* was the only word that I could think of. I didn't bother to reply, I just left.

***

I was back on I-95 South headed home. I guess another night in the office for Jacob Richardson. "Bang 'em and go." No time for small talk after a great night of sex. I started to gather that I was better at a conversation with a woman before sex than the aftermath of being intimate with her. I ran from intimacy. I couldn't give any woman my time or my real thoughts. I would have hurt every one of them. No woman just wants to be seen as a sexual object. Even a prostitute wants to know her pimp cares about her. Even if it's a slap across the face out of love. No matter how many women I've slept with, I honestly couldn't be satisfied. I was numb. I started to think if I could really change.

# Changed

To get my mind off everything, I turned on the radio. I didn't know if it was a sign from God because Sam Cooke's *A Change Gonna Come* was playing on Hot 105. I was now trying to figure out if God was trying to tell me something or was this a coincidence. My grandma used to always tell me that God worked in mysterious ways. The proof was definitely in the pudding. This couldn't be a coincidence.

I thought about the Malcolm X movie when Denzel Washington drove alone while his family trailed him in a separate car. I could recall the uncertainty in his face as a woman drove closely to his car. I was honestly feeling uncertain, just like him. To continue my goal of 20,000 women or to stop was the question? I had a son on the way who needed my attention more than some silly sexual conquest. There was a possibility that I could do it and there was a possibility that I couldn't. Sex with so many women was now starting to be more of a burden than pleasure. I shouldn't have ever married Kim.

# Chapter 16
# Mockery of a Wedding

The next day, Kim and I found ourselves in the sixth row from the altar. We were at Carl and Melissa's mockery of a wedding. Melissa and Carl stood face to face. They were on the verge of saying their vows. I felt my stomach turning. I was starting to get nauseous. I couldn't move.

The preacher then ran me to the restroom when Melissa repeated after him, "To be my lawfully wedded husband, to have and to hold from this day forward, for better, for worse, for richer, for poorer, in sickness and in health, until death do us part."

When they kissed, I excused myself from the wedding silently. I rushed down the back aisle to the restroom. I pushed opened the restroom door. I made it to the stall in a blur. I threw open the door and started puking in the toilet. Once I emptied out everything I had in my stomach, I rose feeling a little dizzy. I stood up slowly thinking, *what am I doing at this wedding?!* Was I there to mock Carl or to keep my promise to Melissa? Either way it went, I needed to get out of there.

I could hear the wedding ceremony ending. I made my way out of the church doors before the groomsmen and bridesmaids exited the chapel. I sat in the car alone waiting for Kim to come out. I felt like shit! I was emotionally distraught. I slept with Carl's bride the night before. Oh my God, what was wrong with me? Hell wasn't even good enough for me. I thought to walk back into the church, but I saw Kim walking up from my rearview mirror. I unlocked the doors.

"Jacob, what is wrong with you? Why did you leave me in the wedding? You know I really don't know those people," she said sounding irritated.

I was still feeling the effects of the sudden case of nausea.

"Kim, I'm sorry. It must have been something that I ate at the bachelor party last night. I did drink a little more than what I was used to. Forgive me, babe," I said, lying through my teeth.

"Well, let's get home. You need to get some rest," she insisted.

I laid in the bed that night thinking about needing some serious help. I had always thought going to see a psychologist was only for loony tunes. I didn't think that I was crazy, but there was something wrong with me. I had to tuck in my pride if I wanted to get better. I knew I would have to see Benny the next day. I remembered once before him, and his wife had to see a shrink for their alternative sex life.

***

The next day, I found myself at Benny's doorstep unannounced with my head in my palms.

"Jacob, what the hell is wrong with you?" He said as he opened the door.

It was hard letting another man see me like this. Especially my longtime friend.

"Man, I need to talk to you," I confessed.

"What happened? Did Kim finally catch yo' ass cheatin'?" He asked.

"Naw man, it ain't nothing like dat," I said, holding on to my toughness. At least, whatever was left of it? The look on my face told Benny that it was serious.

"Okay Jacob, let me go tell Patricia not to come out of the bedroom," he said. When he came back out, Benny told me that it would be cool to talk on the balcony. He lit his cigar while I stared into space.

"So, Jacob, lay it on me man," he insisted.

I almost became insecure with the thought of expressing myself to my longtime friend. In all the years I'd known Benny, he'd never seen me in a moment of weakness. But I had nowhere else to turn.

"Benny, I had sex with this woman last night who got married to my old track mate," I said.

Benny looked at me strangely.

"Jacob, what's new? You're always having sex with someone's wife," he said sarcastically.

It was obvious that he thought I was joking.

# Changed

"No man, it wasn't like that. I slept with his wife the night before and still went to the wedding the next day," I said with hurt on my face.

"Damn Jacob, you had sex with your old track mate's wife and you still went to the wedding the next day? Jacob, you ain't shit," he said mocking me.

I couldn't be angry with his harsh language towards me, but that wouldn't solve the problem that I was having. Benny said exactly what it was.

"Benny, I need help. I'm scared that I can't control myself. I don't want to fuck until my dick falls off. I'm about to be a father and I don't want to start it by being a baby daddy because Kim caught me with my pants down. I mean literally," I said searching.

Benny inhaled his cigar then blew the smoke out. I moved back to avoid the smoke.

"Yeah man, you don't want that. Child support can be a muthafucka! Especially if you're dealing with a bitter woman. She will make your life a living hell," Benny finished.

I nodded my head in agreements. "So, Benny, didn't you and Patricia go see a psychologist when y'all first started swinging?" I asked being nosey.

Benny hit his cigar again.

With smoke coming out of his mouth he answered, "Yeah Jacob, we went to see a psychologist. That white boy was worth every dime, too. We didn't know what direction to go in. She caught me cheating, and I caught her cheating. We both wanted to leave each other, and at the same time, we wanted to stay together. It was some difficult times, but we got through it with the help of Dr. Gallagher. Though we loved each other, we still liked to have sex with other people. Alongside Dr. Gallagher's advice on human sexuality, we decided that it would be best that we didn't hide our sexual desires for other people anymore. It cut the bullshit out. We both felt free. Whatever we did from that point on, we did together."

I thought it was so awkward that a man could let another man have sex with his wife.

"Benny, one question," I said inquiring.

"Wuz up Jacob?"

"Benny, how can you sit there and watch another man have sex with your wife?" I questioned.

Benny put a weird smirk on his face. "Well, that's easy. She watches me have sex with other women. What makes me better than her? That's that male chauvinist crap. Besides, I don't just sit there. I be fucking, too," he explained.

I never thought about it that way. I just knew I couldn't deal with it. I couldn't imagine another man on top of my wife, but to each is his own.

"Jacob, before you lose Kim and your unborn child, go see Dr. Gallagher. He will help you get through this," he promised.

I shook his hand and thanked him. I felt confident that through counseling I could get better. I left Benny's condo feeling like there was hope for me.

# Chapter 17 Satyriasis

I got in contact with Dr. Gallagher's secretary later that evening. I was scheduled to meet with him in a week. I prayed that he could help. I was a car wreck waiting to happen. I just needed polyethylene foam to ease the impact.

***

A week later I took the elevator down to find my Maserati with a flat tire. I was pissed!

"How in the hell did I get a flat tire?"

I thought *It must have been some drunk ass kids who broke their Heineken bottles after a night of partying.* I didn't have time for that shit. I had to meet with Dr. Gallagher at 10 AM in Coral Gables. It was going on 9:15. The time it would take to change a tire. there wasn't any way that I could make my scheduled appointment. I pulled out my cell phone and made the call to push my time back. His secretary didn't have a problem with it. Once confirmed that it would be okay to be late, I turned to the task at hand. I grabbed my black gloves out of my glove compartment. They so happened to be the same ones I used if a woman wanted me to portrait a robber in a role-play situation. Those definitely were some fun nights. But today they would be put to better use.

I took loose the bull crap that held down the donut that was almost the size of the actual tire. I took off the busted tire first then put the donut on. It didn't take me long, but it was a waste of 30 minutes of life. I drove out of the parking garage like a bat out of hell. It didn't matter because traffic was its usual horrible self in the morning. The feeling of driving on a donut in morning traffic pissed me off more. Assholes who were late for work didn't make things any better by not being courteous to any cars. They either cut drivers off or wouldn't let them over. Then at the same time of the macho man contest, it was a honking the horn competition as well. Every five minutes someone was honking their horn at another asshole late for work. Drivers flipped each other off in momentary road rage. It was ridiculous and unbecoming, but I became one of the crazies because I had to make it to Dr. Gallagher's office at a reasonable time.

Once I got through the renegades, it was clear for me to hit the gas further down US-1. I pulled up to Dr. Gallagher's building at 10:30 am. I was 30 minutes late, but I didn't care. I was still feeling the after-effects from changing my tire and jammed-packed traffic. I managed to find a parking space in front of the building. I rushed in. I went up to the third floor where his office was located. I checked in with his secretary who gave me a questionnaire to fill out. I sat down and filled out the lengthy form. It had to be at least a hundred questions on it. Just about every question dealt with sexuality. Still feeling heated about the earlier events, I answered every question with brutal honesty. I didn't have time to sugar coat anything. I handed back the clipboard with all of my answers to the secretary. She told me to wait until Dr. Gallagher called me to the back. I texted Kim while I was waiting.

"Good morning babe."

A few minutes later she texted back, "Good morning honey. How is your training going?"

I couldn't mention to her that I was at a psychologist's office because of my fear of not being able to stop cheating on her.

So, I texted back what was best: "It is really going well. I will see you later. Get some rest. Make sure you rub your stomach for me. Lol!"

Just as I finished the text, Dr. Gallagher came out.

"Jacob Richardson!" He called standing by the door leading into the corridor.

"I'm Jacob Richardson," I replied.

Before he greeted me, Dr. Gallagher walked over to the secretary's desk to grab the form that I filled out. He scanned over it before turning to me.

"Hello, Mr. Richardson! My name is Aaden Gallagher, but everyone calls me Dr. Gallagher," he said laughing.

He then shook my hand firmly. He towered over me. He had to be at least 6'5". I didn't run into many men that I had to look

# Changed

up too. He was a redhead with freckles. He was a slender man and looked like he would pass up a gym for a library in a heartbeat. He had a full sandy red beard. His khaki pants and plaid long sleeve shirt went perfectly with his geeky look. He didn't have anything ostentatious about himself.

We walked back to his office. I sat down in his brown leather chair. I could see from the looks of things his practice was doing well. He began diligently looking over my questionnaire. While he studied over it, I let my eyes roam around his office. His bookshelf was filled with what looked to be books on sex. I saw a few that I've read. *The Origins of Sex* written by Faramerz Dabhoiwala was a good one. Jennifer J. Harman's *Psychology of Human Sexuality* was definitely on the top of my list. Robert Staples' *Exploring Black sexuality* was a must read. Then I saw a few books that I had never read. John Harvey Kellogg's *Plain Facts about Sexual Life and Later Plain Facts for Old and Young* didn't ring a bell. Nor did most of Dr. Gallagher's Psychology books. I knew a little about Ivan Pavlov and Sigmund Freud clinical studies because I needed to take psychology for an elective in college, but I never had enough interest in them to read their books outside of that.

On the side of his elaborate library of books were autographed pictures of celebrities. There was a picture of Tom Brady with his hands over his head after winning his first Super Bowl. Next to the Tom Brady picture was a picture with him and Mark Wahlberg standing together. A little further over was a framed poster of the movie *The Departed*. He looked to be a true Bostonian at heart.

I then gazed over his office desk. He was very organized, just like me. I admired that. His credentials were right above his head. It seemed like his journey to becoming a therapist was a tedious process. Alongside his degrees were several certifications. I was taken aback by a picture he had directly in front of me. His wedding picture was sitting right in my face, and I didn't notice it at first. Dr. Gallagher was married to a Black woman. She was bad at that. She was dark chocolate. Her hair was long and silky. Apparently, she was in better shape than he was. I couldn't believe it. There was also a picture with them on a skiing trip. They looked like the odd couple. I guess he had good credit and a drawer full of MaxiDerm.

"Jacob, let start by telling you a little about my background. I'm originally from Boston, Massachusetts. I received my bachelor's degree in psychology from the University of Massachusetts. Tired of the cold weather and snow, I came down to sunny South Florida to get my Doctoral Degree in Human Sexuality at UM. The weather and beautiful beaches made me stay after completing my studies. I met my wife, Shanique, while attending UM. We have been married for ten years and had two kids together. Little Matthew and Lovely. Matthew is a ten-year-old misfit, and Lovely is my three-year-old sweetheart who loves being up under me. That is the summary on me. Now you Jacob."

I wasn't totally ready to introduce myself to Dr. Gallagher, but I didn't drive all the way down to Coral Gables to start acting shy. Besides, it wasn't like something I haven't done before. I took a deep breath and went for it.

"My real name is Pierre Jean-Baptiste II. My parents were from Haiti. Like most Haitians during that time, they were smuggled into this country. My dad was a hard worker. From my understanding, he did whatever it took to put food on the table. My mother, on the other hand, was a maid at a hotel on South Beach. They worked hard to provide me with a decent home. When I was 5 years old my life changed forever. My dad murdered my mother and the man she was having an affair with. Then he put the gun inside of his mouth and blew the back of his head out.

My name was changed after my parent's murder-suicide. My face was all over the news. My grandma who got me after my parents' death thought it was best that I changed my name to hide me from scrutiny. Besides, she wanted my name to be more Americanized. She thought that Pierre sounded more ethnic than American, so she changed my name to Jacob Richardson. I grew up poor in Little Haiti. My grandma did the best she could with me. I was determined to make it on my own; and so far, so good," I finished.

# Changed

Dr. Gallagher gave me a long stare. It looked as though he was trying his best to sympathize with me. I hadn't talked about my parent's death in a while. The anger and pain were still there in my heart.

"Jacob, I'm sorry to hear about your parents. Were you there when it happened?"

He asked probing for answers. I felt my body tensing up. My throat started feeling like it had a lump in it. Nevertheless, I had to recall a dark time in my childhood.

"Yes, I was."

Dr. Gallagher took a deep look into my eyes.

"So where were you when it happened?" He asked going further.

I closed my watery eyes to take me back to a day I would never forget.

"I was in my bed sleep. It had to be around 3:00 in the morning when I heard a loud bang at the door. I jumped out of my bed. My momma went to see who was at the door. I came out of my room to see what was going on. Then I heard my father's voice from outside. "Where dat nigga at?! Where dat nigga at?!" My father screamed at the top of his lungs.

My mother yelled at him to go away. My dad sounded like a madman from outside of the door.

"Open the muthafuckin' door, Esther!"

My mother stood up strong behind the door. I heard some noise coming from the back room.

"Pierre, leave! I told you it was over a long time ago! I'm calling the police!" My mother yelled back.

That was when everything went terribly wrong. My father kicked in the door. My mother tried to get in his way, but he slapped her down with the gun in his hand. I recalled him saying to my mother, "Bitch I don't give a fuck 'bout the police! Where dat nigga at?!"

My Mother wouldn't say anything. He left her in a puddle of blood. As he walked down the hallway, I thought I could stop him, but he pushed me back as if he didn't know I was his child. He walked into my mother's bedroom ferociously.

"Nigga, where yo' punk ass is at?"

The bedroom was silent. It didn't stay that way for long as I heard shots and cursing. I can't remember how many shots were fired, but when the gunfire ceased, the worst part was yet to come.

My mother jumped up off the floor to check on whoever it was shot in the bedroom. She pushed past my father to comfort the deceased man. That is when my father blew his top.

"Stupid bitch, you're gonna comfort a dead nigga in front of me? You deserve to die too," my father said as he started gunning down my mother in cold blood.

I came out of the bedroom screaming, "No daddy, no daddy!" By then, my father was too far gone. His face looked like a deranged man who was torn between insanity and sanity. He turned to me with a blank stare on his face. I was too confused to be scared of him.

He looked me directly in my eyes and said, "Son, don't trust dese hoes!" He said it as he blew his brains out.

I threw up! It didn't stop me from grabbing hold of him. I hugged him tightly while blood dripped from his mouth on me. We both were covered in blood. I cried out loud holding his limp body in my arms. He didn't move. He was dead. I pushed him off me to check on my mom.

Her body was riddled with bullet holes. It was obvious that they were fatal because she wasn't breathing. I held her in my arms. With tears in my eyes, I remembered what my kindergarten teacher taught me. I called 911. In a matter of minutes, police were all over the apartment. They questioned me later at the police station, but I couldn't tell them anything. My ability to speak was gone. I was mute for at least six months after that. Therapy helped somewhat to get me to speak again, but the damage was done. My parents were gone. My heart was empty. And worse of all, my father's words *don't trust dese ho's* was forever embedded in my mind.

\*\*\*

# Changed

I finished my backstory as both eyes poured with tears.

Dr. Gallagher looked like he needed a tissue as well. But he remained steadfast in his professionalism as a psychologist.

"Jacob, do you need a moment?" He asked with sympathy.

The macho man came out of me. I wiped the tears from my eyes. "Doc, I'm okay. We can continue," I persisted.

"So, therapy helped you talk again, but it didn't help you with you?" He replied.

I began fidgeting. "No. No, it didn't," I replied.

"So, what happened to you after therapy?" He asked.

"In my opinion, I had a somewhat normal childhood. My grandma was the best. She didn't have much, but her love for me was more than enough. She made sure I was raised upright. She instilled morals and values in me at an early age. She disciplined me when I was wrong and rewarded me when I did something right. Her love for God kept her strong dealing with me. Church was her second home. Every morning she would read the Bible. She sheltered me from the mean streets of Little Haiti, but once I had sex for the first time, I became a sexual deviant," I finished.

"How old are you now? And how old were you the first time you had sex? And how many women do you think that you have had sex with?"

I replied, "I'm 28 years old. I was only twelve years old when I lost my virginity. If I remember correctly, it was with the neighbor down the street. She was my babysitter. When my grandma had to go to church service at night, she would ask the neighbor's daughter to watch me. She was around eighteen. Her idea of babysitting was fondling me. We never got caught. From there, I learned how to be sneaky. For your last question, I've had sex with 3,000 women," I said.

You could hear a pin drop when I told Dr. Gallagher how many women I had slept with. His facial expression went from curious to how-in-the-hell.

"Jacob, let me get this right. You have had sex with 3,000 women?" He asked making sure I wasn't lying. I stopped fidgeting with my hands at that point. I sat up straight. I looked Dr.

Gallagher straight in the eyes. "Yes, I've had sex with that many women. The reason why I know this is because I write down every woman that I have slept with in my little black book. My goal is to sleep with over 20,000 women. I want to beat Wilt Chamberlain's record. It became an obsession once I read up on him." I finished.

Dr. Gallagher looked disturbed. His eyes got big, but he moved on to the next question. "Okay, Jacob. When you initially see a woman, what do you see? And how do you feel about women?" He probed for more information.

"To be honest, I see objects. I see different shapes and sizes. Tall or small, doesn't really matter to me. Hips and ass are a plus. But a woman doesn't have to have that for me to have sex with her. However, I do prefer shapely women. A woman's facial features aren't that important, but I do prefer pretty over ugly. The level of education isn't a big deal either. Sometimes, the dumber, the easier. High class or hood rat is all the same to me. Race has never played a factor in my sex life. Black, White, Hispanic, or Asian can all get it. Nothing matters to me about a woman outside of what she has between her legs,"

I took a brief moment to remember what other question Dr. Gallagher asked, "Oh yeah, how do I feel about women? They feel good when I'm inside of them," I stated simply.

Dr. Gallagher looked more perturbed than before. His secretary came over his small intercom box. "Doctor, your 11:30 appointment is here," she said over the intercom. He reached for the button and said, "Could you tell Mr. Lautner that my meeting is running late? Explain to him that he can either wait or cancel." We waited for a moment before he answered. A few minutes later his secretary returned to the intercom. "Mr. Lautner said he will reschedule. He didn't sound too happy," she expressed. Dr. Gallagher smirked. "Tell him I apologize. I will have to make it up to him one way or another."

"Sorry for the interruption, Jacob. Please go on," he said.

I gathered my thoughts again. "I guess I'm a nympho. It's been an ongoing problem ever since I could remember. Sex and women stay on my mind every minute of every day," I stated.

# Changed

Dr. Gallagher started pulling at his long scruffy red beard. He then pulled himself closer to his desk. "Jacob, you are not a nympho. Society makes this mistake all the time. Only a woman with a sex addiction can be a nymphomaniac. A man, on the other hand, can only be satyromaniac. By definition, satyriasis – or satyrmania - is an uncontrollable sexual desire in a man. You definitely have that," he explained. I wanted to learn more, so I remained silent.

"Jacob, I don't mean any disrespect, but I have to ask this question," he said in an effort to ask respectfully.

"Go ahead Doc," I said permitting him.

"Jacob, do you have homosexual tendencies? Or do you have bisexual fantasies? The only reason I asked is that you might get bored of having sex with so many women. Do you think that you might explore other oppositions?" he asked.

I couldn't help but laugh. "That is an impossibility. I will slap the shit out of a bitch if she ever tried to play around my ass hole. I only like women. I like to look at what is opposite of me. I have never been attracted to a man. I like pussy! Matter of fact, I love pussy, Dr. Gallagher! There is no word great enough to describe how pussy makes me feel. I don't know how men get off by looking at the same things they have. To each his own. But for me, I could never be gay because I'm addicted to pussy. Pussy will never get boring to me," I said being amused by the mere question.

Dr. Gallagher wrote down something on a notepad. I wasn't sure if he was writing down what I was saying or jotting down a few notes. Once he finished writing down whatever, he continued to pick my brain.

"So, Jacob, can you tell me how is it possible to have sex with that many women being married? And why did you marry Kimberly if you knew you weren't gonna ever be faithful with your lofty goals?" He said while looking over the form I filled out earlier.

There wasn't any simple way to answer this. My tactics weren't easy to understand. But I gave it a shot. "Well, Dr. Gallagher, my wife works weekends. Her schedule changes occasionally, but it mostly stayed the same at the hospital. The graveyard shift on top of her twelve hour work days equals room to roam. The women that I've had sex with, I never get emotionally attached to them. It's sex and nothing more in my mind. They can believe what they want, but I know what it is once I walk in the room."

I continued, "Most of the women I have sex with for the first time end up being the last time. Their calls go to my block list. If I see them in public, I act like I don't know them. I don't believe in continuing a casual sex relationship. Eventually, they will get emotional, and I refuse to have that. Yes, I do cheat on Kim, but I will never do anything on purpose to hurt her. I hide my alter ego from her very well. And the reason I married my wife is because I followed tradition. Men on my father's side got married. Plus, Kim took the place of my mother," I explained.

Then Dr. Gallagher asked his next question. "Jacob, do you love your wife?"

I felt myself squeezing the handles of the chair hard. My skin became warm. "I know this is gonna be hard to believe, but I do! I love my wife very much. Kim means the world to me. Unfortunately, I'm a selfish corrupted son of a bitch! I'm good to my wife. I think the most difficult part is that I know how I am on the inside, but for selfish reasons, I don't want her to be with anyone else. If I have to remember every lie that I have ever told to keep her, so be it. I can't lose Kim. She is about to have my first child. I'm about to be a proud father! That is why I'm here. I wanna change for the better. I don't want to lose my family," I explained.

Dr. Gallagher nodded his head in agreement. "Jacob, trust me, you are doing the right thing by seeking help. Most who have a mental illness never seek help. The world would be a better place if more people did," he said sadly, then continued his questioning, "How do you get to meet all these women that you have slept with? Do you use dating sites or social media or solicit sex?" He asked.

With a smirk on my face, I answered. "I don't do any dating sites or social media. As crazy as this sounds, I like my privacy. I train people through word of mouth. I have too many clients as is. I don't need social media for that. If I'm ever on social media, it's through my modeling agencies to promote their brand and not me. Kim has social media, and that is the number one reason I stay off it. Social media is the devil when it comes to relationships. I will never get caught up in that mess. There are too many eyes on it. Besides, people are getting divorced every other day because of Facebook, Instagram, and Twitter. You can't even like or comment on a woman's picture without being accused of cheating. I will never be a statistic of a woman who is looking for attention by taking a selfie of herself half naked. I can't do what I've been doing by being dumb. Social media is good for business, but most people use it to live in their past. I'm not the one to live in the past. I'm always in search of new pussy. And no, I have never paid for pussy, but I've had women pay me for sex," I said proudly

"Are you saying that you take a more traditional approach?" Dr. Gallagher asked.

I replied, "I wouldn't see why not. There are too many problems meeting a woman online. People try to be too perfect on social media and dating sites. I'm a person who likes to meet women in person. That cuts out the catfishing. A woman can write a book of lies behind a computer, but in person, the truth is right there. I'm a social butterfly. It's easier for me to find an angle with a woman who's having a drink after work or partying than to type characters on a keyboard trying to pry open information that is needed to have sex with her. I pay attention to body language. Doing that on a computer is impossible. Though social media and dating sites have helped some people with dating, I on the other hand, still like to meet women in person."

"That makes sense Jacob. So, you basically stay off social media because it is an easy way for you to get caught cheating. It is also a way for a woman to hide who she is because she can characterize herself any way she chooses. Moreover, the pictures women put up can be someone else's. Interesting." He finished. I was getting a little tired, but I did want to finish my first secession with Dr. Gallagher. He looked on his clipboard again. He combed over a couple of question before speaking. "Mr. Richardson, we will be done shortly." He persisted. I was relaxed at that point. "Dr. Gallagher I'm okay. I don't have anywhere to be." I said. "Okay,

Jacob here we go. Why do you think it is so easy for people in general to cheat? Can you tell me from both sides?" He asked. This was the granddaddy of them all.

"Well Dr. Gallagher, I think human nature is to never be satisfied. No matter what happens in life, people will always want more. Greed shouldn't be just used for money. Greed is in all of us. Some of us act on it and some don't. There aren't too many people walking on God's green earth that won't believe there isn't something better out there for them. For that fact, I believe cheating is inevitable. The first sign that someone starts feeling unfulfilled, the thought of breaking up comes to mind. Most don't act on it, but the mere thought gets the mind racing. A better life appears before their eyes. But one problem, they don't have the wherewithal to leave. Then that cute guy at the job who is always flirting now looks more appealing. Or the chic who keeps saying you can do better starts looking more fuckable by day. Your mind says leave but looking at the kids, time spent, and bills, people will stay praying it gets better. However, the person who once knew everything to do to make their honey or boo smile is now the creator of frowns. Complacency sets in. He or she forgets how the relationship starts is how it should remain. In order to handle the BS at home, cheating is no longer an option; it becomes a must.

Dr. Gallagher took more notes. He then checked his silver Fossil watch to see what time it was, "Jacob, I have time for two more questions. I'll give you a short evaluation after. With all the women you've slept with, have you ever had an STD? Or have you ever gotten another woman pregnant?"

It was clear he was trying to get everything out of me on the first session. "Doc, this may sound crazy, but I'm an immoral man with morals," I said.

Dr. Gallagher began massaging his beard again. "Jacob, explain how a man without morals can have morals?"

My eyes shifted back to all of his books. I stared aimlessly before entertaining Dr. Gallagher's question. "I can't explain in words what Kim means to me and how much I love her. Though I cheat, I will never bring a disease or an outside baby to my wife. I might as well be the poster boy for Magnum condoms. They

# Changed

should be paying me to be the face of their brand. If I have had sex with 3000 women, trust me I have used over 3,200 condoms. No matter what I do outside of my marriage, I still love my wife. As a model, I'm required to take STD tests every six months. Sometimes I go a step further by getting tested myself. Though I live a reckless life, I'm still disciplined. No pussy is worth being sick for. I'm not a fool. God looks over people like me. He has granted me clemency over and over again. But I know in my heart, karma is a relentless hunter for justice. No crime will ever go unpunished. It will not stop for nothing to rage its revenge. Karma is another way of God telling us life is fair even when it seems like it isn't. What we do in the dark will eventually come to light. No one can escape karma once it finds out what you did right or wrong. I'm on the run right now. My only protection from it is a condom and a good memory." I clarified.

Dr. Gallagher started tapping his desk. He looked like he was internalizing everything I said. "Jacob, what do you mean by having a good memory?" He questioned.

"Well, in order to be good at cheating, you must remember every lie you have ever told. My life is based on a book of lies." I finished.

Dr. Gallagher made in an uneasy giggle. "Let's move on to the last question. Jacob, do you masturbate?"

I thought about it for a moment. Why would he ask me about jacking off? Did I look like I jerk off? "No. I masturbated one time and didn't like it. In my opinion, masturbation is for the unconfident. It is too easy. There isn't a challenge to it. Why jack off imagining to be with a woman you want, when you can go after her? Porno movies do nothing for me? I used to watch it to find out what made a woman go crazy about another woman eating her out, but that was it. I don't know what is fun about jacking off to a man having sex with a porn star on TV or phone? I rather pass. I'm a hunter. If I'm horny, I will go find what I need. And damn sho won't be in a bedroom jacking off to a chic I wish I had." I explained.

Dr. Gallagher then wrote something else down in his notepad. After completing his scribbling, he grabbed my questionnaire again. He surveyed it briefly. He looked up at me and gave his evaluation. "You're on to something because over time masturbating too much to pornography movies can make a man have erectile dysfunction or become impotent. The mind will eventually become desensitized to actual sexual situations.

Moving forward, let me be frank with you. You are a danger to yourself and your wife, Kimberly. In 2013 Florida ranked number one with HIV cases. In 2014 it dropped down some, but Miami statistically became the number one city for new HIV cases. Orlando and West Palm Beach aren't far behind. It is becoming very serious in South Florida. Now, the majority of the new HIV cases are MSM. MSM means men who sleep with other men. This doesn't affect you but in a way it does because some of these men sleep with women. Some come from prison and some come from being molested as children. Either way, it goes, it is never revealed to the woman that they are sleeping with.

Furthermore, according to the Florida Department and Disease Control, one out 50 of every African-American female living in South Florida is HIV positive. As a whole, African Americans make up 38% of the HIV population in Dade-County. Hispanics make up about around 51%. Miami is becoming like a Third World Country. It isn't safe out here anymore for people such as yourself. Have you ever heard of the Murphy Law Jacob?" He asked. "No," I answered. He tapped again on the desk. "It is the law that states anything that can go wrong, will go wrong. You have been lucky so far that you haven't caught an STD or had an outside baby. You have over pushed your luck. You need to consider not only your life but Kim's too. She has nothing to do with your sex addiction. You may want to tell her or divorce her." He finished.

I haven't had anyone speak so bluntly to me since my days of track. My old track coach used to tell me, "Jacob if you don't come out of the block right, you can sit yo ass home for the next meet." I couldn't believe that he told me that I should consider divorcing Kim. "With all due respect, Dr. Gallagher, divorcing my wife is a bad idea. That is why I'm here. I wanna change for the better. I thought your counseling could help my craving for sex to stop." I finished

"I'm here to help you, but you have to be able to handle the truth. Jacob, to be honest with you, you don't love your wife," I tried to interrupt him, but he persisted to speak, "Jacob, hear me out on this one. I know you don't like the way that sounded, but you need to hear it. How can a man love his wife if he cheats on her all the time? If we were in another country or if your marriage was based on polygamy, then your action would be fine. However, we live in America, and that isn't acceptable for any woman. The only reason I said consider divorcing your wife is because it best to let her go than hurting her. If you can't tell her the truth, what do you all have?" He explained.

I was really tight then. I almost felt myself sweating. No matter what he said, divorce wasn't even a consideration. I knew someway or somehow, I could get better for my family. There wasn't anything more important to me. I started feeling like pussy wasn't that important to me.

Dr. Gallagher moved forward with his consultation. "Jacob, I have been with my wife ten years faithfully. So not everyone is caught up in this world of cheating. You need to consider taking that out of your thought process. As a man thinketh so is he. You have to start having more positive thoughts about women. They are not just shapes and sizes. They have brains and feelings. In out of that womb that you call a pussy brings life to the world." He said right before I interrupted him.

"Doc, I can't help how I see women. I definitely understand what you are saying, but I can't help what's going on in my mind. I just think I can sleep with every woman I meet. Make it stop, make it stop Doc!" I said in mercy.

"From listening to you, everything that you are going through stems from childhood. You have never gotten over your father killing your mother. I'm going to take a wild guess. You are more upset with your mother cheating on father than him killing her, I bet?" He blasted me.

The anger in my heart started resurfacing. I had to rekindle a place in my heart that I thought died. The real reason that I went on a sexual onslaught was about to be exposed. "You damn right I'm pissed at my mother for making my father kill her! If she wouldn't have ever cheated on him, we would still be a family till this day. But, no she wanted to go out and have sex with another man. So, I said to myself if my mother cheated on my father, what would stop another bitch from doing it to me? Cheeeaaattt! So before a woman gets me, I will sleep with the entire world if I have to. I will protect myself," I looked over to his wedding picture, "Dr. Gallagher, see that sweet innocent chocolate thang standing next to you, she will cheat on you to one day." I said without thinking about any consequence.

Dr. Gallagher stood up and slammed his open hands on his desk. He hit the desk so hard that his wedding band made a loud clink sound. "Listen, Jacob, don't ever disrespect my wife like that ever again! I will kick yo ass out of my office. And I won't need any security to do it!" He said in a fiery voice.

I had to back down from my statement. I was totally out of line. "Doc, I'm sorry. I do apologize. I didn't mean what I said. I just having been taken to that place in years. I don't know what came over me. I guess I have some issues that I haven't addressed." I said in apology. Dr. Gallagher seemed like he was calming down after I apologized. The rage was slowly going away. The color in his face started changing from purple-red to just red. His veins that were popping out started going back down to normal size. His eyes went from fiery red back to blue.

"Jacob, I accept your apology, but please leave my wife out this. I'm only trying to help you. I see people like you all the time. Maybe not to your extreme but you still can be helped," He finished. I concurred with him. I had to calm myself down as well. I started counting to ten in my head. I felt myself breathing properly once I was done counting. When I was finally relaxed, I was ready to face the music. I needed to hear the rest of what Dr. Gallagher had to say. "Once again, I apologize Doc. Please continue." I said. Dr. Gallagher by that time, facial color returned back normal.

"Now, where was I? Oh yeah, your childhood. Listen, Jacob, what happened to you as a little boy is still affecting you till this day. Seeing your parents getting murdered in front of you was a traumatic experience. It would be difficult for any kid to get over that. Most kids who have dealt with that type of traumatic episode usually end up being sociopaths. They can't handle society anymore. A high percentage of them end up in prison. But, someway or somehow, you didn't end up that way. However, you do have some form of it. You have no morals when it comes to women outside of your wife. Your mission to beat Wilt Chamberlin 20,000 is the only indication that you are out to hurt as many women as possible. The sex is only a small portion of a greater scheme.

Furthermore, you need to find out more about what happened between your father and mother. I believe there is more to the story than what's being led on. If you can find any relatives who were close to your parents, you might find out the truth. Do you have any relatives that you can contact?" He asked.

I had lost all contact with my relatives after my grandma died. I didn't have any brothers or sisters. I wasn't close to my cousins either. My mother's sister was the only one I could think of. My Auntie Fabiola moved to Cincinnati years ago. I didn't know where to start to find her. "I have an auntie in Ohio somewhere. I haven't spoken to her since we buried my grandma?" I explained.

"Jacob, it will be a good thing to get back in contact with her. She may know what really happened between your mother and father. Women normally don't cheat just because. There are usually are variables that bring them to that point. You also need to come to grips with the fact that you may hate women because you hate your mother." He said as I interrupted him again.

"What the hell do you mean I hate my mother, Doc?" he tried to calm me down, but I was gone, "I can't believe you said that shit to me! There is no way in hell that I hate my mother! She may have cheated on my father, but that doesn't mean that I hate her. By the way, I don't hate women. I make them feel good." I said with anger. Dr. Gallagher didn't back down. "Okay, hate may be too harsh of a word. But you do have a strong dislike for her. You becoming a satyriasis started when you didn't forgive your mother for supposedly cheating on your father. Your behavior won't stop until you forgive her and yourself. You are not only a danger to yourself but to your wife." He finished

"Fuck you Doc!" I said as I swiped his paperwork off his desk. "Jacob, I'm trying to help you. You have to face yourself," he screamed back. I sized Dr. Gallagher up. I felt my temper erupting. "No, you face the fact that the only reason you got your wife is because you have a good credit score and you take pills to make yo dick bigger. Fuck you!" I said as I made my way out of the door. Dr. Gallagher walked from behind his desk as if he wanted some. I looked at him directly in his eyes without blinking. He saw it in my face that I was ready to kick his ass. He didn't take another step forward. Once I saw that he was intimidated, I made my way out of the door.

As I passed the front desk, I noticed his secretary looked petrified after hearing all the commotion. She went to pick up the phone. "Don't call anyone. Everything is okay," I overheard him say to her. I slammed the door behind me. I didn't bother to take the elevator. I ran down the stairwell. I burst through the door. I jumped into my car and smashed on the gas. As I drove back home, I thought what was I thinking? No preacher or slick mouth shrink could help me. What did they know? They like pussy just like me. What man didn't? We are all the same. Going to see a shrink was really a waste of time. I couldn't wait to call Benny about this bullshit. I could figure this one out on my own. I would just have to learn how to focus on my modeling career.

# Chapter 18
# Ish Got Real

Once I walked into the house, I smelled the comforting aroma of pasta. My mood changed somewhat, but I was still a little heated.

Kim greeted me with a smile. "I cooked," she said.

I needed to rest my nerves. "Thank you, babe, but give me a minute. I need to lay down," I said.

Kim looked as if she was disappointed. "Jacob, I got up just to cook for you, and you aren't hungry?" she said sounding pissed.

I had to ease the situation as fast as possible. "I'm sorry babe, but I had a rough day. I just need to lay down for a minute to get my mind right." I finished.

Kim looked perplexed. "Jacob, what's wrong with you?" she asked.

I wasn't in the mood to go back and forth. If I had kept going, it would have ended up in a bad argument. "Kim could you please just give me a break? Once I get up, we will talk," I said firmly.

Kim stood still, but her face relaxed, going from frustration to mild disappointment. She simply replied, "Okay Jacob. But I'm hungry, so I'm going to eat now. When you wake up, explain to me what's going on with you. This isn't like you."

I nodded but said nothing further as I went into the room to catch some shut-eye. I laid in the bed and stared at the ceiling. As upset as I was with Dr. Gallagher, my mind returned to what he said during our session. Divorcing my wife wasn't something that I could come to grips with. Yeah, I know she didn't deserve my crap, but as the old saying goes, what she didn't know wouldn't hurt her. Then I thought about what if she caught me. Would she accept me or leave me? More than likely she would leave me. She and my firstborn son would live apart from me. All I could think about was fighting over custody and child support. I figured it would be best to tell her who I really was. Before overthinking things, I fell asleep.

***

I woke up 2 hours later. I felt refreshed. The short nap was everything. Kim entered the room to check on me. "Jacob, are you okay now?" She asked.

I did a long stretch before answering. "Yeah babe, I feel a whole lot better. And I'm hungry as hell!" I expressed.

She went back into the kitchen to fix my plate. I didn't bother to take a shower. I sat at the table quietly. My mind wondered as Kim brought my plate of food to me. She prepared a big plate of fettuccine and shrimp and chicken. She then walked back into the kitchen to get me a bottle of water. I said my prayers to myself as she sat next to me at the table.

She stared at me while I ate. I guess she wanted me to open up. I wasn't ready.

"Jacob, so what was the problem earlier?" she asked.

The best excuse I had for not answering the question right away was that I was still chewing my food. I raised one of my hands, pointing up with my index finger as a signal to give me a minute to chew. She let me chew all my food before answering. To give myself a little more time, I sipped from my Smart Water bottle.

"Kim, do you mind if we talk about this when we go to bed?' I said not having a clue what to say. Kim looked bothered but silently nodded her head in agreement.

After finishing my awesome meal, I laid on the couch with Kim. We watched her favorite shows *Grey's Anatomy*, then *Scandal*. Both shows ended in suspense. Kim couldn't wait until next week's episodes. She had been following both shows from the beginning. She never missed an episode of either. If she was too tired to watch them, they were definitely recorded. I would usually go into the bedroom to watch sports or watch TV in the living room and she could have the bed. But with the dilemma I was facing, it was better to soften her up by watching TV with her.

We went into the bedroom once the news came on. It was the usual madness that plagued the inner city. Though it was a higher percentage of Hispanics in Miami, Black faces always seemed to make the news for violent crimes. I wondered why they couldn't find one positive thing to say about Black people. Outside of the weather report, the news was always negative toward inner-city youth. If I were White, once I got done watching the news, I would probably be scared of Black people, too. Hell, even I was scared of my own kind once I was done watching it. It was so bad that I started calling the news "Nigga News." As I needed to change, so did the pulse of Miami. Yet neither of us were ready to do it.

I turned the madness off once we confirmed it was going to be another high-80-degree day. Kim scooted her booty next to me. I reached under her arm to hold her stomach. It was starting to get out there. But I held her as if her stomach was still flat. The one thing that I was so proud of was I never lost compassion for her. Kim felt so good in my arms. I didn't even get an erection. Tonight, was more about being intimate than being horny. Kim put her closed hands underneath her head. She looked like an angel lying next to me. After snuggling for a while, Kim couldn't hold back anymore. "Jacob, so you not gonna tell me what's going on with you?" she asked.

*Damn!* I thought to myself. The moment had arrived. I had to man up. *Where was the macho man now?* I thought again. "Kim, I've been going through something lately. I really can't explain it," I said.

Kim wiggled her body in discomfort. I still held on to her tightly. "Jacob, I know you. There's something wrong. Are you nervous about being a dad?" she asked.

That was the last thing on my mind. What was truly on my mind, I wasn't sure if I could muster the courage to say. So I lied.

"I'm not afraid to be a father. I'm over ready to be that. Michael will want for nothing. I will give him the things he needs, but I won't spoil him. But there is something else," I said without going into details.

"Jacob, you're making me nervous. Is it my shape? Since I've been pregnant, you've barely touched me. Is it me?" she asked with insecurity in her voice.

I was surprised by the question. I really didn't take notice of my actions, but she was right. I recalled only having sex with Kim once a week after her 16-week mark. It wasn't on purpose, but after how Dr. Gallagher labeled me, I was grossly underachieving with my own wife.

"Kim, you are beautiful. I'm more attracted to you pregnant than when you weren't," I said, praying she would believe it and leave it at that.

No such luck. "Jacob, you mean to tell me that I look better pregnant than when I wasn't?"

I was fucked. *How in the hell do I get out of this one?* I thought. The old saying, "The ways of a woman shall never be understood" was an understatement. I violated the woman's code of insulting without trying to insult. It's like asking a woman if she ever thought about joining a gym. In a man's mind, he may have meant get in shape for health reasons. But in a woman's mind, he just called her fat.

I put my foot so far in my mouth that I thought Shaq kicked me. But I was going to have to soldier on.

"Honey, I don't mean it that way. What I meant is you are still as sexy as the day I met you. Even with the extra weight."

Kim was dead silent, then she said, "Fuck you, Jacob! I'm still sexy with my cute belly nicca!" We both burst out laughing because Kim barely cussed. It kind of eased things.

"Kim, it isn't that. I think I'm going through some changes. I'm not sure what it is," I said again not giving the low down.

Kim moved her body again, shifting to find a comfortable position. "Are you seeing someone else then? Do you want to be with someone else?" She asked with uncertainty.

The pressure was on, but I was not going to fess up. I was ready to fail every question on a polygraph test before that happened. Thankfully, Kim didn't have one.

"No Kim, I would never leave you for anyone else. I want us to be a family. There isn't anything else that I would want to do other than be a good husband and father," I explained.

Kim sighed strongly, but not with relief. It was obvious that she caught on that I bounced around the question. With that, the grilling continued. "Jacob, you didn't answer my question," she said in distress.

I played stupid. "I thought I answered it," I said.

Kim pulled her body away from me. "Jacob, it's a yes or no question," she said with an attitude.

I didn't hesitate this time, "No," I said in short.

Kim seemed like she wasn't satisfied with my answer. "So, do you ever think about cheating on me or have you already?" She asked.

If I were hooked to a polygraph machine, it would have said *this nigga is guilty as hell*. I couldn't just dodge the question as if I'd never heard her. I did what any sensible liar would do. I answered it like a true liar.

"No, Kim! That is the last thing on my mind. I'm too busy trying to get my career off the ground. I need to be in a position to take care of my family forever. I want to leave a legacy. I want the Richardson's to be a household name. I know you don't want to be in the spotlight, but I will handle the brunt of that," I said like a coward who was afraid, to tell the truth.

Kim slumped her body over further. It seemed like she was going to sleep. But I was wrong.

"So, Jacob, it seems like you're unsure of yourself. You are one of the most confident men I have ever met. When we were in college, you weren't afraid to talk to me, even as an underclassman. Other dudes were intimidated by me, but not you. That was the reason I fell in love with you. Don't lose that about yourself. I believe in you. You just have to believe in yourself. You will be okay. Just stay focused. In time you will get there," she said motivating me.

"Okay, Les Brown's little sister," I teased. "You're right. I think that's what it was. I was losing my confidence. I need to believe that I can do this. Thank you, babe!" I said while kissing the back of Kim's head. The few strings of hair that got into my mouth tasted good. It was a testament to the fruity smelling shampoo she used. I held her close to me so that my penis could rub next to her soft buttock.

"By the way, Jacob, if you ever cheated on me, I will do something awful to you. While you're sleeping, I will cut your thang off, and run over it. Then I will go be with this cute doctor at my job who keeps staring at me," she said to get up under my skin. And that she did.

"Kim, what do you mean you'll cut my dick off and run over it? Listen, I need my dick. It ain't nothing to play with. And who the hell is this doctor? Don't make me hide in the bushes at your job," I said to strike fear in her heart.

Kim began giggling. "Jacob don't get uptight. I said, 'if I caught you cheating'. And since you're not cheating, you don't have to worry about me cutting your thang off," she said hysterically laughing.

Kim had me heated, but I couldn't help but laugh.

"Well babe, I ain't gotta worry about that. You are the only one that I wanna be with," I said telling the truth. Yeah, Kim was the only one that I wanted to be with, but the rest I just wanted to have sex with.

# Chapter 19
# Taking off

My career progressed right along with Kim's pregnancy. Midway through her second trimester, things finally got busy for me. The New York modeling agencies came calling. Mr. Grey and his staff gave me more than enough work. Thanks to Benny's deal-making, I was actually overwhelmed. I would be working five days a week with a busy traveling schedule. I would have to be in both coasts to do photoshoots and runway events. On the East Coast, I would have to travel to North Carolina, Washington DC, Pennsylvania, Massachusetts, and New York. And of course, Miami. Mostly on South Beach to possibly model swimwear. On the West Coast, I mainly had to be in Los Angeles, California. I was booked solid for two months with all-expense-paid trips. I even got per diem. Everything I made would just go directly to my bank account. It was perfect!

I was promised that I would make the inside cover pages of *XXL*, *Hip-Hop*, and *Vibe* magazines. In addition, I would be featured in the top fashion magazines such as *GQ*, *Cosmopolitan*, *Men's Fashion*, and *Vogue*. The brands that recruited me to model their clothing lines were high-end men's fashion that included Armani Exchange, Gucci, Dolce & Gabbana, and of course Ralph Lauren's Polo Purple Label. I even got some lower end spots with Gap, Old Navy, American Eagle, Timberland, and Abercrombie. With the opportunities that were presented to me, I knew I was about to be a star in the spotlight. Jacob Richardson was about to become a household name, just like I told Kim. *Lights, camera, action, you're on!*

It wasn't easy telling Kim that I would have to travel for two months, but someway she understood. I hated leaving her behind. I didn't know much about being pregnant, but from my understanding, it was an emotional rollercoaster for a woman. With my fear of Kim becoming depressed and having a miscarriage, I almost wanted to cancel my trip, but she reassured me that she would be okay. With those assurances, I also promised myself that I wouldn't fuck anyone while I was gone. No matter how difficult. My word was my bond. I made sure all the bills were paid up for two months. The less concerns Kim had the better. When I left, I felt that I was walking out the door to my destiny.

***

My first stop was to New York. I had to be there for three days. I had to be out of the hotel room by six every morning. It wasn't a real problem. The modeling agency made sure to put me in one of the best hotels that New York had to offer after the last debacle. The Four Seasons more than made up for it! The décor was beautiful, people were very polished, the elevators didn't shake, and the breakfast, lunch, and dinner were on point.

Every morning through the afternoon was the same. Turn this way. Turn that way. Keep your chin tight. Smile. Show more teeth. Maintain good posture. Keep your back straight. At times, I felt like a slave being examined by top slave bidders. The only difference was that I was getting paid (okay, BIG difference, but you get my point).

I must have changed outfits over a hundred times. Some days the shoots would drag on to the evening. I would be so tired coming back to the hotel, but I would never forget to check on Kim. We either talked by phone or text. She was holding it down back at home like a champ.

She would mostly complain about feeling sluggish from carrying Michael. She would always tell me that she missed me. I felt the same way. I even passed up a couple of gurls who were trying to flirt with me. That was a first. I also didn't pay attention to the other female models who were on set with me. In my heart, I believed I had the willpower to make it back home without having to wash my dick in the sink one time. I was proud of myself for ignoring women who I could've slept with. I celebrated by sleeping in the hotel bed alone every night. Alone, damn it!

After my three day stay in New York, I was off to Boston. It was only a two-day trip. I modeled alongside a couple of White models. They were cool. Some of the White gurls were as sexy as

# Changed

Black gurls. I wondered why Dr. Gallagher left Boston. I guess the old cliché, "Once you go, Black, you never go back," held true. I couldn't believe that they could be built the same way. Some of the female models tried to get me to hang out at pubs after our photoshoots. I hated drinking beer. So, I passed on it every night that I was invited. They probably wanted me to put my meatloaf in their ovens after a long night of drinking. I wasn't gonna be the one to break their taboo of sleeping with a Mandingo. I did the same thing that I had done in New York. I went back to the hotel room to take a cold shower and get straight into the bed.

It was the weekend, so I had to text Kim since she was working. Sometimes she would answer back fast, and sometimes she didn't. It depended on her workload. I never felt so alone in my life. I would ignore my stash of women who tried to get into contact with me. I wasn't in the mood for frivolous conversation. I was on a mission: get money and keep my dick in my pants. So far, so good.

The next stop was Washington, DC, for another two shoots. I was surprised to see that the Capital of the United States of America was a Black town. I did more sightseeing than modeling. Most of my shots were done in the afternoon which gave me the opportunity to be a tourist. I caught the shuttle to every historical monument I could think of. I saw the World War Two Museum plus saw the monument. It was with soldiers pushing together to hold up the American flag. I thought what courage it took for a man to sign up for the military. I then made my way over to see the Lincoln Memorial. It was a sight to see. Abraham Lincoln's large white carved out sculpture was larger than life. He sat in his chair watching over Washington, DC, as he once watched over the whole country. I went from the man who signed the Emancipation Proclamation to free slaves to the man who had a dream that we would all be treated equally. Martin Luther King, Jr., stood tall with his arms folded. His face looked like he meant business. Or, depending on who did the sculpture, made him look like an angry Black man. I would be mad, too, if I had to grow up in those times. I probably would've been lynched for fucking all the white girls in Alabama.

Anyway, as I stared at him, I wondered what he would think of African-Americans if he was alive. He would probably roll over in his grave for some and others, he would have laid his life down again. That thought made me head over to the proudest example of the Dream coming alive – The White House. The White House was no longer white. It now had a Black family in it. I stood across the street from the Obama's residence. A Black man was the president of the United States of American. A cool one at that. Plus, he had the sexiest First Lady ever. From my point of view, Michelle Obama was the cream of the crop. President Barack Obama. "Yes, We Can," I said to myself.

My parents came to mind. I wished they were alive to see this. I walked away from the White house feeling a sense of pride. Even though I was a Haitian, I was still an African-American who understood the struggle.

***

My next two trips were long ones, both a week apiece. My flight arrived in North Carolina at 8:45 AM. It came in late because the airline was going back and forth with some fat man they made get off because he was overweight. I passed him one of my business cards as security guards escorted him off the plane. To make matters worse, my luggage took a year and a day to come through the baggage claim. I was pissed! The ride to the hotel wasn't any better. My Uber driver kept getting lost. The signal on his phone was terrible which made the ride longer than expected. I hated the fact that my credit card was automatically charged. I would make sure to email corporate later.

Furthermore, the photographers sucked. They were incompetent. The imbeciles posing as trained photographers couldn't figure out how they wanted me to pose. They also couldn't get the scenery right. We drove for hours trying to find a location to do the shoot. To top it off, their lenses were outdated. The pictures they took didn't come out crystal clear. I got up every morning with an attitude dreading the idea of working with those clowns. I honestly felt like I was having a male period. I didn't feel photogenic, but I stood in front of the camera anyway. I had the worse time in "Baby Atlanta." It wasn't North Carolina as a whole

# Changed

per say, but no pussy and a whack camera crew almost drove me crazy.

Pennsylvania wasn't any better. My whole concern there was to take as many photos as possible and bounce. I was one week away from being back in Miami for a photoshoot back home. For a week I dreamed of being on the beach doing a hot photoshoot. I pictured myself posing in the heat of the morning while the sun beamed off my back. My shadow would be in the midst of the horizon glistening off of the tides that blew into the shore. I would have some real photographers who knew what they were doing.

Moreover, I was ready to get back home to Kim. I had never missed my wife so much. I ruminated over the idea of life without cheating. I had a sudden epiphany. I realized that there was another nuance to being faithful in marriage. Being in a monogamous relationship was more about enthusiastically anticipating having sex with the one you love compared to just having sex with one person. Having sex with one person would never be easy for anyone. It was quite natural for one to become bored with having sex with one person for a long period of time. However, sex with one person was possible only if the one you love is willing to give of him- or herself what was necessary to be done in the bed to please the other person.

From that, I discovered that I couldn't wait to make love to my wife again. I had an urge to, not just a desire. That feeling of contentment was something I needed consistently. Without those thoughts, I would think about having sex with other women. It wasn't like she was bad in bed. She actually could be awesome when she felt like it. She needed to work on giving head better, but her sex appeal made up for it. I started fantasizing about having sex with Kim. I felt an erection come on. I normally would have gotten out of the bed to find a woman to help relieve the pressure, but not this time. This dick was going home where it belonged, and safely.

# Chapter 20
# Home

The Pennsylvania photo shoot was finally done. I boarded the plane back home with a smile on my face. I couldn't wait to hold Kim in my arms again. The thought of kissing her brought chills through my body. I knew in time I would be a better man. For the sake of my family, I would have to be.

My flight got me home around 7:45 pm. Kim was probably hard at work. I made it my business to go home and drop my stuff off. From there, I took off to Jackson Hospital. I grabbed a bouquet of roses on my way. I didn't text Kim to let her know that I was coming to see her. I wanted to surprise her. I also wanted to see this doctor who thought my gurl was pretty. I know Kim was just playing, but just in case she wasn't, I was ready to go postal in the hospital.

I signed in at the front desk, and the nurse paged Kim. I sat in the waiting room patiently. It was rough waiting there. There were people dealing with all types of illnesses and injuries. One person in the back coughed uncontrollably. It was annoying. People came in on carriers with bullet wounds. The paramedics rushed them to the back. I could hear the moans as they passed by. The women behind the check-in mirrors looked unbothered. I guess it came with the job.

Kim walked from the back in her scrubs. She looked cute with her little pudge sticking out. We both rushed over to each other with opened arms. I bear-hugged her. She felt so good in my arms. I held her for a while before letting her go. I kissed her on the forehead, then her lips. I got a hard-on as if I was a teenager finally kissing his crush. I handed her the flowers. She wiggled her nose before smelling them. I could see from the smile on her face that the scent from the roses was pleasant.

"Jacob, what are you doing here?! You didn't tell me anything!" she exclaimed happily.

I laughed. "If I would have told you, then it wouldn't have been a surprise," I replied.

Kim got on her tippy toes and kissed me again. "So, how was your trip?" she asked.

"It was good. I got a chance to do a lot of sightseeing. I'll tell you all about it when you get home. I just needed to see you," I said with love.

Kim had to get back to work. We kissed again before she turned to walk away. I stood and stared at her like I was the only one in the room. It became obvious that I wasn't when the crowd of people in the waiting room started clapping. I was embarrassed. I smiled and gave a halfhearted wave to my "audience." Once Kim was no longer visible, I strolled out the waiting room feeling like a million bucks.

***

I was awakened by Kim's entrance into the bedroom the following morning. She came straight to the bed and laid on top of me. I became touchy-feely. I grabbed her butt and squeezed it hard. She jumped a little, but not enough to get away from my grasp. I was horny as hell! Love was in the air. It was so thick that I could barely breathe.

Then Kim hit me with a whammy. "Jacob, you just want you some, huh?" she said busting my bubble. It was like the breath was knocked out of me.

"Kim, what you mean 'I just want some?' You know I want some. And I know you want some," I said still kissing on her. I didn't feel that the affection was mutual. I kept going, but I struggled with the fact that she wasn't reciprocating my passion.

"Kim, what is wrong," I asked insistently. She put her hands on my chest to stop me from groping her. I was confused. I didn't bother to tussle with her. I rolled over to the other side of the bed. I searched for answers in my head.

She hit me with it. "Jacob, I'm really tired. I've been on my feet all night. They are swollen. It has been so busy at the hospital. I just need to rest. We can talk if you like."

I was devastated. Why my babe didn't want to give me some? I had been gone for a month, came home to my wife without messing around ONCE while out of town, and couldn't wait to give her all the pent-up passion I was feeling to be met with... I'm tired? It was disheartening. It was a slap in my face.

"Kim, I understand that you've been busy at work, but I thought you would be in the mood when I came back home?" I questioned.

Kim looked with disgust on her face. "Jacob, I understand that you don't know what it feels like being pregnant, but we women go through things that men will never understand. It's like a chemical imbalance. Trust me, Jacob, you're gonna get some, but for now, let me deal with what I got to deal with," she finished firmly.

I couldn't say anything. As much as I wanted to go on and on with her, I couldn't. I had to fall back. "Okay, Kim I think I understand. It has been a long trip, and I just thought we could be spontaneous," I finished.

Kim turned and grabbed my face with her soft hands. "Jacob, I'm all for being spontaneous, but give me time," Kim said as she pulled one of my numbers by kissing me on my forehead.

# Chapter 21
# Slippin' In

At the crack of dawn, I found myself trying to slip my dick in from the side. Kim didn't wear panties to bed. What I thought to be easy was more difficult than I expected. She let me play by her vagina, but wouldn't let me stick it in. I almost put it in her anus by mistake until she almost fell out of the bed. "Jacob, what I told you? I'm serious! I'm just not in the mood!" She yelled.

My ego took a hit that it couldn't recover from. All the hard work I did on the road to keep my dick in my pants wasn't being rewarded. I suddenly began resenting Kim. I felt betrayed.

"Kim, I'm horny as hell! You not gonna make me beg are you?" I said feeling insecure. For the first time in my life, I felt human. I was the type that was used to getting what I wanted when I wanted it. Especially from my wife.

"Jacob, I understand that you're horny, but please understand me. Maybe sometime this week," she said patronizing me.

***

One week later and no pussy. It was already Saturday night and Kim was at work. It had been a total of 38 days since I last had sex. I almost thought about jacking my dick but thought better of it. I sat at the computer looking over the itinerary for my next trip. I was headed to Los Angeles. Long legs and Palm trees were right up my alley. I read carefully over it before clicking out that message to review the others. As I scrolled further down, I came across AWOP. It was another email invitation, and I wondered for a moment if I should click on it. I'd been behaving myself, but the demon whore took over my body. It said, "Nigga what the hell you thinking about? Kim ain't putting out right now. We need what we need."

I clicked on the message. I read over everything first. It was the same protocol. One week before the orgy, everyone participating had to take an STD test. No one was exempt. It didn't matter what the STD was if something showed up, that person was excluded from the orgy. Olivia was a freak in a half, but she didn't play when it came to diseases. On top of the extensive STD test, every man had to wear protection. No ifs, ands, or buts about it. There were too many body fluids running rampant and too many random people to take any chances.

This particular orgy would have twelve women and six men, including me. Twelve women didn't sound bad to me. I looked through the pictures of the women who were handpicked by Olivia's careful eyes. All of the women were of the mature age. Their ages ranged from 35 to 55 once again. Surprisingly, there were five Americans chosen: two from Alabama and three from Atlanta. The rest were from Austria, Great Britain, Argentina, and Canada. Olivia normally didn't choose women from America, but I guessed because she was having her first orgy party in the United States, she decided to step out of her comfort zone. Georgia was the chosen state. That was perfect. Georgia peaches went through my head. I loved me some cornbread eating women.

I then clicked on every woman's picture to see what they looked like, and their disposition. There were two pictures of each woman. One picture was with them in their business attire and the other was in a swimsuit. Most of their bodies were banging. Some were pretty and some looked okay, but they could all get it.

- *Amelia Jones, Australian, 48, Married, Occupation: Top executive at Bank of Australia. Vice: likes dominatrix.*
- *Bella Wales, Great Britain, 39; Single, Occupation: Owner of several vineyards and Wineries. Vice: likes double penetration.*
- *Dawn Morgan, Great Britain, 52, Divorced, Ex-model, Creative Director of Fashion Design Shows. Vice: likes anal stimulation.*
- *Valentina Garcia, Spain, 55, Married, Occupation: Housewife to a multimillionaire. Vice: likes well-endowed Black men.*

# Changed

- *Martina Lopez, Argentina, 35, Engaged, Occupation: Owner of several deluxe boutiques. Vice: likes bisexual pleasure.*
- *Audrey Cote, Canadian, 44, Complicated, Occupation: Owner of Cote's jewelry. Vice: likes being spanked with a paddle.*
- *Sandy White, USA – Alabama, 46, Single, Occupation: Owner of several farms. Vice: likes being tied up while having rough sex.*
- *Jean Carson, USA – Alabama, 37, Married, Occupation: Owner of a horse ranch. Vice: likes oral and penetration simultaneously.*
- *Nakisha Caldwell USA - Georgia, 49, Divorced, Occupation: District Attorney. Vice: likes being choked and spanked from the back.*
- *Tasha Mitchell, USA – Georgia, 54, Separated, Occupation: Judge. Vice: likes submission.*
- *Roslyn Smith, USA – Georgia, 42, Single, Occupation: Owner of a high-end pet grooming service. Vice: likes voyeurism – spectator.*

Olivia, the brains behind everything, rounded out the bunch. It was a fine assembly of cougars. It looked like this orgy was going to be epic.

It was the first time Olivia used America for one of her orgy parties. It was also the first time she ever selected African-American women to partake in her sinful weekend. I reflected with the respect that Olivia understood the demographics of Atlanta pretty well. I figured that she thought it would be best to add some ebony and caramel skin into the fold of her quarterly orgy parties.

The chocolate city was great for my craving for women. The orgy was gonna be held on the outskirts of Atlanta in the suburb Stone Mountain. Olivia had rented out a cabin for the weekend. I was ready for a wild three days in the mountains. Being faithful was starting to be aggravating. A sleepy giant was beginning to awaken. I didn't hesitate to confirm my reservation.

I got in touch with the NYC Modeling agency to inform them that I would be taking a detour from my scheduled photoshoot in California. I explained that I could only do four days instead of 5. I gave them some bullshit excuse. Mr. Fitzgerald okayed it. Benny later called and cussed me out. I didn't give a damn. I needed what I needed. I knew no one would ever understand me but me.

# Chapter 22
# Going to Get What I Need

I took my STD test early that morning before heading off to the West Coast. I got another pardon from God. All my tests came back negative. I was still a black card walking. After the good news, I made my way over to the airport. Before I left, I made sure to kiss Kim on the forehead and rub her stomach. One-week home without having sex took its toll. I felt a little hostile, but I kept it on the inside. I didn't want Kim to see my disdain for her on my face. I simply played it off by pretending that there wasn't anything wrong. I was ready to bounce. I needed some fresh air. The flight to Cali was going to help me escape my wife's in consideration of my needs.

***

The flight was tedious. I was tired but couldn't really sleep. I didn't get a window seat, so I had to sit uncomfortably between two people. Trying to take a nap was impossible being sandwiched between two assholes who smelled like they both fell out of a liquor bottle. The liquor reeking from their pores made me never want to drink again. Horrible, just horrible!

Once the plane arrived at Los Angeles Airport, I ran to the baggage claim. The modeling agency out there sent a driver to get me. Some little short fat man with a sign that read "Jacob Richardson" was waiting by the exit door. I raised my right hand so he could see me. He put his sign down as I approached and shook my hand. We walked out to his newer black model Lincoln. It wasn't like my father's old Lincoln that made noise when it came down the street. I chuckled at the memory; when I heard it, I knew it was dinner time.

We drove off and entered the highway. I've never seen so many people drive so fast. It was like there wasn't a speed limit. It almost gave me the impression that the State Trooper Union was on strike. We pulled up to Malibu Surfrider Hotel. It was alongside the beach and was beautiful. I checked in without incident, and from the balcony of my room, I was able to see beautiful women walking in their bikinis with long legs. I wanted to run behind every foxy momma I saw but couldn't find the energy. I was preparing myself mentally for the orgy in Stone Mountain. I was excited. I decided staying away from women for the next four days wasn't such a bad idea. The couple of orgies I attended before were exhausting. Even a person that trained as religiously as myself would have to come home and regroup for a week. I needed my stamina for the trip.

The photo shoots went smoothly. Everyone was professional. There wasn't any confusion. The locations were great. We took pictures at the beautiful Getty Villa. The garden was to die for, and the long crystal-clear pond sitting in the middle of the largest Villa I had ever seen in my life was breathtaking. I felt like I was in Heaven. The only difference was that I wasn't dead. I felt natural as the photographers snapped their pictures. It was for Gucci, so I had to leave a good impression. The shoot was for their upcoming Spring collection, and I killed it.

Mount Baden-Powell Self-Realization Fellowship Lake was no different. Once again, my breath was taken away. At the crack of dawn, Mother Nature and I became as one. Timberland picked the perfect location. The boots I wore were ideal for the burnt colors of the Spring leaves in the background as they emerged from the trees after the Winter cold. I gasped at the lake's stillness. I saw ducks floating looking for their daily bread. I heard frogs croaking and squirrels running up trees as if they were evading the law after a morning heist of walnuts. The sun smiled at me as it rose from its sleep. I vicariously lived through nature. I felt like a breeze flying through the air. I floated with the gentle currents that went upstream wandering. I was the creatures that crawled and the birds that soared through the air. My body was no longer mine. It belonged to everything that man took for granted. There wasn't a building on earth that could take the place of what trees did for mankind. I was high off oxygen.

With the purity of the scenery, I almost forgot that I was there to do a photo shoot. The hairy-faced photographers got me back into my zone. The poses weren't that difficult, and I lost

# Changed

myself in every one of them. On some occasion, leaves fell in the backdrop to give the photos a surreal feel. The pictures by the lake were even better. The little white shore homes gave more appeal to an already spectacular view. Ducks photo bombed what was supposed to have been just the lake and vacation homes in the background. It was a perfect mistake because the photographers were more impressed by those photos than the ones without the ducks. The photo shoots ended at 1:00 PM.

The drive back home was amazing. Looking at the forest kept my attention. I saw a few deer alongside the rocky roads. I thanked God that they didn't jump out at us as we drove by. There were grassy mountains to the sky that were covered by clouds. Outside of pussy, Getty Villa and Mount Baden-Powell Self-Realization Lake were the most beautiful places I had ever seen. I prayed that global warming would reverse itself. Such beauty should never be tampered with.

We arrived back at the hotel a little after 4:30 PM. It was a long ride back, but I wasn't bored at all. The first thing I did when I got back to the hotel was text, Kim.

"Wuz up babe?" My text simply read.

In no time, I received a text back, "Hey babe! How was the photo shoot?"

I had to think for a moment. It would take too long to text her everything. I decided to take the easy way out. "It was 2 die 4. I want us 2 b buried next 2 each other n The Getty Villa. And if four some reason we can't b buried properly, then I want our ashes 2 b thrown into Lake Mount Baden-Powell Self-Realization Lake."

I sat back and waited for her response. It came back faster than I expected. "That's so sweet Jacob. I don't know what you are talking about, but that's sweet," she finished her text.

I was anxious to know how my little man was doing. "How is my lil man doing?" I asked.

"He is kicking me hard. It feels like he is moving around every minute. And he is making me fat," her text replied.

I laughed out loud and texted back, "Kim, do those exercises at home I showed you."

Kim didn't hesitate, "You come do them for me." I could hear the sarcasm even through the text.

I shook my head. "Kim, you never listen to me. I love you anyway. I miss you. I can't wait to come home." I finished my text.

"I miss you to. I do listen to you, but I don't wanna workout, I just want to drop this load off. I might let you train me after Michael is born. By the way, I want some of your lightening rod when you get home," she texted.

I had to giggle again. I guess she was over whatever she was going through. I thought of something nasty to say. "As long as I don't poke my lil man in the head."

The reply was swift. "Jacob stop it, your rod isn't that big. Lol! Just joking. You are packing. Good night honey."

Oh, she had jokes, huh? "I know you are joking. You know you be running from me. Lol! I will handle my business when I get home. Good night my Mrs. Everything!" I ended with a bang.

# Chapter 23
# The Carousal

The next morning, I woke up to board a plane headed to Atlanta. I slept the entire flight. My hormones were out of control. I almost got on hard when the flight attendant touched me slightly on my shoulder to wake me up. As I walked through Hartsfield-Jackson Atlanta International Airport, I noticed that the majority of people working and passing through were Black. The women were beautiful. Even the girls working in the fast food joints were pretty. It was like I was in the Twilight Zone. Everything seemed to be strange and unbelievable. From the looks of things, it looked like Black people were in charge in Atlanta. It was a culture shock. I truly was in a Black town. Or better yet, Black Hollywood.

I caught a service train to the baggage area. I couldn't wait to get my bags. I was ready to explore. They came, and I was off to the rental spot. Olivia didn't spare any expense; she had a hook up at SIXT luxury rental cars. I looked over every car before making a choice. My buddy Shawn would be hanging with me for the weekend, so I considered what would look best for our styles. The BMW was so cliché. The Mercedes-Benz gave me the creeps. I hated the Benz because it was the typical car everyone bought when they felt like they finally "made it." The Audi was cool, but it didn't feel like a chic magnet. Then I saw a silver Range Rover. That was gonna be my babe for the weekend. It was luxurious, yet it had a sense of roughness to it. I wanted to ride high and hug the road. The Range Rover gave me all of that. Once my reservation was confirmed, I hit the Atlanta streets.

As I drove down Interstate 85 North, I received a phone call from an unidentified number. I already knew who it was.

"Hello," I said.

"Jacob, I hope that everything went well. There shouldn't have been any problems. Were there?" Olivia asked. Olivia was a serious woman when it came to business.

"No, Ms. Olivia. Everything was in order," I replied. "Jacob, please call me Olivia. I told you before not to call me Miss. You make me feel so old. Okay, that's good," she said laughing.

I needed to drop off my luggage before heading out. "Ms. Olivia, am I meeting you at the cabin?" I asked, forgetting to not call her Miss.

"Jacob, what am I going to do with you? Olivia, Olivia, I said!! Jacob, you are lucky you are my favorite," she gently scolded, then continued. "Change of plans. All the men will be staying at the W Hotel downtown. All the women will be staying in the cabin. We will all meet up Saturday night," she finished.

I was more excited now. I made sure to get my thoughts together before answering. "Olivia, that sounds good," I replied.

"Okay, I'm about to forward you all of the information," Olivia paused. "Jacob don't waste all of your energy. We need you ready for Saturday night." I simply replied, "I aim to please!"

Shawn would be landing in about an hour. Though I was hungry, I decided to grab a smoothie real quick. I sat in the parking lot of Smoothie King observing the people that walked by. Atlanta had a different feel to it. It felt like a country version of Miami. The Black men and women who walked by were well dressed. I assumed that Atlanta was a great place to come up. As I was thinking, I received a text from Shawn indicating he'd landed. I finished the rest of my smoothie and pulled off. It was mid-day, so traffic haven't picked up yet. Thank God, because I heard how Atlanta traffic could be.

I got back down to the airport in no time. I saw Shawn standing in front of the Delta emblem. I scooped him up, and we were off.

"Jacob, wuz up cuz?" He said with a California accent. I greeted him back with my Miami dialect, "What they do homie?"

Shawn was a cool dude. He had gotten into some trouble when he was younger before making the cover of *Men's Health* magazine. He was once part of the notorious Crips gang. He gangbanged until his early 20s. From what he told me, he put in some work in his younger days. I wasn't sure if he meant that he

# Changed

killed someone or spent time in the joint, but either way, it went, he was a new man when I first met him.

A couple of photographers stumbled across him while on lunch break. They saw past his mean look and gangster clothes. What they saw was a tall well-built light-skinned man with blue eyes like the old pictures my grandma had of Jesus. The tattoos he had only accentuated what he already had. They talked him into removing his AK-47 tattoo off his arm and tattoo tears. He replaced the AK-47 with a scripture from the bible. Isaiah 54:17, "No weapon formed against me shall prosper." Go figure. He got permission from the Big Homie to get out of the gang with the promise that he would still pay his dues. And the rest was history.

"I've been good man," I said.

Shawn replied, "Datz wuz up!"

I kept the conversation going. "So, how are you and Karen doing?" I asked.

Shawn looked a bit uneasy when I asked. He took a deep breath before answering. "We are getting a divorce. She caught me cheating again. It was like her fifth time catching me. She couldn't take it anymore. Now, I got to go through this alimony and child support bullshit!" He finished sounding disheartened.

"Dude, I told you what to do to not get caught. You didn't listen," I said.

Shawn shook his head. "Jacob, my gurl ain't like your gurl. Mine should have worked for the Feds. I couldn't put my phone down for a minute without her going through it. After getting caught the first couple times, I couldn't have a lock on my phone anymore. Bitches would call me all times of the night. Then to top it off, she put a private detective on my trail. He brought her back a couple of pictures with other bitches and me. He even had one of me doing a chic in the pool. That was the icing on the cake."

I shook my head. Unlike me, Shawn was always sloppy when it came to his infidelity. The worst cheat is a sloppy cheat. "So, what are you gonna do?" I asked.

"Like any man would do in this situation, hope for the best and prepare for the worst. Anyway, how are you and Kim doing?" He asked trying to change the subject.

"Well, we are about to have our first baby. It's a boy!" I said. Shawn congratulated me with a pound and kind words. We continued talking about nothing and made it to the hotel safely.

We checked into our rooms right before brunch was beginning. A Mimosa sounded really good. I didn't have time to change clothes. I rushed down to the W's restaurant leaving Shawn to catch up. It was a sight to see. It was upscale with pizzazz. The waiters were awesome! Even if my waiter weren't around, another would check on my table. The atmosphere was exciting for a mid-day brunch. The women looked high class. Their expensive purses matched their expensive heels. Everyone mingled with each other.

Shawn finally made his way downstairs. I could see that he caught a few of the women's eyes. I could tell his ego went up. "Jacob, man, why did you leave me?" He asked.

"Man, I was hungry as hell! I needed a drink and some food," I replied.

Shawn's eyes roamed around the dining area. "Jacob, I think I see a few ladies I can hook up with, they look thirsty." He said.

I saw a few myself but wasn't interested. I honestly wanted to see more of Atlanta before making a rash decision. "Man, do what you do," I said feeling a little buzzed from the multiple Mimosas.

I decided to leave the hound dog downstairs. We would meet up with the rest of the fellas later on that night. "Shawn, I'm about to bounce. I need to rest for later on tonight," I explained. Shawn looked somewhat disappointed. "Well, aight cuz," he said surveying his victims for the night.

Three hours later I woke up. I was ready to get out. I wondered what the hell they had put into my Mimosa. It was strong as hell. I took a shower and got dressed. It was a Gucci night. I walked across the hall to Shawn's room. He came to the door with a towel on. As I expected, he had two women lying in his bed. Typical Shawn. "Shawn, you haven't changed. We got to get out of here; we have to meet with the rest of the crew downstairs," I said.

# Changed

He tried to get me to come in but I declined. I don't know if I was going soft or really wanted to hit the Atlanta streets. "Okay, man. Suit yourself," he said as he closed the door.

I caught the elevator down to greet the other four participants. They were all sitting in the lobby together. "Hey, I'm Jacob Richardson," as I began shaking their hands one by one.

"Armando from Columbia. How you are doing, Jacob?" He said in terrible English. Armando was a 21-year-old potential Olympic swimmer. He was a lanky 6'3" with short dark hair.

"Hugo Santos from Brazil. How are you?" He asked sounding a little better, but with the same terrible accent as Armando. He was a 20-year-old freelance model. He was 6'1" with an afro of curly hair.

"Daryl Barley from Jamaica. How are you?" He asked with a heavy Jamaican accent. He was better known to the ladies as Mandingo. The reason could have been because of his 6'8" and 265-pound body frame. He was as dark as the ancient African warrior Shaka Zulu and as big as the Incredible Hulk. A true specimen.

"Roberto Rodriguez from Puerto Rico. How are you?" He asked in almost perfect English. He was a fitness guru. He was the shortest of the bunch at only 5'10". He was known as a homewrecker back in his native country.

After the short greetings, we contemplated what we were going to do for the night. After a few minutes of debating, we decided to bar hop and possibly end the night at a strip club. Shawn finally made his way down. I told him the plan and he agreed. We all headed to the valet and me and Shawn jumped into my Range Rover and the rest got into their cars, excited to take on the ATL.

It looked to be a busy night in downtown Atlanta. Traffic was bumper to bumper. We didn't have any idea where we were going. Shawn google mapped popular night scenes in Atlanta. The M Lounge was the closest spot. We pulled up shortly past 9 PM. The parking was terrible, but we managed to park in an over-charging lot. We reluctantly paid the parking attendant. Shawn had a few choice words for him.

It was early, so the lines weren't long. We walked into a friendly crowd. The women were hot, and the men were cool. We all went to the bar to order drinks. We all promised to buy rounds. The first one was on me. Everyone got their chosen drink of trouble. We all sat together at a booth. The waitress that came to the table was fine as hell. We all flirted with her. From the look in her big gorgeous eyes, she didn't mind. Chics were dancing in a small area of the lounge. It was ass everywhere shaking. It didn't matter if they were fake or not, they were jiggling in their dresses. Some even came over by our table dancing in front of us. The fellas started getting restless. We began mingling with the hotties. From the look on Shawn's face, he was ready for round two. I flirted with a couple of females who made it evident that it was a strong possibility that it could be a one-night stand. My two Hispanic brothaz made a move to the dance floor. The music was nice and smooth. I considered dancing but thought better of it.

Shawn was making his move on two more chics. I could see that he was working his magic. The more they laughed, the more I felt like he would have them in his room later. An amazon from Venus kept my attention. She sat close to me. Her perfume smelled lovely. I looked down to see that she had calf muscles like a cantaloupe. I could see that she trained in the gym. We talked like we knew each other for years. It was a clear indication that I could get lucky that night.

I turned to see that Daryl had a sexy one hemmed up in the corner of the dance floor. It looked like everyone was having fun. I then noticed something a little awkward. Everyone was indulging in the pleasure of talking to women, but Roberto. He was talking to a man that seemed to be a bit feminine for my taste. That was when Shawn came over and pulled me to the side.

"Jacob, wuz up with Roberto? Why is he over there talking to dat faggit? You know I don't play that shit! If Olivia gets wind of this, his ass is gone," he said angrily.

I wasn't one to speculate nor was I the one to quickly overreact. "I'm not sure, homie, what he's doing. I don't think that he's that way. You know he's a fitness guru. Maybe he's tryin' to gain a new client. I really don't know man," I said.

# Changed

Shawn looked even more pissed from my response. "Jacob, you can't be serious! That dude is already in shape. He doesn't need a personal trainer. He looks more like he likes to take it up the ass and Roberto looks like he's ready to oblige him," he said with more fire in his voice.

Still being uncertain, I simply said, "Well, we can ask some of his buddies when we can." Shawn simply nodded his head in disgust.

Though all of us had chics hanging from us, we decided to bar hop some more. We all got the chics numbers which were all over us. We promised to hook up later at the W hotel. We were off to the races again. I could tell that Shawn was still steaming about his seemingly newfound revelation about Roberto. It had to be a way I could find out. But my immediate thoughts were on where to go next.

We found another spot. It was called Suite Lounge. The line was long, but we were stuck there. The women looked grown and sexy in their dresses. Daryl, Armando, Shawn, and Roberto started macking while they were in line. I decided this would be the best time to pull Hugo to the side for answers.

"Hugo, my friend, I need to speak to you," I requested. Hugo humbly put his arms around my shoulders.

"Jacob, wuz up my friend?" he asked.

"Shawn is a little concerned about Roberto," I said.

Hugo laughed. "Jacob, I think I know what you're talking about," he said looking me directly in my eyes.

"Is he?" I asked.

Hugo didn't hesitate. "No, Jacob, he's not. I have never heard anything about that. I would know. Besides, Olivia will have him killed if he is." He said with full confidence.

Properly reassured, I had one less problem to think about. About 30 minutes later, we were in. The Suite Lounge was popping. It was a Jazzy spacious spot. It was a mixed crowd. Most of the people had a hookah at their tables. It was so crowded that we couldn't find a seat. We mingled among the party goers. Everyone looked like they were enjoying themselves. I normally hated the smell of smoke, but the aroma from the hookahs didn't bother me.

The fellaz were at it again. Everyone was talking to chics. I wondered for a moment would they be worth a damn for the orgy. Then I thought, *If they weren't, I would just have to put more work in.*

After an hour of flirting and juking, I was ready to go. I wasn't interested in trying to take anyone back to the hotel room. Now, looking at some ass before going back to the W made more sense to me. I gathered everyone up and suggested going to a strip club to end the night. They all agreed. Once again, they got whatever cell phone numbers they could.

We debated if we should go to Magic City, Onyx, or Blue Flame. After debating for 10 minutes, we decided Blue Flame was best. After being price gouged in the parking lot, we made our way inside of Blue Flame. It wasn't upscale, but the dancers were worth every dime of admission. They ranged from all shapes and sizes. From fake butts to real ones. Dark skin to light skin. Tall to small. Big titties to bee stings. There were dope boys making it rain, and those who could barely afford to be there, penny-pinched every stripper that they could. Some of the men looked like husbands who believed there wasn't anything wrong seeing a lil ass before going home to their wives. I guessed it made having sex with the Mrs. more pleasurable. Their wives probably wouldn't know why the best sex they had all week was because their husbands were fantasizing about strippers at the strip club while on top of them. if they made it home after tricking off their paychecks. Couples sat together enjoying naked dancers and fried food and drinks. Some of them had strippers shaking their ass in front of them. They slapped on strippers' asses together. *Happy couples*, I thought. Kim didn't play the strip club life. Boring, just boring!

We all exchanged our one hundred-dollar bills for ones. We sat in front of the stage and made it rain for a fine ass gazelle shaking her money maker. She was slim and tall. She had a nice feminine six-pack. Her ass and hips were well proportioned to her sexy body. We made it rain collectively as she bent over to show her pink lips. Her butt had a nice jiggle to it. While bent over, she smiled at me between her legs. I couldn't help but throw more money on the stage. The waitress, who was thick enough to be a stripper, too, brought our drinks. I was already feeling buzzed from before but didn't want to stop drinking.

The music was pumping. They played mostly Atlanta based artists. It was one trap music song after another. I didn't mind because it seemed like the dancers danced harder to each new track that came on. I had never seen so many fine women in my life. If I didn't know better, I would've married 25 out of the 30 dancers on physical appearance alone.

We were enjoying ourselves until a fight broke out. Hands were being swung, and bottles were being thrown. Shawn got his gangsta on; his instincts went into effect!

"Jacob, I don't have my fire on me! We need to hurry up and get our asses out of here," he yelled.

We rushed towards the exit door. He pushed niggaz out of the way to make a way out. Ducking for cover, we followed his lead. We quickly made our way back to the cars. It was no way we were gonna get caught up in a shootout. We made it back to the hotel safely. I don't think any of them were thinking about taking a gurl back to their hotel rooms anymore.

***

Although I woke up with a slight hangover, my mind was on exploring. I called Shawn, but his phone kept going to voicemail. I decided to head out alone. As I was exiting the hotel, I saw Roberto walking in sweaty. His clothes were damp, and face was red. His eyes were half shut. He staggered as he made his way to the elevator. He looked like he had a long night. I didn't think much of it as I walked out of the W.

I took a tour of Atlanta's outskirts. I drove as far north as Buckhead and as far south as Riverdale. The homes were huge and cheap. I couldn't believe the prices for four-bedroom homes. What they were asking for, in Miami I would have been living in a two-bedroom shack fighting drug dealers from selling crack in front of my house.

I loved looking at the trees as I drove from one neighborhood to the next. I could see the rich empowerment of Black people in Georgia. It just seemed like African-Americans as a whole were doing better in a city that presented so much opportunity to get ahead.

After taking my tour, I headed back to the hotel. I felt inspired by every luxury car passing by with someone Black driving it. I thought to myself that I might relocate to Georgia one day. Then I wondered how Kim would feel about it. She could transfer her job. I didn't see a problem with her going from Jackson Hospital to Grady Memorial. Little Michael could grow up at a slower pace. Miami was becoming too fast for my taste.

I made it to the hotel. Time was flying. It was getting to the moment of truth. It was around 3 PM, Olivia was probably discussing business at her workshop. It would go from 9 AM 'til 5 PM. After that, they would kill some time until 9 PM. That was the time the orgy would start.

The rest of the fellaz were out shopping. Hugo texted me and told me that they were at Lenox Square Mall. I tried calling Shawn again and it was the same result - voicemail. So, I decided to knock on his room door. He came to the door with a towel on again. He opened the door slightly to let me see that he had a different set of women in the room from the night before. He asked me to join again, but I turned him down again. I needed to rest for the big night.

I went to my room to get some shut eye. After taking a long nap, I woke up to a call at 7:00 PM sharp.

"Jacob, darling are you ready? The gurls are about to get ready." Olivia stated.

I wiped the cold out of my eyes first before answering. "Olivia, I'm about to wake up right now. I will get in contact with everyone," I said. I was groggy but slowly coming to alertness.

"Okay, be on time. We are ready for a wild night. I hope y'all are ready to satisfy us," she stated with flair.

Once I contacted the fellas, they all responded back that they were ready. We headed downstairs to meet. Once everyone was present, we proceeded to the cabin. Even though the drive

# Changed

was far, it wasn't that bad. The traffic god prevented any accidents from happening as we zoomed up Interstate 285 North. We made it to the cabin in about 45 minutes.

We each jumped out of our cars not knowing what to expect. It was dark outside. The porch and room lights were the only things to illuminate the forest where the large cabin sat in the middle of nowhere. Behind it was a little man-made lake. I could hear owls hooting from a distance. Daryl's big ass looked scared. I couldn't believe it. *What a waste of muscles*, I thought. After Daryl got himself together, we all walked towards the cabin. I could hear the wood cracking as we stepped up to the door. I took the honor of knocking on the door first. I heard a scatter! Shortly after a few knocks, Olivia came to the door. She was wearing a Moulin Rouge costume with a black mask covering her face. She looked sexy for her age.

"Come in boys," Olivia said, looking at us with flirtatious eyes.

We entered a large living room. We looked around trying to figure out where our Scarlets were for the night.

"Don't worry fellas. The girls are in the back," Olivia answered our silent question.

She then passed every one of us a bag. "Go to the back and change. Wait for my word to come out. Someone will come to get you all shortly."

We walked to the back of the spacious cabin. It was state of the art. It had all new appliances. It was fully furnished with beautiful handcrafted pieces, and the floors were polished cedar wood. The flat screen TV that hung over the fireplace was a few inches from being movie theater size.

We took our bags back to separate rooms. Inside of the bags were a black pair of pants and a bowtie. Nothing else. We got dressed. Once dressed, I looked in the mirror to see that I looked like a Chip and Dale dancer, or possibly a waiter working at the Playboy Mansion. Either way, it went, the excitement was starting to build up.

Hugo, out of the blue, made an announcement: "If anyone has a problem keeping themselves up for a long period of time, I have blue pills!"

Everyone turned to each other like they weren't sure or not if they needed it.

Daryl, being confused, spoke up. "What is a blue pill?" He asked in pure ignorance.

Everyone shook their heads. And all together we said, "It's Viagra!" We looked at him like he was stupid. Daryl burst out laughing and said, "I never used one, but I heard it keeps your dick on hard all night. Yeah man, give me one." Everyone else followed behind him, and so did I. I wasn't sure how long it would be before I felt the effects, but I was ready to fuck.

We all waited patiently in the room for our call. The fellaz seemed anxious. They started talking about what they were going to do and how they were going to do it when suddenly, we heard bells ringing from outside the door. This was our cue.

We heard a booming voice say, "Men, get ready to serve the women of AWOP!" The voice had our attention. We stood up.

The voice began again. "Stand in formation and come out one by one." We lined up one after the other. I was the last one in line. Shawn was in the middle and Armando stood in front. The door was opened by a woman dressed in the same type of Moulin Rouge outfit as Olivia was at the front door. She was a short haired Black woman with ass for days. Her mask covered her face just as Olivia's did.

"One by one, you will walk out!" she said sounding like a drill sergeant. I thought for a moment. *Could the woman hiding behind the mask be Judge Tasha Mitchell?* It didn't matter because I knew when I got ahold of her, I would fuck her into submission. Armando walked out to a hallway of hungry pack of wolves who were ready to eat him alive. He was a piece of meat, as we all were. One by one they grabbed his dick and slapped him on his backside as he passed. They did us the same way. The groping of my dick was cool, but I felt uncomfortable when they slapped my butt. Nevertheless, it was the opening ceremony to the fuck fest. I guess it was a part of our initiation.

# Changed

We were led to the living room area. There was every possible liquor, wine, and champagne sitting on top of the long coffee table. Next to the alcohol was a bowl filled with a white substance. My gut said cocaine. There was also a pile of marijuana by the bowl. The aroma from the bud was strong. On the corner table next to the couch were sex toys and lubricants. There wouldn't be any dry pussies in the house that night. A cooler probably filled with beer was sitting alongside a sectional in the kitchen. It was gonna be a party!

We were aligned adjacent from the thirsty cougars. For the first time, we all stood in the same room. The men and women sized each other up. I could see behind their masks that they were ready to let loose. Olivia made her way towards the fireplace. She stood on top of the hearth to make an announcement.

"I would like to welcome everyone to the quarterly AWOP gathering. I hope everyone has been accommodated. I did my best to make everyone feel comfortable. And I hope everyone has found Atlanta to be exciting! I searched long and hard before selecting this as our location." There was a murmur of appreciation heard through all who gathered.

Olivia continued, "For the first-timers, it's about to be a long night. I hope you all got your rest," Olivia giggled. "Jacob, I think you are the only one who is familiar with the proceedings," she looked me in my face. "Men, your jobs are to please the women. You are our slaves and what we command is what we are going to get. I hope you all took the time to read these beautiful women's vices. We expect every fantasy to be fulfilled - no exceptions!" Olivia surveyed the men with a hard eye to ensure we understood she meant business.

She then turned to the women. "Women, your jobs are to give these sexy men all you have. Give them what you are not getting at home. No exceptions! With that being said, it is now time to start the party!" She shouted with glee.

Everyone rushed towards their choice of drugs. I poured a glass of Louis XIII. It was the finest cognac I ever sipped. My Hispanic compadres went straight for the Tequila. A few of the women joined them. They used small shot glasses along with sprinkles of salt on their wrist. They downed the tequila after every cheer like water. They took one shot after another. Shawn rolled up blunts. I wasn't sure if I would be joining him. Olivia and a few of the concubines started making rows of cocaine on the table. I knew at that point it was about to go down.

Once drugs and drinks started mixing, everyone became more at ease. Conversations flowed and touchy, feely began. I could see the free spirits of the women coming out. I tried to remember each gurl's vice. After downing one glass of cognac, I poured another. Shawn had finished rolling the blunts. I decided to smoke with him. After he hit it a few times, he passed it to me while he choked.

He said, "Jacob, this is some fie! Your lungs may be too young for this."

I took the blunt from him. "I got this homie!" I said. I took a toke of it and began gasping for air. I choked like crazy.

Shawn started laughing. "Nigga, I told you! Dat ain't dat Reggie Bush you be smoking back home," he said laughing.

I didn't find it humorous but couldn't find the air to say anything back. When I finally found the breath to speak, my first words were, "Fuck you, nigga!" We then laughed together. I was instantly high. Everything was funny to me after that point.

Armando and Roberto joined the women at the table. Roberto dove his nose into the cocaine like the scene from *Scarface,* before Tony Montana's demise. Armando and another chic did a straw race to see who could snort the coke the fastest. It was becoming a drug fest. Daryl was the only square in the room drinking a Corona. Some of the other women who didn't do hard drugs smoked weed with the fellaz. They puff'd, puff'd, passed like the earlier days of Woodstock.

Things were becoming sensual. I was becoming aroused looking at the women in their sexy costumes. The Viagra was kicking in. My dick got extremely hard watching the cougars with their legs opened without panties on. The short carouse was now leading to the orgy.

With coke and everything else in his system, Roberto pulled out his dick first. I could see the lust in the members of

# Changed

AWOP's eyes. O' Canada took the lead. Audrey caressed his dick, then put it into her mouth. The other members followed. All at the same time, they started sucking dicks like synchronized swimmers. For the ones who couldn't find a dick to suck, they massaged the men's chests or rubbed on the women's breasts.

I had Nakisha, and she laid down the law on me. She was a pretty Black woman with a few strings of gray hair. Her youthful look escaped the wrath of Father Time. She sucked my dick with her eyes closed. I could feel the passion in her mouth with every slurp.

I turned to see Daryl had Bella sucking his dick and Dawn tea bagging him. I was astonished how nasty they were. Roslyn laid next to them watching while rubbing on her clitoris rapidly. I could see that she was enjoying herself. On the other couch, Olivia was getting her pussy ate by Martina. She held Martina's ponytail tightly as she controlled her head motions. It looked like Martina could barely breathe, but she kept licking and sucking to the delight of Olivia. Hugo and Roberto stood side by side getting their dicks and balls sucked by Tasha and Sandy. Hugo laid back with Amelia's pussy smothering his face and Jean giving him fellatio.

Everyone looked like they were getting their fair share. Nakisha was doing a damn good job on me. She massaged my balls and drooled while deep throating my dick. She would go from gagging on my manhood to nibbling on the head of my shaft. I bit my bottom lip while staring directly in her eyes to express how good it felt. It looked like it turned her on even more. Without me saying anything, she then started sucking my nuts. With her ass in the air, Tasha snuck up from behind and started spanking her rear. With each spank, Nakisha sucked on my scrotum harder and harder. The Viagra pill had me feeling like a teenager with a hard-on. She came back up to suck my dick more. It was becoming time to fuck!

Hugo, Roberto, and Armando were eating pussy like they were at the buffet. Their appetites were big. It was enough pussy to go around to satisfy their hunger. Their tongues traveled down between each woman's legs that were available for their tongue lashing. The moaning and groaning echoed throughout the cabin. I prayed that we didn't wake a sleeping bear. I meant it literally. We were in the forest in the middle of nowhere. We were on their turf.

Anyway, some of the women had all of their clothes off, and some still had parts of their costumes on. That was about to change. Once the men and women were taken care of orally, the fun began. Hidden underneath the women's garter belts were condoms. They slid them out then put them in their mouths. Whatever man was lucky enough to be in front of them, they sucked them on with their mouths. I figured they learned more than just business ideas at Olivia's workshop.

Since Nakisha never left my side, she sucked mine on. She pushed her body back as far as she could on the couch with her legs spread. She pulled her pussy lips open as wide as possible. All I could see was a deep hole. I jumped into it like a skydiver without a parachute. She licked her lips. Her eyes rolled back. She then made fuck faces while I penetrated her mature kitty cat.

The other fellaz were knee deep in pussy as well. Shawn had Olivia bent over beside me. He was hitting the old lady like she was still a spring chicken. Daryl showed his muscles off by picking Valentina up off her feet. He rammed his dick in her while he held her in the air. Age was just a number; how she was able to hold herself up and still throw the pussy back was amazing. Roslyn continued watching and finger fucking her pussy. I could see that she was having one orgasm after another. It looked like everyone was into what they were doing. I could smell the fumes of sex in the air.

All of a sudden things changed when Shawn screamed, "Switch!" Everyone started changing sex partners. I could see in Olivia's face that she was waiting for me. She opened her legs wide and signaled me to come to her with a seductive finger motion. She probably was pissed that Nakisha had me first, but she still summoned me. I knew I had to make up for it. I left Nakisha for someone else to have. With the wetness from Nakisha pussy still dripping from my dick, I came over to Olivia.

# Changed

She pulled herself to the edge of the couch. I immediately penetrated her. She was so wet. I felt like I was in an ocean without a lifejacket. "Deeper, deeper, deeper," she repeated loudly. My dick was drowning, but I refused to let it die in the deep currents. I pulled my dick out to regroup. Olivia looked as if she was disappointed that I couldn't keep going.

"Jacob, what's wrong?" she asked.

"Ms. Olivia, yo' pussy is too good," I said, feeling a little embarrassed.

"Jacob, I told you not to call me Ms. Olivia," she said with a smile. No woman could stay mad after hearing how good her pussy was. I turned to see that there was a little bit of the Louis XIII left in the glass I drank from earlier. I took a swig of it. It hit the spot. I was ready to explore the deep blue seas again. I felt harder and stronger inside of her this time. I couldn't let Olivia get the best of me. I gave it to the old gurl. I had to let her know who she was dealing with.

Right as I was getting the pussy good, Roberto now yelled, "Switch!" I pulled out of Olivia's soaking pussy. I turned to see naked bodies moving throughout the living room. I became hornier. The demon whore became stronger. Armando, Roberto, Daryl, Shawn, and Hugo were going in. They had no mercy on their new partners. In between the fucking, was snorting and smoking. It was intoxicating. What it looked like everyone's body was being taken over by drugs and sex.

It had been over an hour and a half, and I still hadn't nutted. My dick felt like it wasn't going down no time soon either. I noticed no one touched Roslyn, so I stuck my dick in her mouth to show her someone was paying attention. Martina swooped over and started eating her out. She tried to push Martina's head away but couldn't resist her cunnilingus. She squirmed for mercy to no avail. Although Martina wouldn't grant her mercy, I did by pulling my manhood out of her mouth. My attention went somewhere else.

Bella Wales was one of the finest in the whole group. She was in the middle of sucking on Dawn's breast when I grabbed her away. Dawn instead grabbed the anal beads and stuck it up her asshole. I sat on the couch next to Hugo who had Audrey on top of him. Bella began riding me with her wide, white ass. She rode my dick like Great Britain royalty. She felt so juicy. As she went up and down, I felt something different going on with me. It felt more powerful than being high or drunk. I couldn't put my hands on it. I just couldn't move anymore. My dick stayed hard, but my body was paralyzed. I was stuck to the couch. Bella continued to ride me wildly. The room started spinning. People's faces looked distorted. All I could see was that Roberto's condom was off. Everyone was too high on drugs to say anything. Daryl was the only one who could have caught it, but his big ass was fucked to sleep. I panicked as he approached us. Even with blurred vision, I could still see the coke on his nose. All I could do was stare at the ceiling. He held Bella down while he laced his dick with anal ease. Once he was lubricated, he rammed his dick into her rectum. Bella jumped in pain but didn't push him away. I figured, she couldn't feel or see that his condom was off. No matter how hard I tried, I couldn't budge. We penetrated her at the same time, unfortunately. His dick in her anus and my dick in her pussy. He kept ramming her while I prayed that my penis would become soft. The blue pill didn't give my penis a fighting chance.

After busting Bella's asshole wide open, Roberto left to raw dog any woman he could find. Everyone was too drunk or high to see this jackoff walking around breaking the rules. Bella finally got up and what I saw next was devastating. My condom had popped. I felt a chill through my body. A tear came down my face because I couldn't move. I had never had a condom pop on me before. This had to be the worst time ever. Even though I was out of it, the soon to be affluent cougars kept jumping on and off my dick. They showed no regard for me being unprotected. Roberto ran around the room like a jackrabbit humping one after another. I tried so hard to warn them with eye contact, but they all laughed in their stupidity. Being frustrated, I closed my eyes and let the whores have their way with me.

# Changed

# Chapter 24
# Home

I awoke the next day with a hard-on, but I could finally move. Everyone was knocked out in the living room. No one had clothes on. I could barely remember what happened. I just felt like something was wrong. I went in search of my clothes. I stepped over the zombies to walk to the back of the cabin to find them. I didn't bother to shower, I just quickly got dressed and made my way out of the cabin. I didn't care who knew I was leaving.

I headed south on I-85, straight through the city. I took the Range Rover back to the rental place and took a shuttle to the airport. I didn't even bother to make arrangements for my things back at the hotel. I just wanted to get the fuck outta there. I purchased a ticket for standby. I got lucky. Someone didn't make the first flight. I jumped on the plane feeling like I was out of it. I slept the whole way back.

When we landed, and I deplaned, I walked through the airport in a daze. When I could walk no further, I sat down. My body couldn't take it anymore. I blacked out.

When I came to, I was sitting in the same spot. I tried to figure out what happened. It appeared that a couple of hours had gone by since I landed, but my memory was gone. I checked the time, and it was about 5 PM. All I could think about was Kim. Kim had to be to work by 7 PM. I thought for a moment whether I should go home or not. Then I thought it would be best not to let her see me like this. Too many questions would be asked. Before leaving the airport, I took a birdbath in the restroom. The restroom was empty. I had washed my dick in many places, but never in an airport restroom. Once done cleansing myself, I headed towards the transportation area to grab an Uber.

By the time I made it home, Kim was gone. I crashed on the couch. The next thing I could remember was waking up to a hot towel on my head with a thick blanket over me.

"Jacob, are you okay?" Kim asked.

# Changed

I was still disoriented. It took a moment to gather myself. Once I did, I mumbled, "Yeah-yeah Kim."

She looked over me like a concerned nurse. "Jacob, you don't look too good. You need to go to the hospital," she persisted. I pulled the warm towel off my head. "Naw Kim! I'm not going to the hospital. I'll be okay," I replied.

Kim looked like she was ready to throw a hissy fit. "Jacob, you have a slight fever, and your pupils are dilated. Have you been smoking weed again? I thought you stopped!" She said sounding like my mother. She basically was bringing up when she caught me smoking in college. I wasn't in the mood to argue.

"Kim, I don't smoke. I'm just suffering from jet lag," I said trying to sound convincing.

Kim sighed. "Jacob, I'm about to call a doctor," she said.

I grabbed her arm as she picked up her phone. "Kim, I said no! I will be okay!" I yelled.

Kim fell back. The third degree wasn't over though. "So, who is Roberto? You said his name in your sleep."

I was thrown for a loop. My memory still wasn't back. Why would I say Roberto's name? *Who the hell was Roberto?* I thought. Even if I did or didn't know who he was, I had to lie just in case.

"Roberto was one of the photographers. I guess the reason I said his name in my sleep was because he did a great job." I said with a straight face.

Kim twisted her lips in disbelief. "Okay Jacob, you don't have to go to the hospital, but you have to break this fever. Let me run to my mom's house real quick. She'll have something over there to break the fever. Until then, I'll put another hot towel over your head." She said.

She left me alone on the couch. I tried my best to remember who Roberto was. Trying to strain my brain ended up making me fall back asleep. I awoke to a thermometer in my mouth with a bunch of leaves covering me.

"What the hell are these leaves on me for?" I questioned while damn near swallowing the thermometer.

Kim, with her hand on my forehead, replied, "Palmer Christian leaves. They will help you break the fever. Drink some of this," she said with a green cup of juice in her hand.

"What is this?" I asked. "Jacob, this is papaya leaf juice. This will help even more."

I drank the gross green juice and laid in the leaves on the couch. Kim then covered me with thick blankets again. After covering me, she checked my temperature. It was still over 100 degrees. Kim looked very concerned, but there wasn't anything that she could do about it.

She kissed me on the forehead and said, "Jacob, get some rest. Sleep out here tonight. I'm going to the room. I will check on you in the morning," she said before leaving my side. I fell to sleep shortly after.

    ***

I woke up from the best nap in my life. I could tell that my body needed it. I felt normal. The fever felt gone. Thank God for Kim's mom's old remedies. I smelled like leaves. I needed to take a shower. I was funky, and the sweat from my pours didn't make anything better. Kim walked out of the room with the thermometer in her hand. She shook it.

"Jacob, open," she said.

I opened my mouth for her. After a few minutes, she pulled it out.

"Jacob, your fever is broken. I'm relieved," she said showing compassion for me.

I removed the leaves off me. I immediately went to the bathroom to wash my stinkin' ass. As I took a shower, my memory slowly came back to me. I now knew why I said Roberto's name. He was at the orgy party. Then it hit me; he didn't have a condom on. *Oh my God*, I thought to myself! I needed answers. Even though everyone had to take STD tests, I needed to know for sure.

I scrubbed myself quickly. I panicked as I jumped out of the shower. My mind started racing. I knew before I could search for answers, Kim needed her peace of mind.

# Changed

"So, Jacob, who is Roberto?" she asked as if she was probing to see if I was a down-low brotha. *Preposterous*, I thought.

"Kim, Roberto is one of the last photographers that I worked with. He gave me the best pointers on posing in front of the camera. I guess the reason I said his name was because no one else ever took the time to make me a better model. Besides, I told you this already," I said with my fingers crossed.

Kim gave me a look of disbelief. "Jacob, that doesn't make sense. Since we have been together, you are always practicing your poses in the mirror. Besides, I don't know another man who is into their craft as you. So why do you sound unsure now?" she said making me feel uncomfortable.

"Listen, Kim; I don't know everything. If someone gives me pointers to make me better, so be it."

Kim looked insulted. "'So, be it' Jacob? Don't talk to me like that!" she said with anger.

I had to think quickly. "I'm sorry Kim, but I have no reason to lie," I said lying.

Still, with uncertainty in her eyes, Kim moved on to her next question.

"Jacob, how did you catch a fever?" she asked.

My head was starting to hurt. "Kim, I guess I caught it on the plane. There are more than a million people who travel a day. I honestly don't know. It could have happened when I was in California or on the plane. I really don't know," I said in frustration.

After hearing the tone in my voice, Kim backed off. "Okay, Jacob if you say that's what happened, then that's what happened. I'm just concerned about you," she said.

I needed a moment to myself. "Kim, if you don't mind, I need to take a breather," I said gently.

Kim didn't argue. She simply said, "Okay."

I went down to my car. I finally looked at my phone. I had over 40 messages. I didn't have time to check them all. I only wanted to speak to one person.

"Wuz up, Jacob? Man, what the hell happened to you?" Shawn said anxiously.

"Shawn listen man, I had to get out of there. I'm sorry, but I had to go," I explained.

It didn't seem like it really bothered Shawn. "It's cool, Jacob. The fellas dropped me off to the airport. I'm back home. At least what is left of it. Anyway, wuz up Jacob?" I wanted to get things clear and get to the point.

"Shawn, what the hell happened at the orgy party? I came home and completely forgot everything. I think I was drugged?" I said with a questioning voice.

"Jacob, I'm not quite sure because I woke up feeling the same way. I felt sick the next day. I think someone drugged the drinks." He explained.

I thought for a moment that it could be true. I shouldn't have drunk from that glass after putting it on the table uncovered. I wondered what type of drug it could have been.

"Shawn, did you know that Roberto was having sex without a rubber?" I said.

I heard Shawn drop the phone. Once he gathered it back up, he went off. "Jacob, you got to be kidding me! Got damn it, I woke up with my condom off. I'm gonna kill his little nasty bean eating ass!" Shawn screamed through the phone.

I heard Shawn's frustration. It was nothing else we could do but get tested. "Shawn, we got to get tested!" I said.

Shawn was quiet for a moment then exploded, "Fuck dat Jacob! We all had to take a test before going to the orgy. I ain't got shit! All I want to know is where the fuck dat fagget muthafucka live?" He yelled.

I tried calming Shawn down, but he wasn't hearing it. I let him vent then hung up with him. *Damn*, I thought. But Shawn was right. Why would anyone in the orgy have anything if we all got tested? That was my ace in the hole. I had nothing to worry about… or did I?

# d

# Chapter 25
# Kim

Not being totally convinced I was in the clear, I scheduled an appointment with my primary doctor the same day. I wanted to find out if I had something to worry about as fast as possible. However, Kim was going on maternity leave, and she wanted to have sex as fast as possible. I would have to dodge her for at least two weeks before having sex with her again. She wasn't going to make it easy.

After meeting with Dr. Naftali, I found out that the drugs in my system were Rohypnol, Molly, and of course marijuana. The Molly alone contained LSD, cocaine, heroin, amphetamine and methamphetamine, and possibly rat poison. I was distraught after getting the news. With the combination of those drugs, the doctor was surprised that I was able to get up the next day.

But the drugs were the least of my troubles. Dr. Naftali had one of his nurses to take blood from me. With each needle that entered my arm, I thought, *how in the hell did I get myself into this mess?!* For the first time, I didn't have the usual confidence. But once again, I found refuge in the fact that everyone had to take STD tests before the orgy. I kept repeating that in my mind.

After the blood was drawn, Dr. Naftali gave me some medicine for any possible after-effects of the drugs and explained that he would call if anything were wrong with my blood work in two weeks.

\*\*\*

I would practice in the half-bathroom in the living room how I would tell Kim that we needed to start using condoms.

*"Honey, I think we need to start using condoms."*

*"Babe, I think it will be best that we start using condoms to protect Michael."*

*"Kim, I heard somewhere that semen could make a baby come out deformed. So I think we should use a condom."*

# Changed

I said each sentence to myself out loud slowly. Then suddenly I felt a touch on my arm. I pulled away. I turned to see Kim standing by the door.

"Kim, what the hell are you doing? I told you don't sneak up on me!" I blasted at her.

Kim didn't budge or looked startled.

"Jacob, who are you talking to?" she said looking puzzled.

"I was talking to myself. I don't see anything wrong with it," I said being snappy.

"Jacob, I know you are crazy, but not that crazy. What do you mean we need to start using condoms?"

With my back against the wall, I had to tell the greatest lie of all time. "Kim, what the hell are you talking about? I said we need to get a bigger condo. How did you mix up condo for condom? They don't even sound alike," I said throwing the Hail Mary of Hail Marys' of lies.

"Jacob, I'm pretty sure you said condom. Are you sure you didn't say condom?" she probed further.

To defuse the situation, I made a joke. "Kim, you need to get a hearing aid. I didn't know pregnancy affected your hearing," I said giggling.

Kim didn't find it funny. She just stared at me again with untrusting eyes. Then she reminded me again, "Jacob, remember if I ever caught you cheating, I will cut your dick off and run it over. I mean it," she said sardonically.

I wasn't pleased, but neither was she. "Kim, stop accusing me of cheating. I'm not doing anything but thinking about you and the baby. I was just thinking we needed a bigger place. Forgive me for being considerate," I said throwing the guilt trip on her. That was the normal protocol of a liar. Kim simply rolled her eyes and walked off.

For the next couple of days, I acted off the women's manual on how to avoid sex. When Kim asked, "Could we do something tonight?" I would reply, "I have a headache." When she said, "Could I get some tonight?" I would say, "I'm tired." When she said, "I know tonight is the night I get some wood?" I would say, "Tonight I'm hanging out with the fellaz." When she said, "I want to have sex!" I would reply, "That's all you want from me?" When she would stand in front of the TV naked for my attention, I would say, "Kim, could you get out of the way? I'm watching the game."

That went on for a couple of days, but her tactics got more intense. She would sleep purposely naked next to me. Every morning Kim would push her butt back against my morning hard on. She knew my horniest moments were in the morning. Kim knew how I liked to get a quickie before I went to the gym. I did what I had to do to prevent having sex with her. I would sleep with my back turned. Kim was a total wreck. It got to the point that she didn't wear clothes around the house. Our everyday topic was about sex. Sadly, my wife was becoming a nympho. She needed dick on demand, and I wasn't available. I couldn't wait to get past this. In the meantime, I was still Jacob Richardson.

One day while I was training Michelle's crazy ass, I got a phone call out of the blue from Simone.

"Jacob, how are you handsome?" She asked in a seductive voice. It had been a while since I touched Todd's wife. The more guilt I felt, the less I wanted to sleep with her. I hoped that she didn't want to have sex.

"Simone, wuz up?" I said trying to sound uninterested. "Well Jacob, it has been a while since you have been to the house. Todd took Sasha and Albert out of town for the weekend. I'm bored and feel so alone. I was wondering, will you come to keep me company?" she asked.

I knew it. "I think I will take a rain check," I said.

"Jacob, I just wanted to cook you something, and that is it," she persisted.

I thought for a moment while Michelle stared me in my face. I frowned at her before walking off to answer Simone. "I'm not sure about coming over to your house. That could be dangerous," I said.

"Jacob, you have been over here before when Todd wasn't home. Nothing happened with us then, and nothing will happen now. You know we go to the hotel when it is time for that. Besides, my sinuses are acting up," she said.

# Changed

"Okay Simone, I might come by and grab something to eat, but nothing more or less." I finished. She agreed, and we hung up.

It was a Saturday afternoon when I made my way over to Todd's house. I parked at a nearby park. I took my bike out of the trunk. I rode down a couple of blocks before making it down the street Simone lived on. I pulled up to an open gate. Her neighbors seemed like they were gone. No cars visible. No kids running around and no old people sitting on the porch being nosy. The coast was clear. I could see that Simone planned it well.

I knocked on the door one time. I was a little nervous, but I knew how careful Simone was. She didn't want to mess up her alimony due to infidelity. Scandalous! Simone came to the door with a short nightgown on. She instructed me to put my bike in the back of the house. She opened her backdoor for me. She hugged me tightly as I entered. When she turned to go into the kitchen, I could see that she didn't have on any panties. Her butt cheeks moved up and down. *She tricked me*, I thought. So, I let myself believe it. I knew what I was doing when I went over there.

"Jacob, I made some grilled chicken, homemade garlic mash potatoes with shredded cheese on top, and mixed vegetables." She said gladly.

I was hungry. My morning training was a bit tedious since I decided to workout with one of my older clients. We sat and talked about the usual bullshit. She said negative things about Todd who had her living comfortably. Simone sounded more like an ungrateful bitch who did the bare minimum to keep her husband happy. I even tried defending Todd, but she kept going on and on about his shortcomings. Underneath the table, I started rolling my condom on. I was tired of listening to her foolishness, so I picked her up and started doing her on the dining room table with our plates still there. I gave it to her. I hated the way she talked about Todd, so I thought I would seek revenge for him by fucking her brains out. I rammed her just like she liked it. I had to put my hand over her mouth to stop her from screaming so loud. When I got done banging her up, I pulled out to see that my condom was missing in action. I just looked at her with a blank stare and began pulling my pants up. I almost stretched my shirt by forcing it on. Simone looked at me crazy. I had no time to explain. I couldn't believe that my condom was lost somewhere in her vagina.

I ran out of the back door without saying a word. I jumped on my bike and hauled ass to my car. I sweated like a Hebrew slave the whole rout. Once I got to my car, I slammed my bike into the trunk without any regard for scratching the paint. It didn't matter at that point because all I could think about was my penis raw dawging again. *Why did I ram her so hard?* I thought. Stupid! Stupid! Stupid!

***

After the situation with Simone, I decided to chill. No more women period! I strictly stayed home tending to Kim. I made sure she didn't have to do anything. No physical work was allowed. I gave her the much-needed rest she deserved. Kim hated being treated like she was helpless, but duty called. I still dodged her sexual advances. I had never seen her so frustrated with me. Every night it was the same discussion.

"Jacob, am I fat? Am I still attractive? Are you seeing someone else? What is wrong with me?" Yada yada yada bullshit. My decision was final. I wasn't gonna have sex with Kim until I found out my results.

Monday night I found myself drinking my misery away at a local bar. I took one shot after another of 1800. The bartender watched me closely. I managed to handle my alcohol until I got a call from Simone. I didn't want to answer, but I did anyway. "Jacob, you wouldn't believe this, but Todd came home early from the trip. He was so horny that he took my coochie from me. I tried to stop him, but he wouldn't stop. I gave in so he wouldn't think that I was stepping out on him. Besides it isn't like I could call rape," she explained. I immediately spit my Tequila out over the bar counter. The bartender jumped out of the way. He was looking pissed. I didn't care nor did it matter.

"Simone, you had sex with Todd? Man!" I said in disgust. Simone, thinking I was jealous replied, "No matter what Todd and I go through, he is still my husband. If I decide to have sex with him, there is nothing you can do about it."

# Changed

I was baffled by her comment. I wondered for a moment was she trying to make me jealous. Her Jezebel trait was now showing up on me. I wasn't going to entertain it. "Okay Simone, I understand. I'm just saying," I said before hanging up in her face. She tried calling and texting me back, but I ignored her. First thing went through my mind was Todd, but I was interrupted in thought when the bartender asked me to leave after spitting alcohol over the counter. I knocked my shot glass over on my way out the door.

*Roberto better not have shit*, I said to myself. Things were getting deep. I had been through a lot of things in my life, but none like this. The people I loved the most could be affected by my iniquitous behavior. The shame it would bring to my family and me if I had an STD. In addition to the shame, the pain of being a married man would be irreversible hurt in Kim's heart if I gave her something incurable. But, once again I held onto the fact that I got tested before the orgy. My ace in the hole was all I could hang on to.

It had been almost two weeks and still no word from the doctor. I was starting to get comfortable with the idea that I had escaped again. My old swagger was coming back. It was a few times that I wanted to stick my wood into Kim, but I thought better of it. I wanted to make sure two weeks had passed. I knew the routine: if I didn't hear Dr. Naftali's African accent over the phone, I was okay.

The time was coming for me to be a free man. Waiting on an STD test was like doing time in the joint. *Do the time, but don't let the time do you until your release date*, was the best way to think about it. It was easier said than done.

***

One night after wrestling Kim off me, I had a wet dream. It felt like I was in the ocean with a whale on top of me. I felt like I was drowning, and the whale wouldn't get off me. I fought as hard as possible, but the whale was too heavy for me to lift up. I cried for help, but there wasn't anyone around to save me. I was in the middle of the ocean being tormented by a whale. The shore was miles away. There wasn't any possibility for me to swim that far.

As the whale was about to drown me to the bottom of the abyss, I woke up to see that Kim was on top of me. I pushed her off.

"Kim, what the hell are you doing?" I yelled in a fury.

Kim didn't know what was going on. I was pissed!

"Jacob, why did you push me off? I'm your wife and not some type of hoe!" She blasted back.

Kim had every right to be mad, but I was trying my best to protect her from me.

"Kim, I'm sorry I haven't been in the mood lately, but I need you to understand that this relationship isn't based on sex," I said, not believing that I said that.

Kim wasn't having it. "Jacob, I have been here since day one. I'm loyal and faithful. The least I deserve is honesty. You have been acting strange lately. My mother always said when a man starts acting strange, get tested," she said coldly.

I was stung by her comment. "Kim, why would you say that? I love you! You are the only woman I wanna be with," I said with the hope that she believed me.

"Jacob, you better not have anything! It's obvious that you are fooling around on me," she said.

All night I tried to convince her, but Kim's mind was already made up. The only thing that I could do to fix this was to come back with all negative results.

***

Tuesday morning marked two weeks and a day since I initially took the STD test. I felt better about it. No call from the doctor meant everything was all good. Though things were becoming shaky between me and Kim, I knew over time I could fix them. Even though Kim had made a threat two days before about going to get tested, she never made it. She complained about her back and feet hurting her. I assumed that she would go today. I wasn't afraid if she did or didn't. I was confident that I was in the clear.

I did as I normally did. I kissed her on the forehead in her sleep before leaving for the gym.

My clients did well that morning. They worked out hard. I was pleased that I was doing a great job. I knew I wasn't going to be home long. I had a feeling that I was going to be back on a plane headed to another photoshoot.

Moreover, it was getting closer and closer for Michael to be born. I was euphoric about having my first child. To make things better, it was a boy.

The morning was moving fast. To celebrate my passing my STD tests, I would take Kim out that night, but I had counted my chickens before they hatched…

***

Around noon, I received a call from an unfamiliar number. I thought for a moment not to answer it, but then thought it could be for some work. I answered it, and to my chagrin, it was Dr. Naftali on the other end.

"Jacob, I need you to come to my office to see me immediately," he said with urgency in his voice. My heart dropped. "Doc, what do you mean you need to see me immediately? Is it bad?" I asked with the early stages of denial. He simply replied, "Jacob, I can't talk over the phone. Just come in as fast as possible," he said hanging the phone up.

My whole body went numb. I couldn't believe that it came down to this. In my denial, I still tried to believe it was something else other than what I feared the most. I could've taken the less of two evils. Chlamydia, Gonorrhea, and even Syphilis I could've lived with, but not HIV. Then I thought about Kim. No way in the hell I could explain this to her.

I had to take a mental break before going to see Dr. Naftali. I drove to a nearby gas station. I never smoked a cigarette in my life, but today was a great day to start. I pulled into a local gas station in the city that sold loose cigarettes. I asked the clerk for a loosie. He said that he could only sell two at a time. I gave him a dollar and gave the other cigarette to a bum sitting outside. I stood a good distance away from the gas station with my first cigarette in between my fingers. I took my first puff, and it was nasty. I didn't care. I kept smoking as I hoped for the best. Once I was done, I threw the cigarette butt to the ground. I jumped back into my ride and headed to my destiny or doom.

After I checked in, I went to sit down. I was called to the back after sitting in the lobby for a while. I walked to the back with an aggrieved look on my face. I recited every scripture I could think off. I entered Dr. Naftali's office. He sat behind his desk with two other doctors standing behind him. There was one woman in a business suit with a clipboard in her hands standing beside his desk. Dr. Naftali had his hands folded.

"Jacob, please sit down," he said gesturing with his hand.

"Okay, Dr. Naftali, why is it so urgent to see me?" I questioned nervously.

Dr. Naftali began rubbing his hands together before answering me. "Jacob, I don't know how to tell you this, but you are HIV positive," he said with the least amount of emotion as possible.

I immediately went into a panic. Tears uncontrollably started running down my face. My body felt limped. "What the hell do you mean I have HIV?!" I screamed at the top of my lungs.

Dr. Naftali became uneasy. The doctors behind him drew closer. The woman grabbed her clipboard tighter. "I'm sorry Jacob, but the results came back positive. Having HIV isn't a death sentence anymore. There are all types of medicines you can use to live a long and healthy life. Dr. Goldberg is a counselor on our staff who can help you through this," he tried to explain.

I was too livid to understand. "Fuck you, Doc and those two dopey looking muthafuckaz behind you! And fuck dat lil Orphan Annie looking bitch posing as a caseworker! I don't have shit! You are lying. I will go and get another diagnosis," I hollered as I got out of my seat.

"Jacob, please calm down!" Dr. Naftali said firmly.

At that point, there wasn't anything to calm me down. I had zero understanding. I kicked down the chair I sat in. I stormed out of Dr. Naftali's office. The worst was yet to come.

As I drove in limbo, my phone went off. It rang and rang. I chose to ignore it, but the calls wouldn't stop. I was too pissed to look down at them. At that point, I didn't give a fuck who it was. I almost cut off the phone until I saw it was my wife calling me. I wasn't sure if she took the test or not, but all I could see was that she continued to call. My texts were going into overload. I chose not to look at them. With the pressure of each ring, my heart grew softer and softer. I started to wonder what Kim could want. I prayed it had nothing to do with what my result was. Maybe she was having early contractions. Then I thought about her earlier back pains and swollen feet. Maybe she needed my help.

Then I thought she could be the ear I needed to vent out about the vicious lies Dr. Naftali told me. I was being tormented with each ring. I drove through a couple of streetlights before answering her desperate phone calls. I finally came to a red light. With sweat pouring down my face, I finally answered her call.

"Jacob, I don't believe yo muthafuckin ass gave me HIV!" Kim screamed through the phone.

*To be continued…*

## ABOUT THE AUTHOR

 Jay Welsby didn't always believe he'd be a good writer. But one day God said, "Do the best you can with what I've given you." And he did.

After winning a writing contest and writing a few short stories, Jay stopped fearing his God-given gift, relentlessly pursued his writing career in spite of his flaws. Knowing he needed to leave the comforts of his native Miami, he selected Atlanta to be his new home so he could learn and grow in his gift. His reasoning: "I believe it's better to write in a situation that isolates you from every distraction possible."

Since the move, Jay has experienced many challenges and obstacles, but choses to focus on the many opportunities and blessings that have come. One of those being his first book *Changed,* an incredible inside look at the mind of a serial cheater and the devastating consequences of his actions on every person he encounters. "After pouring my heart, sweat, and pain into a book that I believe will change people's lives, I'm proud to say that the task is finally complete."

To learn more about Jay Welsby, visit his website at www.JayWelsbyAuthor.com, follow him on Instagram at jay.welsby, and Facebook as Jay Welsby.